REBELS OF THE SKIES, CAPTIVES OF THE HEART

ROOK CALDWELL. The woman who put her life on the line every day, who behind the stick of a helicopter had nerves like steel cable, was hauntingly, vulnerably human . . .

JIM BARTON. A wealthy, young lumber baron, he took his chances with everything he had: his pride, his fortune—and Rook, the woman he loved . . .

GIL LOGAN. Flying was his passion, and it never let him down—unlike the girl he married for love . . .

EVE LOGAN. A tempestuous Southern belle, she married Gil Logan for better or worse. But wasn't the Coast Guard his real wife?

NOAH CALDWELL. His long talks with his sister Rook were a process of discovery for both of them. Painfully, wonderfully, they were learning how to be a family again . . .

BEGINNINGS

"Combining riveting adventure with perceptive characterization, this enthralling novel should appeal to anyone who appreciates quality reading."

—*Rave Reviews*

Eileen Nauman

BEGINNINGS

POPULAR LIBRARY

An Imprint of Warner Books, Inc.

A Warner Communications Company

POPULAR LIBRARY EDITION

Cover illustration by Franco Accornero

Popular Library books are published by
Warner Books, Inc.
666 Fifth Avenue
New York, N.Y. 10103

A Warner Communications Company

Printed in the United States of America

First Printing: April, 1989

10 9 8 7 6 5 4 3 2 1

To Captain Roland "Bud" Breault, USCG—teacher, mentor, and friend. Without your generosity, and that of the Coast Guard personnel you allowed me to interview, this book could not have been written. My thanks and salute to all of you for sharing your experiences with me.

and

To the unsung heroines and heroes who wear the U.S. Coast Guard uniform daily in our behalf. Thank you.

and

To Kathryn Falk, Carol Stacy, and my editor, Beth Lieberman.

CHAPTER

One

LIEUTENANT Rook Caldwell was pleased with her decision. The primal forest beauty of Route 101, heading north to Port Angeles, was healing some of her tension. She had decided to drive her red Toyota MR2 sports car up the coast of Washington, coming in the back door via the Olympic National Park. Today was April second. Tomorrow she was to report to her first Coast Guard station as a helicopter pilot—one of only six women in that particular arm of the service to fly Search and Rescue aircraft. Her stomach rolled—butterflies. Would she ever outgrow them? At twenty-five, she should have been rid of them forever. A silly smile touched her lips and she glanced into her rear view mirror out of habit. She was on the final, gentle grade that would lead her into the seaport of Port Angeles. A number of timber trucks had already whizzed by her. Another one, its grille gussied up with highly polished chrome, was stalking her. *Let him pass,* she thought.

The FM music was a perfect background for the mountains that rose on either side of the two-lane highway. Douglas fir, western white pine, alpine, and balsam fir covered the slopes. This was heavy timber country, and both man and machine had left scars. There was something sacrilegious about that, Rook decided. The slopes were scraped naked of trees, and looked as if they'd never recover.

Rook's gray eyes darkened with the pain of memories. Men meant pain, separation, and anger. Her full lips tightened as she thought of the years she and her mother had been hounded by her father's vindictive detectives. She hated Jack Caldwell and everyone in his family. Noah was no longer a brother to her; just a faint memory. He had volunteered to go back East with Jack after the divorce. Her stepmother, May Caldwell, was the daughter of a U.S. senator, and had tried to make Rook "mind her manners."

A devil-may-care smile came to Rook's mouth. May had called her a "wild little animal." When cornered, Rook would rebel, regardless of the abuse Jack meted out, because of her stubborn refusal to change. May wanted her to wear dresses, not jeans. She wanted Rook's shining black cap of hair to grow so that she looked less like a boy. And makeup! May had tried to get her to wear perfume, lipstick, and a bit of blusher over her high cheekbones. Rook could almost look back on those rare "visits" to the Georgetown house with humor. She would let the detectives take her back, stay a week—maybe two, at the most—and then sneak out a window, fade into the dark of night, and make her way back to Texas and her mother, whom she loved fiercely.

Mom . . . too bad you didn't live to see me graduate with honors from Pensacola. You'd have been proud of me . . . Tears blurred Rook's vision for a moment until, with a sigh of frustration, she wiped her eyes.

The deafening blast of an air horn filled the sports car. Rook instinctively cringed, glancing into her rear view mirror. Her heart thudded heavily in her breast. The timber truck with the fancy grillwork was careening down on her. She glanced at her speedometer which read sixty miles per hour, then up at a sign just ahead that said: 45 MPH. They were getting ready to enter the outskirts of Port Angeles.

Again, the air horn blasted—frantically, now. Rook refused to speed up. Ahead, she could see another timber truck laboring slowly up the hill, making it impossible for the one behind her to pass. *Tough, he can put on the brakes and slow down, then. Just like a man,* she fumed, *to push something smaller and weaker than himself around.*

The grille loomed in her mirror. Rook watched, mesmerized, as the hurtling truck continued to bear down on her. Was he going to bully her off the highway just because he was in a hurry? The air horn sounded again and again. Rook tightened her hands around the wheel. *All right, big boy, you're not going to get away with this.* She lightly touched the brakes in warning. Again, the air horn bellowed and the grille inched closer.

They passed the 45 MPH sign, and the grade became steeper. To her left, Rook could see the dark blue Straits of Juan de Fuca. To her right, she caught her first glimpse of the fish and timber town of Port Angeles. Disbelief ballooned in her as the timber truck moved within a foot of her bumper. One part of her wanted to slam on the brakes and make the bastard hit her. Another part of her—the mature one—decided evasive action was the better part of valor.

Rook was totally unprepared when the bumper of the truck solidly struck her sports car. The rear window shattered, sending a shower of glass across her shoulder. The air horn screamed. The Toyota was being pushed along by the truck. Rook pressed her foot down on the accelerator, and the needle shot up to seventy-five. The shoulder was muddy and rocky. She had no choice; it was either try for it and let him by, or end up flying into Port Angeles as the hood ornament on the timber truck. What a hell of a welcome to her new home!

Her reflexes were fast. She knew her Toyota as intimately as she knew the helos she'd flown the last eight years of her life. Whipping the sports car onto the three-foot-wide muddy shoulder, Rook down-shifted to fourth, then third, not touching the brake. The timber truck careened by, missing her slewing car by fractions of an inch. The mud was thick on the shoulder, and the wheels on the passenger side dug in. The car was headed toward the high wall of the rocky bank; she turned the wheel fractionally to the left, and it steadied momentarily. Rock and soil flew in all directions, and smacked and grated along the belly of the vehicle. Her car would be scratched, and the oil pan would probably be torn off because she was sinking so deeply into the mire.

Despite all her efforts to maneuver the car to a safe stop, Rook had managed to memorize the license plate on the truck as it had sailed by, disappearing around a long curve at high speed. "Easy, easy," she crooned to the car, gently bringing it to a halt. Silence suddenly surrounded her. Her hands were white-knuckled on the steering wheel, and her breath was coming in sobs. Gradually, she released her grip, sinking back against the seat. She had almost been killed. What if she hadn't had the skill to stop the car? Thank God for seat belts.

Rook opened her eyes, now a stormy gray with shock. "I'll find him," she muttered. Checking for traffic, she eased the muddied and scraped sports car back onto the highway. Shifting rapidly, she roared down the road, through a series of snaking curves that finally shallowed out into a flat half mile of road. Rook spotted the timber truck, now halted alongside the road not far from the tee intersection and stop sign. She saw the driver get out of the cab and walk past the load of timber chained to his truck.

Rook pulled up directly behind the vehicle. The driver quickened his pace toward her, relief etched in his features. Jerking the door open, she leaped out and walked rapidly toward him.

"Hey! You, there! Just who do you think you are, bullying a small car off the road?" Rook tried to take the anger out of her voice. After years of working around men she knew from experience that a low tone of voice and reasonableness were better than sharp words.

Jim Barton girded himself when he heard the woman screaming at him. He stared down into her eyes, which were narrowed with silvered anxiety. Barton glanced beyond her to the battered red sports car. Immediately, he became apologetic. "Hey, look, I tried to warn you. Didn't you hear me on that air horn?"

Rook hated having to lift her head to look up into his face.

She planted her fists on her hips, because her hands were shaking, forced into standing her ground with the driver. "Sure, I heard your air horn! How could I miss it when you drove through my rear window? You almost killed me back there! And my car—"

"I'll pay for any damages, lady." Christ, she was madder than a wet hen. Jim almost smiled, but the situation was too serious. In her own way, she was attractive. He liked her oval face—her stubborn chin, those petulant full lips, and her large gray eyes. She wore a plain white blouse, and a pair of well-worn jeans that showed off her long legs to a decided advantage. And there was no ring on her left hand. He hadn't seen her around here—she was probably just another tourist.

"I'd hope so, mister," she gritted out. When Rook saw the expression lighten his dark blue eyes, it shattered her attempt to recapture her anger. "You think this is funny? If I hadn't had the reflexes I've got, I'd have plowed into that rock bank! But you don't care, do you?"

"Hey, wait! My brakes failed! If I could've stopped, I would've."

Rook stared at him, disbelief etched into her face. "Sure they did!" Oh, why was she being antagonistic? This just wasn't like her. Rook wrestled mightily with her shaken emotions.

Anger tinged his amusement. "I don't make a habit of tapping people's cars for the hell of it."

"Tapping?" She pointed toward her car. "That's hardly a tap you gave me! My window's busted and the entire trunk and bumper are caved in."

Nostrils flaring, Jim held out both muddy hands. "Look, I told you the truth. My brake gave way. Now, if you don't believe me, you can climb under the truck and take a look for yourself."

Rook was trembling visibly and she didn't want him to see it. She used his invitation as an excuse to move away from him. Her nerves were unraveling. "I'll do just that."

She walked quickly to the rear of the eighteen-wheeler, got down on her hands and knees, and crawled beneath it.

Nonplussed, Jim watched her. "Why, you little hellcat," he muttered, and then went to join her.

Glancing over at him when he crawled up beside her, Rook continued to examine the brake area. She reached up.

"Don't!"

Shaken when his large hand clamped around her wrist, Rook jerked away from him.

Barton bit back a curse. "Just for your information, those brakes are hotter than hell. They'll burn your hand."

"If they're not working, you're right. But I don't trust you enough to take your word. I'll find out for myself." Rook leaned up, placing the back of her hand close enough to find out. They were hot. She could smell the odor of burned, tortured metal. She wrinkled her nose. Meeting his dark look, she muttered "You got any more brake equipment on this rig?"

"Yeah, under the hood. I suppose you want to look at it, too?" It was almost on the tip of his tongue to ask her if she was a mechanic, but he didn't.

"No." Rook crawled out, wiping her hands across her thighs. She walked around the truck. All her anger turned into admiration. He'd had the good sense to use the rocky shoulder and steep bank as a brake, maneuvering his truck into it. A lesser driver would have flipped the loaded truck once it sloughed into the foot-deep mud. The entire right side of his rig had been badly damaged.

Rook felt him come up behind her and stepped away. There was something disturbing about him. She didn't trust him. Maybe it was his rugged good looks. He appeared to be around thirty, his hair a dark brown with red highlights, tousled by the inconstant breeze. He was wearing a faded red and black checked flannel shirt, a pair of jeans, and rough-cut boots. His Levi jacket emphasized the breadth of his shoulders and his masculinity.

"Now I don't feel so bad," she whispered, trying somehow to apologize for her over-emotional reactions to the accident. "You beat up your truck worse than my sports car."

"Yeah, and it will cost a hell of a lot more to repair it, too. Look, just give me your name and an address where I can reach you. I'll have our insurance company contact you to fix the damage to that foreign machine."

Rook bristled, but kept her irritation under control. The rush of adrenaline had caused her initial display of feelings. He was probably a union redneck who only bought American products. She walked back to her car and retrieved her purse. Disliking him for the way he was affecting her, Rook leaned against the fender of her car, retrieving a pad and pencil. She scribbled down her name and the station address, then ripped off the paper and handed it to him. His hand was large, and his fingers were blunt, with a number of scars across the hairy tops of them.

"Give me your info, please. And I want some proof of identity."

Jim wiped off his hand, then dug in his back pocket for his wallet. "Trusting creature, aren't you?"

"Of you, in particular," Rook took the proffered license and wrote down his name. Finally, her voice was normal: low and calm.

"Sounds like you think men are little more than a virus."

Rook couldn't ignore the amusement in his baritone voice, relaxing slightly. "What I think is of little concern to you, Mr. Barton. Who do you work for?"

He dug out a business card and handed it to her, enjoying her reaction as she read it. "My father and I own Barton Industries, Miss—" he looked down at her name.

"It's Ms., Mr. Barton. And the last name is Caldwell." She wrote down the rest of the information, and handed his credentials back to him.

Jim settled the billfold into his rear pocket and glanced at the paper she had given him. He cocked his head. "The Coast Guard station? Is that where you work?"

"It will be as of tomorrow, Mr. Barton. You can contact the personnel officer over there when you want to get in touch with me. He'll know where I'll be assigned." The redneck probably thought she was a secretary. Let him. Rook closed the note pad and stuffed it back into her purse, then pushed off from the fender to leave.

"Hey..."

She stiffened when his hand went around her upper arm and drew her to a halt. Rook turned, barely tolerating his grip. "What is it now?"

"We got tangled up in conversation over the brake situation. Are you okay? Any injury?"

If she didn't know his type, Rook would swear that the concern in Barton's voice and face were genuine. She shrugged it off, realizing he was asking from a business standpoint. If she were injured, she could sue the hell out of his timber company. "Don't worry, Mr. Barton, no whiplash. I came unglued after the emergency situation, but I'm fine now." She pulled her arm free of his restraining hand.

He stood there, watching her slip back into the sports car. Tongue of a viper, eyes of a dove. What a combination. Defensive, too. Jim scratched his head and waited to see if her car would start. Looking down at the paper, he noticed her letters were painfully clean and precise. But those eyes, and that mouth of hers, shouted of something else—something far more interesting, that he wanted to investigate. *Well, Ms. Caldwell, in a few days, you and I are going to meet again. Next time, we'll see who gets the upper hand...*

He didn't have to wait those few days. Jim heard the engine grind. Seeing the frustration in her face, he girded himself for another round, then ambled up to the car and leaned down, placing his hands on the door.

"Won't start?"

Rook gave him a distraught look. She wanted to cry, but hid the reaction.

A bit of a grin edged his mouth. He quickly swallowed it, struggling hard to remain sober about her predicament. The gods were with him. Maybe... If only he could get her to climb down off her high horse. She was as touchy as an old brood hen sitting on a clutch of eggs.

"Want me to try it?"

That did it! Rook, staring straight ahead, fists wrapped tight around the steering wheel, struggling to remain composed. "No, I don't want you to try it."

Rook didn't need any of this—especially such a smart-aleck trucker. He was laughing at her; she could feel it. "Just because I'm a woman, I don't know how to start this car. Is that it?"

"No way, Ms. Caldwell. I'd never say that about you."

I'll bet you wouldn't, she thought to herself.

"Want me to look under the hood?" Jim offered.

"No," she sighed. Why wouldn't he just go away? There was something about him that stripped her, made her feel vulnerable. That was something Rook had never felt around a man before—ever.

Jim straightened up. "Okay, how about under the car?" He glanced at the furrowed soil, where the sports car had run along the muddy bank. "Chances are, there's something torn loose under the carriage."

Rook got out and shut the door. "You're probably right." She dropped to her knees, ignoring the mud. Barely able to see daylight between the undercarriage and the ground, Rook reached out, sliding her hand along the soil, hunting for the telltale oil slick.

Barton got down on his hands and knees, opposite her. "When you were a kid, did you like to play in the mud?"

Rook almost laughed, the tension dissolving around her. She managed a slight smile. "My mother told me that when you got handed mud, you made mud pies, Mr. Barton."

He grinned affably, placing his large hands across his tightly muscled thighs. "Well, I suppose we could do that here and now, if you want, because your car isn't going to start." For a split second, he saw the wariness thaw from her gray eyes. There was amusement in their silver depths. Just as quickly, Jim saw her replace it with a wall of coolness.

"Or, I could give you a lift into town in my rig. There's a garage down the way. I could get Charlie, the owner, to retrieve your car."

Rook pulled her hand from beneath the car, the sleeve of the blouse muddied, and studied her fingers. She groaned, thrusting her hand up under Barton's nose.

"I've got a busted oil pan, just like I thought."

He tried to appear contrite. "I'm sorry." He dug in his back pocket for his handkerchief, and held it out to her.

Rook stared at it.

"It's clean," Jim said drily.

Taking it, she got to her feet and wiped off her hand the best she could. "It looks like I don't have a choice, Mr. Barton. Thanks for the offer. Let me get my suitcases. . . ."

The trunk had been smashed so that nothing was coming out of it. Rook groaned as she stared at her car. "I can't believe you did this! I guess the suitcase I'm going to be able to get is the one in the back of the car." Despair filtered into her voice. "Do you know how much trouble you're causing me?"

Jim came and stood at her shoulder, running his fingers through his hair. "It's a lousy welcome, I know. Look, when Charlie brings your car in, he'll pry open the trunk and retrieve your belongings. Where are you staying?"

Disheartened, Rook dug back into her black shoulder purse. In one of the many neatly kept compartments, she drew out a small black address book. "The Red Lion Inn."

"Yeah, I know where it's located." Jim went back and pulled her other suitcase from the back seat of the sports car. "Come on, Ms. Caldwell, I'll get you safely into Port Angeles."

"You haven't so far, Mr. Barton," she said testily, walking at his side. He had a long, fluid stride, and Rook tried to ignore the animal image that it conjured up in her mind. Jim Barton reminded her of a cougar: lithe, tightly muscled, and highly dangerous.

Grinning, Jim opened the driver's door. "Climb in." If he'd expected her to fuss or ask for a boost because of the height of the first step into the monstrous rig, Jim was wrong. Ms. Caldwell appeared completely at home around machines. She probably got along better with them, too, he thought with amusement. Still, as she hefted herself up and onto the seat, Jim admired her long, thoroughbred legs once again. Graceful, too. That was four things to like about her. If only she'd get rid of that sourpuss personality of hers, he might have a chance.

On the way into Port Angeles, Jim noticed she kept to her side of the truck, blatantly ignoring him. He shifted the growling truck into a higher gear.

"So, you're going to live here?"

"That's right, Mr. Barton."

"Ouch. I haven't exactly been the Welcome Wagon, have I?"

Rook grinned slightly, trying to ignore the warmth in his voice. Barton had an incredible effect on her. What was going on? The men she'd been around lately saw her as nothing more than competition for a flight slot. This redneck truck driver seemed to actually be enjoying her company—what little of it she was giving him.

"You've earned a permanent place in my memory, Mr. Barton."

Jim winced. "Talk about getting off on the wrong foot . . ." He downshifted, taking it easy with his air brakes, which were still low on pressure. Once he dropped her off and got to Charlie's, he was going to park this monster and hitch a ride back to the office to get his Corvette.

Rook studied his rugged profile. "There was no foot to get off on, Mr. Barton."

It felt as if a hand had gripped his heart. "You married?"

Panicked, Rook muttered, "That's none of your business."

"There's no ring on your left hand." The words were out of his mouth before he could take them back. Normally, he thought before he spoke. This raven-haired woman was wreaking havoc on his normal tact and diplomacy.

Heat crawled up into Rook's cheeks. This guy was *worse* than a virus! "I'm not up on the meat market block, Mr. Barton, so forget it."

Jim studied her for a moment, dividing his attention between driving and absorbing the fervor of her reaction. She was scared—genuinely scared. *I'll be damned. In this day and age, too.* He laughed to himself. Maybe she'd just come out of a nunnery or something. Yeah, that would fit: no makeup, plain, simple clothes.

"Peace?" he asked, holding up his hand in a Boy Scout salute.

"I don't hide behind the Boy Scouts."

He chuckled indulgently, watching a grudging smile come to her mouth. Some of the caution had fled from her eyes. "Do you trust anyone?"

"Yes, myself."

"Good place to start," Jim agreed. He slowed down, bringing the truck along the curb. "Here we are—the Red Lion Inn. I'd drive in, but I'd never get this monster out of that parking lot." He reached for the suitcase, but she grabbed it first.

"Thanks for the lift, Mr. Barton," Rook said, prying open the door. The metal protested loudly, but she used her foot and pushed it wide enough to slip out. The less she had to do with this man who rattled her senses, the better.

"But—wait!" Jim got out, walking quickly around the truck.

The salt air was invigorating; Rook took a deep breath of it. "I can find my way to the lobby," she told him.

Jim took the suitcase from her hand. "I'm sure you can, Ms. Caldwell, but where I come from, a man is taught to carry a woman's suitcase."

Rolling her eyes, Rook shook her head and marched on ahead, leaving him to follow. "This is the late eighties, not the fifties."

"Guess it's the backward ways of Port Angeles that did it," Jim teased good-naturedly.

"I can tell a feminist is out of place here." *Especially with you.*

In the lobby, Jim put the suitcase down and waited while Rook checked in. He noticed a Coast Guard symbol on it. Maybe she had a boyfriend at the air station. Damn.

"What room are you in, Ms. Caldwell?"

Rook wondered if she was getting used to Jim Barton's

persistent presence, because the question didn't rankle her as much. "Twelve."

"Great. Listen, I'll take care of your car." He saw her full lips twitch. Was it a sign of distrust? Frustration? Or just pure annoyance? Probably the latter.

"Fine."

"I'm really sorry for the accident."

Rook melted beneath his utter sincerity. Who was immune to that kind of warmth in his blue eyes and the dark tenor of his voice? Suddenly very tired, Rook nodded. "I'm sure you are. Thanks . . . for everything."

He nodded. "I'll be in touch."

Right now, all Rook wanted was a hot bath and to relax. She needed time and space to get her head on straight about tomorrow. "Okay . . ."

And sooner than you think, he promised her silently. Jim didn't take her preoccupation as an insult. There was a faraway look in her gray eyes, faint circles forming beneath them, too. The accident had drained her. The adrenaline high she'd been on had suddenly disappeared, and now, exhaustion was setting in.

It was nearly one o'clock. Rook headed for her room, glad to be alone. She had all day tomorrow to get herself together. Her car wouldn't be fixed soon enough to drive on base, so she'd have to rent a car.

Sighing, she threw her suitcase on one of the double beds, turned on the lights and the television. The first thing she wanted to do was take a shower. She shed her clothes immediately.

Hot streams of water pummeled her, and Rook turned her face into it, letting it wash away the last hour's fear and terror. To be honest, she was still afraid—of Jim Barton. How could a man trigger such an incredible array of emotions from her? No one ever had before. Scurbbing her face with the fragrant bar of soap, Rook tried to wash away all thoughts of the man.

Instead, she allowed her drowsy mind to dwell on the fact that tomorrow, the base of Port Angeles would be getting a new captain. At least she didn't have to attend the ceremony. No, tomorrow she'd wander around the area on foot, and get acquainted with the town that would be her home for at least the next two years.

As she shut off the shower and toweled herself, Rook wondered what the new skipper was going to be like.

CHAPTER

Two

CAPTAIN Ward Stuart straightened his tie one final time—a nervous habit he'd never been quite able to break. The highly polished halls of the 13th Coast Guard District of Seattle reflected his image. Cabin call . . . that's what this little tête-à-tête with Rear Admiral Pete Savage was fondly called. Actually, Ward thought, it was more like an inquisition, complete with veiled threats about the victim's career prospects if the admiral's ideas weren't followed exactly.

At forty-three, Stuart thought he cut a fairly decent figure. He didn't have a potbelly, like a number of his contemporaries. He was lean, and walked with a slight cockiness. The only thing he regretted was his small size: five-foot-six was really short. And it didn't help psychologically in command situations. Over the years, Stuart had heard it whispered behind his back that he had a Napoleonic complex. According to his eldest son, Kenny, who was seventeen and a real problem, he *was* Napoleon. Ward considered himself tough but fair. With a slight frown, he dismissed thoughts of the problem between himself and his rebellious son. First things first. He had to get this cabin call out of the way, then assume command of the station, and then, make another effort to square his son away. Ward slowed and made a right turn into Admiral Savage's outer office. His yeoman looked up and smiled pleasantly.

"Captain Stuart. I'll tell the admiral you're here. It will be just a moment."

When Ward entered the spacious office, Rear Admiral Pete Savage rose from behind his highly polished bird's-eye maple desk, his hand outstretched.

Ward quickly came to attention, saluted, and then offered his hand. "Admiral."

"Ward, good to see you. Sit down, sit down." He pushed a buzzer and his secretary, Chief Yeoman Gent, appeared. "Two coffees, Mildred. Ward, you still drink it black?"

Sitting down in a chair angled toward the desk, Ward nodded. "Black, and strong enough to throw a salute, sir."

Laughing pleasantly, Savage waved the yeoman out the door. He tapped his fingers on Stuart's personnel file, which was spread out neatly before him. "You're looking fit, Ward. Lean and mean as ever, I see. That three-year stint back in Washington, D.C. didn't hurt you a bit." He raised his gray brows, the rest of his angular face remaining impassive. "I'm impressed with your record. It isn't often we get a non-Academy man who not only makes captain, but also gets command of a group/air and cutter station."

Stuart had the good grace to blush; his cheeks were ruddy anyway because of his Irish and English lineage. The inference was there: Ward had used the "system" at the main office of the Coast Guard to get what he wanted. *You bet your sweet ass I did.* Ring knockers from the Academy didn't like nonring knockers getting their favored positions. Yes, he had maneuvered politically, but any officer who wanted command did.

"I felt very honored to be considered, sir." Humility was best at this stage. Ring knockers didn't like upstarts in the ranks, and he was definitely listed in that category.

Savage scratched his thinning gray hair, making a pretense of studying Stuart's record. "You've got all the earmarks of a fine commanding officer, Ward. You flew fixed-wing up in Alaska for two years, helos at every other base. I'm particularly impressed with your stint in Puerto Rico as base supply officer. You not only created a better accounting system, but one that has now been adopted servicewide by the Coast Guard. Impressive."

"Thank you, sir." And no thanks to his commanding officer in Puerto Rico, who had tried to bury his career by giving him bad marks on his fitness report. No, Ward knew the C.O. hated his guts. It was a mutual and natural animosity. Ward had no respect for a C.O. who put his own welfare above that of his men and women. The mayhem Ward had created in trying to protect the enlisted from the C.O. had been considerable and cataclysmic, almost sending his career down the drain. The fact that he had streamlined the accounting system had saved him. Bad officers could make even great junior officers look like unsalvageable material doomed to be drummed out of the service. He never forgot that lesson.

The yeoman came back with their mugs of coffee and then left. Ward relaxed only slightly. He could see a strange light in Savage's pale blue eyes. The admiral wanted something; he could sense it. Ward squirmed. Some officers made ridiculous demands upon their people, and he knew that Savage was bucking for promotion to Commandant of the Coast Guard.

"Just how much do you know about the Seattle District, Ward?"

"That it's one of the busiest on the West Coast for drug interception, sir."

Savage was pleased. "Correct." He leaned forward, elbows on the bird's-eye maple, buttonholing Stuart. "Which leads me to a topic of prime importance to me and the base commanders within my district." He cleared his throat, his brows moving downward. "As you know, I'm sector commander for the Maritime Defense Zone. In December, the Joint Chiefs of Staff will be conducting a major military exercise, which will involve the Coast Guard, Navy, and Air Force. The exercise will be held in the 13th District—my turf. I need all my commanders to have their individual bases in top form." Savage leaned back in his expensive leather chair, a pleased look replacing his intense expression. "Bluntly, Ward, if I look good in this interservice exercise, I'll improve my chances for commandant. If just one of my commanders screws up, my aspirations for that position are scuttled."

"Yes, sir." Great. The handwriting was on the wall: if the admiral was scuttled, the offending commander's career would be down the tubes, too.

"Now, let's talk about your base. Port Angeles has had a fine skipper, a personal friend of mine, for two years. Unfortunately, Bob Crane is retiring after thirty years of unblemished service. Bob is a fine officer and has left Port Angeles shipshape for you to take over. I'll expect the same response from Port Angeles under you as I did from him. He was one of my best station commanders. I could always count on him when I needed help keeping things under control."

Crane was a ring knocker, so of course he was nothing but Superman in Savage's eyes. Ward nodded. "I've never had the pleasure of working with Captain Crane before."

"If you can be half as good as Bob was, I'll be satisfied."

Great. From the stories Ward had heard, Crane was a real bootlicker. He grimaced to himself. Superman, he wasn't, but he had a hell of a lot of horse sense, and he was good at managing people—all except for his son, Kenny. There, he was failing—badly. Ward forced his concentration back to Savage; the problem with his elder son was never far from his mind.

"Naturally, I'll preside over the change-of-command ceremonies tomorrow at 0900."

"Thank you, sir. I'd consider it an honor."

Savage smiled paternally. "Port Angeles has just been given another honor. Do you know that you'll be getting our first female helicopter pilot day after tomorrow? Lt. (jg) Rook Caldwell. I've seen her service record. Been flying helos since she was sixteen. Graduated from Texas A and M with honors. She went to Pensacola and outscored the boys at their own flight games. At Mobile, she was one of the best. Quite frankly, I think she's going to be a fine asset to the 13th District. I hope you will feel the same."

"Lieutenant Caldwell sounds sharp, sir. I'm sure she'll fit in just fine at the station."

Ward left the office mulling over several potential problems. Tomorrow he'd find out what shape the station was in. Nagging questions about Lt. Rook Caldwell hovered in front of him as he walked down the hallway toward the exit. She could turn out to be a royal pain to his career, or a blessing in disguise.

CHAPTER

Three

JIM Barton's eyes narrowed on the door leading into the Red Lion Inn's restaurant. It was 6 A.M., and as usual for that time of day, he lounged at a table with his father and three other timber truck drivers. Rook Caldwell had just stepped through the doors, her eyes still puffy with sleep, her sleek cap of black hair combed to perfection. She was wearing a decidedly feminine pink blouse and khaki slacks.

He watched her progress into the restaurant, picking up his mug and sipping the coffee, tuning out the table conversation. She threaded her way through the busy establishment, finding an empty booth at the rear. Smiling to himself, Jim watched her sit down, her back to the wall so that she could look out into the area. Trusting wasn't one of her watchwords, he thought, rising to his full height. Excusing himself from the table, he walked slowly in her direction, wondering when she would spot him.

Rook nearly choked on the ice water she had swallowed when she saw Jim Barton walking toward her. He was clean-shaven, his blue eyes dancing with deviltry. A lock of reddish brown hair grazed his broad, unlined brow. Maybe it was the lopsided grin on his mouth that was making her heart thump hard to underscore this unexpected meeting. Dressed in a blue chambray shirt with the sleeves rolled up on his elbows, and pair of clean jeans, he looked incredibly alluring, and Rook found herself unable to resist staring at him in open admiration. Maybe it was the glint in his eyes. Whatever it was, Rook didn't want any part of it.

"Good morning," Jim said, halting at the booth. He saw color rise in her cheeks and her gray eyes grew suspicious. "I can tell that you think I came here deliberately to meet you this morning." He smiled broadly.

Flushing, Rook grabbed the water with both hands. "You read minds, too, Mr. Barton."

"Actually," Jim began, gesturing toward the table in the distance, "my dad and I come here every morning before we start cutting timber. They've got the best eggs and bacon in Port Angeles."

Was he lying? Rook craned her neck, spotting a table with four men sitting around it. "Your father?"

Returning his attention to her, Jim nodded. He put his hands on his narrow hips. "Yeah. He's the tough old Irishman with the red beard sitting over there. Dad's seventy-one and doing the work of a forty-five-year-old man."

A smile edged Rook's lips. No, he wasn't lying. She saw the sudden warmth in Barton's eyes and heard the underlying pride in his voice. "There are days I get up feeling like twenty-five going on eighty."

Good, she was relaxing. "Is this one of those days?"

Rook sipped her water. She ought to invite him to sit down. But if she did that, he'd take it the wrong way. Jim Barton was like a summer cold—hard to get rid of. "I look that bad, huh?"

Shaking his head, Jim met her small, hesitant smile. Her entire faced eased when her lips lifted at the corners. "Actually, considering the hell I put you through yesterday afternoon, you look pretty good." Better than that, but Jim sensed that if he said she was beautiful, she'd consider it a line and ask him to leave.

Leaning back, Rook realized that he might be inquiring about her health for insurance reasons, and not stalking her. "I feel fine. No neck pain or backaches from yesterday."

"Great. Mind if I sit down for a moment?" He gave her a hopeful look.

"Well—I. . . ." How could she say no to that innocent look on his face?

"Look, let me make up for yesterday's crash. You're going to live here in Port Angeles. At least let me buy you breakfast, and then we'll call it even." He slid into the booth opposite her before she could open her mouth to ask him to leave.

Rook stared at him. "Mr. Barton—"

"Call me Jim. And I've been wondering what your first name is." He knew he had her buffaloed by the confusion on her face. "Are you a Jennifer, I wonder? Maybe a Susan or Katherine?"

The waitress came over. Helpless beneath Barton's dazzling Irish blarney, she ordered a breakfast of orange juice, toast, and coffee.

"That's all?" Jim demanded.

Rook gave him a flat look of annoyance. "I'm not a timber truck driver, Mr. Barton."

Jim shrugged and nodded to the waitress. "Millie, just bring me a cup of coffee, please."

"Sure thing, Jim," and the waitress left.

"You know," he continued conversationally, "I think you ought to eat a little more. Sort of skinny, aren't you?"

Meeting his friendly blue gaze, Rook gritted out, "I like myself just the way I am."

Damn! She'd taken that the wrong way. Sure enough, Jim saw her lean back, that same distrust coming back to those large gray eyes of hers. "Well, what I meant was—"

"Save it, Mr. Barton. I know where you're coming from, and where you want to go."

"What's your first name?" he asked quietly, refusing to be drawn into her assessment of him.

"Rook."

"Rook?"

"That's right. Rook." She sat there smiling to herself. For once, she had him on the defensive.

He lifted his eyebrows. "That's quite a name."

"I like it. That's all that counts."

"I imagine there were a few kids who might have made fun of it when you were growing up."

His insight was startling, unexpected. Rook moved nervously around in the booth, her appetite completely gone. "A few."

Jim grinned. "Let's see . . . a rook is a crow."

"I've eaten some now and then. Haven't you?"

His smile broadened, and so did hers. When she relaxed and dropped those walls, she was like blinding sunlight. Jim liked her self-inflicted sense of humor. "Oh, yeah. Like yesterday: I ate a plateful."

"At least you aren't so stuck on your ego to admit that much." Chuckling, Rook met and held his warm gaze. A delicious sense of protection overwhelmed her in those fleeting seconds. It was a feeling she'd never experienced around a man before. And, just as quickly, Rook shielded herself from it.

Spreading out his long legs on either side of where hers were tucked beneath the booth, Jim nodded. "Well, I don't see any resemblance between that kind of crow and you. So, Rook has to mean something else." He rolled his eyes toward the ceiling in thought. Her low chuckle had moved through him like a warming spring breeze, eliciting and tugging at all his senses. "You know, crows and ravens are real tight family members. In fact, no one in the bird kingdom is as family-oriented as they are." He glanced at her significantly. "Does that part fit why you have that name?"

Uncomfortable, Rook stared down at the glass of orange juice the waitress had placed in front of her. "I don't discuss family matters, Mr. Barton."

Ouch. Strike Two. Frowning, Jim nodded. "I know what you mean. My father's always trying to tell me he can do the work of any man in our outfit, and I keep trying to put him in safer jobs. Sometimes, parents don't do what you want them to," and he gave her a brief smile. There was no thaw in Rook's features. Sensing that he'd hit a real sore spot with her, he left it alone.

"Well, everyone knows a crow or raven is smart. Matter of fact, they're downright clever." He cocked his head, studying her. "Are you?"

"What?"

"Smart?"

"I can hold my own."

"Clever?"

If I were, Rook thought wryly, *I'd have found a way to get out of this breakfast with you*. "Practical. Not clever."

"A good dose of horse sense is worth its weight in gold," Jim agreed, suitably impressed. "So, you're a lady with intelligence coupled with common sense. That makes you as rare as your beautiful name."

"You're impossible, Mr. Barton," Rook growled, gripping the glass.

Holding up both hands in a sign of surrender, Jim said, "Whoa. I just paid you an honest compliment. Since when is honesty wrong?"

Her eyes narrowed. "Where I come from, Mr. Barton, men give lines like that every minute of the day."

He sat up. "Oh? And where do you come from?"

Rook blew out a breath of utter exasperation. "Mr. Barton, I don't *want* to discuss my personal life with you. I don't mean to hurt your feelings, but—"

Jim got up and gave her a one-cornered smile of apology. "No problem." He took the check the waitress had left, noticing the nonplussed look on Rook's face. "I don't intend to make your second day in Port Angeles a pain in the rear, too. I'll see you around."

She watched Jim saunter off, heading for the cashier at the end of the counter. Rook felt like a first-class heel for her less-than-polite reactions. Dammit, he was stalking her, and she knew it. So he went slinking off like a hurt puppy dog, trying to get her to feel sorry for him so the next time he made a hit on her, she'd allow it to happen.

Well, there would be no next time. Having lost her appetite, Rook picked up her purse and left the restaurant. She had to rent a car, and find an apartment. It was going to be a royal pain.

The gray clouds that lay above Port Angeles like a soft, quilted blanket were beginning to darken. Any minute, it was going to start raining. Great! Rook ducked into her room. At least she didn't have to attend the change-of-command ceremonies that would be taking place shortly over at the Coast Guard station. Her luck hadn't totally deserted her. Opening the newspaper to the rentals section, Rook tried to concentrate, but Jim Barton's affable, smiling face kept appearing.

Rook muttered an unladylike oath under her breath. Okay, so she had acted like a first-class bitch to him! *Admit it.* She wasn't sure of his motives, but her instincts told her he was stalking her for whatever selfish goal he had in mind. As she leafed through the ads, Rook reconsidered. He really had looked hurt when she rebuffed him, but some men, she knew from experience, were *very good* at playing a role in order to get a woman to fall into their arms.

CHAPTER

Four

CHANGE-of-command ceremonies were a royal pain in the ass as far as Gil Logan was concerned. Thanks to the outgoing captain's inefficiency and shortsightedness, the pilots were standing SAR duty every other day. At any other station, it would have been duty once every four days. This had been going on for two weeks, and it was wearing everyone down. It was Saturday, his only day off before duty again on Sunday. The last place he wanted to be was in dress blue uniform, waiting for Admiral Savage to arrive by helo so the ceremony could begin.

Logan hid in his office, catching up on some badly needed work regarding housing for the personnel. Each officer had "collateral" duties besides flying SAR. Some jobs, such as public relations, which Gil considered a candy position because there was so little responsibility, were in high demand. Usually ring knockers got those. Safety, personnel, and housing were the toughest. As always, he got lucky and was assigned to housing.

He glanced at his watch. In a few minutes, his wife, Eve, would meet him. Gil gathered up some brochures, placed them in a manila envelope, and marked *Lt. Caldwell* across it. When she came aboard on Sunday, he'd give it to her. He picked up his white cap, careful not to get fingerprints on the black patent leather bill, and settled it on his head. He knew he was running late, and Eve didn't tolerate tardiness.

Just as he emerged from the side door, he saw her enter the building at the far end. She looked luscious and feminine in her lavender raincoat, her umbrella a dainty concoction of her Southern heritage. Her pale blonde hair lay around her proud shoulders, emphasizing her flawless complexion, high cheekbones, and pouty, full lips. Gil felt himself tighten with desire, as he always did when he was around her. Automatically, he checked her forest-green eyes for telltale signs of how she was feeling. There were emerald flecks of anger in them.

"I hate this rain, Gil," she complained, shaking the excess water from the sleeves of her raincoat. Folding the umbrella and placing it under her arm, she gave him a frustrated look. "I'll be so glad when this tour is over. Washington State is nothing but rain or fog, three hundred sixty-five days a year. I hate it!"

He came to a halt and placed his hands on Eve's shoulders. He wanted to kiss that little-girl pout off her lips. More importantly, he needed a few moments in her arms. The last SAR case they'd had yesterday had been a gut-wrencher. They had been called out to locate an eleven-year-old boy who had fallen overboard from a yacht that was sailing the straits. When they located the boy, around midnight, Marchetti had paled as he pulled the lifeless form onto the platform attached to the H-52 helicopter. Sam Talbot had vomited, never having seen a dead person before. Gil had wanted to cry when the family, waiting at the hospital, had seen their son's lifeless form rolling away from the '52 on a gurney.

"Come here," he said thickly, taking her into his arms. "I need you . . ." He had wanted to talk to Eve about the boy they had plucked from the straits, to release the pent-up emotions that he had held so tightly in check. By the time they had flown back to the air station, it was one o'clock, and he knew from past experience not to call Eve after ten because it would ruin her beauty sleep. Blindly, Logan crushed her curved, pliant form to him, hungrily soaking up her feminine warmth and the White Shoulders perfume she always wore. He kissed Eve's cheek, searching for the warmth of her mouth to drive the knot of coldness out of his gut.

"Gil . . .! Not here!" Eve struggled free of his grasp, taking a few steps back from him, looking around. "What will people think if they see you mauling me in public? Where are your manners?"

Frustration thrummed through Gil and he angrily smoothed his rumpled jacket. "Sometimes I wish you weren't so sensitive about what other people think, Eve. I haven't seen you in damn near two days. I'm human, in case you've forgotten."

Stung by his growling, Eve pouted. "Believe me, after seven years of marriage, I know just how human you are."

Gill hung on to his shredded patience. It was on his lips to tell her how much of an insecure child she always was. Dammit, he needed an adult sometimes—someone who could be strong when he got tired. And right now, with all the flying, the lousy collateral duty, plus an absentee commanding officer, Gil desperately needed a harbor of peace and warmth. But Eve wasn't going to provide him that shelter—not now, not ever. Swallowing his frustration, he took her by the arm, leading her toward the rear doors.

"Come on, the admiral should be landing shortly, and we can get this show on the road."

Eve gave him a sour look. "Do you think the new C.O.'s wife will be like the old one? All Mrs. Crane did was fish with her husband. She never threw one party. Really, she had the manners of a boor, Gil."

He opened the door for her and waited patiently while she opened the dainty umbrella. He'd never tire of her graceful movements. What was it about Southern women that kept men snared in their trap? Whatever it was, Eve possessed that mystique. She was a delicate, sensual creature, given to fits of temper and whim, but he loved her anyway, faults and all. God knew, he had enough of those himself.

"You ought to be glad Mrs. Crane didn't invite you aboard their boat. How'd you like to bait a hook?" He grinned down at her as they huddled under the umbrella in the steady downpour, making their way toward the huge hangar.

Eve shivered dramatically. "Gil Logan, you love to torment me with these awful things you say! A lady would not pick up those squirmy worms and put the poor things on a hook! It's unthinkable."

"The Cranes are outrageous," he agreed, unable to halt his smile over her response.

"I'm so glad we're getting rid of them. I wonder if Mrs. Stuart will be more like a real C.O.'s wife? She ought to invite the officers' wives over for a luncheon within the first month, you know."

Gil ignored Eve as she rambled on about military protocol. His wife had become an expert on that topic, there was no doubt. Eve had trained hard to be an exemplary military wife, but the twist was, she hated the military. Gil wasn't getting promotions fast enough to suit her. She wanted him to get a better paying, more prestigious job on the outside, in the civilian world. With a shake of his head, he dismissed that particular can of worms. They had enough arguments without him bringing up another of their sore spots now.

"Hey..." Lt. Taggart Welsh said, sidling up to Gil, "where'd you get this scrumptious-looking Alabama peach?" The ceremony was due to start in an hour, and a number of personnel had arrived early, before the call to muster in the ranks was given.

Eve colored beautifully beneath the officer's obvious flattery. "Oh, Tag, you're such a gentleman. Always flowery words for us poor, bedraggled women. I'm dying in this horrible rain and fog." She reached out, squeezing Tag's long, slender hand. "How are you? More importantly, how's Paula doing?"

Gil flinched inwardly. Paula had leukemia, and it was slowly draining the life out of Tag. He had known the tall, gangling officer since Pensacola. They were the best of friends. Eve's light banter on such a painful topic made Gil boil. Couldn't she see the haunted look in Tag's hazel eyes? Or the fact he was losing weight when he had none to spare? Why the hell couldn't she have just asked politely about Tag and left Paula out of it?

Tag gave her a forced smile, stretching the paper thinness of his long, horselike face. "Oh, we're fine, fine. And I might say, despite this rain, you're looking as lovely as ever, Eve." He nudged Gil in the ribs. "All the pilots are jealous of Gil, you know. We all wish we had such a good-looking woman around."

"You're so sweet, Tag. Tell me, how's Paula?"

"Eve, they're going to muster the ranks shortly. Why don't we leave serious talk for later?" Gil gave her an imploring look, trying to save Tag.

She frowned. Gil was always trying to orchestrate her behavior. "You see, Tag? Now he's trying to tell me what I can and can't talk about."

Tag shrugged good-naturedly. "Aw, I think he means well. We've got a few more minutes before the head honchos arrive. I'd like to pass the time of day with you until then. Any objections?"

"Just as long as you don't start cracking those corny jokes of yours," Eve warned, smiling up at him winningly.

Tag came around and stood next to Eve. "Now, now. Hey, did I tell you two my latest joke? It was so hot when I was stationed in Alabama, the eagles on the captain's shoulders were Southern-fried."

Tag glanced down at Eve, who was pointedly trying to ignore the joke. He looked over at Gil, and saw his friend's blue eyes alive with amusement. "You liked that one, huh, Gil?"

Gil tried to keep a straight face. "Yeah, Tag, I can identify with it."

"Gil!" Eve gave him a dirty look. She knew he hated Alabama, her home state.

"Don't worry, honey. Tag knows our marriage wasn't made in heaven, like his and Paula's."

She crossed her arms, embarrassed. Eve wanted to die.

No matter what she tried to do to make their marriage work, it just kept crumbling before her eyes. "You shouldn't be talking about our marriage in public, Gil."

"I know . . . it's bad manners."

Tag looked around. Operations, aviation engineering, and the cutter officers were beginning to muster. "Well, hang on to your hats, boys and girls. We're about to witness the event of the year: a new skipper is coming on board."

Ward Stuart tried to look relaxed as he and his wife, Marcia, stood next to Admiral Savage. The air station's four helicopters had been placed outside the hangar for the duration of the ceremony. The cold April wind whipped through the cavernous, well-lit structure, rain pounding unrelentingly on the glistening black asphalt ramp outside the opened doors. Captain Bob Crane had said little to him upon their arrival; a few polite words, that was all. One comment stuck like a thorn in Ward's side: Crane had said he could fish full-time now that he was retiring from the Coast Guard. Previously, he'd confided, he'd only been able to pursue his passion part-time. Stuart grimly wondered what "part-time" meant.

Judging from the sloppily uniformed enlisted personnel, Crane's part-time was probably closer to full-time. Either that, or Crane hadn't run a tight ship. The officers from the 82-foot and 210-foot cutters stood in their own formation. As he perused each formation, he saw tension-lined faces, dark circles under the eyes of his pilots, and wives shifting nervously off to one side where they sat. No, if his sixth sense was operating, this group wasn't a happy one—not by far. Damn.

Logan remained at attention throughout the mercifully brief change-of-command. His gaze strayed to Ward Stuart. The new skipper had an alert look on his square-jawed face. He reminded Gil of a wolverine: small but dangerous. Maybe it was the man's large, intelligent green eyes or that mouth, compressed into a thin line, that rang a warning bell in the back of his head. Gil wasn't sure. Stuart, compared to Crane, looked fresh out of boot camp: all spit and polish.

Glancing down at his own black shoes, he realized too late that Stuart had zeroed in on him and them. And if Gil could read the new skipper's mind, he was mentally putting him on his shitbird list right now because his shoes were dull-looking, the brass buttons on his uniform unshined, and God only knew what else.

Logan's gaze moved cautiously around the assembly as the ceremony progressed. The admiral was presiding over it like an indulgent parent with his two favorite sons. He saw Chief Aviation Machinist Chappie Jarvis weaving slightly while at attention. Christ, was the man drunk at an event like this? Everyone knew Jarvis was an alcoholic—even Crane, who didn't care. Had Stuart spotted Chappie's weaving? Flicking a look in the new skipper's direction, Gil's stomach knotted. Yep, Stuart's intense gaze was lethally pinned on him. Did the man miss anything? Groaning to himself, Logan rolled his eyes upward to look at the superstructure of the hangar. Stuart was going to be one of those C.O.'s who had eyes in the back of his head. Great . . .

Ward glanced toward the rest of his family. Marcia looked elegant in her dark blue suit and ruffled white blouse. Her dark, walnut-colored hair was drawn back into a chignon, her cheeks flushed with excitement. Pride moved through him. Marcia had been his childhood sweetheart; they had married right out of high school. She'd stuck with him through good stations and bad. He admired her grit and he loved her. Next to her was Robby, their fourteen-year-old, red-haired, freckle-faced son. He was dressed in a dark blue suit, which matched his mother's outfit to a degree. His light blue tie was knotted painfully tight at his neck. Ward smiled down at his son, wanting to tousle his hair.

Ward was embarrassed by his seventeen-year-old son's obvious absence. Earlier that morning, Kenny had sullenly come downstairs, dressed for the ceremony. His dark brown hair was long, and would have been unkempt if Marcia hadn't begged him to comb it. What grated on Ward even more was the two-day growth of sparse beard Kenny was trying to grow in order to more closely imitate the Don

Johnson look. Damn television. It did nothing but sway gullible children. And when he saw Kenny's outfit and appearance, Ward's heart sank. The pale pink wrinkled cotton slacks and mint green T-shirt, along with the white cotton sport coat, had triggered Ward's anger. Kenny looked slovenly—certainly not someone he wanted to parade out in front of his new command. Why couldn't Kenny understand that he had to be a model citizen because of his new status?

A heated argument had ensued over Kenny's attire. Ward absolutely refused to allow him to come to the ceremony dressed in that manner. Kenny had slunk off to his room, but not before Ward had made his son promise to come and pick Robby up shortly after the ceremony—and in decent attire, or else. The admiral began to speak, and Ward shifted his attention to him.

"Port Angeles is in for two top flight changes," Savage began, his voice rolling across the one hundred and fifty assembled Coast Guard people. "The first is that a new group commander, Captain Ward Stuart, will be taking the helm. I don't need to repeat his credentials, which are considerable and available for you to read in the Change-of-Command brochure handed out to each of you. The 13th District is proud to have him aboard, and expects great things of him in his two-year stint here at Port Angeles. You'll benefit from his experience. The second change is that tomorrow morning, Port Angeles will be getting something rare: a female helicopter pilot—Lt. (jg) Rook Caldwell. She is the sister of Lt. Noah Caldwell, skipper of the *Point Countess*. The Coast Guard, as you know, has been a leading proponent of utilizing women in all career categories. Lieutenant Caldwell is the sixth woman to graduate from the Academy and, of course, we'll expect great things from her." Savage looked meaningfully over at Stuart, who sat to his right on the platform. "And I'm sure, with Captain Stuart's leadership, everyone will move ahead at full speed."

Eve twisted a look at Gil. A woman pilot? He hadn't said anything about a woman being in the men's ranks here at Port Angeles! Heat fanned across her cheeks. Eve chewed on her lower lip, a nervous habit she'd had since childhood. Her father had cheated repeatedly on her mother. Eve's greatest fear was losing Gil to another woman. What was Rook Caldwell like? Was she pretty? Single? Probably out to snag a husband! Eve's stomach knotted painfully. Why had Gil hidden this fact from her? He'd tell her sooner about this . . . this so-called woman SAR pilot! That meant Gil would be flying with her for at least a year or more, and with the duty roster the way it was, *often*. Eve shut her eyes, each breath painful.

Perhaps Noah could tell her more about this sister of his. Eve had always liked the stalwart skipper of the 82-foot *Point Countess*. He was a gentleman in every way, and Eve had often entertained sexual fantasies about him. Noah was single at twenty-six. Why some clever woman hadn't caught him yet as a husband was beyond her. If she were single, she'd have gone after him—just as she had gone after Gil. Eve didn't hear the end of Savage's droning speech, or the order to dismiss. As soon as protocol would allow her, she'd slip free of her obligations to chat with the new commanding officer and his wife, and then corner Noah.

Ceremony over, Noah took off his cap for a moment and ran his spare fingers through his short, black hair. The groups were breaking up, and people were milling around. Settling the cap back on his head, he turned to get into line and meet the new C.O.

"Noah . . . Noah Caldwell?"

This wasn't his day. Eve Logan was the nosiest busybody on base. She carried more gossip per square inch on her tiny frame than anyone he'd ever come across. Eve was one of the most insecure women he'd ever met. He almost felt sorry for her. Flashing a smile of greeting, Noah nodded deferentially in her direction.

"Mrs. Logan."

"Call me Eve. When are you going to drop the formality, Noah? We've known each other over a year!" She came up and draped her arm around his, lightly pressing herself against him.

A year too long, Noah thought. He was aware of the brush of her breast against his arm and politely disengaged himself, putting a few feet between them. "How are you, Eve?"

She smiled genially. "Miserable, as always. The flying certainly keeps everyone busy enough. I barely see Gil anymore. It gets awfully lonely at home without a man around."

"I'm sure it does."

"Yes, well, I just wanted to come over and congratulate you on your sister coming on board. You must be terribly excited."

He kept his expression carefully neutral. "Terribly." Actually, scared to death was a better description. He hadn't seen Rook since she was thirteen. That was a long time—too long.

Laughing gaily, Eve asked, "Tell me, what's she look like?"

If his stepmother's father hadn't sent him a recent color photo of Rook graduating from Pensacola, Noah wouldn't have known. "About five-foot eight inches in height, short black hair, and gray eyes."

"Did you two ever get called fraternal twins? You have black hair and gray eyes, too."

"No, she's the spunky one, and I'm considered the quiet one. It was easy to tell us apart." *We didn't live together long enough to remember much of anything,* Noah thought, pain and then sadness moving through him. "She's the far better looking of us." She was attractive in an arresting way, Noah had realized when the photo had arrived. His baby sister had grown up, and she was a looker. She was a fighter, too, and Noah admired her for that. Not many people had taken the world by the tail and given it a successful shake or two. Rook had. He alternated between absolute fear and heart-hammering joy over the prospect of meeting Rook tomorrow when she came aboard the base. She had been the missing part of the family. And even though they were born only eighteen months apart, Noah could almost swear he felt like her twin sometimes. As much as he yearned for the family closeness, Noah knew that Rook hated him and the idea of family ties with equal fervor. He wiped his sweaty palms on his trousers.

Eve felt her world collapsing around her. Rook was beautiful. "I think you're very handsome, Noah. I can't conceive of your sister outshining your looks."

He laughed softly. "She does, believe me. You'll have to excuse me, Eve. It's time for me to meet our new skipper."

Eve stood there alone in the midst of the swirling activity, lowered voices echoing in the cool dampness of the hangar bay. How dare the Coast Guard bring a woman into a man's occupation! Rook Caldwell was just looking for a husband, that was all. Would she try to steal Gil? Gripping her purse tightly beneath her arm, Eve sought to find him, her heels grating against the concrete. Within the hour, all the officers and their wives were expected to appear at a cabin call ordered by Stuart in the wardroom. Fighting back her tears, Eve could pry more information out of the new C.O. about this superwoman who was coming on board shortly.

Captain Crane and his wife had left early; so had Admiral Savage. That was all right with Ward, as he looked around the room where the first cabin call would take place. He wanted to roll up his sleeves and get down to the business of assessing the officers of his cutters and helicopters. Kenny had driven Robby home, and Ward had been relieved when he had grudgingly shown up in a nice pair of slacks and an ironed shirt. He'd given them both strict instructions to keep a low profile for a few more days, until he could get them enrolled in their respective schools. Robby had his painting, and would be content at their new home, but he knew Kenny would take off. He tried to screen out the word: cocaine. Was Kenny using coke? He worried that his son would never get along in the world.

He couldn't have his son using drugs—the Coast Guard just wouldn't tolerate that from a commanding officer. His people would lose respect for him. The consequences of such a catastrophe were frightening to Ward—it was the worst nightmare in the world for him. Somehow, he had to reach Kenny and make him understand just how important this command was to him and his career. He'd busted his tail all his life for this moment, and no one—not even his son—was going to taint it for him.

Marcia gave her husband a ferreting look, as if sensing the turmoil of his thoughts. She checked with Robin Lipton, the executive officer's wife, to make sure the punch and cookies had been attractively laid out. Small groups were beginning to wander into the blue-carpeted room. The huge picture windows afforded a view of the small airstrip and the gray-green straits just twenty-five feet away from the rock embankment. Marcia slipped her hand around her husband's arm, and gave it a small squeeze.

"Stop worrying about Kenny. He'll be all right, Ward."

He managed a slight, strained smile. "I'm in hot water if all these officers can read my face as well as you do, sweetheart."

She warmed to the endearment, leaning up and giving him a peck on the cheek. "They haven't been married to you for twenty-five years like I have, darling, so relax. You know Kenny: he's as restless as that water out there. He'll probably change clothes, drive around, and get acquainted with the town."

Ward snorted and picked up a small cup of punch, handing it to her. "Sure. He'll be looking for the first dealer he can find. I kept hoping that moving to a small town might help him settle down."

"Shhh, let's talk about this later. Here comes the X.O.—Commander Bruce Lipton, if I'm not mistaken."

Giving Marcia a wink, Ward murmured, "You've got the whole roster memorized already, don't you?"

"I sure do, Skipper. A good military wife makes it her business not only to know the wives, but to learn about the men as well. After all, how else can I be of help?"

Ward wanted to put his arms around her, draw her close, and kiss her hard and long, right here on the spot. "Tonight," he promised, "you are going to be amply rewarded for all your diligent work, Mrs. Skipper."

Marcia glowed, and her lilting laughter floated across the room. "I can hardly wait."

Neither could he, but right now, serious business was ahead. Although this cabin call was supposed to be informal and filled with chitchat, it was anything but that. From years of experience, Ward knew how to use his body language and tone of voice to put an individual at ease. When Commander Lipton stepped forward, looking pale and nervous, he smiled warmly and thrust out his hand.

"Bruce Lipton, correct? Glad to meet you." And so it went for the next two hours. Marcia circulated through the clusters of nervous wives and soon had them at ease, laughing occasionally and planning parties.

Ward memorized key words for each officer he met. Tag Welsh, the aviation engineering officer, looked ill. He appeared gaunt, and he had dark circles under his eyes. AEO and safety officer were the most important jobs in Coast Guard aviation. Although Tag seemed pleasant enough, Ward picked up some undefinable emotion around him. His hands shook imperceptibly when he held the glass of punch, and there was a nervous tic under his right eye. What the hell was affecting Welsh so much? He was a case of nerves. How did he fly SAR missions? Had the old skipper worked this man to death, or what? He'd find out by perusing those personnel files that Captain Crane had promised to have waiting for him tomorrow on his desk at Admin.

Lt. (jg) Ty Scanlon, the personnel officer, was an easygoing extrovert, with a lovely wife named Jordanna. They made a nice couple. *Solid* was the key word for him. There didn't appear to be any major marriage or personality clashes between them. That was good, because in Ward's experience, a marriage going to hell in a handbasket rode roughshod on a man. He was particularly keyed to that with his officers.

Lt. Gil Logan and his Southern belle wife, Eve, were a whole different matter. Ward's key phrase for the tall, broad-shouldered helicopter pilot was *bad attitude*. His sloppy uniform screamed of insubordination, and his insecure, flighty little wife possessed the smile of a cream puff, but she had a backbone of pure, unbending steel. Logan seemed aggravated when his wife started pumping him for information on Rook Caldwell. She was a very jealous, territorial wife, Ward decided, which meant there was potential trouble ahead with the addition of a female to the helo ranks.

Lt. Noah Caldwell was quiet and alert. *Sharp* was the key word for him. Ward liked the thoughtful cutter officer. If his sister Rook was anything like Caldwell, he could rest easy. Savage had been right about him, it seemed. He was cut from a superior piece of cloth, and probably deserved a shot at Surface Effect Ship duty. Ward made a mental note to pursue that with Caldwell at a later date.

At the end of the two hours, Ward dismissed everyone. It was early Saturday afternoon, and he knew how important it was for the men to share quality time with their families. He read anger in Eve Logan's eyes as she left, and wondered who she was upset with.

Gil had sensed the impending explosion from Eve all evening. Each time he tried to caress her shoulder or put his arm around her, she pulled away. That, coupled with her silence, warned him that a serious storm was brewing.

Sitting at the Formica table in the kitchen, he went over some office paperwork. The new skipper would haul him in very shortly and want answers about housing. And judging from Stuart's look, he'd damn well better have them—or else. Glancing at his watch, he saw it was nearly 11 P.M. God, tomorrow afternoon at three, he had to relieve the duty officer and take over. Rubbing his face tiredly, Gil reminded himself that not only would the new skipper probably be anchored to his desk reading key personnel records, but that the new female helo pilot was supposed to come on board. It was going to be a hell of a day, no matter which way he cut it.

"I'm going to bed."

Gil lifted his head and twisted around toward the door to the living room. Eve stood clothed in one of her favorite satin negligees—an apricot confection that emphasized her flawless complexion and silky blonde hair. "I'm right behind you. I've had enough housing work tonight." Suddenly, Gil's depression lifted as he gazed hungrily at Eve. More than ever before, he needed her arms around him. He wanted to make love to her, but that was only part of it. She gave him an undefinable sustenance in bad times like this.

She lifted her shoulders in an elegant motion. "I really don't care, anyway. The Coast Guard has become your wife. I'm just someone left at home. Good night, Gil."

He stared at her, stunned. The rustle of satin disappeared; only the faint fragrance of her perfume was left to entice him. Rising slowly, Gil realized that there would be another showdown in the bedroom.

Eve pretended to be asleep when Gil slid into his side of their double bed, unsure of how to broach the subject of Rook Caldwell. She lay there for at least fifteen minutes, sensing he was awake and troubled. Well, so was she.

Gil stared up at the ceiling, hands tucked beneath his head as he lay there. Eve wasn't asleep; she was merely waiting, like a huntress, to pounce on her prey. With a loud exhalation of breath through his nostrils he muttered, "All right, Eve, what's eating at you? You've been sulking like a child all evening. What have I done now?"

Eve remained in her curled up position, with her back to him, for several more minutes before answering. "It's what you haven't done that disturbs me, Gil."

He glanced at her blanketed form, outlined by the thin stream of moonlight filtering through the lace panel at the window. Holding on to his mounting anger, he gritted out, "What is it that doesn't please you, Eve?"

Rising like a sleek cat, Eve sat up and leaned against the pecan headboard. She tucked her knees against her and wrapped her arms around them. In a hurt voice she said, "I'd like to know why you hid the fact from me that you were getting a woman pilot in with the group." Possibly losing Gil to the woman pilot scared her badly.

Gil sat up, his eyes shining like obsidian in the darkness.

"Dammit, Eve, I didn't purposely hide anything from you. It just slipped my mind, was all."

Her large eyes were huge with hurt. "That's an awfully big thing to forget!"

He raked his fingers through his recently washed hair. "Jesus Christ, Eve! It isn't like we haven't been a little busy the last three months at the station. Due to Crane's screw-up, the pilots have duty every other day. We've had more SAR cases than normal. We're all tired and whipped to the bone. Quite frankly, hearing about that broad coming on board was the last thing on my mind. We've had a record number of transfers in the past quarter, and I've been working my ass off with housing duties." He met her mutinous stare. "And what have you been doing? You're here at home. You have no job to make a demand on you." He avoided dredging up the fact that they didn't have children—another sore spot between them. "All you have is your weekly bridge club, the library meeting, and a few do-gooder organizations. You try living the schedule I've been on, and see just how damn much you forget."

"I don't care, Gil! And stop making fun of the organizations that I volunteer my time to! It's the proper thing for a military wife to do." Wasn't he proud of the fact that she tried hard to be exemplary?

With an explosive curse, Gil got out of bed. He stood naked against the moonlight, every muscle in his body taut. "I'm so sick and tired of hearing about what's proper, I could—"

"Stop behaving like an animal! All you can do when you're angry is shout and curse. A gentleman wouldn't do either." Insecurity jagged through Eve, and she wanted to cry.

Knotting his fists, Gil glared down at her. She looked so slender and vulnerable to him. But she was defensive when her security was threatened. "Shove this 'gentleman' crap. I've never been one in your eyes, so why keep harping about it?"

"You were one when I met you."

He laughed harshly, pacing back and forth in the large master bedroom. "The only thing you were hot about was getting a husband, and we both know it." He stalked over to the bed and leaned down, gripping her soft, delicate wrist. "Let's face it, Eve, I was your meal ticket out of a miserable existence in that tin shanty town you left behind. I didn't know it then, but I know it now. And all these airs you put on about who's coarse and who's a gentleman is rubbing me raw." He released her and sat down, holding her glare.

"I'm doing the best I can for us. Things are tough now, like they were when we were stationed in Alaska."

"That was a hell hole!" she spat, shrinking away from him. She rubbed her wrist tenderly. Gil had barely held her in check, but she wanted to make him think he had hurt her. "And the last six months have been hell on me!" Why couldn't he understand when she was bored and unhappy?

"You?" he roared. "Well, what about me? I drag my ass home after twenty-four hours of duty, with the probability of SAR cases thrown in on top of it. The next day I have eight hours of collateral duty to perform. And when I finally get home, the dinner's cold. You haven't even had the decency to keep it warmed up in the oven."

"How dare you! I cook all day long for you, and what do I get? Abuse!"

"I'll trade you," Logan snarled. "I get heartburn. Your food isn't cooked with love, it's cooked with venom."

Tears glittered in her eyes that were filled with genuine hurt. "Get out of here, Gil! I can see talking isn't going to help a thing. Take your blanket and sleep out on the couch."

He jerked the sheet aside and climbed back into bed. Pulling it up to his waist, his back to Eve, he growled, "You feel that way, you take the couch. I've got a tough day ahead of me tomorrow, and there's no way in hell I'm losing any more sleep tonight."

With a little cry of exasperation, Eve leaped out of bed and ripped off the bedspread, her head held high as she marched imperiously from the room. Gripping the knob, she slammed the door shut just as hard as she could.

Standing in the middle of the living room, Eve dropped the bedspread and sobbed. Oh, why couldn't he realize that she was important, too? Him and his damned beloved Coast Guard! She clenched her fists, walking the length of the room, trying to get rid of all her frustration.

Sniffing, Eve scrubbed her cheeks dry. She had to do *something* to show Gil that she was worthy of his attention. She was just as important as the Coast Guard. Wasn't she? Eve picked up the bedspread and dragged it behind her to the couch.

Sitting down, she pulled the silk coverlet across her legs, staring into the darkness. There had been an ad in the *Star* for a reporter. Suddenly, hope filtered through Eve. She pressed her brow against her hands. If she became a reporter, that might give her stature in Gil's demanding eyes. He might pay more attention to her.

Still, fear ate at her. The only things Gil respected were his fellow pilots and his father's thirty-year marriage. He admired longevity and toughing things out, obviously. Well, maybe if she took an important and glamorous job, he'd ignore this Rook Caldwell who was coming on base tomorrow morning.

Lying down, Eve closed her eyes. Gil always respected fellow pilots. Rook was a woman pilot. She gave a shuddering sigh. As much time as he spent at the station, it would be easy for Gil to fall in love with this woman. She flew aircraft and God knew, Gil rated that career as the most important in the world. Opening her eyes, Eve blinked away fresh tears. How could she compete with a woman pilot? Somehow, she'd have to get that job and make a name for herself fast—fast enough to grab Gil's attention and make him proud of her, for once. That way, he'd not be enticed into falling into Rook Caldwell's scheming clutches.

CHAPTER

Five

ROOK'S overall expectations of Air Station Port Angeles dimmed as she drove out the thin, curved ribbon of road toward the end of Ediz Hook. Within the safety provided by the rock retaining wall and narrow sand spit lay a natural deep-water harbor. Embraced within the hook was a busy timber operation. Hundreds of logs floated within corrals, waiting to be picked up by foreign freighters out in the harbor. Off to her left stood a huge pulp and paper mill, its stacks spewing out tons of steam and white smoke. She wondered how much pollution was tolerated by the state of Washington. At 0745, the day was crawling over the horizon, the sky an overcast gray. The straits were a muddy green color, but calmer than the day before. Rook felt as if the whole world around her was holding its breath.

God, I'm nervous, she thought. Then, she smiled wryly at herself; something she did in times of high stress. Her mother had taught her to make fun of her own frailty in moments like this. A sharp memory of the timber truck accident entered Rook's thoughts. After driving into Port Angeles, and checking in at the Red Lion Inn for the night, she'd collapsed on a chair after taking a shower. It was then that her hands began to shake and the tears came. Her mother had taught her to never be afraid to cry. It was the human thing to do, and it served as a natural vent and escape valve to one's emotions. .

She slowed her rental car to a stop at the front gate. There was no guard—just a button to press. A metallic voice answered, and she explained that she was reporting for duty. The chief manning the SAR desk told her to come on board, and gave her directions to the Administration building. Crawling at fifteen MPH, Rook gazed at her new home. On the left was a newly built commissary, a few small white stucco structures, and finally, Admin. Across from it was the hangar. She longed to go there first, but vetoed the idea. To the left, she spotted the cutters anchored at their respective docks. As Rook parked the car in the designated visitor's space, she got out. The quiet station was nearly deserted. Port Angeles lay across the harbor, oblivious to the importance of this Sunday morning.

Nervously checking her dark blue uniform and straightening the colorful tie at her throat, Rook settled her hat on her head. She slung her purse over her left shoulder and picked up her orders and other records. Then, mouth dry and heart pounding in her constricted throat, she entered Admin.

Gil Logan was behind the Operations Center desk at the other end of the hall when he heard the door open and close. He glanced down at his watch: 0755. Caldwell was due to report in at 0800, and the chief who had just spoken to her had informed him of her arrival. At least she was on time, unlike Eve, who was perennially late. Grabbing his third cup of coffee for the day, which had started at 0600, Gil scalded his tongue. Muttering an oath under his breath, he set the cup aside and wiped his mouth.

"Hot as it is, I think I could use a cup of coffee, too. Lt. (jg) Rook Caldwell reporting as ordered, sir."

Gil managed a sheepish smile. His first impression of Caldwell was far from what he expected. She wasn't ugly, her voice was a pleasant contralto, and—surprise of surprises—she had a sense of humor. She was tall for a woman, though. He liked the alertness he saw in her wide, gray eyes. Eyes of a hawk, maybe.

"Take it easy," Gil murmured, noticing how stiff and formal she was. He took the pack of orders she offered him and placed them on the desk. "I'm Gil Logan, the senior duty officer for the day." He offered his hand, shocked at himself. He was treating her as if she were a newly arrived male helo pilot. Well, why not? He had enough problems to juggle without trying to play the wounded, defensive, macho male, too. "Welcome aboard."

Relief flooded through Rook as she gripped his hand. "Thanks, Mr. Logan."

"Call me Gil, if I can call you Rook. You still want a cup of this coffee? It's guaranteed to eat chrome off a car bumper."

"Yes, to both questions." The bulk of her nervousness passed and Rook removed her hat, setting it on the counter. Behind Logan was a detailed map of the straits, British Columbia, and Northwest Washington. There were a bank of phones of various colors on the desk console, and bulletin boards with lists of telephone numbers. This was where the SAR calls came in. Excitement began to thrum through Rook.

Gil poured her a cup. "Black, or sweet and blond?"

She smiled. "Will you hold it against me if I say sweet and blond?"

Placing the creamer and sugar bowl toward her, Gil shook his head. "I haven't got a thing against you, Rook. If the truth be known, we're so short on pilots right now, if a pelican came through those doors and said he could fly, I'd sign him up." And then he grinned, belatedly. "Not that I'm comparing you to a pelican."

It was her turn to smile. "No offense taken."

Gil sat down and opened the manila envelope that contained her orders. "No chips on your shoulder?" he teased.

"None that I know of."

"Good. You'll get along fine here, then. With the few pilots we have, we're a close-knit family in many respects." He separated the papers for Admin and for Operations. "And, I've been assigned as your sponsor, to help you get the lay of the land here at the station. We'll start that at 0755 tomorrow morning." He glanced up to see what kind of effect that had on Rook. Sponsors were assigned to every newly arriving person. He wasn't about to tell Eve of this latest assignment, which would put him in close contact with Caldwell for the next couple of days, until she got acclimated to Port Angeles.

Rook gratefully sipped her coffee. She liked Gil Logan. "I'm in good hands, then." When she saw a red flush crawl up his neck and into his face, Rook's heart went out to the pilot. He was just as nervous about this first meeting as she was. Logan resembled many of the inspector pilots she'd flown with at Pensacola and then, later on, in Mobile: fairly tall, well built, and lean. He had dark brown hair, intense blue eyes, and pale skin, as if he saw very little sun. The one-piece, olive-green flight suit he wore was what she longed to wear. They were comfortable compared to the uniform skirt and jacket she was currently wearing.

"Why are you short on pilots? I thought each station was given enough of a complement so that duty was only every fourth day or so."

Although he liked Caldwell initially, Gil didn't feel comfortable spilling the ugly truth about Port Angeles. He had yet to be called in by the new skipper, and she might be a gossip, like Eve. Instead, he said, "Just one of those situations you run into occasionally. We're in the midst of quite a few changes. We just got a new skipper yesterday."

"Uh-oh."

Gil glanced up. She had grasped the implications immediately. "Captain Stuart's aware you're coming on board this morning. He wants to meet you as soon as I'm done with the initial paperwork here."

"Great." The word mirrored her pained expression.

He grinned. Rook was going to get along fine with the troops. He gave her back some of the necessary papers, and was about to alert Captain Stuart of Rook's presence, when the red phone rang shrilly. Frowning, Gil picked it up. It was the SAR telephone, a direct line to Seattle office, which received most of the distress calls and then sent them out to the appropriate base nearest the SAR case for action.

Rook listened closely as Logan took down the necessaary SAR information. Her heart began to pound. She wanted to take part in the rescue, but there wasn't any possible way. In order for her to begin to fly on a regular basis, she had to go through at least a week of orientation.

Gil hung up the phone, leaned over, and keyed the SAR alarm. He gave Rook an apologetic look as he leaned down and flipped a switch on the console. "Men overboard at Pillar's Point." He released the key on the mike and glanced over at Caldwell. "Gotta run," he told her. "I'll see you a little later." He headed for the door. With Annie Locke on board as their enlisted flight mechanic, Gil felt good. She was reliable and cool-headed.

Rook stepped aside, out of the way, when a shorter, sandy-haired officer in a green flight suit came down the stairs double-time. He gave her a piercing look—one laced with curiosity—and then raced out the doors, running toward the hangar that sat across the parking lot from Admin.

Walking to the doors, Rook watched as both pilots disappeared through an open door at the rear of the hangar. Envy ate at her. If only she could be going along. *Soon,* Rook promised herself. *Soon, I'll be a copilot flying with someone like Logan.* Taking a last sip of her coffee, Rook picked up her purse, set the mug on the console, and headed up the stairs in search of the C.O.'s office.

"What have we got?" Lt. (jg) Reno Gunnison asked, strapping into the copilot's seat.

Logan glanced up from his preflight duties, already strapped in, his helmet on his head. "A distress call from a fishing vessel near Pillar's Point in the straits. The boat hit something, and the two crewmen jumped overboard." They quickly went through the mandatory preflight checklist together.

"How long ago?" Reno was thinking about hypothermia, from the low water temperature, which killed most people within half an hour to an hour after jumping off a sinking vessel.

"Ten minutes. We still got hope." In no time, they were ready for liftoff. Annie Locke gave a thumbs up, taking the last chock away from the tail rotor wheel and climbing aboard. The blades swung faster and faster above them, the '52 shaking with the additional power Logan was feeding the engines.

Reno calculated in his head. It would be fifteen minutes before they'd reach Pillar's Point, which lay west of them on the coast. "We've got Annie with us. That's a good omen."

Logan pulled up on the collective, feeling the aircraft lift off immediately. "Yeah, we got lucky," he agreed, watching the instruments closely. Sun glared through the plexiglass, heating up the cockpit immediately. Already, Gil could feel the familiar trickle of sweat from beneath his armpits as he jockeyed the '52 to an altitude of one thousand feet. The green landscape raced beneath them. The dark marine blue of the straits was off to their right.

"Hey, was that the new woman helo pilot there at the desk?"

Logan nodded. "Yeah. Seems like an okay sort. I feel for her. She's gotta meet the new skipper."

Reno grinned, busily coordinating radio broadcasts between themselves and the air station. "Better her than us. Our turn's coming soon, though!"

Ward lifted his head when a firm knock sounded at the inner door to his open office. He saw a woman officer standing there uncertainly.

"Ah, Lieutenant Caldwell. Come in, I was expecting you." Ward wondered why Logan hadn't brought her up himself. He got his answer when he heard the whine of a jet engine on a '52 starting up. There must be a case.

"At ease, Lieutenant. Sit down," he invited, gesturing toward one of the two leather wing chairs that sat positioned at either corner of his massive cherry desk.

Managing a slight smile, Rook tried to relax. "Thank you, sir."

He gave her a nod, hoping to make her feel more comfortable. "Well, you and I share one thing in common."

"What's that, sir?"

"We're both brand spanking new to the base. I arrived yesterday and you, today."

"Is that an omen, sir?" she asked, smiling.

"Omen? That sounds sinister. I'd hope our showing up here isn't a negative. Let's just say it's symbolic—of what, I'm not sure yet." He liked her sense of humor. She was attractive without makeup. Her fingernails were blunt-cut and unpolished. Her hair was short and shined like the wing of a raven. The cut was appealing to the structure of her facial features. Ward was pleased that her uniform was meticulously kept, but then, she was fresh out of boot camp.

Rook sat stiffly in the chair, hands clasped in her lap. Captain Stuart was short. It was a shock—at first. But she saw the glint in his eyes and sensed he missed little. That kept her even more on guard. Was he pro- or anti-woman helicopter pilots? She'd find out soon enough. Stuart could either make her first tour—the foundation of a career she wanted for the next thirty years—a positive experience or a disaster. If he was a dyed-in-the-wool male chauvinist, he could make it so tough on her that her fitness reports would get her drummed out of the service after her first five-year stint. Sweat popped out on her upper lip.

Rook hung on to all her questions, realizing silence was proper while Stuart read over her personnel file. She wanted to fidget. Instead, she swung her attention to the white H-52 helo with the international orange stripe on its tail as it lifted beyond the hangar, heading out in a westerly direction over the straits. She ached to be on board, to be part of the team trained to save lives. Would Gil and Reno arrive in time to save the two fishermen?

"Your credentials are impressive, Lieutenant," Ward complimented her. "I see you've been flying rotary-winged aircraft since you were sixteen. How did you get into that?

Most sixteen-year-old girls have more pressing interests." He was thinking of Kenny, who mimicked the latest fashions and made dating the highlight of his life.

"We . . . my mother and I . . . lived near Brownsville, Texas, at the time. I hung around a crop-dusting airfield after school every day, sir. The money a pilot made was pretty good, so I asked Old Jake if he'd teach me to fly. I was fifteen at the time. He sort of liked me. His daughter had died two years before, and I guess I reminded him of Becky. So, he'd take me on crop-dusting flights, and by the time I was seventeen, I had my license."

Ward leaned back, folding his hands across his stomach, studying her. He saw Noah Caldwell's stubborn chin and high cheekbones in her face. In some ways, they were similar, possessing that necessary drive to make something of themselves. "And you did this flying for the money?"

"I did at first, sir. My mother would never accept welfare, even though things were pretty tight. I had a newspaper route in the different towns we lived in, from the time I was eight, and that helped. Money was my first objective, but as soon as I flew in a helo, I changed my mind."

"Oh?"

Rook gave Ward a shy smile. "I fell in love with flying, sir. From sixteen on, I ate, slept, and breathed it. Old Jake made me see the importance of top grades. He was the one who suggested the Coast Guard as a place to use my talents."

"Wise man, this Old Jake."

"Yes, sir. He was more of a father to me than my real one. During college, I made my tuition and living expenses by crop-dusting in the summer with his company. I flew on weekends, too."

"Earning your own way through college is something very few young men and women do nowadays," Ward observed wryly. Good, she had backbone and tenacity. He liked that kind of attitude. The distaste in her voice—a slight tinge of bitterness about her real father—pressed a warning buzzer in the back of Ward's head. No one had the perfect family—

he knew that from personal experience. Camelot existed in fairy tales, not reality.

"It appears that Lieutenant Logan has a SAR case."

"Yes, sir. One came in while I was checking on board with him."

Ward smiled again and picked up the phone. "That means you'll have some time to kill before he gets back. Why don't you have a seat in my secretary's office? I've got a pleasant surprise for you."

Frowning, Rook stood up. "Surprise, sir?"

Ward nodded. Connecting with the cutter, he said, "Yes, this is the captain. Have Lt. Noah Caldwell come to my office immediately. Thank you."

Noah! Rook's mouth dropped open and she staggered back a step. *My God, no!* Not her brother!

"Lieutenant?" Ward demanded, watching her face drain of all color. Scowling, he watched her eyes darken with what could only be called pain. What was going on here? When the station secretary had made a note that Rook's brother, Noah Caldwell, was stationed here, he felt they should get some time together. Now, watching her reaction, Ward wasn't so sure.

"Uhh . . ." Rook stumbled badly, trying to think, but only feeling. Her world was coming unhinged. She had to get hold of herself! The captain was staring at her. He mustn't know the awful truth! That was one of the two worst secrets she'd carried, like a living nightmare, within her each and every day.

"I think you'd better sit down," Ward began, rising.

Before, Rook had always been able to cap her feelings. Now, it was impossible. Struggling, she shook her head. "I-I'm sorry, sir. It's just that—well, this is a surprise. I-I didn't know my brother was here."

Smiling weakly, Ward watched her closely. "Yes, according to the personnel records, Noah's been here a year." Odd that she wouldn't know that. He gave a mental shrug. There were too many other things pulling at him to give much credence to her reactions.

Faintness swept across Rook and she deliberately moved toward the door. "It's been a long time since we saw one another," she whispered huskily. "Is he on his way?" How was she going to deal with this? *How?*

"Yes."

"I-I'll meet him out in the hall, sir."

Perplexed, Ward nodded. Of course, she wanted their reunion to be private. He was sure that they had a lot to catch up on. "I understand, Lieutenant. Dismissed."

"Yes, sir." Coming to attention, Rook made a miserable about face and groped for the doorknob, her hand shaking visibly.

Ward watched Rook close the door to his office. What the hell, this was Sunday. Give her a few minutes alone with her brother while Gil was on the SAR case. Right now, Ward wanted to make the transition for Rook as painless and pleasant as possible. On Monday, Lieutenant Logan would begin her orientation phase, and she could sink her teeth into some real work.

Once out in the hall, Rook stood motionless, then buried her face in her hands. She had to get herself together. She had to! Noah was coming. Hatred mixed with anger, and then anguish. She choked back a sob.

Noah removed his baseball cap as he entered the Admin building. He wore the dark blue work uniform and foul weather jacket that cutter crews donned when at sea or at work when docked. He wiped his hands on a rag, trying to remove the grease. The morning had been spent with his engineer chief, Dave Harper, tinkering with a valve problem. Noah had asked the new C.O. to call him when his sister came on board.

Taking a deep breath, he slowed his ascent on the stairs leading directly to the captain's office. Admin was empty, as usual on Sunday. For that, Noah was grateful. Rook hadn't seen him face to face since she was fifteen, the last time she had run away from their home in D.C. Would she recognize him now?

His eyes grew dark and troubled. Fear gripped him as never before. He couldn't even remember feeling this scared—even when boarding a druggie's boat in search of marijuana or coke. What would Rook do? He prayed she'd have the good sense to be calm, cool, and collected. For all he knew, the captain might be waiting there with her.

Rook heard someone coming up the concrete steps; the echo floated up to the second floor. A gasp escaped her as she recognized her brother.

Noah hesitated on the last step, six feet separating them. He saw Rook's ruddy-complected face drain of all color. Swallowing hard, he took the final step. He knew that she had had no idea that he was stationed here, or that Grandfather Rufford had had a hand in having her transferred to Port Angeles. She would never know.

"Rook?"

Shock turned to rage. Rook retreated back a step as Noah moved forward, his hand offered to her. "What are *you* doing here?" she rasped.

Noah halted, before offering her a faint, shy smile of apology. "I'm stationed here, like you are. When I found out you had arrived, I wanted to be the first to welcome you on board." He cleared his throat, nervously searching her wan features. "Are you going to be all right? Do you want to sit down? I know this is a hell of a shock. I tried to contact you at Mobile after you graduated, but you left a week early, and—"

"Get out of here, Noah," Rook grated under her breath. She caught and held herself in check, her emotions boiling wildly just beneath the surface. "I told you before: there's nothing left between us. I don't have a brother. I never did. Just get the hell out of my life and leave me alone!"

He winced, hearing the raw pain and desperation in Rook's husky voice. Fingering his cap nervously, he said, "That's going to be a little hard to do. I'm stationed here, too. Look, there's a pilots' lounge right down the hall. Why don't we go in there and talk?"

Rook realized with a start that they were standing right

outside the captain's office. The door was shut, but that didn't guarantee that Stuart hadn't heard her snarling rejoinders to Noah. She straightened up, squaring her shoulders, chin tilted in a defiant position. Whether she wanted to or not, Rook had to admit that Noah had grown tall and strong and handsome. His face had matured into that of a man. She'd seen enough officers in the last eighteen months of training to acknowledge that Noah had the look and carriage of a superior commander.

"We have nothing to discuss, Noah, and you know it."

"Please, Rook, can't you give me . . . give *us* a chance?"

Damn him! He was going to press her, as always. Rook looked down the deserted hall. Their voices carried too easily. She didn't want their personal family problems to become gossip. "All right, let's go to the lounge. But what I have to say to you is going to be short."

He shrugged. "Okay. Come on, I'll show you where it's at—that is, unless Gil gave you the tour already."

Irritated that Noah talked about Logan as if he'd known him forever, she muttered, "He's on a case, and we barely got past formal introductions."

Heartened, Noah said, "Great. Maybe you'll let me show you around the base. It's quite an impressive operation."

Rook said nothing, following at a safe distance. Noah led her through one room, down a hall, and then made a sharp left. The pilots' lounge consisted of a television, a telephone, plus a few couches one could doze on, and a large table with plenty of chairs around it. A number of pieces of art—one depicting a duck holding an umbrella over its head—were visible on the walls. Noah sat down, tossed his cap on the table, and looked up at her expectantly.

Shutting the door to the ready room, Rook turned, a scowl on her set features. "All right, Noah, what's this all about?"

"What are you talking about?"

"Us. Stationed here together. How'd you manage to pull that off?"

He feigned surprise. "I didn't pull anything off."

"That's an outright lie! You forget, I'm used to your

stepfamily's meddling! How many times did they send those detectives out to Texas to haul me back to D.C.?"

Noah saw tears in her gray eyes. He felt for her, and for himself. He placed his hands flat on the table, and spoke, his voice quiet. It was a tone he used when in a boarding or emergency situation on the *Point Countess*, when his men were relying on him to keep calm. "Look, we've got to sit down, behave, and talk like adults about this sometime, Rook. Sure, we were separated, but that doesn't alter the fact we share the same blood. It was Father who sent those detectives to find you—not my stepmother or Grandfather Rufford. Jack was wrong to hunt you down."

She glared at him, folding her arms against her breast. "Noah, you can't atone for what Jack or that foster mother of yours did to Mom and me, so quit trying!"

"Then stop blaming me for it, dammit. I'm your brother, Rook. Look, I can't help it if Jack found you and brought you back to D.C. Every time he did, you ran away." He shook his head. "To this day, I don't know how, as a nine-year-old kid, you made it back to Texas by yourself, and in one piece. So many things could have happened to you . . ."

"If I'd stayed, worse things would have happened!" Rook cried. "And you—you sided with Jack. You stayed with him when Mom and I left . . ."

Her breath was fast and shallow. Rook allowed her arms to drop to her sides, fists clenched. "As far as I'm concerned, I have *no* family. Mom died a month before I graduated from Pensacola." Tears blurred Rook's vision, and with a croak of frustration, she turned her back on Noah to wipe them away.

Noah rose, moving quickly to his sister's side. The instant he put a hand on her shoulder to comfort her, she jerked away from him. She whirled around, her face etched with anguish.

"Don't touch me! Just get the hell out of here, Noah! Get out of my life, once and for all!"

He stood there patiently. "I can't do that, Rook. I never could." His voice grew hoarse with feeling. "Whether you accept it or not, we're brother and sister. I love you; I always have. I want us to be family again."

She took a step back, swiping at the last of her tears. "I'll **never** call those monsters who raised you family."

He frowned down at the carpeted floor. "Okay, okay. You never did like our stepmother or Grandfather Rufford. I don't expect you to like them now. I can understand how you feel, Rook. Mom needed you and you needed her."

"Mom loved *both* of us, Noah, but you moved back East with Jack without a fight—without even a whimper. You gave up Mom's love. Do you know how many times she cried herself asleep after you abandoned her for Jack? Do you know how many times I woke up as a kid and heard her sobbing your name? That so-called father of ours split us apart, Noah, just as surely as if he'd taken an ax to all our hearts. He killed Mom by having detectives chase her all over Texas to find me and drag me back East. She had high blood pressure when she was twenty-eight. She died of a broken heart at forty-five, for Christ's sake." Rook sobbed, burying her face in her hands, "Alone in a little apartment in Odessa. I-I couldn't even be there for her."

Tears blinded Noah and he turned away, unable to stand the suffering in Rook's torn voice. He rested his hands against the table, staring vacantly off into space. As badly as he wanted to, he knew Rook wouldn't let him help ease her grief. Heart attack—that was what the detective agency had said. Melody Caldwell had died alone, thinking that her son didn't love her, when he did—fiercely. As a boy, and then as a teenager, Noah had written to his mother. His father, Jack, had said that the letters were being forwarded by the detective agency, but he'd lied. Noah found out about it only after entering the Coast Guard Academy. The post office had sent back his mail, address unknown. When he got his first leave from the academy, he had cornered Jack about it.

Noah dragged in a breath of air and recalled that wrenching confrontation. At eighteen, it was hard for Noah to understand the depth of hatred his father held against his real mother. He never realized a human being could hate so deeply and for so long. Jack Caldwell had hated her enough to lie to his son. When asked where all his letters had gone, Jack stalked into his study and unlocked a drawer in the huge oak desk. There, neatly wrapped in rubber bands, were the hundred or so letters Noah had penned to his mother, hoping someday for a response from her. Jack had taken every opportunity to prove to him that his mother never loved him because she'd never written him. Somehow, Noah had never wanted to believe his father, but he had never understood why his letters went unanswered.

Now, Noah knew why. And for the next two years, he understood what the word *hate* meant, because he hated Jack for what he'd done to him. The letters he'd written to Rook were also in that drawer. He looked across his shoulder at Rook, who was trying to dry her face. He ached for her. How could he get her to understand how much he'd always loved her and Mom? How?

Straightening up, Noah grimly settled his cap back on his head. He dug into his breast pocket. "Look, I've got to get going. We're having some trouble with one of the engines on my boat, and I promised to get back over there to help." He cleared his throat and turned, walking over to Rook. She stared up at him, her eyes red-rimmed and filled with anguish.

"I—uh . . ." He grimaced and held up a pair of gold wings. "I know when you graduate from Pensacola, family is supposed to pin on your first set of wings. No one was there to do that for you, Rook. When Captain Stuart found out that we were going to be stationed together, he thought it might be a nice gesture if I did it. He ordered this pair for me to give to you. It's a little late in coming, but the sentiment is still the same." He looked her squarely in the eye, his voice choked with emotion. "I'm proud of what you've accomplished. And I know Mom is, too . . ." The gold wings glittered in his fingers. "I'm sorry I wasn't there to see you graduate. I wanted to be, Rook, but I was in the hospital at the time, and they wouldn't release me so I could make the trip." He pressed the set of wings into her hand. "Here," he muttered thickly, "these are for you. Maybe, if you want, we'll see each other again."

Rook stared down at the wings. Noah turned and headed toward the door, shoulders hunched forward, hands deep in his pockets. "Wait!"

Noah's fingers hovered over the doorknob. He barely turned his head, trying to prepare himself for another explosion from Rook. There was so much to talk about and to explore. All his hopes had been crushed by her anger. What had ever led him to believe that Rook would forgive *and* forget? She was human—hauntingly human—and, if he didn't miss his guess, very fragile right now. She'd just lost the only person in the world she thought had loved her. That wasn't so. He loved her, too, but she didn't know that, and refused to accept it. Noah tasted bitterness in his mouth as he stood there, waiting for her to speak.

"You were going to come down to Pensacola and see me graduate?"

Noah nodded. "Yeah."

"Well—I mean, how did you know I was graduating, or even in the Coast Guard?"

"Grandfather Rufford always kept tabs on you. He was proud of you, too, Rook. Every once in a while, I'd get a note from him about how you were doing, your grades . . ."

"I—see." She closed her fingers around the wings. "You said you were in the hospital? What happened?"

"Nothing much," he muttered, unwilling to discuss it.

"I want to know."

Noah hitched up one shoulder, holding her wavering gaze. "Two days before I was to get leave to fly down and attend your graduation, I got an attack of appendicitis."

Rook saw the tension in his broad shoulders, the stiffness in his posture. Noah had planned to come to her graduation . . . Rook stared down at the wings, touched far more than she wanted to be by his admission. But one humane gesture didn't make up for the years of pain she'd endured from Noah and *his* family. "I see."

"I've got to go, Rook. I'll see you around."

"Yeah . . ." He opened the door, walking away and leaving her alone.

Silence filled the ready room. Somehow, it felt empty without Noah's larger-than-life presence. Rook sat down, her knees suddenly weak. She sat there, brow resting against the hand that held the gold wings. How could Noah be so thoughtful, and yet, beneath it all, be such a callous liar? In all those years, she'd never heard one word from him—ever. The only time she had seen him was on her infrequent visits back to D.C. And then, Jack had made sure they were kept as far apart as possible.

Gil guided the small but ungainly looking '52 toward the eastern end of the city, where the hospital was located. He could see a trauma team standing by with two gurneys and oxygen equipment, just outside the yellow circle where he'd land the bird. "How bad is that one guy?"

"Not breathing well," Annie responded worriedly, staying with her two patients in the rear of the '52.

The landing was uneventful, as was the transfer of the two fishermen. As Annie Locke secured the cabin for the quick flight back to base, she smiled up at Reno.

"Good job, sir. You pumped a lot of air into him when we had to give CPR."

Reno gripped her shoulder and smiled. "Are you saying I'm a bag of hot air?"

Annie smiled, her homely, freckled face lighting up, front teeth white and pronounced. "I guess we both are, sir. That fisherman stands a better chance of making it because we are."

"I hope so, Annie." Reno went back to the cockpit. In no time, they had landed. Both Annie and the copilot were wet, and would have to go for a change of clothes. The '52 would be brought into the hangar, washed, and refueled, so it would be ready for another SAR case if one was called in. Gil praised Annie and Reno for their professionalism on the rescue. He was the last to leave the craft. As he walked away, he saw Chappie Jarvis glowering in Annie's direction. What was his problem? The protective hackles on Gil's neck rose. He slowed his pace, waiting to see if Jarvis, whose nose was a bright red, was going to intercept Annie. The chief was drunk again—as usual. Luckily for Jarvis, he let Annie pass without comment while she went to retrieve a dry flight suit.

Heading through the hangar, Gil went to the line shack to fill out the maintenance sheet and pilot's flight record. Then, he walked back to Admin. He would be senior duty officer for the rest of the twenty-four-hour period. A situation report would have to be filed with the SAR coordinator for the 13th District in Seattle. After that, he'd have to inform the Ops officer, plus call the local newspaper, the *Port Angeles Star*, to give them the details regarding the case. Paperwork was the great enemy of a pilot, he groused to himself, getting writer's cramp. He'd forgotten about Rook Caldwell until he saw her waiting patiently by the SAR desk.

Rook saw the strain around Logan's mouth and eyes as he placed his log on the counter. "How'd it go?"

"One alive and the other, who knows?"

Rook was taken aback by his callous comment. Didn't he care what happened to them? Emotionally spent herself, she didn't pursue the topic. In the next few weeks she'd find out what SAR cases were like, and maybe she'd end up just as flip and hard as Logan. She hoped she wouldn't.

Shaken from her confrontation with Noah, she walked around the desk, unable to sit still. Gil gave her an assessing look.

"Look," he muttered, continuing to fill out paperwork, "I'm going to be busy until about 1400. Haven't you got unpacking to do or something?" And then he forced a smile for her sake, not wanting Rook to take his brusqueness the wrong way. "Take the time off and come back."

Grateful, Rook nodded, picking up her cap. "Sounds good, Mr. Logan."

"Gil," he reminded her, holding her gaze. She looked positively ill, or close to it. Why? Too harried himself, Logan let his observation go. "See you at 1400, okay?"

"Fine." Rook headed out the side door and to the rented car. If she hurried, she'd be in time to meet the movers. Again, her luck was holding—in some ways.

CHAPTER

Six

AT noon Rook sat on one of the unopened boxes, silence surrounding her. The movers had arrived at nine o'clock—right on time. Her stomach grumbled. After not eating any breakfast, and then having her confrontation with Noah, she should be starved, but she wasn't. This was only the third time in her life that she'd felt this kind of terrible, weighted depression. And as much as she fought to get rid of it, she couldn't. It was demoralizing.

Glumly, Rook looked around her newly leased two-bedroom apartment overlooking the straits. She should be happy, but she wasn't. Her first duty station was turning out to be a nightmare. Noah . . .

Tears welled up in Rook's eyes and she sniffed. There was a soft knock at the front door. Getting off the box, Rook dug around in her jeans pocket for a Kleenex. There was none. She walked to the door, not caring if her visitor saw her tears. Rook knew then she'd hit bottom emotionally. The only other times she'd felt like this were when Noah had decided to stay with Jack, and when her mother had died.

Jim Barton's smile faded when he saw the tears in Rook's eyes. There was a smudge of dust on her cheek, and her once neatly brushed hair looked as if someone had tousled it playfully. Her eyes were red-rimmed.

"Looks like you need some help," he said huskily, and

held up two sacks from McDonald's. "I got a couple of hamburgers, some french fries, plus a chocolate and strawberry milk shake." He couldn't tear his gaze from the misery he saw in her gray eyes. "I figured you'd be moving today and you'd be pretty hungry by now."

Touched beyond words, Rook stepped aside, motioning for him to enter. "Come in," she said in a strained tone.

Jim looked around the apartment. Boxes were scattered everywhere. He was bothered by the fact that Rook had been crying. The door shut quietly, and he turned.

There was compassion in Jim's face. A wall of pain burst from Rook's heart.

"Thanks," she whispered, gesturing to the lunch he'd brought.

"You didn't eat anything this morning over at the restaurant."

Rubbing her brow, Rook stood there, unsure. "I know..."

"It was my fault." He shrugged and opened one of the sacks. "Come on, let's get you to take a break and eat."

Rook took a seat on the plum-colored couch. Jim brought over the food and sat down opposite her on an unpacked box.

"What do you want to drink?"

"I—pick one. I don't care."

Frowning, Jim chose the strawberry milk shake and handed it to her. He noticed her hand shaking when she gripped the container.

They ate in silence. Occasionally, Jim would glance up at Rook. It was as if someone had taken all the spirit and fire out of her. What the hell had happened between this morning and now to do that? He finished off his sandwich quickly, throwing the wrapper back into the sack.

"Looks like you've got a big job ahead of you," he commented, trying to keep things conversational. If Rook wanted to talk about it, he'd let her take the first step.

"Yeah, it looks impossible right now." Rook chewed on the food, not tasting it, staring down at the floor.

Jim sensed she was talking about something other than her

apartment. "Sometimes, a little help gets things moving in the right direction. A little talking . . ."

"No," Rook muttered, "nothing's going to help me."

He cocked his head, studying her morose features. "I'm a pretty good listener, Rook."

Why was she eating? It was just sitting in her stomach like a huge, heavy rock. Putting the hamburger aside, she sipped on the cool, sweet milk shake. For some reason, she felt her spirits beginning to lift. Was it because of Jim Barton? No, that was impossible.

Yet, when Rook lifted her chin and looked over at him, her entire being responded powerfully to the hope and care she saw in his eyes. She made a weak gesture around the room.

"Have you ever had your life resemble what this place looks like right now?"

Jim studied the apartment for a long minute, ferreting out what she meant by her question. "I believe there are times when everyone's life seems to fall apart. And when it does, it can be pretty confusing for a while."

"Has it in yours?"

He pursed his lips. "Yeah, a few times." And then he smiled over at her—a smile meant to heal her. "My mother died when I was ten, and I was in a shambles for a long time after that. It made this room look picked up in comparison."

She understood that. Rook set the milk shake aside, the need to talk clawing up her throat. "My mother died less than a year ago. I was away . . . She was alone in Odessa, Texas. She had this heart condition. I knew she was getting worse." Rook rested her hand against her brow, closing her eyes. "I was praying to get done with school and get home before . . . When I graduated, I'd have extra money. Mother needed a full-time nurse. I couldn't afford one on my paycheck—just a part-time one."

The terrible softness of Rook's voice tore through him. "You're blaming yourself for something that was out of your hands, Rook. It sounds like you were doing the best you could."

Sighing, Rook looked up at him, tears filling her eyes. This time, she didn't care what he thought. Somewhere inside her, she knew Jim wouldn't read them as a sign of weakness. "I had two lousy months to go, that was all. Maybe, if she'd had that full-time nurse on duty, she'd have gotten her to the hospital in time to save her."

Rook's vulnerability was excruciating in that moment. It was the first time she'd allowed Jim to see her—the real woman who hid inside those hard walls she erected so easily to keep him out. Gently, he said, "I'm sure your mother loved you for all your efforts, Rook. And I'm sure she understood right down to the last moment of her life." He saw her shrug, her shoulders, which had once been proudly thrown back and square, now broken by the unknown load that had struck her in the last few hours. "What about your father, or the rest of your family? Were they doing anything to help your mother?"

Hardness returned to Rook's eyes. "My father is a bastard. Unfortunately, he's still living and my mother is dead, thanks to him." She stood up suddenly and went over to a box, unpacking it with renewed fury.

Jim assimilated the hatred and vehemence in her contralto voice. He watched Rook for a while as she began to unpack another box. That incredibly mobile and beautiful face betrayed her real self, the woman he wanted to know. Getting up, he walked over to her. His head was screaming at him to do one thing, his heart another. A long time ago, he had found out that his heart was his best guide. Reaching out, he wrapped his fingers around her arm, pulling her to him.

She stood there, looking like a disheveled and lost child in his eyes. The shirt she wore hung down across her long, curved thighs; her hair was mussed and endearing. Reluctantly, Jim released her. "Look, something happened to you between breakfast and now." He searched for the right words, his voice low. "I know you think I'm trying to get you into bed, but I'm not." *Liar.* "I'll admit, I'm damned attracted to you, but Rook, a man can be a friend to a woman, too."

She searched his face. His honesty pared through all her experiences with men and her confusion mounted. She'd never had a man as a friend. Only Jake, but he was more like the grandfather she'd never had. "I don't have the strength to argue with you, Jim. And right now, I've got bigger problems—problems I never anticipated."

A frisson of joy raced through him. Rook had called him by his first name. It was a step in the right direction—a small, but important step of trust. "We have nothing to argue about between ourselves, Rook. Besides, that's not important right now. You are. Come on, sit down. You don't have to tell me the details, but get some of it off your chest."

Rook moved to the couch and sat down. Jim remained where he was. She gave him a curious look. "You're different now. Why?"

"Different?"

"Before, you were chasing me. You aren't now."

"I'm glad you can tell the difference." His smile was encouraging. "Give me the straight scoop. What happened this morning?"

Rook held his unwavering gaze. Before, she'd always had her mother to talk with. Now, she had no one. "I barely know you."

"Maybe we knew each other in a past life."

She gave him a wry glance. "You believe in that stuff?"

"We're comfortable with one another, Rook. It's important that we recognize that, no matter what the reason."

Jim was right, she conceded. "I feel stupid, but it doesn't matter anymore." Gathering her thoughts, she finally spoke. "I just found out that my brother, Noah Caldwell, is stationed here. I didn't know that. It's like a bad dream, Jim."

"You don't get along with him?"

"Not since our parents divorced. Noah could have come with us and helped. Instead, he stayed with Dad. Then, it was up to me to care for Mom."

Barton ambled over, sitting down at the other end of the couch, purposely keeping the distance between them so Rook wouldn't get the wrong idea. "Go on," he coaxed.

Rook launched into the details, leaving out the fact that she was a Coast Guard helicopter pilot. Something inside her said Barton wouldn't like to know that. She was purposefully vague on her career, but filled him in on other pertinent details. When she had finished twenty minutes later, she looked up to see what kind of impact her story had had on him.

Rubbing his jaw, Jim stared back at her. There was so much to digest, and it began to explain why Rook had behaved the way she had with him. Men meant abandonment. When the chips were down, they had proven completely unreliable in her child's eyes. That feeling ran just as deep today, he realized. "A broken home hamstrings everyone," he began. "You were a victim—a helpless pawn on the battleground between your parents. That's a pretty good blow to your sense of self-worth."

"Believe me, my self-worth is in fine shape. And I've got confidence, to boot. I just didn't plan on Noah being here, that was all." Rook stood and went to the kitchen, getting a glass of water. Oddly, she felt better having told Jim about Noah and her family relationship. When she came back into the living room he was still sitting there, frowning.

Jim wasn't so sure about that, but didn't say anything. Her face had color to it now, and her eyes no longer appeared dull. Just talking it out had helped Rook get over the worst of it.

Setting the glass aside, Rook began to unpack another box. "It's been a long time since I confided something this important to anyone."

"See, it didn't hurt, did it?"

She rallied beneath his teasing. "No . . . not yet."

"Oh? You think later on I'll spill this deep, dark secret of yours to the world?"

Rook drowned in his amused features. "No, there's something trustworthy about you, I suppose." A small smile tugged at her mouth.

Placing his hand on his heart, Jim dramatized her statement. "I don't believe this! Finally, she realizes I'm not such a bad sort, after all."

"I have a feeling you know yourself and people a lot better than I do."

"It's our age difference," Jim assured her lightly, watching her respond beautifully to his efforts to pull her out of that darkness that held her in its invisible grip. "How old are you, anyway?"

"Twenty-five. You?"

"Thirty-two. See, I'm an old man in comparison to you."

Jim didn't look that old. He was darkly tanned from working long hours outdoors, physically in peak condition, and bursting with an inner vitality she'd not seen in many men. "I don't see you as an old man," she murmured.

"Whew, that was close."

Rook smiled. She carefully unwrapped the picture of her mother and held it for a long time. Walking over to Jim, she offered it to him, her voice unsteady with emotion. "This is my mom. I mean, it was."

The color photo revealed a woman almost identical to Rook. "She'll always be alive in your heart," Jim told her. The woman in the picture couldn't be more than in her mid-forties. She was small-boned, fragile-looking, with Rook's black hair and incredible, dove-gray eyes. "Tell me about your mom," he coaxed softly. By knowing her mother, he would learn much about Rook that she wouldn't ordinarily have shared with him until much later in their relationship. Jim shook himself inwardly. *Relationship*. Funny, from the instant he'd met Rook, that was what he wanted with her—a long-term relationship, in order to search and explore one another. She had that kind of complexity that drew him, called to him, and he couldn't help but respond to it. Nor did he want to. Jim looked up at Rook, who stood near his right shoulder.

Rook began awkwardly. She had never really had to describe her mother to anyone before. "Her name was Melody, because she had such a beautiful singing voice."

Jim ran his fingers around the gold frame. "She looks a lot like her name: fragile and sensitive."

Sitting down on the floor, back propped against the couch, Rook nodded. "Yeah, Mom was incredibly sensitive to all things. She could smell rain before anyone was aware that it was coming And hear sounds that maybe only a dog could hear." Rook's voice grew with enthusiasm. "When I was a kid, and not working a paper route, we used to go out in the country and pick wild flowers or hunt for special rocks, or wild bird feathers. She knew so much about nature and animals."

Warmth flowed through Jim as he studied Rook's animated features. She didn't realize how much she was like her mother. He said nothing, cherishing all the information because it confirmed what he'd sensed about Rook all along. "I'll bet you like to do those things even today."

Laughing, Rook nodded. "I love animals. And flowers! I used to stop at certain houses on my paper route and smell them."

"What's your favorite flower?"

"Roses. Mom had this wonderful bed of roses that she tended. As her heart condition got worse, she couldn't go out every day. . ." Sadness flooded Rook. "I tried to send her a bouquet every time I got some extra money when I was at school."

He slid his hand over her shoulder, giving it a squeeze. "I have a hunch you really made her day doing that."

Picking at a piece of lint on her jeans, Rook shrugged. "I hope so . . . she deserved so much more happiness than she ever got, Jim. From the minute she married Jack, her life was one miserable nightmare after another. He just kept beating her down. Every time the detectives located our new address and took me back to Washington, D.C., it killed another part of her." Sighing, Rook glanced over her shoulder at Jim. His hand felt reassuring to her. "That's what made me run away. I knew she needed me."

"She loved you."

The words struck deeply through Rook and she nodded,

tears welling up in her eyes. Valiantly, she swallowed the reaction. "Yeah, she loved me a lot. And I loved her, too. I always will."

"She's alive in your heart and mind. That's all that counts." Jim didn't want to remove his hand, but he knew he must, or Rook would interpret his action the wrong way. Now, he understood so much more about her distrust of him. If he was careful and planned his steps, maybe he could get her to like him as much as he liked her.

When Jim removed his hand, Rook felt suddenly bereft. It was a startling realization. And then, she remembered his words about a man being a friend. At no time in the last hour had Jim made a sexual advance. That in itself was jolting to Rook. The pilots at the school were always making remarks about taking her for a romp in the hay. It had been the same in college.

Looking up, Rook studied Jim Barton in the gathering silence. She compared him with the men she had known. There were differences. His face was open and honest, and so were his guileless azure eyes, which contained such life in their depths. He had a broad, generous face with crow's feet at the corners of his eyes and lines around his mouth, indicating that he laughed a great deal. He gave her a slow smile that found its way into her guarded heart. It was a smile that welcomed her examination of him.

"You don't play games, do you?"

Jim shrugged. "No."

"Why?"

"A long time ago, when I was a lot younger, I found out it wasn't a very smart thing to do," he admitted, lulled by the softness coming to her fatigued eyes. "Being myself is important to me. If a woman wants labels, she's looking at the wrong man."

Jim didn't want to overstay his welcome now that he had gained her trust. "Look, I've got to get back to work. My dad will be stripping gears if I'm not hauling a load of timber out of Alpha area by two o'clock." He rose, rubbing his sweaty palms on the thighs of his jeans.

Rook scrambled to her feet, giving him a shy smile. "Listen, I owe you—"

Opening the door, Jim hesitated, casting a glance over his shoulder. "Friends don't owe each other anything. Deal?"

Heat flooded her cheeks and Rook died inwardly. Would she ever outgrow blushing? "If you say so. To tell you the truth, I haven't ever had a man for a friend, so this is new ground to me. I don't know the rules."

Stepping out onto the concrete steps, Jim gave her a nod. "What do you say we make them up as we go?"

"Sounds good," Rook answered fervently.

"I'm going to be kinda busy the next week—"

"So am I."

"Mind if I call you sometime after we both get past our individual workloads?"

Lowering her lashes, Rook saw the longing in Jim's eyes. Panic ate at her. "I don't know. Call me then. I'm going to have a terribly busy schedule . . ."

"Fair enough. See you later, Wild Rose." Jim skipped down the stairs, not even feeling his feet touch the ground.

Rook stood there, watching him walk toward the battered red Ford pickup with the company name emblazoned on the door. Jim walked so proudly, his head held high, his grace undeniable. *Wild Rose* . . . A flutter swept through Rook as she went back inside, mulling over the endearment. The words had come out soft and deep, feathering through her.

"Hey," Tag called in a conspiratorial whisper as he poked his head into the communications room opposite the SAR desk, "you know why your first wedding anniversary is called the paper anniversary?" He looked expectantly at both people. When they shook their heads he said, "After one year you're beaten to a pulp, that's why."

Rook grinned and the enlisted man laughed. She was standing to the rear of the communications room, where the petty officer on duty was explaining some of the intricacies of the air station's radio procedures. She liked the tall, gangly officer immediately.

"Your jokes are as bad as ever, Mr. Welsh," Radioman Third Class Joe Lieber spoke up, smiling.

"I know, but what would you people do without my sick sense of humor around here?" He slipped in and offered his hand to Rook. "Hi, we haven't been formally introduced, but I'm Tag Welsh, AEO officer. Gil said you'd probably be in before 0800 this morning, and I wanted to be the second guy to welcome you on board."

She shook his thin hand. His grip warm and firm. "Thanks, Lieutenant Welsh. I'm Rook Caldwell."

"Call me Tag. Rook's an unusual name. How'd you get nailed with it?"

Noticing that Lieber was listening, she smiled. "Because I was the black crow of my family."

"Is that anything like the black sheep?"

"One and the same. How about your name? Tag."

"Ahhh, my wife Paula chased me until I let her catch me. You know, play tag."

He was incorrigible, Rook decided, with a broad grin. But there was something wrong; she could see desperation in his eyes.

"Hey," Logan called from across the SAR desk, "the skipper wants to chat with you, Tag."

With a good-natured groan, Tag mock-saluted Rook. "My turn on the firing line."

"I already had mine."

"Is he as mean as he looks?"

Rook followed Tag out into the hall. "He appears to be a decent C.O."

"They all do, at first." Tag scratched his head. "But anything's an improvement over the one we just got rid of, believe me. See ya later, boys and girls."

Ward made a cursory inspection of Tag Welsh when he entered the office and shut the door quietly behind him. He invited the AEO to sit down.

"Your record is impressive, Mr. Welsh."

"Tag, sir."

"Tag? As in catch as catch can?"

A grin spread across Tag's long face. "Being aviation engineer officer sometimes forces you into that position, sir."

"I know it does. Tell me about the state of our aircraft."

"All helos are operational."

"Excellent." Ward looked into Welsh's eyes. "And the morale of our people out in the hangar?"

Tag squirmed. So far this morning, Stuart had interviewed nearly all the key officers. He was one of the last to be called in to brief the C.O. Had anyone else spilled the beans yet? Breaking out in a sweat, he muttered off-handedly, "Well, sir, you know. . ."

"No, I don't know. Spell it out for me, Tag. I can't help you or your people if I'm not apprised of a potential crisis."

Crisis was the correct word. Someone must have hinted to the captain about the problems out in the hangar. Tag felt slightly relieved. "Uh . . . well, there is a morale problem in general, sir."

"Why?"

"The last C.O. sort of let things slide around here . . . sir."

Ward saw the officer break out in a sweat, making him look paler than before. The man had to be ill or something. "Let slide in what way?"

"Well, uh, to give you an example, right now, all helo pilots are standing duty every second day."

"I noticed that this morning. How did that occur?" Ward had talked earlier with Bruce Lipton, who had hemmed and hawed around, but not really explained the situation. He was protecting his backside politically by refusing to make an accusation against a fellow officer.

"Two of our pilots requested leave, for different reasons, sir. Both put in for thirty days. I brought it to the attention of Lt. Comdr. Bob Nelson, the Ops officer, who immediately denied their requests. Both pilots asked to see the captain, and he gave it to them without ever consulting the Ops officer. The entire station got shortchanged as a result. It's created plenty of hard feelings between the helo pilots, generally."

"Didn't Commander Nelson try to deny their leave?"

"Yes, sir, he tried to, but the X.O. said the captain didn't care, so it was approved."

"Didn't care?" The words came out in a grate. Holding on to his simmering anger, Ward switched topics. "You followed correct procedure, Tag. Otherwise, how's the morale out in the hangar, in general?"

"Pretty low, sir."

"Why?"

Tag stared down at his highly polished shoes for a moment. "I don't know if I should say anything, sir. But I am AEO, and people's lives are on my hands."

"Go on."

"We've got a chief aviation machinist by the name of Chappie Jarvis who, I believe, is an alcoholic."

Ward's brows dipped immediately. One thing the Coast Guard would not tolerate were drug addicts and alcoholics in its ranks. They got an automatic release from the service if they didn't agree to get off the substance and get professional help. He picked up a pencil, studying it darkly after writing Jarvis's name. "You can prove this?"

"I've tried, sir."

"What are Chief Jarvis's duties over there?"

"He was the line crew chief, in charge of air crew and maintenance, sir."

Ward held the panic deep inside him. The line crew chief oversaw the servicing and maintenance of the aircraft. "What do you mean, *was*?" If Welsh was telling the truth, it would be only a matter of time until a helo wasn't serviced properly and an accident occurred.

"I tried to bring this to the attention of the last skipper, but he told me to handle it. Captain Crane is from the old guard, sir. I feel that since Chief Jarvis has only two years until retirement, a number of people, including the skipper, felt his problem should remain hidden. My people's lives were on the line over there, and although I couldn't prove the chief was drinking directly, I took matters into my own hands. Without support above me, I isolated Chief Jarvis into a paper chase job to keep him away from the helos as much as possible. As a result, the crews are pretty competitive with each other."

"Because Jarvis plays favorites on the duty roster?" Ward guessed grimly.

"Yes, sir. Some flight mechs stand more duty than others."

Making notes, Ward nodded. "You're to be commended for your action on this matter." He knew that a young officer like Welsh could have had his entire career destroyed because he bucked the system and went over the C.O.'s authority. Grimly, Ward added, "I'm ordering Jarvis in for alcohol screening. We can demand that he go whether there's actual proof of his drinking problem or not. I won't tolerate drugs or alcohol among my people. I'll look into this, Tag."

Welsh had no doubt that the C.O. would by the set of his jaw and the flash of contained anger he saw in Stuart's eyes. "Yes, sir."

"Are there any other problems?"

"No, sir."

Ward scrutinized Tag closely, the silence growing in volume. "Sure?"

With a scowl, Tag muttered, "None that I can think of, sir. If you can help me help our people over there, I'd be deeply grateful. They're a fine bunch, but they've been beaten down for the past year pretty badly. That schedule has to be straightened out so that it's fair to everyone."

Ward glanced down at Welsh's personnel file. "How about your personal life? Everything all right?"

Tag squirmed. Crane's attitude about bringing family problems to work had been well-known—he didn't want to hear about them. "Great, sir," he lied. And then he managed a nervous laugh. "That's the only thing that's gone right for me since I got to this base. If it weren't for the support and understanding of my wife, Paula, I'd probably have thought about hitting the bottle, too." And then he quickly added, "That was just a joke, Captain. I joke a lot, so don't take me seriously unless I tell you to."

"Fair enough. So, how long have you been married to this fine woman of yours?"

"Ten years, sir. Paula and I met right after I graduated from high school. She's stuck with me through thick and thin."

"Sounds like a fine partner you have on your team, Tag."

Tag felt a warm flush crawl up his face, his voice fervent. "She's made my life worth living, sir. I'd always heard about these dream marriages, but never personally believed in that myth. I came out of a broken home, where my old man kicked us kids around a lot. I was used to shouting matches. Paula taught me love could be gentle, giving."

Ward nodded, understanding all too well what Tag was saying. Marcia was his mainstay, too. There weren't too many women who were equally strong as the men they married. He gently hedged toward the next problem he saw with Tag. "There's a comment here on your record from the X.O. that your wife's been ill. Can you fill me in, Tag?"

Tag remembered the last skipper's attitude about bringing serious family problems to work. He tried to gauge Stuart's show of concern. "She's dying of leukemia, sir."

"I'm sorry."

Wrestling with an unexpected surge of emotion, Tag choked up. He could only nod.

"How long have the doctors given her?"

Eyes watering dangerously, Tag got up. He thrust his hands into his trouser pockets and turned away, staring out the window toward the hangar. "Six months, maybe less . . ."

Ward got up, poured two cups of coffee, and handed one to Welsh. Tag nodded his thanks and gripped the mug tightly between his fingers.

"She's a fighter, sir. Paula started getting tired about two years ago, but she just shrugged it off. She was teaching kindergarten. She loves kids, sir. We tried for so many years to have some of our own . . . The doctors said that her state of health before she contracted the disease could possibly have made her infertile." He gulped down the scaldingly hot coffee.

Ward waited several minutes while Tag stood stiffly at the window, drinking his coffee. His mind swung to other questions—ones of equal importance. How was Welsh flying? Was his attention one hundred percent on his job, or was part of his mind and heart back with his ailing wife? How much did he worry, and how did it affect his performance. Welsh was an easygoing, likable sort of individual. The air crew personnel probably worshipped him. But with his present stress, Welsh could be slipping in his assigned duties. How were the crews affected? He'd have to find out. Was air safety deteriorating as a result? Morale could plummet dangerously in a situation of this magnitude. And if it did, people could make mistakes—deadly ones—in servicing the helos.

"You know," Tag spoke softly, breaking the silence, "she refused chemotherapy and any other kind of treatment. She said that leukemia was sort of like going to sleep. You just get tired, close your eyes, and one day, you don't wake up." Tag shut his eyes tightly, a tidal wave of grief overwhelming him. The captain wouldn't want to hear his sob story—he had a base to run. How many times a night would he suddenly jerk awake and roll over to see if Paula was still breathing? God, how many times had he thought she wasn't? Her breath was so shallow anymore that Tag had to lie above her, his ear close to her lips, to hear that soft, wispy breath that promised him she was still alive.

"I'd like to meet her," Ward said, meaning it. "I'm sure our wives would have a lot in common."

Tag turned and set the mug on the desk. He managed a painful smile. "Oh, you'll get to meet my Paula, sir. Your wife is having a luncheon for all the officers' wives next week. Paula promised that she'd be there."

"Anything else you'd like to discuss with me, Tag?"

"Uh, no, sir." He smiled shyly. "Here I am, dumping my problems on you. You've got a base to run."

"It's my business and nature to know my people, Tag. I

wouldn't want it any other way. Any time you want to talk again, come and see me."

"Sure you aren't part preacher, sir?"

Stuart grinned and walked Tag to the door, opening it for him. "Oh, I've got a preacher part, all right. But most people wouldn't say it was the inspirational kind."

Tag responded to Stuart's teasing. "I see, sir. More like raining fire and brimstone?"

"You've got it. Thanks for coming in and talking with me, Tag. With your help and care, we'll get this station back on its feet."

"It needs a shot in the arm, sir. This place was dying before you came. I just hope you have a big enough Band-Aid for it."

"The patient's wounded, not dead. We'll bring the air station back. You can count on it."

CHAPTER

Seven

WHEN Annie Locke saw the new C.O. snooping around the line shack and talking with people, she wished she were an ostrich. Instead, because she was working on her helo, she hunched a little more deeply under the engine cowling to continue her inspection of the jet engine. Out of the corner of her eye, she saw Chief Jarvis walking in a hurry toward his office, where Stuart was heading. One of his "favorites"—probably Marchetti—had tipped him off that the new skipper was sniffing about.

Word was circulating like wildfire that Stuart was a tough, no-nonsense officer with a strong streak of fairness in him. Annie prayed that was so. After a year of constant harassment from Jarvis and his groupies, she was ready to slit her wrists. Being one of the few women flight mechanics in the Coast Guard hadn't made it easier on her. When she had heard a woman helo pilot was coming on board, Annie had jumped up and down, clapping her hands. Marchetti had glared at her. Seth Davis, a black aviation metalsmith who had been one of the few men to befriend her and treat her like an equal, had grinned, showing his row of incredibly white teeth and pink gums. And Yeomen Third Class Jody Theron, the "body works" from Admin, who happened to be hanging all over Marchetti at the time, wrinkled her pert nose in disdain.

A new hope thrummed through Annie as she carefully tested each nut and bolt on the engine mount. Her hands were greasy, but she loved the machines. With them, she had magic; she always had. Would Lieutenant Rook Caldwell be similarly mechanically minded? She hoped so. Sometimes, Annie simply wanted to sit down and shop talk about an engine. Most of the line crew and other flight mechs refused to allow her into their circle. She was female; therefore, an outsider. Oh, it wasn't anything so obvious, but when she entered the line shack, all the joking would die away in silence. She would do what had to be done and then leave, feeling the unspoken rejection.

"Petty Officer Locke?"

Annie jerked up, hitting her head on the cowling. Ruefully, she rubbed the spot tenderly after resetting the cowling cover. Turning around on the side of the aircraft, Annie looked down. There was the woman helo pilot, standing beside Mr. Welsh. And when she smiled, Annie sensed instant camaraderie from her.

"I'm sorry, I didn't mean to startle you," Rook said, "I'm Lt. (jg) Rook Caldwell. When Mr. Welsh told me there was a woman flight mech over here, I had to meet her." Rook offered her hand to the young woman.

Heat stole into Annie's face as she leaned down after quickly wiping her hand free of the grease. "Gosh, it's great to meet you, Lieutenant Caldwell." She pumped her hand an embarrassingly long time before releasing it.

"Hey Annie, I told Ms. Caldwell that you were our best flight mech," Tag said. "How'd you like to take some time off from that engine and show her around?"

Annie could have thrown her arms around Welsh and kissed him. "Yes, sir! I'd love to, sir . . ." She scrambled down off the platform, her eyes shining with enthusiasm. "Gosh, when I heard you were coming, I jumped up and down for joy, Ms. Caldwell."

Tag laughed and shared a look with Rook. "She did. That's the truth. I heard later that Annie was dancing all across this hangar floor."

"Ahh, that's an exaggeration, Mr. Welsh."

"Go on, Annie, show her around. Bring her back to my office when you're done. I've got to meet the skipper over at Chief Jarvis's office. See you later, Rook. You couldn't be in better hands. Annie won't brag about herself like some of our guys do. There isn't a pilot here who wouldn't jump at the chance to fly when Annie's on duty. She's top drawer all the way."

Rook smiled gently over at Annie. She was pathetically homely, and yet her blue eyes sparkled with incredible life. There was a constant smile on her face, showing her bucked teeth. Somehow, the obvious deformity didn't lessen Annie's inner beauty. It simply enhanced the radiance that poured out of the woman like sunlight. "I can attest to that, Annie. I was at the SAR desk yesterday morning when the call came in. Later, I overheard Mr. Logan praise your abilities."

Bashfully, she avoided Rook's direct gaze. "I'd fly with any of these pilots any day, Ms. Caldwell. They're a super bunch. Just super!"

As Rook walked around the white H-52 with the orange stripe on the tail, she met the flight mech's smile. "I hope someday, Annie, that you'll say the same thing about me."

"Oh," she gushed, throwing up her arms, "I just know I will! You don't know how lonely it's been out here without someone to talk to."

"Or confide in, maybe?" Rook baited, hearing the pain and loneliness in her voice.

"Yes, ma'am."

Rook liked Annie immediately. She was enthusiastic, and yet she possessed a solid stability. Despite her childlike joy over meeting another woman in a male occupation, there was a strong streak of responsibility to the red-haired petty officer. "Make you a deal. When things get bad and everyone's ignoring you, come on over and talk to me, okay?"

Annie turned and looked at Rook, gratefulness written all over her freckled face. "Thank you, ma'am. You don't know how much that means to me. Have they assigned your collateral duty yet? Do you know where you'll be working when you aren't flying?"

Rook hid the grimace she felt. "The X.O. assigned me as public relations officer."

"Great."

Not so great, Rook thought. She wanted a meaty job—one with responsibility—Not a cushy candy job. Being in P.R. wasn't going to advance her career one bit. After things settled down, maybe she'd go to the X.O. and ask for a different job. She had her sights set on the future safety officer job. That would require three months of school. Well, what had she expected? That the men would think that she was automatically mechanical-minded? Rook knew she'd have to prove herself—as usual.

"Uh-oh," Annie warned. She motioned for Rook to follow her around to the nose of another H-52.

"What?" Rook looked in the same direction.

Annie chewed on her lower lip, worry in her voice. "Chief Jarvis is getting mad. See how his face is going red all over? The skipper just went into his office ten minutes ago. The chief came galloping out of the men's room when someone told him that the skipper was snooping around."

Rook couldn't see what the two men were saying behind the glass-paned door, but it was obvious that Stuart was already beginning to stir things up. She noticed the scowl on Annie's face. "Does Chief Jarvis have anything to worry about?"

With a snort, Annie nodded. "He's a drunk."

Rook blinked. She remembered how tired the pilots she'd met already seemed, and the sour feelings in the Admin office between the yeomen and other people. There weren't many good vibes anywhere, she decided—not even out in the hangar, her future turf. "Are you sure, Annie?"

"Yes, ma'am. Oh, don't worry, I'm not snitching on the chief. He's been drunk every day since he came here a year and a half ago. I ought to know an alcoholic when I see one. My mother was one. And the old C.O. wasn't around enough to care what happened to any of us. Mr. Welsh tried his best to get the chief removed, but it didn't work. What he did do was slot him into a desk job to protect the rest of us." Annie made a face, turning her back on the scene, looking across the apron to the straits, no more than three hundred feet on any side of Ediz Hook, where she stood. "This is my third air station, and I sure found out fast that the chief didn't like women in a 'man's world,' as he called it."

Rook frowned. "Has he made it tough on you?" She was thinking that the pilots could make it tough on her, too, if they wanted.

"I get twice the duty as any other flight mech. At first, Mr. Welsh would make the chief rework the duty roster. But when his wife got ill, he sort of let things slide around here, and I didn't try to get it changed. Fighting Chief Jarvis was like fighting city hall. After a while, I got tired and quit trying."

Anger moved through Rook. Would Stuart find that out and correct it? If he didn't, she would make it known through the proper channels and get it changed. "That's a lot of time spent here."

"I don't mind, ma'am." Annie lovingly patted the sleek, satin surface of the '52's nose. "I'm not married, there's no action in Port Angeles, and there's nothing I love more in the world than flying and SAR cases." Her eyes shone with fervor as she met Rook's measured gaze. "Believe me, there's nothing like rescuing people from life-threatening situations. I live for it." She raised her arm, gesturing around the hangar. "This is my calling, Ms. Caldwell. I don't need a boyfriend or husband. The helos are my friends, my lovers, in a way. The people I rescue are my friends, too." She laughed softly. "You heard about the SAR case on Sunday?"

"Only that one man wasn't breathing when you pulled him from the straits."

"Mr. Gunnison and I took turns on that fisherman. He'd been floating facedown for fifteen minutes. We administered

CPR. And do you know what? He's alive. They brought him back in the emergency room over at the hospital." Satisfaction laced her voice. "We saved him, Ms. Caldwell. We gave him a second chance. Do you know, that's the greatest high in the world for me—the greatest."

As Rook rounded the '52, she could well believe it. She had no boyfriend, no husband, or family, either. Suddenly, as never before, Rook was infused with excitement. Finally she'd found someone who understood, who loved flying as much as she did.

Chappie Jarvis kept a broad smile on his square, weathered face while Stuart was in his office. Unlike everyone else, he wore his service dress uniform with light blue shirt and tie, denoting his authority in the hangar. He stood by the window, hands behind his back, carefully watching the C.O. Ward sat in front of his desk, idly going over some past pink sheets on the '52s. What the hell was he snooping for? Had someone ratted on him? Probably that little buck-toothed bitch, Locke. He ran a damp hand across his balding head. At forty-one, he was not only going prematurely gray, but losing hair as well.

Ward looked up. "Chief, I'd like to have the last three months of maintenance records on my desk by 1600. I also want to see the duty roster for the same time period."

Chappie nodded brusquely. "Yes, sir." The short little bastard of a commanding officer was going to try and get the goods on him. Now he knew Locke had squealed to the new skipper about the extra duty he'd given her. Chappie was sweating profusely. He knew he didn't have time to fix all the records. He'd seen Stuart's kind before: an officer who brooked no shit from anyone. This was probably his last command before they gave him mandatory retirement, so he was going to be a hard ass on everyone. After Stuart left, Chappie walked to the rear of his office. Hands shaking, he fumbled with the key to the file cabinet. There was a fifth of vodka in there, and right now, he needed a drink to fortify himself. If he didn't have those records on Stuart's desk at 1600, his ass was grass.

Tag stuck his head out of his office, and spotted Rook and Annie across the hangar. They were in deep conversation with one another over a jet engine that was being serviced.

"Hey, Lieutenant Caldwell!"

Rook lifted her head. "Excuse me, Annie, I'm being called."

"Yes, ma'am."

When Rook drew closer so that Tag didn't have to shout, she saw him jerk his thumb toward Admin.

"Just got a call from Ty over in Personnel. Said for you to hightail it back to your office. There's some guy waiting over there with a bunch of flowers for you." Tag smiled and wriggled his eyebrows dramatically. "Anyone we should know, Rook? Geez, two days in Port Angeles, and you already have male admirers bringing you flowers. That's impressive."

She snorted softly. "You're jealous, Tag." *Who the hell can it be? Not Noah! God, please don't let it be him.* But that'd be just like him: to show up with flowers and an apology. Rook wanted to crawl into a hole and pull it in after her.

"What's his name?" Tag called.

"None of your business."

"Funny name . . ."

"Tag—"

"Okay, okay, just teasing, Rook. I promise I won't spread word of your new boyfriend all over the base."

Rook pulled open the hangar door, and sunlight cascaded down on her. Tag was endearing. She would bet that he could keep a hundred secrets. The man had a certain air of honor about him. As her heels clicked along the asphalt, Rook took a look around her. The early afternoon had left the skies a clear blue, the sunlight dazzling on the calm waters of the straits. The temperature was in the low sixties, and a hint of ocean salt, mingled with the scent of forest, bathed the air station.

On Sunday, Admin had been deserted and ghostlike, with few people on duty. Today, it was a beehive of activity. Rook was sensitive to the stares she received, and tried to pretend she didn't see or register them. Jane, the phone operator in the small office to the right, waved to her. Rook smiled back.

Stilling her jangled nerves, Rook tried to prepare herself to meet Noah once again. Damn him! He couldn't play fair. He knew she wouldn't react when ten other people were watching them. Taking a deep breath, Rook pushed open the heavy maple door that led into the secretarial pool and her public relations office.

The air she'd inhaled escaped in a rush. Rook stumbled to a halt. There, in a dark blue business suit, white silk shirt, and expensive light-blue tie, was Jim Barton. And in his left hand was a bouquet of the most beautiful red roses Rook had ever seen. The once busy office quieted.

Jim's smile faded when he realized that Rook Caldwell was not a secretary.

"You're an officer."

Her heart pounded hard. Rook didn't know whether to be relieved or not that it wasn't Noah. "And you're wearing clothes—I mean, a business suit!"

"You aren't going to hold that against me, too?"

Heat flamed into Rook's face. She was acutely aware that everyone had stopped work to watch and listen. Her eyes narrowed and she met the gazes of the people in the office. The clatter of office machines and computers promptly began again.

"Follow me, Jim Barton, and don't say another word until we're behind closed doors," Rook whispered in a strangled tone.

Rook walked into her new office and waited until Barton entered before shutting the door. She had an urge to slam it shut, but decided it wouldn't be a mature thing to do. Placing her garrison cap on the desk, she stood opposite him.

"All right, what's this all about? It's been less than twenty-four hours since I saw you last. I thought I'd made it clear I was going to be very busy the rest of the week." Her eyes flashed with disgust. "All this talk about being friends was nothing but a cover, wasn't it?"

Jim gave her a nonplussed look. "Hold on, Rook. I just—"

Compressing her lips, Rook planted her hands on her slender hips. "Do you know what you've done, Barton? You've embarrassed the hell out of me out there! I haven't been on this base two days and *you* show up looking like some fresh college kid, bearing flowers!"

He grinned lopsidedly. "You'd better thank your lucky stars, Lieutenant, that I didn't come in here dressed in my normal work clothes. Think of all the juicy gossip if I'd showed up as a muddy, unshaven lumberjack."

"Jim Barton, you are the most unpredictable man I've ever had the bad luck of meeting!"

"Now, I know you don't mean that."

"Oh, yes, I do!" Rook rolled her eyes. "I don't believe you're for real. Why don't you take yourself and those flowers and get out of here now if you really care about saving what's left of my self-respect with these enlisted people." She groaned and sat down.

Ignoring her plea, Jim took a chair opposite her desk, holding the fragrant bouquet in both hands. "I came for two reasons," he muttered, digging into his breast pocket. "Charlie's got your car running now. He gave me the address of a good foreign car mechanic over in Sequim, where you can finish having it repaired." He handed her the business card. "Terry said for you to bring it over anytime."

"What's a squim?" she asked, eyeing the card.

Jim tried not to smile. "That's Sequim," and he spelled it out for her. "It's an unpronounceable Indian word for the town down the road a ways from Port Angeles." One corner of his mouth twitched as she softened toward him. "Do you have a way to get back? It's only eight miles from here."

Rook muttered, "No, but I'm sure I can catch a bus out to the station."

"There aren't any buses that come out this far."

Rook refused to meet his amused, dark-blue eyes. Why did he have to be so handsome? "Oh . . . well, I'll have one of the other pilots swing by and pick me up." It was going to cost her too much to continue to rent a car right now.

"I've got an even better idea."

Rook gave him a guarded look and glanced out the glass windows to see if the office personnel were still watching. They were. She groaned. Reluctantly, Rook returned her attention to Barton. "Why do I feel I should immediately distrust any idea you might come up with?"

Jim grinned, his tone amicable. "Even though I drive a truck for a living, I happen to own a nice gray Corvette."

"No."

"Don't be so damned contrary."

Rook glared at him. "Could we just limit our conversation to getting my car repaired? You've put me in a highly embarrassing position here at my office by bringing the flowers. Just for your information, I'm one of only six women helicopter pilots in the Coast Guard. I'm the first to be stationed here."

His brows rose. "A lady pilot. I imagine that is rare. I knew you were unique the day I met you."

"I knew you'd have a macho reaction to the fact that I work in a male-dominated occupation."

Jim swallowed his smile. Rook Caldwell could be a wench when she wanted to be. That was part of what drew him to her, he guessed. And, she was a looker—a wild, blushing rose right now. "I don't have a problem with you being a helicopter pilot, but you obviously do."

"I do not."

"You've accused me of being prejudiced against you, when the real truth is, you're prejudiced against timber truck drivers."

"Well, I wouldn't be if the only one I've ever met hadn't plowed into the rear of my car and damn near killed me!"

"I'd be upset for a while, but I wouldn't hold a grudge, like you're doing. After all, it was an accident. Believe me, we timber truck drivers don't make a practice of running over every pretty girl we see in a sports car."

He was right. Contrite, Rook said, "I can't spend office hours chitchatting with you."

Jim slowly unwound from the chair, laying the roses on the desk in front of her. "I understand. Here, these are for you. After yesterday morning, when you were feeling pretty rough, I thought these might cheer you up. Your cheeks turn this color when you get angry or shy."

Rook watched him amble to the door and place a hand on the knob. He turned, and she met his amused gaze.

"When will you take your car over to Sequim?"

"That's none of your business."

He smiled confidently. "Why so defensive around me, Rook? Could it be you're a little bit drawn to me, too, but are afraid to admit it?"

"Get out of here, Barton. I have work to do."

"I thought so." He winked. "I'll be seeing you around—sooner than you think. Oh, yes, what is it those civilized white collar workers say: have a nice day? You have one, too . . ."

Rook pretended to stay busy the rest of the afternoon. She tried to ignore the roses on her desk, refusing to touch them until the beautifully formed buds began to droop. Nothing that lovely should be punished just because she was upset with Jim Barton. Yeoman Third Class Jody Theron assisted Rook in locating a vase. As the secretary arranged the roses, she said, "These are just beautiful!"

"Thank you, Jody." Rook pretended to be hard at work at her desk, hoping Jody would get the hint not to ask any questions.

"And he was so handsome! Wanda recognized him! That's Jim Barton, the son of Howard Barton, and one of the richest men in the area."

Rook riffled through the pile of brochures "Yes, I believe he said his name was Barton."

"What a catch," Jody sighed, standing back and admiring her handiwork.

Rook lifted her head, pinning the woman with a black stare. "Just for the record, Petty Officer Theron, Mr. Barton plowed into the rear of my sports car two days ago with his timber truck. He was just here to apologize and give me the name of a good mechanic in Squim, or whatever it's called."

Jody smiled weakly and retreated. "Yes, ma'am."

The door shut quietly and Rook stared blindly down at the paperwork. Dammit, she shouldn't have to explain herself to anyone—especially nosy office personnel. Men! They had always been a pain to her. Could anyone have had a worse first day than she had?

Chappie set the maintenance and duty roster records down on Captain Stuart's desk with as much decorum as he could muster. It irked him when Stuart barely looked up to acknowledge his dramatic flourish or presence.

"Thank you, Chief. That will be all. Please close the door as you leave."

"Yes, sir."

Ward pushed the other paperwork aside after the chief had left. He picked up the March duty roster, rapidly perusing the names on it. A scowl started to form on his broad brow, and he jotted down the last names of a couple of people who, it appeared, were standing more than their fair amount of duty.

Minutes stretched into an hour, and then two. The next time Ward looked at his watch, it was six o'clock. He was supposed to be home for supper. He picked up the phone and called Marcia.

"Captain Stuart's residence."

He smiled, relaxing when he heard Marcia's voice. "You don't say."

"Ward! Where are you? Don't tell me: you're still at the office. I should have expected this."

"Sorry, honey, but I tripped over a potential problem and I got lost in the details of it."

"Uh-oh. Bad?"

Rubbing his face, Ward said, "It has all the earmarks of being a mess, but I can't tell until I investigate some more. Look, I'm going to be late. I'll probably get home around ten."

"No problem. I'll put the pot roast in the microwave and heat it back up when you get here."

"Thanks, honey. How are the boys?" More specifically, How was Kenny?

Marcia's tone lowered a bit. "Robby's in his room doing homework."

"And Kenny?"

"Out."

"Out? Where?"

"Now, Ward you can't dog his heels every minute of every day."

"Dammit, Marcia, we've been through this before. I gave him specific instructions to leave word where he was going to be and with whom."

"Kenny was here for dinner, then some boys in a car came by and picked him up."

At least Kenny was leaving his grounded car alone—so far. "Who were they? Did you meet any of them?"

Apologetically, Marcia said, "No. It was dark, and they just drove up and honked the horn for him. He said it was some new friends he'd made at school today."

"I'll bet. Did you tell him he had to be home by half past ten?"

"Yes," she said tiredly. "Ward, just relax. You know if you pressure Kenny too much, he'll explode like he did last time. We can't afford to have him cause a similar embarrassment here at Port Angeles. The town's too small."

With a snort of frustration, Ward growled, "How is it I can demand and get the respect of three hundred base personnel, but not my own son? Just where the hell did I go wrong?"

"Honey, don't do this to yourself—or me. When you get home, we'll talk more."

"I suppose. Okay, look, I'll see you a little later. I love you."

"And I love you, Ward. Don't worry, everything will be all right. Kenny will be home on time and things will work out fine."

Marcia tensed when Ward entered the house. She gripped the cup of tea she held in her hands a little tighter. It was eleven o'clock. She saw how tired he was—the corners of his mouth were pulled in and his eyes, which normally held a devil-may-care glint, were now dull. He carried not only a bulging briefcase, but a huge stack of records beneath his left arm.

"Here," she said "let me help you. What did you do? Bring all of Personnel home with you?"

"This isn't from Personnel. It's the line crew roster and maintenance records of the '52s." Wearily, Ward allowed her to take the parcel. He placed the beeper, which was with him twenty-four hours a day, on the counter, along with his hat. He dropped the briefcase beside the table, thinking that for a woman of forty-three, Marcia had one hell of a figure beneath the simple pink cotton robe she wore. He could see the feminine ruffle of her silk nightgown as he slid his arms around her, drawing her hard against him.

"Mmmm, you not only feel good, Mrs. Skipper, but you also smell good . . ." and he released her enough to tilt her face upward and kiss her.

Reluctantly, Ward let her go afterward. He gave her a faint smile, brushing a strand of hair from her cheek. "You grow prettier every day, did you know that?"

She warmed to his roughened voice, sliding her hands up his arms to his shoulders. "And you look whipped. Come on, I've got some lemon spice tea just about ready to brew. The den is about the only room in this house that's free of boxes and paper. I started a fire in the fireplace. Why don't you go sit in there and I'll bring you the tea. Did you grab a bite to eat?"

Ward nodded, bussing his wife's cheek before releasing her. Marcia instinctively knew when he was at low ebb, and tried to be there for him when he needed her the most. Grateful for her care, he asked, "Are the boys in bed?"

Marcia's hands froze in midair above the tea tray. "Robby is."

Ward hesitated in the doorway, the beginning of a frown working its way across his brow. "And Kenny?"

Turning, she said, "He's not home yet," and then quickly held up both her hands. "I'm sure he'll be home shortly. He's only a half hour late."

Hot rage welled up in Ward. He felt Marcia's cool fingertips on his arm. "Damn that kid—"

"Please, Ward. Don't upset yourself about this. He's a half hour late, not two or three hours. He was so excited today that he'd made some friends right away that he's probably lost track of time."

Compressing his mouth into a thin line, Ward muttered, "That's the way it started last time, Marcia. First, he was fifteen minutes late, then forty, and finally, hours at a time. Dammit, I can't afford to have my son embarrassing my command by getting lousy grades, carousing around at all times of the night, and getting into drugs again! This isn't D.C., where one kid's screwup goes unnoticed because the city's so big that word doesn't circulate as quickly."

"Ward, give him a chance, will you—"

The front door opened and then closed. They both turned toward it. Kenny ambled in, hands in the pockets of the pale pink cotton slacks he wore. His hair was long and uncombed, giving a slightly wild appearance to his lean face.

"Hi, everybody."

"You're a half hour late, Kenny."

Pouting, Kenny leaned against the wall and crossed his feet, digging his toe savagely into the pale gold carpet. "I'm sorry, sir."

Marcia gripped Ward's arm tightly, a silent plea not to

start another quarrel with their son. She heard the belligerence in Kenny's tone.

Ward measured his son's sullen response. He distrusted anyone who couldn't stare him straight in the eye, and Kenny never could. "I'm sorry, too. For that half-hour error, you're grounded for the rest of the week. You'll come straight home from school, do your homework, and stay *here*."

"That isn't fair!" Kenny shouted, jerking upright.

"You made a contract with me and your mother, and you blew it, Kenny. You gave your word. We talked long and hard about what it meant to transfer here to Port Angeles. You've been part of a military family for seventeen years, and you know what it means to be conscious of the image it carries with it."

"Dammit, I wasn't late on purpose! Steve's car had a flat tire between here and Sequim, or I'd have been home on time."

"Why didn't you get to a phone, then?"

Disbelief shadowed Kenny's features. "Because there wasn't any . . . *sir*. Have you been out on that portion of 101? If you had, you wouldn't ask such dumb questions. It's nothing but farms and forest. There are no phone booths."

Trying to throttle his heightening anger, Ward growled, "Can you prove the car had a flat tire? Or is this just another one of your convenient lies?"

Marcia stepped between them. "Now listen, both of you. You're both tired, and the day's been long. Kenny, go get washed up and get to bed. Any homework you have can be done tomorrow morning. Just set the alarm earlier. Ward, I'll see you in the den. Now, go on, both of you."

Ward stared steadily at his son. He raised his finger, jabbing it toward him. "You're grounded. Just remember that, or else."

"Or else what?" Kenny shouted shrilly. "You've already taken my car away from me. Jesus Christ, I just got here to this stinkin' one-horse town and you're on my ass already! As usual!"

Ward brushed by Marcia, halting inches in front of his son. "And I'll be on your ass every second, if I have to be, until you no longer live in this house."

Kenny whirled around, heading for the stairs. "You don't give a damn about me! All you care about is your career. You're so afraid I'll tarnish your good-guy image. Well, don't worry, *sir*. No one wants to stay the hell out of your way and that Super Coastie image more than me." He saw his father's face tighten and fled up the stairs to his room before Ward could retaliate.

Ward halted at the bottom of the stairs, cursing softly beneath his breath, turning and almost running into his wife. He glared down at Marcia, frustration written in every crease of his face. "Sometimes I wonder how we managed to have a kid like that. Robby's so damn good in comparison to him." He brushed past Marcia, heading toward the den. When days went bad, they went all the way.

CHAPTER

Eight

GIL greeted the next morning with bloodshot eyes. He hadn't slept well because he had missed Eve's presence in the bed. She was still acting like a child, sleeping out on the couch. Needing her warmth, Logan had tossed and turned all night. Later, he'd nicked himself shaving, and he knew it was an omen. He glanced down at his watch, and realized it was nearly 0630. He had to hurry.

Eve forced herself to get up and put on her peach-colored silk robe. She heard Gil bumping around in the study of their small, two-bedroom house. Halting at the doorway, she saw he was dressed in uniform, with an olive green flight suit tucked beneath one arm. That meant he had duty for the next twenty-four hours, beginning at three today—again.

"You said you'd attend my club's dinner tonight."

Startled, Gil jerked up from his crouched position at one of the file drawers. "I forgot, Eve. Things are crazy over at the station right now, and it slipped my mind." Normally, Eve slept until ten every morning. Eve's blonde hair was mussed about her fragile face, giving her an ethereal look. Her voice was husky with sleep, and her eyes were barely open. Her lips were soft and inviting. Gil ached to take her back to bed with him. Things always got repaired between them when he loved her. Gil struggled for words to pacify Eve. "Look, I'm sorry, honey. I know how much this dinner meant to you."

Crossing her arms, Eve muttered, "You forgot? You always forget, Gil. If it has anything to do with your precious Coast Guard, you automatically remember it! But if it's something that's important to me, you forget it."

Gil raked his fingers through his hair and stood up, shutting the file drawer more loudly than he'd intended. "Dammit, you *are* important to me, Eve."

She gave him a scalding look. "My body's important to you. I'm not."

He jammed several files into his leather briefcase. "That's not true, and you know it." He allowed his hands to drop to his sides and faced her. "What the hell's happening to us, Eve? All we've done the last six months is fight. I try to find some neutral ground between us, but you always find something wrong with it. I'm sorry I forgot about that dinner tonight, but you know what kind of shape the air station is in. Now, this new C.O. is really stirring up the pot. All of us thought things were chaotic as hell before, but we were wrong. The shit is really going to start hitting the fan today. The captain ordered all the flight records from maintenance, and Jarvis knows his ass is going to get burned."

With an exasperated sigh, Eve whispered angrily, "I don't *care* about that station, or the new C.O., or Chief Jarvis! I think he's an alcoholic, and deserves to get punished for everything he's been doing wrong."

"Let's talk about us. How about if I make up for the dinner I'm missing by taking you out tomorrow night? Are you game?"

Eve pouted a few moments and then murmured, "I guess so . . ."

Gil approached her, placing his hand on her shoulder. He leaned down, nuzzling her cheek. "Champagne? Flowers? And the best food in Port Angeles? That little French restaurant on the outskirts?"

Her resolve wavered and she glanced gratefully up at him. There was a catch in her voice. "That sounds nice, Gil. We've barely seen each other the last five months."

"I know, I know . . ."

Eve looked at her watch. "Where are you going so early? It's only half past six."

Gil steeled himself for the inevitable. "I promised Lieutenant Caldwell that I'd give her a ride to the station the next couple of mornings." When he saw Eve's face twist in shock, he quickly added, "Her sports car got rear-ended by a timber truck two days ago. I'm following her to Sequim to drop it off, then giving her a ride back to the station."

"I don't believe this!"

"Eve—for Christ's sake."

"No! Don't you *dare* touch me, Gil Logan!"

Helplessly, he watched Eve march down the hall and disappear into the living room. "Sonofabitch," he muttered, and then walked over and picked up his cap, settling it on his head. His stomach was tied in knots. Picking up the briefcase, he stalked into the living room. Eve was curled up on the couch, face set, lips pouty, staring at the opposite wall.

Gil crouched down in front of her, his hand resting lightly against her robed knee. "Honey, look at me . . . please."

"Go to her, Gil. That's where you want to be anyway."

He squelched the urge to curse. Instead, he said quietly, "That's not true, Eve. I love you. I always have and always will. Look, we're going through a tough time together. And what's making it worse is the hours I've got to spend at the base. But that will ease, sooner or later."

She tightened her arms against her breasts, refusing to meet his searching gaze. All her fears were coming true. "The officers' wives will talk! By noon today I'll hear from Jordanna how you gave Lieutenant Caldwell a lift to the station. It will be all over Port Angeles by nightfall!"

Closing his eyes, Gil muttered, "Eve, to me, she's just another junior officer who happens to fly helicopters—not a potential affair. Have I ever given you reason to distrust me?"

"I've heard of these cockpit romances."

"I've never heard of or seen one in my six years in the Coast Guard." He stroked her knee. "If it will make you any happier, it appears that she has a boyfriend already. Jody Theron was telling us that Howard Barton's son is courting her." Gil saw

Eve barely flick a glance in his direction, but it was a sign that she was listening. She never had been able to pass up gossip. "Apparently, he came over early yesterday afternoon with a dozen roses. No, make that thirteen. Jody counted them. They went into Caldwell's office and talked for another ten minutes behind closed doors. Now, do you feel better?"

Eve's lower lip pushed out a bit more, but she refused to respond to Gil's entreaty. "Jody Theron is the biggest gossip on base and you know it! She deliberately starts rumors that have no foundation."

Releasing a long breath, Gil slowly rose. "Eve, ten people in the office saw Barton walk in with the roses. Do you want signed affidavits from them as proof that it happened?"

She turned her head away from Gil, staring over at the wall. "I'll call someone this morning and verify your story."

He almost smiled. She'd call Jody herself. Gil wasn't sure who was the bigger gossip: Jody or Eve. "Do what you want. I'll give you a call tonight around five if I'm not called out on a case."

"Who else has the duty tonight?"

"It's not Lieutenant Caldwell, if that's what you want to know. Sam Talbot's my copilot."

"Fine."

He leaned over, pressing a kiss to her silky hair. "I love you, Eve. I'll see you tomorrow evening at five."

"Fine."

Gil straightened up, giving her a look of longing. As he turned away, the awful truth that their marriage was crumbling hit him. Had his parents ever gone through times like this? What had they done to solve their problems? Pride prevented Gil from asking his father. Bob Logan had spent twenty years in the Coast Guard, and he had made his marriage work. Why couldn't he? Gil headed out the door, automatically looking up at the sky that he might have to fly in today or tonight. For the second day in a row, it was devoid of the stratus clouds and pockets of low-hanging fog that always plagued the seacoast town. Instead, there was a vibrant pink on the horizon, which meant that the sun would rise in another half hour. Was it a sign that maybe the day would go better than expected? His mind revolved ahead to Rook Caldwell as he backed the two-door Ford out of the driveway and onto the street. If Jim Barton was her boyfriend, that would take the heat off him. He'd have to find out if Jody's gossip was true.

Rook was jumpier than usual. She expected Jim Barton to mysteriously show up at her doorstep at seven o'clock instead of Gil Logan. He didn't. And, as Gil followed her over to Sequim, she expected Barton to be waiting for her at the garage. He wasn't. Terry, the mechanic, was an old man who knew a lot about foreign cars. He promised to call Rook when it was repaired, but told her not to expect it back for at least two weeks. The aged mechanic didn't have a loaner car to give her. Rook's heart sank for the inconvenience it was going to cause her.

On the way back in Gil's car, Rook hesitantly explained the situation.

"That's not a problem. I can come by and pick you up in the morning. Depending on the duty, I'm sure one of the other officers would be happy to take you home. If we pull duty together, I can pick you up and drop you off."

"I can't ask that of you, Gil. It's awfully sweet, but—"

"Pilots stick together, Rook. We're like family, in a way."

She wanted to strangle Jim Barton for all the problems he was causing her. What would the base gossip be about her riding with different male officers for two weeks? If Rook didn't miss her guess, pert little Jody Theron would be there to log it all in and then blast it around the station with that mouth of hers. She was a loose cannon. Already, she'd heard a couple of yeomen whispering about the roses. Rubbing her brow, Rook grimaced.

"Let me think about it, Gil." There had to be a better solution. She absolutely refused to think about taking Barton's offer of his Corvette. Then, the tongues would really wag.

"Okay, no sweat. Whatever you want to do is fine with me."

* * *

At the office, Rook's orientation got underway. To her delight, the Ops officer told her that she'd fly every day, if possible. At 1300, Gil would take her on her first familiarization flight. Already, things were looking up, and some of her depression over the car situation evaporated. Changing into her one-piece olive flight suit, Rook felt good about herself. Finally, she was going to do something she was very good at: fly. If she could do it well and impress Gil, he would tell the other pilots, in turn, that she could be trusted. Throughout the rest of the morning, Rook prayed that she wouldn't screw up on the coming flight. She just couldn't.

As Rook walked down the hall with Gil to take the FAM flight, she saw Chief Jarvis. He didn't look happy, either. She watched the impeccably dressed man walk up the stairs that would lead to the skipper's office.

Gil opened the door for Rook. "The shit is going to hit the fan now," he told her quietly.

"What do you mean?"

"Jarvis has been playing favorites over at the hangar for some time now. The old C.O. didn't give a damn what he did or how he did it. Now, I think Stuart's on to his games."

Rook nodded. "Funny, Annie Locke said the same thing to me about the chief, yesterday."

"Jarvis hates Annie. He's been on her case for as long as I've been here. I don't know how she's hung in there."

"Why does he hate her, Gil?" Rook knew the answer before he even said it.

"Oh, he's one of those throwbacks to the Ice Age who believes women should be barefoot and pregnant. You know the type."

"Unfortunately, I do."

He smiled over at her. "Don't worry, there aren't too many Ice Age types here. I think you'll find we're professionals."

"I'm finding that out already, and believe me, it's a huge load off my shoulders."

Out of habit, because pilots were buddies, Gil placed his

hand on her shoulder. The gesture shocked him as much as it did Rook. He saw the panic in her eyes and quickly broke contact. Had anyone seen it happen? "Sorry," he muttered, "I'm already treating you like one of the guys."

"That's all right, Gil. It was the thought that counted. I appreciate you making me feel as if I'm part of this team before I've even begun proving myself."

Heat crawled into Gil's cheeks over his stupid, unthinking gesture. Was Jody Theron watching through the blinds as they walked over to the hangar? Oh, Christ, if she was, and Eve found out about it, there would be hell to pay. "Anything's going to be easier than what Jarvis is walking into, believe me," he muttered, trying to switch to a more impersonal topic.

"Chief Jarvis reporting as ordered, sir," Chappie snapped in front of the C.O.'s desk.

Ward looked up from the neat piles of paperwork in front of him, allowing the chief to remain at attention. A quick perusal told him that Jarvis knew how to influence a superior. His uniform was clean and pressed. His shoes were like ebony mirrors. Ward studied the man's impassive face. He saw a thin sheen of sweat on it. Had he been drinking prior to coming over here? Anger made Ward's voice clipped and steely.

"Chief, I studied the duty roster for six hours last night, and what I found requires a lot of explanation. For instance," Ward dragged out one of the many lists he'd prepared, "how can you explain the fact that Locke, who's an E-6, has stood forty-three percent more duty than anyone else? That includes almost half of the duty weekends. Davis, who's also an E-6, has stood thirty percent more duty than average. There are certainly plenty of E-4s and -5s who could take up the slack and give those two time to fulfill other, more important duties. And Marchetti, who's only an E-4, has stood less duty than anyone."

Jarvis swallowed hard. The bastard was going to make him stand at formal attention. Normally, chiefs were accorded special privileges by officers, and particularly by C.O.s, because of their importance in the infrastructure between lower enlisted rates and the officer group. He'd swallowed half a pint of vodka this morning before coming to work, and then eaten a chocolate bar to cover any residue of liquor on his breath. God knew, he needed fortification for this confrontation.

"Sir, if I may sit down and explain?"

"You can stand there and give me an explanation, Chief Jarvis."

Hatred exploded within Jarvis. He only had two more years before his twenty years were up, and he was eligible for a pension. Now, this short shit was going to threaten his entire career. "Yes, sir," he croaked in a rumbling voice.

"First, why has Locke stood so much duty?"

"Many of my men were either sick or had leave, and she was one of the few I could pull in on short notice, sir."

"That wasn't just watch duty, Chief. That was ready-crew duty. Weren't you worried about her mental state after a while? Flight mechanics are very special people, in a highly responsible position. The helicopter and two highly trained pilots are in their hands every time they fly out on a case."

"Sir, it was just one of those situations where Locke happened to be available."

"For a year?" Ward exploded. "You're telling me this woman just conveniently happened to be there when another one of your personnel fell sick? You were in charge of deciding who gets leave and when. If you saw too many people were requesting leave at the same time, depriving you of the necessary crew on the line, why did you allow it to be approved?"

Chappie felt sweat running down either side of his rib cage. His pulse began to pound at his temple, creating a monstrous headache. "Sir, things weren't exactly shipshape around here the last year."

Ward ignored his feeble protest. "Let's go to Seth Davis. Explain why he stood so much extra duty. He's got a fine record, and had high marks until he came here. What happened?"

"It was his attitude, sir."

"What exactly is his attitude problem, Chief?" Ward saw the instant hatred in the chief's squinted blue eyes. Jarvis was one of those salty old bastards who wore the label "redneck" well.

Chappie wanted to wipe his forehead; he could feel sweat collecting on it. "He had a bad attitude when he got here, sir. He didn't like being told what to do and when. So, I assigned him extra duty to straighten him out."

"Did you go to Lieutenant Welsh about Davis's attitude problem, Chief?"

"No, sir."

"Why not?"

"I figured I could handle it, sir."

Ward stared at him, allowing a good minute to pass in silence. The chief was sweating profusely. Slowly, he turned the page on his copious notes. "What about Angelo Marchetti? He's a flight mech, too, but he seems to have fewer duty days than anyone."

"He was sick an awful lot, sir."

"Did you send him over to the dispensary to get a chit to prove it, Chief?"

"Uhh . . . no, sir, I didn't."

"So, you just gave him time off?"

Swallowing convulsively, Jarvis croaked, "Yes, sir."

"You know, Chief, I can check all this out. As you can see, I'm writing down your explanations to all the questions I asked."

"Yes, sir." He blinked away the sweat, dragging in a couple of deep breaths. His back hurt from standing at such rigid attention for so long.

Ward pressed down the intercom. "June, get me the personnel files on Locke, Davis, and Marchetti. Also, I want their medical records from sick bay."

"Right away, Captain Stuart."

"Thank you, June."

Ward returned his attention to Jarvis, his eyes hardening. "Chief, I've got to tell you, I'm not happy with what I've discovered so far. The transfer rate, absenteeism, and disciplinary rates are the highest I've ever encountered. They indicate something is wrong. You were in charge of the line.

I've already alerted Lieutenant Welsh that he's to take a stronger day-by-day interest in what is going on over there until this investigation can yield some solid answers. From this minute on, Lieutenant Welsh must approve your duty roster before you can institute it. Is that understood?"

"Yes, sir." Ordinarily, no officer took interest in the duty sections. That was a chief's responsibility. Now, Stuart was taking his power away from him and treating him like an errant child. He was almost twice Welsh's age, and felt humiliated by the order. Stuart was trying to embarrass him in front of the line crew.

"Further, Chief Andy Johnson will take over all maintenance on the H-52s from this day on."

Jarvis gasped, and he lost his stiff posture for an instant. "Captain, you can't do that! I—"

Stuart leaped to his feet, both clenched fists resting lightly on the desk. "You're at attention, Chief," he whispered tautly.

Squaring his shoulders, Chappie stared straight ahead. Controlling his violent emotions, he rasped, "Why are you taking my job away from me?"

"To give you time to think about how you've played favorites with my people, for one. Let's get something real clear between us, Chief: I don't let anyone come down on the people who work under me. They're all treated the same."

It had to be Locke who blew the whistle on him, Chappie thought. He was reeling in shock. Davis had probably squealed, too—the nigger. Gathering what was left of his shredded ego, he muttered, "I *have* treated everyone fairly, sir."

Ward relaxed. "I'll know the answer to that soon enough, Chief. That's all for now. Dismissed."

Silence filled the office after Jarvis left. Ward was angry that the chief had tried to cover his ass and had lied to him. Restless, he got up and paced the spacious office. The wall of windows afforded him a view in two major directions: from the hook, he could look across the straits. In the distance, he could see British Columbia and its capital, Victoria. The other set of windows gave him a view behind the hook. The deep-water harbor was busy with freighters from Japan, hauling logs aboard with huge cranes. His thoughts turned to Rook Caldwell. Logan had taken her out on her first FAM flight, and he wondered how she was doing.

"This is CG 1406, Port Angeles."

Rook glanced over at Gil. He had given her permission to fly and he answered the radio call from their station.

"This is CG 1406."

"CG 1406, we've got a SAR case for you."

"Wait one." Gil always kept the knee board strapped to his right thigh. He took out a pen, ready to write. "Port Angeles, CG 1406, go ahead."

Rook listened intently, her heart picking up in beat. A SAR case! And Gil was going to take the call, even though she was a green copilot! Excitement wove with sudden fear as Rook wondered if she could do her end of the job without screwing up. True, they had an experienced flight mech with them. Angelo Marchetti seemed to know the ropes well enough.

Gil signed off and gestured toward the open ocean just ahead of them. They had flown the coastline in a westerly direction, acquainting Rook with various important points that the pilots used when flying by sight.

"Possible boat sinking about four miles dead ahead."

Rook glanced at him and then increased airspeed. The small '52's rotary blades beat harder, and the shudder within the fuselage increased slightly. "The air station said it was telephoned in. Is that normal?"

"Smart cookie," he congratulated her, pulling the map across his lap. "No, it's not normal. You're going to find out that some idiots think it's funny to call in phony rescue calls. I can't begin to tell you how much time, fuel, and concern have been wasted on these false alarms."

Anger made Rook frown. "Isn't there any way to intercept that kind of call?"

"If there was, believe me, the Coast Guard would have employed it. Okay, let's go down to five hundred feet. We've got good viz and it will give you an edge on spotting the debris, or people in the water, a little quicker. If," he said grimly "there really is a sinking."

Clouds were moving in from the west, blotting out the sun. Rook knew this was ideal. Flight crews had a tough time spotting anything floating in the water when it glinted blindly with sunlight.

Directed by Gil, Rook eased the '52 into the first leg of an expanding square. They both kept a sharp lookout for debris, oil slick, or people on the fairly calm surface of the Pacific.

Gil fumed to himself. They'd dropped a Datum Marker Buoy, which would record, via radio signal, the winds, tides, and current direction. After forty-five minutes of widening the pattern, they'd seen absolutely nothing; not even debris, or a telltale oil slick. "The ocean's fairly calm today, with no strong currents in any particular direction," he pointed out to Rook. "If it was running confused, we might have missed one of the indications for a yacht sinking, but this isn't adding up."

"You think it was a fake call?"

"You bet I do. I'm radioing Port Angeles. I'm recommending they suspend the search."

District 13 Operations Center approved the suspended search. Logan got permission from Port Angeles to continue the FAM flight. At Gil's request, they climbed to a thousand feet. Rook saw the rolling ocean beneath her booted feet. It was a patchwork of greens and grays as the sunlight moved through the swells.

"Hey, Mr. Logan, whales at four o'clock!" Marchetti sang out in an excited voice.

Whales? Rook craned her neck to the right, trying to get a look.

"Roger, four o'clock. Let's go down and take a look," Logan told her.

Excited by the possibility of seeing the large, beautiful mammals, Rook followed his orders. She banked the helo to the right, rapidly descending to a hundred feet. There, just below and a quarter mile ahead of them, was a large herd of whales. Their black, barnacled backs shone sleekly as they surfaced and blew huge plumes of spray into the air.

"Can you see the new calves?" Gil asked, grinning. He pointed to a baby whale between its two gargantuan parents.

"Yes!" Rook's excitement increased. "Aren't they beautiful! There must be fifteen or twenty in this pod. And look! Are those porpoise over there?"

"Sure are. A lot of them, too. Here, let me take the controls. I want to go down for a closer look. I've got a camera I always carry. It's behind my seat. Get it, and we'll try and shoot a couple of pictures for your scrapbook."

Rook hesitated. "Are we allowed to do this?"

Grinning, Gil took over the flying and pointed the nose of the '52 downward. "Of course—it's part of your training. Right now, I'm going to show you some beeps to a hover."

With a shake of her head, Rook reached behind his metal seat and drew out the camera. "I like your training methods, Gil."

"Stick with me, kid, and I'll show you a whole new world."

Rook saw the entire herd dive as the '52 came closer to them. The altimeter registered fifty feet. She got the camera ready, aiming it down in front of the nose, adjusting the focus.

"I'm going to try and guesstimate where they'll surface from here," Gil told her, jockeying the '52 forward and hovering at fifteen feet above the ocean. "They gotta come up for air. We just have to figure out where."

Smiling, Rook waited. Minutes passed without a sign of the mammals.

Gil was almost ready to move ahead when suddenly, a huge whale came boiling out of the depths of the Pacific, water churning and frothing in his wake.

Rook gasped, jerking back in her seat as the whale flipped its huge tail and propelled itself up . . . up . . . until finally, she could see its jet-black eye. Her mouth fell open as she watched its nose come within two feet of the whirling rotor blade above them. His gleaming body filled the entire cockpit window surface, each barnacle and sucker fish attached to him visible. He hovered there briefly before gracefully sinking downward. A huge surge of water shot skyward as he disappeared back into the ocean.

Gil stared, stunned. Marchetti, who had wedged himself between the two seats, gasped. The camera dropped out of Rook's hands and landed in her lap. Finally, reason interceded, and Gil quickly lifted the '52 well out of range of the playful whale.

"Man, I don't believe this," Marchetti whispered. "Did you see that whale, Mr. Logan? I swear, he knew what he was doing and just how close he could get to those blades! That sucker jumped fifteen feet straight up in front of our windows. Outrageous!"

Gil shook his head, exchanging glances with Rook, who had paled. "Incredible," he muttered.

"Impossible," Rook stammered. "How was he able to judge the distance? His nose was barely two feet away from our rotors. My God, what if he'd hit them?"

Gil didn't even want to think about *that* possibility—his ass would have been strung up so fast it would have made his head swim.

Managing a choked bit of laughter, Marchetti slapped the pilot on the shoulder. "Going out with you is downright dangerous, Mr. Logan."

The shock began to wear off Rook as they flew back to the air station. She gave Gil an apologetic look. "I'm sorry, I forgot to snap the photo."

"Don't worry, none of us were thinking too straight when that bastard decided to scare the hell out of us," he grumbled.

Her eyes rounded. "Do you really think that whale knew what he was doing?"

"If he didn't, he sure as hell fooled me."

"And me," Marchetti chimed in, grinning from ear to ear. "Man, wait 'til the guys hear about *this* one. The one that got away, Mr. Logan!"

Gil turned and nailed Marchetti with a dark look. "Not one word of this to *anyone*, Marchetti. That's an order. Understood?"

Glumly, the flight mech nodded. "Yes, sir, Mr. Logan."

And then he brightened. "But what a story! I mean, it's fantastic, sir!"

"My court martial would be fantastic, and my career would be hung out to dry if anyone hears about this little stunt. Understood?"

"Yes, sir. Couldn't I just tell my wife?"

"*No!*"

Marchetti slunk back to his seat near the door and strapped in for the coming landing.

Rook switched both pilots' channels to "Private" so that she could speak to Gil without the flight mech overhearing their conversation. "Has this ever happened to you before? I mean, a whale playing tag with a helicopter?"

He gave a morose shake of his head. "Damnedest thing I've ever seen, Rook. I swear to God, that animal knew exactly what he was doing! Incredible, just incredible."

"And beautiful. Do you know, I could see his eye? He was looking right at us, Gil."

"Yeah, and I'll bet if that whale could have smiled, there would've been a big grin spread across his chops, too."

Giggling, Rook reached over, touching his arm momentarily. "What a FAM flight. Thanks, Gil."

Smiling sheepishly, he brought the '52 in for a landing "Don't breathe a word to anyone, okay?"

"I won't, I promise." And then Rook looked over at him. "My God, do you realize what could have happened if that whale had hit our rotors?"

"Yeah. The score would be Whale 1 and Coast Guard 0. We'd have bought some Pacific Ocean real estate at the cost of half a million dollars for a lost '52. Not a very pretty picture, is it?"

Sober now, Rook agreed. She unharnessed after Gil shut the '52 down. Before leaving the cockpit, they went over their individual procedures. Rook then climbed out on the ramp, and turned to wait for Gil. His hair was mussed as he took off the white-and orange helmet. She moved her hand to her own hair, thinking it must look just as bad.

And then she laughed to herself. Since when did she care

about her looks? Gil joined her and they walked back into the hangar together, their respective helmet bags in hand. Marchetti caught up with them.

"This is one time Bucky Beaver didn't get all the action," he crowed proudly, thumping his chest.

Frowning, Rook said, "Bucky Beaver? Who's he?" Often, the flight mechs had nicknames for one another.

Logan scowled at Marchetti, then answered Rook. "He's referring to Annie Locke."

"Oh?" Rook sized up Marchetti. "She gave herself that nickname?" she asked, thinking that she was terribly self-conscious about her teeth.

"No, ma'am. It's what we call her."

Rook slowed her pace. Gil did, too. "To her face, Marchetti?" she challenged, holding his confused gaze.

Marchetti glanced up at Gil and then back to her, not understanding the sudden anger he heard in Rook's voice. "Well . . . uh, no, ma'am." And then he saw her eyes narrow in fury. "Hey! It's just a joke! The boys call her that when she's not around."

Rook blocked Marchetti's path. "I don't ever want to hear you or anyone else refer to Annie Locke in that derogatory manner again. Do you understand, Marchetti?"

Looking to Gil for help, Marchetti realized with a sinking feeling that the pilot was siding with her. Meekly, he hung his head. "Yes, ma'am."

"Good," and Rook stalked off, anger in every stride she took.

Gil caught up with her in the line shack. Rook gave him a measured look when he entered the small, confined room.

"I suppose you think I was too hard on him."

"No." He opened his flight log and began to write down the hours logged.

"What, then? You're giving me a funny look."

"Don't take it as a negative, Rook." Gil waited until the line shack emptied of enlisted personnel before continuing. "Annie's a good kid. I heard a couple of the other flight mechs call her that nickname off and on, only I didn't say anything."

"The girl's terribly sensitive about how she looks, Gil. You know how much it would hurt her if she heard that."

He smiled faintly, signing the pink sheet. "Yeah, you're right."

"Then, why are you looking at me that way?"

"Let's just call it a look of admiration. I think you're going to add a dimension of sensitivity that's been absent from the air station. You're absolutely right: Annie would cry if she knew these guys were calling her Bucky Beaver behind her back. The rest of us clods just neglected to speak up. Come on, let's grab a cup of coffee over at the SAR desk. We're celebrating your first official flight."

Relieved that Gil wasn't going to chew her out for making Marchetti toe the line, Rook managed a strained smile. "Better, let's celebrate that potential whale strike as an almost 'first' in Coast Guard history, performed by an intrepid, if not dumb, H-52 crew."

Gil laughed. "Agreed!"

CHAPTER

Nine

JIM took a deep breath before pressing the buzzer to Rook's apartment. It had been a week since his debacle with her at the Coast Guard station. Maybe she'd cooled down by now and understood the real reason he'd brought her flowers. He fervently hoped so.

Sunshine fell around his denim-jacketed shoulders. It was Sunday, a rare sunny day for April, and he wanted to take advantage of it in every way. Jim pressed the button. Glancing at his watch, he saw it was nearly eleven o'clock. Rook should be up and about by now. Ruefully, Jim laughed at himself as he stood there, thumbs hooked in the pockets of his well-worn jeans. Here he was, at thirty-two, his palms sweating like an eighteen-year-old boy on his first big date.

As Rook opened the door, her eyes first noticed Jim's broad chest. She blinked once to underscore her surprise at seeing him. "Jim . . ."

Shrugging nervously, he gave her a quick smile. "Hi."

Pleasure flooded Rook, and so did compassion. It was obvious he was nervous. "I'm glad you're here," she admitted.

"You are?"

"I had that coming, didn't I? Yes, come in."

Rook's usual defenses seemed to be down. He was seeing her pleasant side now. Some of his nervousness dissolved.

"Look, I don't want to take up your time or botch any plans you might have for today. I just thought I'd drop over on the chance that you might like to go sailing for a couple of hours with me." He gestured to the brilliant blue sky and blinding sunshine. "It doesn't get sunny like this in late April very often, and the straits are calm today. There's just enough of a breeze to fill the sails." He pinned her with a hopeful look. Rook appeared interested.

All of her worries about the station and the people evaporated under Jim's invitation. "I didn't want to do housework anyway," she began wryly. "Come in, please."

Jim entered. The apartment was neat and clean; there was no evidence that she'd only moved in a week ago. "Place looks nice."

Rook stood in the center of the living room, a few feet from him. "Thanks." For once, she wanted to be wearing something more feminine and flattering than a white shirt with tails that hung to her thighs and a pair of jeans. She wriggled her toes in the dusty-rose carpet. It was her turn to be nervous.

"Listen, I owe you an apology for last week—about the roses, I mean. They were lovely, and I did appreciate them."

Jim glowed beneath her breathless tone. "Looking back on it, I can see why you were upset. You do have an image to protect. I should have called first, but I often do things on the spur of the moment."

Relieved that he understood, Rook chuckled. "I was uptight that day, anyway. You coming in unexpectedly corked it. But it wasn't your fault—not really."

The day was looking sunnier by the moment. Jim ran his fingers through his hair. "Sometimes spontaneity pays off, sometimes it doesn't."

"Sailing sounds like fun. I've never done it before," Rook admitted, moving to the couch and sitting down. Jim remained standing. He filled the room with his presence, and Rook felt as if she were basking in his personal sunlight.

"And you're in the Coast Guard?"

Grinning, Rook tucked her legs beneath her body. "I'm in the air wing, Jim."

"And a landlubber by heart?" he guessed, the tension draining away from him. Even in a simple white shirt and blue jeans Rook looked spectacular. There was less tension around her eyes and mouth. And he noticed a dancing, silvery quality in her eyes. Was that glint a sign of happiness over seeing him once again?

"Yes, I am. Sit down."

Sitting on the other end of the couch, Jim said, "I don't think you have to worry about seasickness. I've got a sweet little sailboat called *The Rainbow.* She's got a good, steady hull and the waters in the straits today are almost glassy smooth."

"You've sold me."

"Great. Just put on a pair of tennis shoes and grab a wind breaker, and we'll be off."

Suddenly, the last week's tension and responsibility fell away from Rook. She leaned down, pulling her sneakers from beneath the couch and wriggling into them. "Sounds wonderful. What about lunch?"

"I brought a picnic basket."

Raising one eyebrow, Rook said, "You've thought of everything, haven't you?"

Grinning bashfully, Jim nodded. "I hope I have."

"Friends?" Rook pressed.

"This is a day for friendship," Jim agreed huskily. Already his mind was racing ahead to the time when they would be on the water of the straits.

When the thirty-foot racer-cruiser listed to port after catching the wind around Ediz Hook, Rook gasped. She had been sitting with Jim in the stern, the tiller between them. Automatically Rook threw out her arm, caught off balance by the unexpected movement of the boat.

Jim switched hands, holding the tiller steady and lifting his arm to wrap it protectively around Rook's shoulders so she wouldn't fall. Both Rook and the boat steadied simultaneously. She was warm and pliant against his side and he laughed, the sea air intoxicating.

Gulping back her initial fear, Rook was grateful for Jim's arm around her, holding her steady as the cruiser leaned even more precariously on her side, the deck nearly in the blue waters.

"A-aren't we going to tip over?" she squeaked.

Laughing, Jim looked straight into her eyes. They were large and wide like those of a child. He glanced at her cheeks, flushed with color, and her beautifully sculpted mouth. It looked excruciatingly inviting. "Relax, we've got a keel under her that won't allow that to happen."

Not quite sure, Rook stayed beneath Jim's arm. The wind came in brisk and fresh from the northwest. She might not trust the boat, but she trusted Jim.

Guiding the boat farther out into the straits, Jim leaned over, his mouth near her ear because the wind was rushing around them. "I think we'll head toward Victoria. You ever been there?"

His moist breath feathered against her temple and ear, sending a ribbon of heat through her. "No, I never have." Rook drowned in the warmth of his eyes, her gaze settling on his strong, smiling mouth. An intense stab of longing for him caught her off guard. It was the first time in her life she had ever felt that kind of molten desire. Shaken, Rook looked away, losing herself in the vivid green and blue beauty that surrounded them.

Jim leaned back, bringing Rook with him. He'd seen the smoldering fire in her gray eyes, and watched her lips unconsciously part. God knew, he wanted to kiss her, but it was too soon. Content that she was in his arms, he guided *The Rainbow* past a buoy. The hull lifted up and then fell, slicing cleanly through the clear water.

"Victoria is beautiful. It looks like Old England. There are quaint houses, and all the buildings have flower boxes—even in the city center. It's a garden spot, and a lot of very rich Canadians live there."

"Sounds beautiful," Rook said wistfully. Giving him a

glance, she added, "Someone in the office said you were rich. Is that true?"

"What if it is?" Too many women stalked him to marry his money. His gut told him that Rook might be bothered by the fact, but he didn't know why. She didn't seem the kind of woman who would marry for money or security.

Rook's mouth compressed. "I was just wondering, that's all."

He grinned, measuring the wind in the sail. For once, the breeze in the straits was holding steady. The gleaming white main sail and jib were filled, and didn't need any trimming. "My family worked half a century to build our lumber business. Money hasn't changed what I am."

"What are you?" Rook asked seriously, studying his rugged profile as he lifted his chin to study the sails through squinted eyes.

Jim slanted a glance down at her, seeing that she was sincere. It pleased him that she was interested in him. It was a good sign . . .

"Instead of giving you a list of adjectives, why don't you tell me how you see me?"

Beginning to believe that *The Rainbow* wasn't going to tip over, Rook pulled up one of her legs, and rested her foot on the helm where they sat. "Easygoing," she began hesitantly, mulling over their previous meetings.

"Usually. That comes from my Scottish mother's genes."

"Irish and Scottish. What a combination," Rook teased. "Hot-tempered, and stubborn to boot."

"Have I been either?" he chided her playfully, watching that wonderful smile he knew had always been there come to life on her lips.

"No. I have, that's for sure. I do have some Irish blood in me, but mostly English. My mother came from English stock, and I always said I was a clone of her in most ways."

"You are," Jim complimented. And equally sensitive, too, which appealed strongly to him. "So, what else do you see in me?"

"You're spontaneous to a fault—and dogged. You go after what you want."

"Such as showing up in your life three days in a row after we met?"

Laughter pealed from Rook. She felt the load she normally carried on her shoulders lift. The brisk April wind sifted through the strands of her hair, blowing her troubles away. The salty ocean scent mingled with the tangy pine fragrance of the forest that embraced them on two sides, its towering trees lifting their arms toward the cerulean sky which was dotted with calling sea gulls.

"It was a bit much," Rook said.

Jim gave her a lopsided smile. "You're right, it was. But you were new in town, and you didn't have a car. I felt responsible, and I wanted to right the wrongs I'd caused."

"I thought you were chasing me," Rook admitted.

"I know."

"I guess I'm a little flightly when it comes to men."

He nodded. "From what you've told me so far, men haven't exactly been good news in your life."

"I'm not afraid of them," Rook protested.

"I never thought that. Wary, yes—but not afraid."

She gave him a searching look. "Just how many layers are there to you, Jim Barton? Are you sure you aren't a psychologist, on top of being a timber baron?"

Jim reluctantly released Rook. He had to tack, and needed both hands to do it. "Thirty-two years of living have provided me with some wisdom about people's ways and motivations. Well," he said, looking over his shoulder at her as he got up, "maybe we can change that image you have of men, with time. Come on, I'll show you how to help tack this lady over to the starboard side. In a couple hours you'll be able to call yourself a sailor. . . ."

"I don't want this day to end," Rook admitted wistfully as Jim lowered the sails. They were about to enter the docking area. She sat on the helm, watching him guide *The Rainbow* with the tiller and the aid of a small, five horsepower motor.

The sun was dipping behind the Olympic National Forest to the west, the shadows deepening around them.

He smiled down at her. Rook's nose was sunburned, and her gray eyes shone with new life. "The sailing did you a lot of good," he noted.

With a grimace, Rook touched her cheeks. "I'll bet I'm red as a lobster!"

"Just your nose. And you look beautiful . . ."

Sliding her hands back into her lap, Rook turned away. *Beautiful.* Coming from Jim, she knew it wasn't a line. It was a husky, heart-stopping compliment. Over a hundred small boats bobbed in individual slips around the huge quay. Rook didn't know what to say.

"Tired?" Jim prodded mildly, swinging *The Rainbow* into her berth with ease.

"Yes." Rook watched as Jim shut off the motor and went forward to tie the boat to the dock. He did everything with such confidence and natural ease. That is what drew her to him: his easygoing nature. The men she'd known had pushed and hounded her: a quarry to be caught, captured, and then coldly released. Jim had put his arm around her only twice.

Torn, Rook stood up as Jim offered her his hand from the wharf. She didn't know whether to be disappointed or relieved. As his fingers closed around her, swallowing up her small hand, she was aware of how gentle he was, despite his bearlike strength.

Jim lifted Rook lightly to the dock and released her. He grinned down at her, his hair tousled by the wind. "Well, what did you think? Do you want to sail her again sometime?"

Reaching out, Rook touched Jim's denim jacket sleeve. It had been an unthinking action on her part. "I'd love to do it. This is so different from flying."

"More relaxing, I'll bet." Risking everything, Jim moved to her side, sliding his arm around her proud, small shoulders. Would Rook tense and pull away, or would she welcome him?

"I think it's the company I'm keeping that makes it so much fun," she teased back. Falling into step with Jim, Rook leaned against him as they wandered slowly down the creaky wooden dock toward the parking lot, where his gray Corvette was parked. Savoring the sense of protection Jim gave her, Rook marveled at the range of emotions he was drawing from her.

"So what's up tomorrow for you?" Jim asked.

"Another day at work. We've got a terrible flight schedule, and the other pilots are working every other day on SAR duty. The captain wants me on the flight line as soon as possible."

"You're going to be busy, then."

Rook nodded. "I was lucky to get this weekend off. I know it won't happen again until the captain can get the flight roster straightened out. That won't be for another three weeks."

"Yeah, we're going into our busy season, too. Dad wants us to open up Bravo area, a new lease we were just awarded by the government. The soil's still pretty unstable up there because of the spring rains, so I'm trying to get him to wait."

"But he's full steam ahead on it?"

Worriedly, Jim muttered, "Dad can't sit still. He finds opening up a new area a real challenge. This is one time when I wish he'd wait." And then he laughed, leaning down to unlock the passenger side of the car. "But who am I to tell him what to do? He founded our company fifty years ago with blood, sweat, and his Irish ethics of long hours six days a week."

The idea of not seeing Jim for three weeks was disconcerting. Rook slid into her seat.

"With our crazy schedules," Jim suggested, shutting his door and putting on the seat belt, "how about it if you call me when you get a free day in your schedule? I'll try to work around it, and we'll take *The Rainbow* out again if the weather's cooperating."

As she held his gaze, Rook felt herself go shaky inside.

Jim hadn't touched her, but the longing in his eyes was enough to make her excruciatingly aware that she was a woman, in every meaning of the word. "Yes," she answered softly, "I'll do that."

Jim started the car. What he'd wanted to do was lean those scant inches and claim Rook's full lips. The desire was in her eyes, but so was confusion. *Patience*, Jim told himself. *Be patient and be yourself.*

Putting the Corvette in gear, Jim guided it slowly out of the parking lot. "Let's hope Monday is a good day for both of us."

Rook groaned, leaning back and smiling. "How do Mondays treat you?"

"Lousy. You?"

"The same."

"Then, expect to find a fresh bouquet of roses on your desk tomorrow morning, Ms. Caldwell. When things start to go wrong, you just lean over and smell them. Think of us, and the day we shared."

Eve could barely hide her nervousness as she stepped into the Personnel office of the Coast Guard station. This Monday morning heralded her new status in the world: as a full-time reporter. Anticipation thrummed through her as she halted, eyeing the secretarial pool in the center of the huge, well-lit area. To the left were the glass-enclosed offices in which the pilots performed their collateral duty.

A shiver of dread ran through Eve as she spotted what could only be Lieutenant Rook Caldwell, working hard at her desk. Her heart sank. She wasn't pretty—she was beautiful, Eve realized with anxiety. And Gil had been assigned as her sponsor, meaning he'd be spending even more time with her during her first months on the station. Gathering what little courage she had left, Eve watched Jody Theron as she approached.

"I'm here to see Lieutenant Caldwell," Eve said, a tremor in her voice.

Jody hesitated. "Well—uh, she's busy right now, Mrs. Logan."

Triumphantly, Eve displayed her press pass. She squared her shoulders, and tried to sound brisk and businesslike even though she was dying inside. "I'm here on official business, Jody, as a reporter for the *Star*. I've been assigned to interview Lieutenant Caldwell."

"I'll tell her you're here—"

Eve stepped past the enlisted woman. She had to move or she was going to lose her nerve. "Don't bother, sweetie. I'll introduce myself," she said as she swept by.

Rook scowled, hearing the door to her office open and then close. She'd given Jody Theron strict orders that she wasn't to be disturbed. Twisting a look to the left, Rook's frown deepened. A sleek, well-dressed blonde woman stood poised at the door. She wore a black skirt, a scarlet blouse that matched the color of her lipstick, and a short black jacket. Rook sensed danger. The woman's green eyes were narrowed and anxious-looking. And there was an aura of tension around her as she clutched a tape recorder in her right hand and a yellow legal pad beneath her left arm.

"Yes?" Rook said, placing the pen on her desk.

Throat suddenly dry, Eve forced herself to speak. "I'm Eve Logan, the wife of Lieutenant Gil Logan, Ms. Caldwell." She moved restlessly, shutting the door with finality behind her. "I'm sure Gil hasn't told you yet, but I'm a reporter for our local newspaper, the *Port Angeles Star*." Eve's heart was pounding so loud in her breast that she wondered if Rook could hear it. Eve set the recorder down and turned it on. Taking out a pen, she smiled. "My editor is just dying to get the scoop on you. Gil told me you're one of only six women Coast Guard pilots. You've got to be proud. So, if you'll give me a few minutes of your time, I'll get my interview."

Hesitating, Rook turned around in her chair. Today she was dressed in her summer uniform and not her flight suit. Her military training had been in aviation. She didn't know what the regulations were concerning reporters coming on base unannounced for impromptu interviews. "Mrs. Logan—"

"Do call me Eve. After all, you're one of us."

"Look, I don't know if I can give you an interview—"

"Of course you can! Why, I'm a member of the Coast Guard family. I can assure you that my interview with you will be very positive and uplifting. And I'm sure the new captain would rather have the wife of a military officer do the story than a civilian." She wrinkled her nose disdainfully, beginning to relax. Being a reporter wasn't so hard, after all. "You know how civilians love to gut the military." Smiling, Eve leaned against the desk. "Now, let's begin at the beginning . . ."

Half an hour later, Rook stared at the red roses that had arrived shortly before Eve Logan. Uneasy, but unable to figure out why, Rook got up. "I think you've got plenty for your interview, Mrs. Logan."

"Eve. Tell me, who gave you these lovely roses? I can tell they must have cost a lot of money."

Rook's jaw tightened. "They're from a friend."

She smiled brightly. "The name?"

"It's not for publication," Rook said tightly.

Shutting off the recorder, Eve continued to smile, feeling much better. She had been successful. "Admirers, already. Of course, you're very beautiful, and I'm sure every single man in Port Angeles will want to go out with you. I just know this is going to be a wonderful article, Rook! You've given me so much material. What a fascinating person you are." Eve tried to look sincere at her through her lashes. "You and my husband must see a lot of each other. He's your sponsor, he drives you to work, and you fly with him."

Warning grated across Rook's exposed nerves. As warm as Eve's voice was, her eyes were brutally cold upon her. Okay, she got the message. Loud and clear. "Not as often as you might think," Rook said, trying to keep her own emotions out of the confrontation. Eve wasn't here for an interview, as much as to subtly warn her away from Gil.

With a weak smile, Eve deposited the tape recorder back into her oversized purse. "I must be going. Deadlines, you know. Thanks so much!"

Distracted, Rook watched Eve float out the door. Shaking

her head, she turned back to her desk. Eve's warning kept nagging at her. Dammit, she was going to have to ask Gil not to drive her anymore. Rook didn't want this kind of warfare with the pilots' wives on top of everything else.

Blowing out a breath of air, Rook stared at her red roses. Yes, Eve had been nervous and unsure of herself. She was obviously upset that Gil was her sponsor. She would draw blood if she didn't do something to parry this first attack. Her stomach began to knot. Who could she get to drive her? Shutting her eyes, Rook realized she had only one option—Noah . . .

Noah couldn't mask his surprise when he saw Rook boarding his cutter. Standing on the bridge with the bos'n, Dave Harper, he watched her progress across the sleek deck of the *Point Countess*.

"Dave, why don't you take the day off? You don't have the duty," he suggested.

The sandy-haired man nodded. "Yes, sir. I'll see you at 0800 tomorrow, then."

Noah nodded, turning and leaning against the steel counter to wait. What did she want? He found himself suddenly hoping that Rook had come to her senses and wanted to talk. And maybe, to make amends.

Rook stood just outside the hatch that led into the cramped bridge of the *Point Countess*. Noah greeted her with an unsure smile. She managed one of her own.

"Permission to come aboard, sir?"

He gestured for her to enter, pointing to the seat in front of the helm wheel. "Permission granted. Come in."

Rook hated appearing nervous in front of him, but she couldn't help herself. She toyed absently with the black leather purse hanging from her left shoulder. "I won't stay long, Noah. I know you're busy."

"Never too busy to see you, though." He gave her all the room there was to spare as she inched toward a chair bolted securely to the deck. Walking over to the hatch, he slid the door shut so that their conversation would remain private.

Most of the men were taking off for home anyway, so the cutter was almost deserted for the night, with the exception of Cunningham, who had to stand duty. The gentle, rolling motion of the boat soothed his jangled nerves.

"Look . . . I have a favor to ask of you, Noah."

He brightened. "Sure."

Rook gave him an I-don't-believe-it look.

Grinning sheepishly, Noah said, "Hey, I'd do anything for you, so don't look so shocked. What is it?"

Fidgeting, Rook slid her fingers along the top of the chair. "I need a ride into the base every day. My car was hit by a timber truck the first day I got here, and the mechanic over at Sequim says it will take at *least* two weeks before I get my wheels back."

"What accident? Why didn't you tell me about this earlier? Are you all right?"

Rook tried to shrug off Noah's concern, and gave him a brief explanation of the accident. Did he truly care, or was he just pretending to? She tried to ferret out deceit on his part, and could find none.

Noah scowled, relieved that Rook hadn't been injured. "I'm glad you came to me."

Rook eyed him. "You weren't my first choice, Noah, but I can't afford to have the pilots taking me to and from work. It wouldn't look good."

"It wouldn't?"

She made a sound of exasperation, dropping her purse on the seat and looking around the bridge. "All the guys are married. Don't you see? I'm single, a *female* helo pilot?"

"Oh . . . the jealous wife angle?"

"You got it." She turned to him. "Will you promise not to say anything to anyone about this conversation?"

Swallowing a smile, Noah nodded. "Sure. Is that why you're nervous?"

Rook nodded, looking out the windows of the bridge, thinking how calm the straits looked in the mauve evening light. "Just an hour ago Lieutenant Logan's wife, Eve, showed up unexpectedly at the station. She just *happened* by. And she just *happened* to find an excuse to check me out, too," Rook rattled on. "You talk about a jealous wife, she's one. God knows, I've got enough troubles of my own to juggle right now without her on my case for no reason."

"Did Mrs. Logan say anything to you?"

Releasing a heavy sigh, Rook held Noah's compassionate stare. "Do you know how many people there are in that one office alone? Ten. That's ten sets of ears, eyes, and mouths. That's not to say that there are ten brains between them, though. Jody Theron is the base gossip."

"I've heard about her," Noah said drily. "Real pretty little gal, but she has a double-edged tongue."

"Yeah, well, it's all true. I was in my office, busting my tail on this P.R. assignment for Captain Stuart, and Eve Logan comes waltzing into my office. She gives me one of these smiles designed to cut you down from forty yards, and then proceeds to tell me she's a reporter from the local paper and would love to interview me. All the while she's scoping me out, measuring me up like I'm a piece of meat to be butchered at some later date."

"Was your office door closed?"

"Yes. But I was too stunned by the whole thing to think straight." Rook rubbed her face. "God, Noah, you'd think that my flying reflexes would transfer over to human crisis encounters."

His smile softened. "It never works that way, Rook."

"So I'm finding out. Well, I got a lift from Gil Logan this morning, and he offered to help me the two weeks my car's in for repairs. But after Mrs. Logan came in and dropped all kinds of catty innuendos, I can't afford to have other wives getting angry, like she is, simply because I'm riding to and from work with their husbands."

"Tell you what. I have a black TransAm. If you want to keep it for the duration, you can pick me up at my apartment every morning. At night, I can get one of my men to give me a lift home."

She stared at Noah, stunned by his generous offer. "But —won't you need the car at night?"

He shook his head. "Captain Stuart, the District, and I are putting together a drug interdiction plan, so I've got plenty of homework to do for the next few weeks." He grinned. "Besides, Port Angeles doesn't exactly have great pickings for a bachelor."

She looked to her left, toward the town of seventeen thousand situated at the base of the Olympic Mountains. "This place is sort of in the middle of nowhere, isn't it?"

"If you're married, Port Angeles isn't a bad town. But if you're single, and looking for a place to meet women other than at a bar, you can hang it up."

Rook caught herself. She was letting down her guard. That wasn't good. "Look, if you mean it about your Trans-Am, I could use the favor. But if you need it some night, unexpectedly, let me know."

Noah picked up his cap and slid open the hatch. "I will. Come on, you can give me a lift home, and the car will be yours."

He lived in an apartment complex at the foot of the mountains. The slopes behind the building were lush with spring grass and newly sprouted wild flowers. Noah glanced over at Rook before he opened the door to get out.

"Sure you wouldn't like to go out to dinner?"

"No. Thanks anyway."

Noah nodded. "Maybe another time, then." He'd never be able to push Rook into trusting him. She'd have to come to him on her own terms. Noah settled for that, silently thanking Jim Barton for the accident that had sent Rook to him for help. Otherwise, he would have been at his wit's end trying to figure out a way to approach Rook and get their relationship on better footing. "I'll see you at half past seven, Sis."

Rook tried to ignore the heat in her cheeks when he called her Sis. "Okay," she agreed, unable to meet his warm gaze.

On the way over to her apartment, which sat near the straits, Rook's thoughts drifted back to Tag Welsh. Near four o'clock he'd received a call from his wife. She knew, from talking with Gil, that Paula Welsh was dying of leukemia.

Her fingers tightened around the steering wheel. Tag was so likable. Why did things like this happen to good people?

Tag couldn't fight the overwhelming fear that gripped him as he raced from the car to the rear entrance of his house. He nearly tore the screen door off its hinges getting inside. Paula never called him home from work.

She opened her eyes when she heard Tag's commotion at the back door, and gave him a soft smile as he raced into the living room. "Tag?" Chilled, she pulled the green and blue afghan across her legs and lay back down on the sofa.

He knelt beside her, one hand on hers, the other on her brow. "What's wrong? Are you all right?' He was gasping for breath, and his hands were shaking badly. Paula's flesh —what little there was of it—was cooler than usual. The house was warm. "Are you cold?"

"Just a little. I'm fine, Tag."

"Are you sure?" Tears glittered fiercely in his eyes as he sat down, facing her, never letting go of her thin, frail hand. She was still so beautiful. Her dark brown hair glinted with red highlights beneath the lamp. And her large, hazel eyes, flecked with gold and brown, held so much life in their depths. Tag could never get over the fact that except for a weight loss, Paula looked the same.

She patted his hand. "I'm positive."

"Why did you call, then?"

"Didn't Jody tell you? I wanted you to pick up a can of soup from the store on the way home."

Tag shut his eyes tightly. "Damn that little bitch! No, she just said you'd called and that you sounded really bad. She said she could barely hear your voice." He opened his eyes. "I thought—I thought—"

Paula slid her arms around her husband, drawing him to her. "Oh honey, I'm sorry. Maybe she just forgot about the soup."

Tag gripped his wife to him, never wanting to let her go. He kissed her hair, brow, and cheek, hungry just for Paula's nearness. Not a minute of his day went by when he didn't wonder how she was. Would he come home someday and find that she had died on the couch, without anyone near to comfort her? A deluge of emotions suffocated Tag, and he buried his face in the thick, rich, chestnut folds of her hair.

"Where the hell have you been, Eve?" Gil demanded as she walked in the door. It was ten o'clock. When he had come home earlier, the house had been empty, which was highly unusual, because Eve was normally either on the phone or in front of the television, watching one of her soap operas. He stood in the kitchen, waiting for her answer. She was dressed in a business suit.

"Out."

"Out where?"

She set her leather purse on the table, along with a slim attaché case. For once, she felt confident, the entire day a glowing success. Shrugging out of her pale-lilac raincoat, she said, "I wonder how you'd react if I told you I got a wonderful job today."

Anger tightened the planes of his face. The day had gone from bad to worse. "That's not even funny."

Eve slipped out of her blazer and walked down the hall to hang it up, her heels echoing sharply against the wooden floor. "And neither is all this extra duty you're standing. Why should I stay home if you're not going to be here half of the time?"

Gil stalked into the hall. "Look, I told you the captain was trying to straighten out the mess, but he can only do so much until Vance and Wingate get back off leave. He's already cancelled Wingate's request for an extra week."

With a shrug, Eve breezed by him on her way into the living room. She went over and turned on the television. "Sure, I hear this same old spiel all the time." She smiled brightly up at Gil as he entered the room. "I did something about it."

He shut the television off and stood in front of it. Eve sat down and crossed her slim legs, her eyes shining with happiness. "All right, let's talk about what you're doing," he said heavily.

She laughed prettily, clapping her hands. "I can't believe it! This is the first time in six months I've gotten your full, undivided attention, Gil."

"You've always had my attention," he said tightly, walking to the couch and sitting down. "Now, where have you been all night? And why didn't you have the common decency to leave me a note? Jesus Christ, I was worried half out of my mind!"

She clasped her hands in her lap, bubbling. "I was out, discussing business."

"Business?"

Eve was thrilled over Gil's interest. Finally, he was paying attention to her, and she gratefully absorbed every particle of it. "I went over to the *Star* and got a full-time job as a reporter this morning."

Gil took a deep, controlling breath, folding his hands in front of him. "Why?" His mother had remained at home, and his father had provided for the family.

Her joy receded and Eve muttered, "Running a house is all you think I'm capable of, isn't it? I've been hired by the editor and owner, Steve Hunter. I've already finished my first assignment: interviewing Lieutenant Rook Caldwell." Pleasure sang through Eve until she saw the look of shock on Gil's face. Eve felt her stomach knot. "I also am being given the society column. Isn't that something?" Her voice grew strained as Gil's scowl darkened. "My hours are eight to five. So far, I've typed up a rough draft of my interview with Lieutenant Caldwell."

The hopeful look Eve gave him made Logan groan. "You know that paper is anti-Coast Guard, Eve!" He halted, trying to get his temper under control. When he spoke, his voice was low and clipped. "Did you ever think about the problems your spur-of-the-moment decision might generate for me at the station?"

Her eyes flashed. "As usual, you're only worried about your precious Coast Guard image! You can't even congratulate me, or thank me for helping to contribute to the income."

"Eve, we don't need the extra money. I make enough to support two people." He nailed her with an exasperated look. "If we had a family, it might be different. But you've seen to that, too. So, you don't need the job for monetary reasons. And why should I congratulate such an idiotic move, when I know I'm going to take heat from the C.O. because you're working for that newspaper?"

She leaped to her feet, tears glittering in her eyes. "How come everything I do is left-overs or second class? Of course, when you come home bragging about your latest rescue and the people you saved, you thump the hell out of your chest! But let me get one small laurel and you're ready to crush it!"

Gil stood ominously over her, his fists clenched. "You twist everything I've ever said to you, Eve. If I talk about a rescue, it's because I've got to get it off my chest. I'm human. I can't sit at the controls crying like a baby! I have to swallow everything I see, hear, or feel. Some of those cases rip me apart. I can't keep carrying that stuff inside me forever. I need to unload and talk about it. I wouldn't call that bragging or thumping my chest, dammit." His nostrils flared and he paced the living room at least another minute, trying to cool down. Changing topics, Gil said, "I don't suppose you know that Paula Welsh is worse?"

Tossing her head, Eve got up and marched into the kitchen. She went to the cupboard that contained the liquor, and poured herself a stiff scotch on the rocks. Nothing she did was ever right. It hurt. Eve sobbed. "I don't care about sweet, kind, selfless Paula. Right now, I care about the fact that you hate whatever I try to do." She saw Gil enter the kitchen and threw some ice cubes into her tumbler. The scotch sloshed out of the glass and onto the formica counter. Turning, she glared back at him.

"You can't be that heartless," he rasped. "Paula's done so many things for you since we arrived here. She was the first to welcome you to the station, and she made special efforts to make you feel at home. Is this how you repay her kindness when she might need some comfort?" Gil walked over to her, his voice dangerously low. "Come on, tell me you don't care."

Eve took a step back, pinned between the counter and her husband. "I don't care! I never did," she rattled. "I'm sick and tired of hearing Paula's daily health report! You won't even congratulate me on a job I love. All you care about is your Coast Guard family, not me!" she cried, and tried to escape from Gil's presence.

"No, you don't," he snarled, clamping a hand around her delicate wrist. He seethed with frustration.

With a cry of pain, Eve tried to twist free. The tumbler flew out of her hand, shattering on the floor between them. She froze and then sobbed. "Damn you, Gil Logan! I hate you! I hate you!"

Thunderstruck by her outburst, Gil released her. Eve flew out of the kitchen, down the hall and to their bedroom, slamming the door shut. Silence filled the house as he stood there, staring down at the broken glass shards scattered over the floor and his feet. Rage welled up through him. He shook his head in shock. Eve hated him . . . She'd never said that before.

Placing a hand against the counter, he waited until his sudden dizziness passed. Hate was a powerful word. What had he done that would make a seven-year marriage go into this kind of a tailspin? Unable to sort through his snarled feelings, Gil left. He'd go to Tag's place and see if there was anything he could do to help.

CHAPTER

Ten

"ROOK?"

She looked up from her desk. It was 0830 and she was just finishing her second cup of coffee for the day. Tag leaned in the door to Admin, dressed in his flight suit. "Yes?"

"Come on, we've got a SAR case. The Ops officer says I can pull you for my copilot. Want to come along?"

Unabashed at showing her eagerness to the secretaries, who had stopped to watch and listen, Rook got up. Once in the hall with Tag, they walked quickly down to the SAR desk. Unable to still her excitement, Rook asked, "What have we got, Tag?"

"We just received a call from the Barton Industries. They're pulling logs out near Thatcher Ridge. It's about a mile outside the Olympic National Park."

Rook gasped. "Oh, no!" She automatically thought of Jim Barton. It had been three weeks since they'd gone sailing, and she had planned to call him tonight to tell him she had Saturday off. Her heart twisted. Jim loved his father as fiercely as she had loved her mother. "My God, what's happened?"

Tag came to a halt at the counter, spreading out a number of maps and other items. "Howard Barton was driving a D-9 Cat up on a muddy ridge. It rained like hell up there last night, and the soil was unstable in their work area. Apparently the old man got too close to the edge of a ravine, and went end over end. I guess the Cat rolled a good hundred feet before coming to a rest at the bottom of it."

Rook tried to control her sudden anxiety, unable to explain her emotional reaction to the news. "Is he pinned?"

"Yeah, but the timber company people are working to free him right now. We're taking the call because there's no access into that area. Guess the guy's got internal injuries. Wouldn't be surprised. This time, we're going to become a medevac, Rook. The trauma unit at Mercy's already standing by for us to fly Barton there, as soon as we can extricate him from the area."

Combating the devastation she felt, Rook fought to pay close attention to what Tag was saying. "So, how are we going to effect this rescue?"

He smiled over at her. "Bingo. You asked the right question." Tag motioned to the local weather report. "We've got a familiar problem here in this area: high altitude. The spot we've got to fly into is at 4,500 feet. That's near the maximum altitude for the '52 for a litter pickup out of ground effect." He showed a couple of graphs in her direction. "I want you to figure out the power requirements we'll need. The '52 weighs a lot, and at that altitude, it will be tough for it to hover over the trees on its own, much less with a load from below. We may have to defuel."

"You're going to lower a litter to pick him up?" The Hover Out of Ground Effect, or HOGE, meant hovering very close to the earth's surface where there was no benefit of downwash air currents to provide the helo up with lift. More fuel was burned as a result.

"We have to. The guy on the radio at the scene said the trees are anywhere from seventy-five to one hundred feet in height. Our basket cable is a hundred feet in length.

Jim had to be the man on the handset, radioing in for help. Rook tried to block out how he must feel, with his father trapped and seriously injured. She grimaced. "That's cutting it close, Tag."

"The name of the game, darlin'. So figure our HOGE power. Tell me how many pounds of fuel we can carry so we can lift this guy out."

Speed was of the essence. Rook got out the performance charts and wrote down all the necessary information on another piece of paper, which would be used by the aircraft commander. A helicopter had its Achilles heels, and this was one of them. When the temperature and barometric pressure combined to create a high-density altitude, a helo would slug along. There might not be enough power for the rotors to lift the aircraft, or much of a load. That was why the helicopter's weight and pounds of fuel became a critical issue. Further, the danger of the situation increased because the HOGE altitude limits of the '52 with a load would be around six thousand feet on a litter pickup. The higher the altitude, the harder it would be for the helo to hover because the air was less dense, providing less lift to keep it in the air. Rook pushed the final figures over to Tag, who was working rapidly on another part of the data.

"I've figured that we can do it with six hundred pounds of fuel on board, Tag."

He rubbed his bloodshot eyes, rapidly going over her figures. "No, we'd better defuel to five hundred pounds."

Rook's eyes widened. Five hundred pounds left them very little air time over the rescue site. They would have only forty-five minutes to fly there, make a litter pickup, and fly to the hospital and allow a reserve. "But, isn't that cutting it close, Tag?"

"Yeah, but we don't have many choices open to us, Rook. This one's like walking the edge of a razor blade, any way we cut it."

"According to my figures, we could still meet power requirements with six hundred pounds of fuel on board."

"Five hundred will do it. Call over to the hangar and have them defuel 1418, please."

Panic started eating at Rook. Tag had looked like hell when he'd come in this morning. According to Gil, Paula was worsening rapidly. Was his judgment impaired on this case as a result? She chewed on her lower lip, trying to decide whether or not to push the issue of the extra fuel on board. In the end, Rook decided not to. Tag had been a SAR pilot for five years, two of them here at Port Angeles. He would know the local weather and terrain conditions far better than she. Rook said nothing further and made the call.

Within fifteen minutes, they were airborne and heading south toward the snowcapped Olympic Mountains. Tied up with trying to read the map and talk on the radios, Rook shoved her emotions aside in order to operate at maximum efficiency.

"We're making good time," Tag said, easing the helo up and over the first mountain, and then dropping to a lower altitude. A green carpet of forest lay beneath them. A straight line would get them there faster, but this one particular mountain was too high, so they had to fly around it. It ate up fuel time. Tag fumed over the delay.

Rook glanced up from her duties. "Do we get many calls from timber companies that are logging in these mountains?"

"We get calls from lumberjacks all the time. Usually, it's a tree that's fallen on someone in an inaccessible area. This is the first time I've heard of a Cat rolling over a hill, but I'm sure it's pretty easy to do out in these places."

In another thirty minutes, they had arrived on station. Rook looked out her window, and her heart slammed into her ribs. There, standing next to the yellow Cat turned on its side, was Jim. From this altitude, Rook could see anguish clearly written across his drawn features. At least ten other lumberjacks stood helplessly in a tight circle, every one of them mud-covered and exhausted. The Cat had been pulled off Howard Barton with steel cable by the timber trucks up on the top of the ravine. Rook saw Jim kneel down beside his unconscious father, who had several jackets thrown across him in an effort to keep him warm. He placed the radio close to his mouth and Rook leaned over, switching one of their many radios to his frequency.

"Coast Guard, this is Jim Barton. What do you want us to do? We've got to hurry. My father's in bad shape."

Tag nodded, giving Rook permission to use the loud hailer. Rook flipped on the switch and picked up the microphone. "Mr. Barton, prepare to receive a litter. We'll winch it out the helo shortly. Once the litter is on the ground, get your father strapped in and then step away from it. We'll winch him up as quickly as possible and take him to Mercy Hospital. Their trauma unit is alerted and will be standing by. Over."

"Rook?" There was disbelief and hope in Barton's hoarse voice.

She tried to ignore the sudden emotion in his tone, struggling to keep hers cool and professional-sounding. "Yes. Have your men clear an area for the litter. I'll continue relaying instructions as needed. Over."

"All right... I'm damn glad you showed up. My father..."

Her voice grew husky with feeling. "Mr. Barton—Jim—just get the area cleared as quickly as possible. Please."

Tag went through the procedures with the flight mech, Seth Davis. To enter a HOGE, Tag made his approach into the wind and gradually reduced airspeed, maintaining an altitude of ninety feet—just clear of the fir trees. Control manipulation and power changes had to be made smoothly and precisely, or the helo could inadvertently begin to descend, which could lead to power settling—another dangerous flight hazard. Rook could feel the helo laboring heavily, and kept an eye on the flight instruments. Below her, she saw the men clearing space for the litter. Jim had moved his father to the most accessible spot. They all stood tensely, looking up at them, waiting.

Sweat popped out on Tag's face, all his concentration on keeping the '52 steady in a hover as Seth got ready to lower the litter on the steel cable. The gray, rain-swollen clouds hung only a hundred feet above them, threatening to deluge them once again. The helo was floundering badly, trying to maintain the hover. His gloved hands tightened considerably around the collective and cyclic.

Rook's job was to act as safety pilot, telling Tag if he got too low to the trees and making him aware of any other possible problems. She also had to monitor all the aircraft instruments. She remained in contact with Jim, leading him and his men through the steps of rescue. Once, Rook saw Jim wipe his eyes free of tears. She realized now how much her own emotional reactions could interfere on a rescue.

Tag was left completely free of all details except flying. And in this situation, Rook knew it would take all his skill to give them a safe margin. She glanced up at the leaden skies. Had the temperature or wind changed? If it had, it might affect their HOGE power. The helo was barely stable now, and they hadn't even started the lift.

How much did Howard weigh? Suddenly, that became a critical issue. She remembered Jim pointing him out to her in the diner that morning, but she'd only gotten a glimpse of him. Should she radio Jim and ask? No, he might panic if he thought there was a problem. The possibility of settling with power shrilled through her mind. If the load was too much, the helo could settle and they'd all drop slowly out of the sky, probably killing some of the men gathered below, not to mention themselves. The only alternative if that situation became a reality was to shear the cable, then drop the litter and the patient. Rook's throat constricted with tension. Automatically, she flicked a glance at the fuel gauge: three hundred pounds left. God, they had to hurry with this medevac, or they wouldn't make it out of the mountains themselves.

"Go on hot mike," Welsh ordered the flight mech.

"Roger, hot mike."

Holding the helo steady at eighty-five feet, the sponsons brushing the crowns of the fir, Tag said, "Conn me in."

"Roger," Seth responded. "On hot mike, have target in sight, litter going out the door." The wire litter hung suspended in front of Seth. He pressed the button that would begin lowering it toward the group below. "Litter below aircraft . . . litter halfway down . . ."

Rook's gaze flew to the gauges. She felt the helo laboring heavily. Would the bird stay in the air, or were they going to settle in? Torque was gradually creeping up. Her gut tightened. That could spell disaster. And fuel? Two hundred and eighty pounds left. Jesus, they had to get that litter down, throw Barton in it, and lift like crazy, or they'd never make it to the hospital!

"Litter on deck."

"Thank God," Rook whispered. She glanced over at Tag, seeing the concentration on his masklike face. He knew they were in trouble, too.

"Seth, can you get a look and see how much the victim weighs?" she asked.

"Good move," Tag growled, his thinned lips barely moving.

"I'm worried, Tag."

"Makes two of us."

Seth craned his neck out over the lip of the deck. "Uh . . . he looks pretty heavy, Ms. Caldwell."

Rook tried to keep her voice calm and patient, but she felt anything other than that. "Seth, give me your best estimate."

"Two hundred and fifty pounds?"

"Christ," Tag whispered.

"Tag?" The question was in her voice. He was aircraft commander. What would he do? Call off the medevac because the situation was deteriorating around them, or try the rescue anyway?

"Seth, motion for them to get that guy in the litter pronto," Tag ordered.

"Yes, sir!"

"What's our fuel look like?"

"About two hundred and sixty pounds."

"Torque?"

"Ninety percent."

"Keep me informed."

Rook's hands hovered near her own set of controls. Anytime a rescue was in progress, the copilot's hands were always near the cyclic and collective, in case something happened to the pilot.

"Taking the load," Seth said.

Rook felt the helo shudder as the cable began to winch up the victim in the litter.

Tag cursed softly, his knuckles whitening. They were just this side of overtorquing it.

"The trees, Tag—you're sinking," Rook said, her voice unsteady.

Gently, he fed a little more power to the laboring '52. Throughout the cabin, the high whine of the winch continued, the gears screeching beneath the heavy load.

"Two hundred and fifty-five pounds of fuel."

Tag's mouth tightened. Hurry up with that damn load! The winching and weight was sucking the fuel tank dry! Why hadn't he listened to Rook? Now they were critical! What thc hell had made him decide on a hundred pounds less?

Seth watched as the litter threaded between two huge Douglas firs, branches swatting at the unconscious victim's legs. He gripped the side of the fuselage hard, feeling the helo stagger perilously. Was Mr. Welsh going to make it? The ground looked a long way away to Seth. *Come on, come on*, he silently begged. Why the hell couldn't they invent a faster-moving winch? Seth saw the blood over the older man's abdomen. From years of experience in rescue, he knew the victim's color wasn't good, either. He pressed his lips to the mike.

"I'm gonna need CPR backup once I get the victim on board. He's going blue on me."

Rook responded, not sure if they were even going to be able to get out of here. "I'll be back as soon as we're clear of the trees."

"Roger."

"Fuel?" Tag demanded.

Sweet Jesus, they weren't going to make it! Rook swallowed against a lump, her voice sounding strangled. "Two hundred and forty pounds . . ."

"Litter outside the door."

"Hurry, hurry," Rook begged.

"Litter in cabin, going off hot mike."

Tag waited long seconds, silently pleading with Seth to say the magic words that would get them to hell out of the hover and to a higher, safer altitude in their run for the hospital.

Seth tow-blocked the hook, leaning across the victim in the litter. He yanked the door shut, breathing in loud, harsh gasps. "Cabin secured! Ready for forward flight."

Rook immediately unstrapped and squeezed between the two chairs, aiming herself for the rear cabin to help Seth. She gripped Tag's tense shoulder, squeezing it once as if to give him hope in their deteriorating situation. Placing all her fears aside, Rook concentrated on helping Seth administer CPR to Howard Barton, who lay waxen in the litter.

Tag carefully eased the '52 up, nose to the wind, to give her all the lift she could grab with her long rotor blades. "Come on, baby, be good to me just this once," he begged her. Had the wind velocity increased? If it had, more of the precious fuel would be eaten up. First things first—he had to climb to altitude. To try to autorotate below a thousand feet was sheer stupidity; few walked away from such a controlled crash at less altitude. And yet, more fuel would be consumed if he tried to reach that safe altitude.

Tag gripped the controls hard. He felt as though his entire body was welded to the thin, pulsating skin of the helicopter. She was a living extension of him now, her heartbeat moving through his body. Silently, Tag coaxed her gently past five thousand feet, then fifty-one hundred, all the while flicking his gaze to the fuel gauge needle, which now hovered close to one hundred and fifty pounds. *Be good to us, sweetheart. You've never let us down yet. Come on, come on, you've got such a courageous heart . . . don't let us down . . .* He continued his silent pleading with the '52 as she climbed to fifty-five hundred feet, far above the snowcapped mountains.

As the helo rounded the peak and started its descent, Tag could see the town of Port Angeles. Everything looked so calm below him. The city was just awakening at barely nine o'clock. Tag blinked the sweat from his eyes, his vision momentarily blurred. Christ, he'd made such a stupid error!

Rook had the correct figures. Why had he changed them? Why? Three people had trusted his skill, his experience in assessing the situation. Now, if they ran out of fuel, they could all either die, or end up seriously injured. His only hope was the fact that they were in a gentle descent using less power and eating up less fuel.

Tag called ahead to the base to alert them to the helo's landing. He saw that they only had one hundred pounds of fuel left in the tanks. *Come on, baby, carry us home. Get us home . . . I promise you I'll never do this to you again. Get us home . . .*

Rook knew something was wrong. After they got Barton stabilized, she climbed back into the cockpit. Her gaze went immediately to the fuel gauge. The needle was perilously close to empty.

"Tag—"

"I know."

Rook strapped herself in, her hands shaking badly as she did so. Tag was descending from a thousand feet on a glide toward the hospital's rear parking lot. She held her breath. Were they out of fuel? Fuel gauges were *never* accurate, and there was always a fifty-pound plus or minus in the tank that the '52 carried. They could have fifty extra pounds still on hand, or less—and have no way of knowing. The needle rested on the fifty-pound mark, and the yellow warning light glared at her. Any time now, the engine might stop.

"Hold on . . ." Tag gritted, gripping the controls, getting ready to push the helo into an autorotation. He'd deliberately come into the wind, wanting that cushion and lift of air, just in case.

Rook grabbed the sides of her seat, eyes bulging.

Three hundred feet.

Working the controls, Tag willed the helo to hold on. Each muscle in his face was frozen; his body was a taut bow as he brought the bird in, the asphalt growing larger and larger below them.

Two hundred feet . . .

The '52 shook, its rotors pulling in the last available air before landing.

"This is it," Rook cried, trying to brace herself. "Seth, hang on!"

No! Tag crooned to the '52. She wouldn't let him down! Not now. She had the heart of a Thoroughbred, this one. Deftly, he lifted the nose at the last possible second. It was enough! Enough! He felt her blades lift, just as her wheels touched the asphalt.

Rook nearly cried out as they jolted to a safe landing. The engine continued to run, the blades whooshing slowly around. They had more fuel than what the gauge had shown. Thank God. Tag began immediate shutdown procedures. Outside the cockpit, the trauma team stood ready for a signal from the flight mech to come forward.

"Get back there and help with the transfer, Rook."

She snapped out of her shock, quickly following Tag's strained order.

In the cockpit, Tag hung his head. His hands were shaking so bad that he didn't know what to do. God, he'd cut it too close—too damn close. When Rook climbed back into her seat after the medical team had taken the victim inside the hospital, he glanced over at her. She was ashen, sweat making her grim face glisten.

"Call the air station and ask them to send over a fuel truck, will you?"

"Yes . . ." She turned on the radio and called, then turned to hold Tag's dark stare. "Are you okay?"

"No. None of us are. Christ, I feel like a wet rag."

She reached over and squeezed his slumped, thin shoulder. "You did one hell of a job getting us here. That was some kind of flying."

Grateful for her unexpected camaraderie, Tag managed a one cornered smile. He fondly gave the helo a well-deserved pat. "She got us here." And then he sobered. "I don't know about you, but these helos are just like people to me. Each one has a separate personality, its own glitches and strong points. This gal has heart—more heart and guts than any helo over at that hangar. Never forget that, Rook—ever. If you have a bad SAR case to go on, pray you get CG 1418. She's quite a lady."

Touched by his fervent admission, Rook smiled gently. "I'll remember that, Tag."

He unstrapped himself and moved dazedly. "How about our victim? Did you get any info on him yet?"

"No."

He moved his head in the direction of the hospital. "Why don't you go see what you can find out for our case report? I'll wait out here with Seth for the fuel truck."

Rook didn't want to leave Tag. He looked pale, and his eyes were like dark holes. "Are you sure? Maybe I could beg, borrow, or steal a couple of cups of coffee for us. I think we need something to calm our nerves. How about it? I can get the report info later."

"Yeah, that sounds like a good idea. Go ahead. I think Seth likes his coffee with a little sugar. You might check with him."

When the fuel truck arrived half an hour later, Rook was feeling more stable. The three of them stood a safe distance away while the '52 was refueled. They sipped their coffee, getting soaked in the pall of rain that had spread from the mountains directly behind the hospital across the city of Port Angeles.

"Miserable weather," Rook commented, bowing her head a little to ward off the misting rain.

Tag nodded, deep in thought. Not only was the Ops officer going to ask questions as to why he ran short of fuel at such a critical time, but so was the new C.O. If his luck hadn't held, they could have been forced to land on a road in the middle of nowhere—if they'd been lucky. The victim's life would have been jeopardized, too. Tag tried without success to analyze his faulty decision-making process. Why hadn't he gone with Rook's recommendation of six hundred pounds of fuel? The numbers supported it. Under the circumstances, higher power might have been required. On the other hand, they might have settled had they carried an extra hundred pounds of fuel. Christ, this was a messy one to call. And it would have to happen with a new skipper on board.

"Well," Tag said glumly, stuffing the styrofoam cup into the leg pocket of his flight suit, "let's get this show on the road. The helo's tanked up and topped off. Once we get back to base, there's going to be a fair amount of paperwork for us to do, Rook."

She nodded and began the long walk back to the '52. She climbed in and began her preflight check-list with Tag. As soon as she got back to the air station, she'd have to call the hospital to find out how Howard Barton was doing. Between Seth and herself administering CPR, the man was breathing again, and he had been semiconscious when the trauma team had taken him into the hospital. It occurred to Rook that today was the first time she'd ever administered CPR to someone. She began to get shaky all over again.

In her office, after cleaning up a bit, Rook called the hospital admitting office.

"Yes, this is Lieutenant Caldwell from the Coast Guard calling. I'm making out our flight report. Do you have the particulars on Howard Barton, the gentleman we medevaced out of the forest?"

Rook waited, tapping the pen absently, glancing out the window of her office toward the secretarial pool. Jody Theron was watching her. Rook stared back. Jody quickly returned to work, pretending she was busy. Her attention swung back to the voice at the other end of the line.

Rook rubbed her brow as she jotted down the necessary information. "Uh, has the son arrived there yet? Jim?"

"Yes, ma'am. I believe he came tearing in here just a few minutes ago. He's mud from head to toe."

Rook nodded. It had probably taken Jim a good hour with a four-wheel-drive truck to get out of that inaccessible spot and drive back down to Port Angeles. Rook cradled the phone more closely to her mouth, aching for him. No one deserved this kind of trauma—especially not Jim.

"Can you tell me how the senior Mr. Barton is?"

"Last I heard, he was being prepped for emergency surgery."

"How was he listed in emergency?"

"Critical, Lieutenant."

Rook tried to stay with the business at hand, scribbling down Howard Barton's address and phone number on the form. After she hung up, Rook stared at the light blue wall in front of her desk. She remembered the roses and turned to look at them. They were still fresh and fully blossomed, scenting the air with their fragrance.

She forced herself to complete the report and bring it to Tag at the other end of the building. Rook walked into his office, shut the door, and laid the report down in front of him. He didn't look very good.

"Want some more coffee, Tag?"

He raised his head from his paperwork. "No . . . thanks."

"You okay?"

"Yeah, just a little stressed out."

"Hey, I got this joke for you. You're always looking for new ones, aren't you?" she asked, forcing a cheerier tone.

Tag gave her a glance.

Rook ignored him. "Come on, you can add this one to your impressive repertoire, and tell it to all the guys."

"I'm not in the mood for jokes right now, Rook."

She sat down on a chair next to his desk. "This one's really good, Tag. Come on, let me cheer you up for once."

He laid the pen aside. "Okay, what is it? And it better be good."

"You'll love it. I laugh every time I think about it."

"Give it to me."

"Okay. What's a doughnut?"

A bit of light came back to his dark eyes. "A doughnut?"

"Yeah, you know, one of those round things with holes in the middle you buy over at Maudie's Restaurant for us every morning."

"I give. What's a doughnut, Rook?"

She grinned. "A fried halo."

Tag stared.

"Get it? You deep fat fry doughnuts, and they have a hole in the center—"

"Rook, do me a favor?"

"Yes?"

"Don't try and tell jokes. You're terrible at it."

Rook saw a tired hint of a smile pull at Tag's mouth. She reached over and patted his arm. Her plan to make him feel just a bit better had succeeded. "Maybe you're right, Tag."

With a groan, he shook his head and went back to writing his report. "I know I am. Now, get out of here. Go powder that cute nose of yours or something."

She rose. "I don't wear makeup, so I have nothing to powder it with, Mr. Welsh."

"A woman like you should wear a little bit, you know—just to show everyone how pretty you really are."

Embarrassed by Tag's honesty, Rook left as quietly as she had come. She had seen the worry in his drawn features. There would be an inquiry on this incident. Tag didn't need this, on top of the rest of his problems. As she slowly walked back to her office, she tried to think of a way to make him feel a little better, despite the dark cloud that seemed to constantly hover over his head.

CHAPTER

Eleven

WARD told Tag to come in and sit down. He had both his and Rook's hand-written reports on his desk. The Ops officer, Commander Bob Nelson, grimly stood nearby. It was nearly five o'clock, and Ward was sure everyone was ready to call it a day. It had been a long, grueling one for the two pilots, and Tag looked worse than everyone else combined. Ward kept his voice soft and low when he spoke to him.

"Bob and I would like to hear your side of the story concerning the reasons for only carrying five hundred pounds of fuel on board this morning."

Tag sat straight in his chair, the olive drab material of his flight suit darkened beneath each armpit with rings of sweat. "Lieutenant Caldwell figured out our HOGE power requirements and told me six hundred pounds, sir. I don't know what made me correct that downward to five hundred."

Ward watched the officer closely. He was coming unraveled right in front of them. His hands shook every time he lifted them to make a gesture. It wasn't Ward's intent to upset Tag even more, but he had to try and find out what had led to the decision.

"It looked like a rough SAR case from the word go," Ward said, watching some relief come to Tag's eyes.

"Yes, sir, one of the worst I've been on in a long time."

"You say you decided not to go with six hundred pounds of fuel. Can you give me any reason for that, Tag?"

Tag shook his head. "No, sir, I can't. I screwed up."

Bob Nelson shot a pleading look at the skipper, then turned his attention to the pilot. "Look, Tag, you've had a damn good flight record. It's not like you to make an error like this. There must have been *something*, maybe even some unconscious reasoning, that made you change those stats for your gross weight?"

Tag looked at each man's grave face. He stared down at his hands, which he had clasped in front of him. "I don't know, Bob. I can't think of anything right now. Rook questioned me on my decision, but I went ahead with it, anyway. It's my error in judgment entirely. She had nothing to do with it. She was right and I was wrong."

Ward straightened up, leaning back in the chair. "More important, Tag, you did a creditable job, flying under some trying circumstances. You got the helo down in one piece and the victim to the hospital."

"Yes, sir."

"All right, Tag, you may go. Send in Ms. Caldwell, will you?" Ward asked.

Ward saw the slump to Tag's shoulders as he left the office. It was as if all the life had been drained from the man. He switched his attention to Rook as she entered the room.

"Come in and sit down, Ms. Caldwell."

"Yes, sir." Rook sat on the edge of the wing chair. She sweated—not for herself, but for Tag. She had expected to get called on the carpet, but not this soon. They had turned in their reports only two hours ago.

"Tell me what happened out at the SAR desk this morning. What were your duties?" Ward asked her.

"Mr. Welsh asked me to compute our HOGE power and max gross weight, sir."

"How many pounds of fuel did it compute with the variables?"

"Six hundred, sir." And then Rook added quickly, "But I think Mr. Welsh was correct in going to five hundred."

Bob gave Ward a quick look. "Why do you say that, Rook?"

"Well, while we were out there, the temperature increased and the weather conditions fluctuated. My nose felt warmer. And with that unexpected temperature change, if we'd gone with the computed gross weight, I'm positive we'd have been unable to hover. Neither of us was expecting the victim to weigh two hundred and sixty pounds, either. When Davis started winching up the litter, I didn't know whether the helo was going to maintain altitude or not. If it hadn't been for Mr. Welsh's fine flying and experience, I don't think any of us would be alive right now to be talking about it."

Ward sat back, digesting her impassioned defense of Welsh. Was Rook doing it to protect him? Maybe herself? She wasn't at fault, that was clear. Maybe she didn't realize that. "Look, Ms. Caldwell, this isn't a Captain's Mast and it isn't an investigation. We're merely trying to piece this whole thing together. No one's charged with anything. Do you understand?"

Rook's heart was pounding hard in her chest. "Yes, sir." She squirmed in the chair. "Originally, I questioned Tag—er, I mean, Mr. Welsh, on his decision. But the weather was so gimpy and changing, plus the x-factor of not realizing the victim's weight, that he was correct on his decision."

Ward nodded. "Anything else you want to add, Ms. Caldwell?"

"No, sir."

"How was Mr. Welsh's frame of mind this morning before the SAR case?" Bob asked her.

Puzzled, Rook said, "Sir?"

"Did he appear absentminded—maybe preoccupied in some way?"

She shook her head. "No, sir. Not in my estimation," she answered slowly. What were they getting at?

"That's all, Ms. Caldwell," Ward murmured. "It's 1700, and I'm sure you'd like to call it a day."

Managing a slight smile, Rook stood up. "Yes, sir."

Ward turned to Bob after she had left. "Well? What's your opinion?"

Bob stood up, his hands resting loosely on his narrow hips. "Originally, I think Tag made an error. However, we both know that a temperature inversion can throw any statistic out the door in a second. Since the victim weighed so damn much, I'd say that Tag lucked out on his error. I think Caldwell's right: if they'd gone in with six hundred pounds of fuel under those fluctuating conditions, they would not have been able to do the job."

"I concur. But Welsh shouldn't be let off that easy. He did make an error that could have cost both lives and aircraft—not to mention a lawsuit, if the victim had died."

"Correct. So, what do you want me to do?"

"Counsel him and note it on his fitness report. There's no reason for anything else at this point. The man knows he was wrong and admitted it. I don't believe in harassing my people if they own up to their errors."

"Sounds reasonable. I'll counsel him first thing tomorrow morning." Bob started to head for the door.

"One more thing," Ward called.

The officer turned around. "Yes, sir?"

"Take Welsh off duty tonight. Call in another pilot to take over. He's in no shape to take another SAR call if we get one. Tomorrow morning, after you've talked with him, I want him here in my office."

Bob nodded. "You going to ground him?"

"I don't know. But it's obvious his wife's illness is affecting his ability to make good decisions." Ward stood and expended a long breath of air. "If he doesn't have the good sense to come and talk to you, and ask for time off because of his present mental state, I may have to do something about it."

Relieved that Ward understood, Bob nodded. "I tried to tell the old C.O. about this, sir, but he wouldn't listen. We were short of pilots anyway, and he didn't want Welsh pulled."

"Any time one of my pilots becomes a danger to himself, I'll ground him or her."

"Yes, sir. I'll see that Mr. Welsh is here by 1000 to see you."

Ward restlessly paced his office, the SAR case report in his hand. He halted at the window that overlooked the parking lot and watched Rook Caldwell, in her blue uniform, climb into a black TransAm. He tapped the copy of the report absently against his leg as she drove away. He knew that Howard Barton was the father of Jim Barton, the man who had come on base to give her flowers. Was she going to visit the hospital and find out how her first rescue victim was doing? Smiling slightly, he turned, deciding to call it a day. It had been a hellish one.

"Jim?"

Jim was sitting in the waiting room of the Intensive Care Unit, lost in a maelstrom of conflicting emotions, when he heard Rook's husky voice. Wearily, he raised his head. She was wearing her blue uniform. His first thought was that she looked good in it. The second, more important emotion, caught him totally off guard when she crouched down in front of him.

"Rook?" There was disbelief in his thick voice. When he saw her smile, some of the awful pain he was feeling went away.

"You look like hell."

He looked down at his filthy clothes. The mud had dried on him hours ago. "Yeah . . . I guess I do."

"Your father?"

Warmth flowed through him, chasing away the coldness that had inhabited him since his father's accident. "He's next door in I.C.U."

"How's he doing?" she asked quietly. Rook tried to hide her shock over Jim's condition. A day's worth of beard had darkened his face, making him look gaunt. His eyes were red-rimmed; he'd been crying. That shook Rook deeply, as it had when she had seen his face wet with tears at the rescue site. Rook had never seen a man cry before. Jim smelled of mud and sweat, and there were dried streaks of blood all over his shirt.

"He's critical, but stable, thank God."

"I called over and found out he got out of surgery about three this afternoon."

Jim was resting his elbows on his thighs, hands dangling limply between his legs. Rook's unexpected nearness and concern nearly unstrung his carefully closeted fears and grief. "Yeah. They couldn't stop the bleeding for a while. They said there were a lot of serious internal injuries." He gave a slight shrug. "You know how doctors are. They talk in a language nobody can understand."

"I know. So, your father's resting comfortably now?"

Jim nodded, feeling a hundred years old. He could smell his own stench—the fear-sweat that had stained his clothes. "They let me go in once an hour for five minutes to see him. He's still coming out from under the anesthesia, I guess."

"It will probably be a while." Rook transferred her hand from the arm of the chair to Jim's shoulder. "Listen, you've done all you can here for him. Can I give you a lift home? Maybe a shower, a change of clothes, and some food will help you."

He stared at her, the silence building between them. "I guess you're right. I smell like hell." Jim straightened up and looked down at his clothes.

Rook stood up, noticing at least two minor injuries to his right hand and arm. "Come on, fella, you need some doctoring yourself. I'll drive; you give me directions to your house."

He was too emotionally and physically exhausted to argue with her. Instead, Jim was grateful for the strength that she was giving him. "Sounds good. Let me tell the nurses at I.C.U. where I'll be."

She nodded.

Rook had wisely gotten directions to Jim's home before they left the hospital, since when she glanced over five minutes into the drive, she found him fast asleep. His hair was mussed, strands dipping down across his drawn brow. There was something vulnerable about him in sleep that allowed her to put down her guard toward him.

Jim gave her the keys as they walked up to the huge cedar home that sat far on the slope of the Olympic Mountains. She led him inside and straight to the bathroom.

"Start stripping off those clothes." Rook leaned over and got the shower started for him. She saw that his movements were slow, and that his hands shook as he tried to unbutton the shirt. "Here," she whispered, "let me do that. How long has it been since you last ate?"

Jim felt light-headed. "Five this morning . . . I think."

"I thought so." Rook pulled the soiled shirt off him, wrinkling her nose when she dropped it on the tile floor behind her. She tried to ignore his powerful-looking well-defined upper chest, dark with hair. Tugging at the belt to his jeans, she muttered, "You do the rest. When you get done in here, come on out. I'll rummage around your kitchen and fix you something to eat. Then you're going to bed."

Jim's reflexes were slow, but not too slow to catch her fingers before they left the belt he was wearing. "Look," he said, his words slurring, "I've got to get cleaned up and go back over there. I want to be there when Dad wakes up."

Rook's hand tingled hotly, aware of the calloused warmth of his hand as it encircled hers. "All right," she said softly, not wanting to upset him further, "we'll do it your way."

While Jim showered, Rook called the hospital. Yes, the head nurse would call if Howard Barton was regaining consciousness. Just as Rook suspected, the nurse felt the senior Barton would come out of the anesthesia and go directly to sleep without waking. But, in the event he woke up, they would call.

Rook tried to still her reaction to the opulence and beauty of Jim's house. It had every conceivable modern convenience, she discovered. Jody Theron was right: the Bartons weren't poor. She whipped up a plate of scrambled eggs and bacon while Jim showered. When she realized that over half an hour had elapsed and he still hadn't appeared, Rook investigated.

She found the bathroom door open and followed the puddle of wet footprints down the highly polished cedar hall. Rook halted at the open door to the expansive master bedroom and smiled. Jim had opened the closet, climbed into a pair of clean gray trousers, and sat down on the bed to put his socks on. But somewhere between getting the first sock on and the second one, he had lain back and fallen asleep.

She moved quietly to the bed. His snore was heavy and profound. As gently as possible, Rook maneuvered him onto the bed. Jim barely stirred from sleep, rolling over on his side and drawing his legs up toward his body. Taking a blanket from the closet, Rook covered him and then tiptoed out of the room, shutting the door quietly behind her.

It was nearly ten o'clock when Jim woke. First, he lay there a good five minutes, reorienting himself. When his fogged brain remembered that Rook Caldwell had brought him home, he sat up. Rubbing his stubbled face wearily, he picked up the phone and called the hospital. Afterward, he shrugged on a clean shirt and padded through the quiet, darkened house.

He found Rook asleep on one of the den couches. Shaking his head, Jim walked down the carpeted steps. This was his favorite room, with the fireplace and floor-to-ceiling windows overlooking the city and straits. Everything looked so peaceful from here. And despite the traumatic day, he felt more solid emotionally than before.

Kneeling down next to the couch, Jim quietly watched Rook. She lay with her hands beneath her cheek, turned on her side, legs drawn up. Her shoes had been placed to one side, and her slender feet were now encased only in nylon. He reached out, barely grazing her cheek, realizing for the first time that she must be as exhausted as he was. Her skin was pliant beneath his thumb as he lightly outlined her clean bone structure. New, unexpected protective feelings moved through him. Rook stirred and he rested his hand on her slender shoulder. Jim watched as her thick black lashes fluttered open to reveal drowsy gray eyes.

"Just lie there," he told her quietly. "It's ten o'clock."

Rook's eyes widened and she looked up at Jim. His face was shadowed in the darkness. Groggy, she muttered, "Your dad? Did they call?" and she groped for the phone, which she had placed next to her on the couch.

Jim caught her hand, and held it gently. "Everything's all right, Rook. They said he's resting well." He looked deeply into her vulnerable gray eyes. The husky quality of her voice moved him.

"You aren't like any woman I've ever met," he said. "First, you rescue Dad, and then you come and take care of me. You don't look much better than I feel. The day had to be hell on you, too, in a different way."

Unguarded when just awakened, Rook's normal defenses weren't in place. She responded to his low, unsteady voice. Despite all that had happened to him, Jim was still aware that the SAR case had affected her, too. But she had been too busy earlier to realize that she'd been in shock herself. "I'm okay. . ."

Jim gave her a slight smile that said he didn't believe her. "Sure, and so am I. You don't lie very well, lady. . ."

Rook slowly sat up with his help, wildly aware of him as a man. His father's accident had stripped Jim, leaving him open and accessible to her. Unable to think coherently, Rook reacted out of instinct when she saw his eyes fill up with tears. Wordlessly, she slipped her arms around him, drawing him to her. Jim gripped her hard, squeezing the breath from her as he crushed her against him.

Rook ran her fingers through his dark, thick hair, feeling the unbearable tension in his body. "He's going to be all right, Jim. I just know it. . ." she crooned near his ear. And then, she felt a shudder move through him and she tightened her hold around him. Rocking him gently, as if he were a hurt child, Rook felt more than heard the sob that escaped him.

She buried her head next to Jim's, tears squeezing from

beneath her tightly shut eyes. She wasn't sure any longer who was comforting whom. It didn't matter, she discovered. For the first time in her life, she had trusted a man with her emotions. Although stunned by that realization, Rook didn't care. What was important was getting Jim through the trauma reaction. She didn't need to ask if he loved his father; she could tell by his wrenching sobs, which seemed to come from the depths of his soul.

Later, after his weeping ceased, Rook managed an unsteady smile and tried to dry his stubbled cheeks with her fingers. "Look at us," she whispered, a catch in her voice. "We're a couple of crybabies."

Jim shook his head. "No, just a couple of human beings caught between a rock and a hard place." He framed her damp face, mesmerized by the velvet grayness of her eyes as she gazed at him. Words were useless to describe how he felt. Instead, he pulled Rook those scant inches forward, finding and drinking deeply of her tear-bathed lips.

Heat throbbed wildly through Rook as his mouth wreaked a fire of its own across her lips. Her fingers dug convulsively into his shoulders as he deepened the kiss between them.

The phone rang.

Easing from the welcoming warmth of her mouth, Jim sat up on the couch, one arm around Rook as he answered the phone. It had to be I.C.U.

Rook gripped Jim's hand tightly. Was the hospital calling with good or bad news? What if his father died? She remembered the awful loss of her mother and the shock of the phone call telling her about it. She tried in vain to read Jim's tense features.

He replaced the phone in the cradle, looking down at her. "He's regaining consciousness." His voice cracked. "The doctor said they're taking him off critical."

Rook made a muffled sound and threw her arms around his neck. "Oh, Jim, that's wonderful!"

"No," he said gruffly, holding her tightly, never wanting to let her go, "you are."

Rook eased out of his arms, Jim's words vibrating through her. She saw the raw honesty in his swollen eyes, and heard it in the shaken tone of his voice. His kiss had been branding, forever changing how she felt about him. She could taste him on her lips. His vulnerability stripped her of her ability to erect a defense. Rook didn't want any barriers between them—at least, not right now. Jim needed her.

"Listen, you've got to eat something. You're shaking like a leaf."

Jim didn't want to release her. Fighting his head and listening to his heart, he allowed his hands to slip from her slender waist. "I guess I'm hungry. I don't feel like eating, but I know I should."

Gripping his hand, Rook led him to the kitchen. "I'll make some more scrambled eggs and toast."

At the table, Jim pushed the eggs around on his plate. Rook sat at his elbow, doing the same thing. "We're both a mess," he muttered. "We can't even force ourselves to eat."

Rook pushed the eggs into her mouth, chewing them slowly. "Eat. Otherwise, we're going to be no good to anyone. Your dad is going to need you more than ever, Jim."

He gave her a faint smile, admiration in his eyes. "Mothering sort, aren't you?"

Wearily, Rook smiled. "Some people tend to bring that trait out in me."

Reaching over, Jim slid his hand over hers, gripping it gently. "That's another thing I like about you. You care."

Her appetite fled completely. The roughened warmth of his hand spread like a soothing balm across her tattered emotions. Placing her fork down on the plate, Rook whispered, "I think I'd better get going, Jim. It's been a long day and a longer night."

His hand tightened on hers and he held her gaze. "Stay tonight—please."

Rook opened her mouth, then shut it. His kiss hovered hotly in her memory, simmering, beckoning. "I—"

"I don't mean in my bed, Rook, if that's worrying you. There's a guest bedroom at the other end of the house." Jim dragged in a ragged breath. "Right now, I need you. Just your presence . . ."

Closing her eyes, Rook hung her head. No man had ever told her he needed her. How could she tell him no? "Okay," Rook choked out.

"Thanks," he whispered, meaning it. Releasing her hand, he got to his feet. "Come on, I'll show you where the guest room is located."

It was nearly one o'clock before Jim felt tired enough to go back to bed. Two hours after Rook had told him good night and disappeared into the guest bedroom, he was pacing the large sun deck that faced the dark straits. The May night was cool and damp, but it relieved the heat that was building explosively within him.

Resting against the cedar railing, Jim watched the low stratus clouds slide silently over Port Angeles. His father could have died today, but by some miracle, he hadn't, thanks to Rook and the Coast Guard's swift response. The kiss he'd shared with Rook had been nothing short of a miracle, too, infusing him with newfound hope and strength. Massaging his face in an attempt to think clearly, Jim felt the stubble of beard beneath his fingers. He raised his head. It had turned out to be a day of miracles, he decided humbly, shivering against the dropping temperature.

Turning, he padded barefoot back into the house, sliding the glass door shut and then locking it. The den was silent. Rubbing his chest unconsciously, he headed down the hall toward the guest bedroom. Knocking softly, he waited to see if Rook was still awake. There was no answer.

Opening the door, Jim stepped inside. Rook lay asleep, dressed in a pair of his pajamas on top of the covers. It was chilly, and she should have covered herself up. *Silly twit*, he thought, going over and picking up the rainbow afghan folded at the end of the bed. Carefully, Jim draped it across her body, taking care to not awaken her.

He stood there several minutes, etching her peaceful, sleeping features into his mind, his heart. There was still darkness beneath her glorious gray eyes, the black lashes thick against her flesh. And that wonderful mouth he'd tasted earlier . . . Jim took a deep, unsteady breath.

Tonight, he knew, Rook had exposed herself to him in many ways. Through this crisis, he'd seen the real Rook who hid behind those walls. Leaning down, Jim threaded several strands of her hair through his trembling fingers. Her hair was silken and clean, like gossamer threads spun from ebony eiderdown.

Crouching down, taking care not to disturb her, Jim placed his hand on the edge of the bed and watched her sleep, her hands beneath her cheek. Her hair provided a soft, dark frame for her face. It was a face he could study and trace for the rest of his life and about which he could always find something new and beautiful.

"I love you, Rook Caldwell." His barely whispered words dissolved into the lulling darkness. Rising, Jim tucked a bit of the afghan around Rook's shoulder and left.

Rook jerked awake when the alarm buzzed at six-thirty. Momentarily confused, she sat up, the afghan slipping off her as she fumbled to shut it off. As she looked around, the chain of events from last night slowly congealed in her barely functioning mind. There was a knock at the door.

"Come in," she croaked, setting the clock back on the bed stand.

Jim smiled a welcome as he entered, with coffee on a tray. "I heard your alarm and figured you might like some coffee."

With a groan of thanks, Rook reached for the cup after he'd placed the tray across her lap. "You're wonderful. God, I need this . . ." and she took a scalding swallow.

Sitting down on the edge of the bed, Jim watched her. Rook's eyes were puffy and sleep-ridden. That glorious cap of hair was an unruly mop that begged to be tamed back into place with his fingers. She looked like an endearing Raggedy Ann doll in his huge pajamas, the sleeves far too long, hampering her efforts to hold the cup between her hands.

"Looks like you need some help," Jim said, taking the cup

and placing it back on the tray. Patiently, he rolled up the sleeves until her hands were free.

Shyly, Rook looked up, drowning in the tender blueness of his eyes. "I'm pretty helpless the first half hour after I wake up," she confessed, her voice still raspy. "How's your dad? Have you heard anything? I didn't hear the phone ring all night."

"He slept well last night—that's why you didn't hear them call us. I just got done talking with Dr. Roher, and she says he's resting comfortably." Jim handed her the coffee, and watched her long, slender fingers curve around the china cup. There was nothing but grace and elegance to Rook, just like the bird she was named after.

Rook reached out, gripping his hand. "That's great news, Jim!"

He grinned at her sudden enthusiasm. "Yeah, it is good news, Wild Rose."

The endearment rippled through Rook, sweet and filled with promise. She drank her coffee. "I've got to get going soon. I'm going to have to pick up a clean uniform over at my apartment before I go to the station." She grimaced, running a hand across her hair. "And this mop of mine . . ."

Catching her hand midair, Jim said, "Beautiful hair. You look winsome when it's tangled like this."

The yearning in his voice filled her like sunshine warming a cold, freezing land. She watched as Jim cupped her hand within his, wildly aware of both his strength and incredible sensitivity as he studied her palm.

"Such small, capable hands," he said huskily. Taking the cup, he placed it on the tray, holding her wide gray eyes. There was so much he read in them as he leaned forward, cupping her cheek.

Automatically, Rook closed her eyes, craving contact with his mouth once again. Last night had been explosive, unexpected, and both had been cheated by the phone ringing. Now . . . Rook whispered his name, wanting to complete what had begun in the fertile darkness hours before.

Jim heard her tremulous voice, and felt the moistness of

her breath against his cheek as he bent those last few inches to claim her. As he moved his mouth hotly against hers, he reveled in her taste and texture. Rook's kiss was at once innocent and provocative. Moving his other hand to her neck, he framed her face, moving his tongue slowly across her lower lip, feeling her tremble subtly beneath his onslaught.

Each caress of Jim's tongue brought another explosion of fire, entwined with melting desire. Rook's hands slid up along the line of his chest, and she became aware of her femininity as never before—her fragileness against his size and overwhelming male intensity. His mouth devoured hers in worshipful adoration, heating her, cajoling her to revel in their oneness.

As his mouth slowly left her lips, Rook felt as if she had been torn away from what had made her whole. Dazed, she lifted her lashes, staring up in confusion at Jim, his face so near to hers. He was breathing hard, his nostrils flared, but so was she. Rook drowned in the azure of his intense gaze, yearning for him.

"I think," Jim began in a strained voice, "you'd better go." He glanced down at the watch on his wrist. It took an embarrassingly long time for him to focus on and read the time. "It's almost seven."

Rook nodded, barely coherent. "I—yes."

Getting up, Jim took the tray and headed to the door. "Let me know when you're ready and I'll drive you back over to the apartment."

She got up after Jim closed the door. Her knees were weak. Weak! How could one kiss so devastate her? Her mind had turned into little more than jelly. Rook sat back down, dumbfounded, trying to think clearly. One kiss—one burning, branding kiss. Rook touched her lips and closed her eyes. Jim was potent, demanding, but his kiss hadn't been any of those things. Instead, his mouth had been coaxing, inviting her to participate in their mutual exploration of one another. Rook wondered how she was going to piece herself together today.

Jim's kiss had made her feel soft and womanly, had put her in touch with feelings she couldn't begin to describe or ignore. Making a concerted effort, she stood up. First, a shower, and then a quick dash to her apartment before she went to the station. Rubbing her face, Rook wondered how she was going to function.

CHAPTER

Twelve

NOAH was in her office when Rook arrived, flushed, almost ten minutes late. She was too vulnerable from the last twenty-four hours to mask her feelings when she saw her brother pacing worriedly in her office. Rook ignored the looks from the secretarial pool.

"Noah?"

"Rook. Where have you been?" he raked his fingers through his hair.

She quietly shut the door so their conversation couldn't be overheard. "I was over at the hospital most of the night with Jim Barton. Why, what's wrong?"

Relief crossed his face. "I heard through the grapevine that you damn near had to crash land on that SAR case, and I tried to call you. God, I must have phoned you twenty times. And then, I borrowed a friend's car and drove over to your apartment, and you weren't there." He grimaced. "I've been in this business long enough to know what SAR cases do to an inexperienced person—especially pilots. We don't get as many shock and trauma situations as you do, usually." He stared at Rook, noticing her pallor. "You all right?"

Rook had to talk to someone. "Yes . . . no . . . oh, hell, I don't know, Noah. So much has happened . . ."

He nodded. "Tell me about it."

She hesitated. "Noah, I'm suppose to be working—"

"What does the SAR manual say about the importance of the victim talking about his tragedy or trauma? Now, talk."

Miffed, Rook sat down. "I'm hardly a victim in this case."

"Like hell you're not. Flight incidents and SAR cases can be bloody, messy situations, Rook. No one can ever adequately prepare you for the emotional shocks you're going to take out there. After you do it for a year or so, you get some distance and objectivity on it. But until then, you're vulnerable, and you're going to feel every victim's pain and anguish." Noah crossed his arms, waiting for Rook's response.

She barely looked at him, noting the stubborn jut of his chin. "Christ, I'm barely awake. I need some coffee. How about you?"

"Yeah, I could use a cup."

She got up. "Okay, don't go away. I'll be right back."

Rook passed Tag Welsh on the way to the thirty-cup coffee maker. If she thought Jim looked like hell, she was wrong. Tag looked worse. She almost stopped to talk to him in the hall, but saw that he was heading toward the captain's office and decided to leave things be for now. Rubbing her temple where a headache was starting, she wondered if every day was going to be like this: an emotional roller coaster. Noah was right: no one had prepared her for the emotions she was now experiencing about the rescue.

When Tag Welsh entered the captain's office, he didn't miss the fact that his log book and files were in front of Stuart. "Sir, permission to speak?" He tried to calm the nervousness he felt deep in his gut.

"Certainly," Ward murmured, motioning toward a chair. Although he had a prepared speech to give, he let the officer go first. Maybe Tag was going to unload on him, and if he was, that was a positive signal.

Clearing his throat, Tag muttered, "Captain, I'm officially requesting the Ops officer take me off flight duty temporarily."

Hiding his surprise, Ward said, "Go on."

"Well, after yesterday's stunt, I figured it all out." Tag opened both his hands, studying them darkly. "My wife, Paula . . . well, my mind's on her every minute. I screwed up yesterday on a SAR case because I wasn't thinking straight. I hadn't slept well the night before, so I wasn't making rational decisions." He grimaced and looked over at Stuart. "I almost killed myself and three other people because I can't keep my mind or emotions off my wife's illness."

Ward nodded sympathetically. "You're a credit to yourself, Tag, and to all of us, for admitting that. I'm in agreement that taking you off flight duty for now is beneficial. I'd like you to talk to the chaplain. He can help support you through this difficult period." He gave Tag a slight smile and pushed a couple of papers toward him. "However, I'm not about to lose your talents as engineering officer. Do you think you can apply yourself one hundred percent to making sure those birds are properly maintained?"

Tag's face brightened a bit. He'd expected Stuart to throw the book at him. Instead, the captain was trying to be humane and fair. Gratefully, he said, "Yes, sir."

"As you already know, Chief Jarvis has been suspended from his duties, and that places a bigger responsibility on you. The new chief is going to need more help and direction for a while until he gets used to all his duties."

"I'm prepared to deal with it, Captain."

"Is there anyone over there who can help with some of the peripheral duties?"

Relieved that he wasn't going to get a Captain's Mast, Tag broke into a smile. "Well, sir, Annie Locke, as you know, just made E-7. She's ready for more responsibility. What you may not know, sir, is that she's been going to night school to get a degree in electrical engineering. She's just a semester short of her degree, and she has a 3.5 average." Seeing that Stuart was pleased with that news, Tag continued, presenting an idea he'd been harboring for a long time. "I'd like to put Annie in charge of quality assurance in helo maintenance, Captain."

Ward's brows moved up a notch. "That's an excellent idea."

"Yes, sir. Believe me, Annie's got everything it takes to be an engineer herself. She's young, bright, and responsible. As a matter of fact, when things started going sour over there with Chief Jarvis, and I couldn't get help from above, I had Annie helping me with helo inspections." He waited to hear Stuart's reaction. When he got none, he went on. "She's stood more than her fair share of duty, and I'd like to reward her for her efforts—sir . . ."

"She'd still have her flight duties," Ward pointed out, delighted with the idea. He was impressed with Locke's personal initiative. And if he didn't miss his guess, she'd be able to correct any errors of omission Welsh made. Ward would have a talk with Annie soon.

"Oh, yes, sir!"

"And she wouldn't be relegated to a yeoman for you?"

"No, sir. I want her out there doing Q.A. I'll let Chief Jarvis handle the paperwork."

"Excellent idea, Tag. I like it. You rearrange your department as you see fit." He saw Tag's face relax for the first time. Ward gentled his voice. "Look, the next six months are going to be hard on you. I'd consider it an honor if you wanted to bend my ear from time to time when you need to talk to someone."

"Thank you, sir. I'm in touch with a hospice group here in Port Angeles, and they're helping Paula and me through this. I think things are going to be okay—well, as okay as they can be, under the circumstances."

Ward smiled. "You've got a lot of common sense, Tag, and I applaud that. Despite some grave personal problems, you're wise enough not to jeopardize other people's lives. Just remember, I'm here if you need to talk." The pilot looked relieved with the mild reprimand.

Standing, Tag went over to the desk, offering his hand. "Thanks, Captain."

Leaving the office, Tag felt a hundred pounds slide off his

shoulders. He knew his decision would put an extra burden on the already depleted pilot roster, but most of them would understand.

"Hey, Annie . . ." Seth Davis called, motioning her over to the helo he was working on.

Annie, who had just come on duty, ambled across the hangar to Seth. "Morning. What's up?"

He gestured for her to climb up on the ladder and join him. When she did he said, "This isn't for everyone's ears, that's why I called you over."

"Yeah? What's going on? This must be big, or you wouldn't be acting so secretive." Her eyes lit up with amusement.

Taking a small pair of pliers, Seth bent down and gently put one of several lock nuts back into place on the main rotor head. "I just heard Chief Jarvis hit the roof over in his office. I happened to be grabbing a cup of coffee in there when Jody came over with a new set of orders for the chief."

Annie's eyes widened slightly. "Yeah? Well, what happened? Tell me!"

"Get this: Mr. Welsh has been grounded."

"Oh, no . . ."

"Not only that, but the chief has been reduced to shuffling maintenance and service reports." Seth chuckled and looked over his shoulder toward her. "And you're going to be taking over quality assurance. You'll be assisting Mr. Welsh in all inspections."

"You're jiving me, Seth."

"Would I lie to you?"

Annie eyed him speculatively. "Are you *sure*? You know how Jody gossips."

"Hey, I was *in* the chief's office when he read the orders. He about tore a new hole in the overhead, let me tell you. You know how he gets when he's pissed."

"Yeah, the original Screamer from the Black Lagoon," she muttered, frowning. Annie allowed the implications to sink in for several minutes before speaking again. "Seth, they probably grounded Mr. Welsh because he's so distraught over his wife's illness."

"That's what I think. I mean, a man can only stand so much. I don't think I'd be able to work if Donna was dying in front of me day by day. I don't know how he's held it together this long."

"I don't know either," Annie admitted, her voice filled with emotion. "He's such a fine guy, Seth. He's always treated us fairly."

"Not to mention being the best pilot we've got."

"Well, one of the best. Mr. Logan's no wimp at the controls, either."

Seth grinned, his teeth white against his sweaty ebony skin. "Yeah, I'll give him that."

"God," Annie whispered, realizing the full implications of the information he'd given her, "this is an awful big step up for me, if it's true. I mean, the responsibility."

"You wanted to apply to Officer's Candidate School after you got your degree. Getting to help Mr. Welsh isn't going to hurt your chances, Annie."

"No, I guess not." She started to climb down off the ladder.

"Hey!" he called.

She looked up at Seth, midway down the ladder. "Yeah?"

"Watch your rear, gal."

"Why?"

"You know who's going to be gunning for you from now on—Jarvis." He waggled his finger toward her. "Watch him—close. Word's out he's got an appointment with the skipper at eleven. I saw him taking a nip from that bottle he hides in the file drawer earlier."

Annie snorted and climbed down off the ladder. "He'll probably hit the bottle in the pilot locker room, too, before he goes over."

"That new skipper's stalking him. The chief's number's up."

"It's about time, Seth."
"Amen, sister, amen."

Chappie wiped his mouth with the back of his hand as he mounted the stairs. This was it. The C.O. had kept those damn files for over a week now. Sweat trickled down his armpit; he absently scratched it through the jacket he wore. What was the captain going to say? How could he get out of the situation? Why did Stuart have it in for him? Any other C.O. would protect a chief's rating and importance when he had so little time left before retirement.

Waiting in nervous anticipation in the outer office, Chappie kept rubbing the palms of his hands against one another. This was just another ploy to get him to sweat some more. He knew officers and the head games they liked to play on the lowly enlisted personnel.

"He'll see you now, Chief Jarvis," June said.

Getting up briskly, Chappie nodded in her direction. He mentally girded himself, pretending that he was going into battle and that Stuart was his ultimate foe.

"Sit down, Chief," Ward invited. His quick perusal told him that Jarvis was on edge. "Coffee?"

Surprised by the change in Stuart's tactics, Chappie's mouth dropped open. He quickly snapped it shut. "No, sir. Thank you, anyway."

Ward smiled and got up, pouring himself a cup. He twisted a look over his shoulder. "Sure?"

"Well, maybe half a cup, sir."

Ward poured a second mug and took it over to the chief. He went behind the desk and sat down. A minute of silence had the effect he wanted on Jarvis: the chief relaxed slightly. Sipping the coffee and appearing totally at ease, Ward pointed absently at the records from Maintenance Control. "I've had the opportunity to look at these things, Chief, and I'd like your explanation on the points we covered last week." Ward wanted to give Jarvis every opportunity to admit that he'd played favorites and wanted to clean up his act. If he'd do that, then Ward knew the man was intrinsically honorable and had a good level of self-respect. Those were qualities he looked for in leaders, whether officers or enlisted.

Chappie launched into his rehearsed speech, basically reiterating what he'd told the captain last week. He emphasized the sick leave, the unexpected emergency leave, and other traceable sources. The expression on Stuart's face didn't alter when he dropped into a wheedling tone.

"I don't like pointing fingers, sir, but the last C.O. really put us under the gun."

"I realize that, Chief, and I'm taking that into consideration, up to a point."

Chappie leaned back, aware of the warning in Stuart's tone on the last sentence. It was a veiled threat to come clean—or else. He fidgeted with the coffee, gulping some of it down. "Sir, I haven't been well myself of late."

"Oh? For how long, Chief?"

Now Stuart's voice was silken and Chappie hesitated, unsure whether the captain was going along with his ploy or not. Damn, he was the toughest C.O. he'd ever had to try and read. "Well . . . uh, a year ago, sir."

"What's the problem, Chief?"

"Bouts of dizziness sometimes. Oh, nothing to worry about—"

"Have you seen a doctor about this?"

He shook his head, gripping the mug hard between his weathered fingers. "No, sir. I just think the combination of the old C.O. and the long hours I've been putting in have caught up with me."

Ward gazed at him, his eyes dark and unreadable. "Chief, I think part of the problem might be tied in to these records, and possibly related to your health situation. What do you think?" *Come on, man, admit you have a drinking problem.* Ward had already been tipped off by another flight mech that Jarvis kept a pint of vodka in the locker room over in the hangar.

With a shake of his head, Chappie muttered, "Not at all, sir. I always try to do my duty. My job comes first."

With a sigh, Ward pulled out a sheet from Jarvis's personnel file. "Chief, I don't want to play games with you. You were put on report for an alcohol incident at your last duty station."

"That was two years ago, sir!" he protested loudly. "And that's all it was! Just an incident."

Ward stared into Jarvis's haunted eyes. "I won't have my people's lives put in jeopardy by anyone on drugs or alcohol, Chief. Now, I've given you the opportunity to talk to me openly about this health problem of yours."

"I'm sober, sir! I swear to God I am! I'd never drink on the job."

Grimly, Ward stood up. "I hope for your sake you're not lying to me, Chief. Because, if you are, I'll string your ass up so fast you'll think hell's a great place to live instead. Do you read me?"

Chappie stood. "Yes, sir. Loud and clear, sir."

The silence thickened between them as Ward stared hard at the chief. "One last chance, Chief, before you leave this office. I've never punished any man or woman who's come to me openly and honestly with a problem. I work hard to rehabilitate my people because I want them satisfied with themselves and their job performance for the Coast Guard. I can forgive human weakness. What I can't forgive is a liar."

Jarvis belligerently met Stuart's hard features. "I don't have a problem. *Sir.*"

"Very well," Ward said grimly. "You've seen the new orders for yourself, Mr. Welsh, and Miss Locke?"

"I have, sir."

"Any questions about my decision?"

"I can't say I have, sir, but I've been in this man's outfit long enough to follow orders."

Ward saw the hatred in the chief's eyes. Disappointed, he waved him toward the door. "Dismissed."

Could he have handled it differently? Better? Ward knew Jarvis was an alcoholic. It was simply a matter of time and gathering up enough evidence to bring him before a Captain's Mast. He wouldn't see flight safety jeopardized for Jarvis's unadmitted problem. No, he'd have to move quickly. And then he wondered how any action against the chief would impact Locke's new assignment. A lot of the enlisted men would be jealous.

Chappie unlocked the file drawer. He glanced out the window of the office door and then slugged down two gulps of vodka, finishing off the contents of the bottle. He knew he'd have to remove all evidence from his office and be extra careful about his hiding places from now on. The alcohol barely took the edge off his anger. If that goddamn captain thought he was going to drum him out of the service, he was mistaken. He moved to the window. It was almost noon, and the hangar was deserted. Everyone had gone to lunch. His eyes narrowed. He spotted Annie Locke in the cockpit of CG 1418. She was doing scheduled maintenance on the bird. A slow smile came to his face.

So, Mr. Welsh and that bastard of a captain thought highly of Bucky Beaver's skills. Well, he didn't get to a chief's rating by being a fool. There wasn't a gold striper in the Coast Guard who could keep up with his maneuvering. The smile widened on Chappie's square face, exposing his teeth. Why hadn't he thought of this before? Not only could he get Locke into hot water, he could embarrass Welsh, and show the captain that the people he thought so highly of were fuck-ups. And, of course, he'd be there to not only expose the problem that Locke had failed to remedy, but to point fingers. That would take the heat off him. Since the captain wanted whipping boys, let him go after two of his own favorites.

Rook sat in her office, her thoughts wandering. She couldn't focus on the public relations drafts that she was supposed to deliver to Captain Stuart by the end of the day. The office was quiet when the secretarial pool was at lunch. As usual, the day was gray and cloudy. She stared out the window, wishing for some sunshine. Getting up, Rook opened the door to her office, hoping for some fresh air. She glumly looked at the calendar: June 25. She'd managed to survive almost three months at the station. She was officially on the SAR duty roster, having completed her initial orientation training, but she didn't feel happy. Paula Welsh's health had declined steadily over the last three weeks, and she wasn't expected to live much longer.

She missed Tag's daily round of jokes, his country boy humor and easygoing manner. Rook tried to give him emotional support, but she realized no one could help him now. She knew from experience that the death of a loved one was something that had to be faced alone. Scribbling idly on a note pad, her thoughts moved to Jim's father, who was slowly recovering but still in the hospital. That one trauma-filled day had driven her and Jim into each other's arms. She didn't regret that, but something deep within her signaled a warning to run from the developing relationship. Rook was unable to understand the wild panic that came and went. Right now, Jim was over his head in paperwork, running the huge business by himself. Before the accident, Howard Barton had been a driving force equal to his son in the company. Now, Jim was laboring under a double work load that would give a Type A executive a heart attack in a week's time. They didn't get to see each other often between his extra responsibilities and her duty.

And then there was Gil. Something was eating the hell out of the man, but Rook couldn't get him to talk about it. It was probably his wife, who had been writing ridiculous things about Coast Guard people. She waited uneasily to see if her interview would appear in the newspaper. It had been almost two months since Eve had shown up unexpectedly in her office. Had Eve used the pretense of an interview to size her up, or was she holding the threat of a blasting article over Rook's head to keep her away from Gil. She had never discussed the interview with him, but it was obvious he knew about it. Gil was short-tempered and growly lately; no one liked pulling duty with him. Tonight, she was his copilot. Rook prayed there wouldn't be any SAR calls.

"Hey, Ms. Caldwell, what are you doing here all by yourself?" Annie asked, standing uncertainly at the door.

Rook lifted her head, warming beneath Annie's infectious smile. Did she ever get depressed, like the rest of them? It didn't seem so. "Hi, Annie. I see you've got duty with us tonight."

Annie gave her a thumbs up, nervously standing there. She was dressed in her olive-green flight suit. "Yes, ma'am, I got the magic combination. Couldn't get two better pilots."

With a laugh, Rook sat back in the chair. "You're good for me, Annie. I'm glad you dropped by, because I was feeling a little down about Paula Welsh."

Everyone at the station knew of Paula's deteriorating health. With a solemn nod, Annie said, "Yeah, Mr. Welsh is going through a terrible time. I just wish there was some way to help."

"It's probably more important that we be there for him afterward."

"To pick up the pieces," Annie agreed softly. She gave Rook a shy smile, her hands stuck in the pockets of the flight uniform. "I just dropped by to sorta talk to you, Ms. Caldwell. I suppose this is a Personnel matter, but I don't feel comfortable talking to a man about it." She hesitated, then, sensing Rook's willingness to listen, continued. "Have you got a few minutes?"

Rook gestured to the chair next to her desk. "Sure, come on in and sit down." Pulling open the desk drawer, she asked, "I packed a lunch. Want to share it? I don't have much of an appetite right now."

Annie shut the door and held up a hand as she sat down. "No thanks, ma'am. I just got done grabbing a bite to eat over at the line shack."

"Okay." Rook placed the sack aside, devoting all her attention to Annie. "What can I do for you?"

Heat crept into Annie's freckled face. "Well, it's not what

you can do for me. I just need another woman's opinion on something."

"Yes?"

Annie pointed to her front teeth. "I, uh, was wondering if I got my jaw and teeth fixed, if it might improve my looks just a little. No, I know I'm homely-looking as all get out." She gave a bashful laugh. "I come from straight Kentucky hill stock, and if you think I'm unsightly, you ought to see some of the folks that stayed home."

"Annie, I think just the opposite about you. You're beautiful, from the heart outward."

Surprised, Annie risked a quick look in her direction. "Really?"

"When you smile, your face becomes radiant, your eyes light up, and we're all the better for it. I don't call that unsightly—I call it beautiful."

Laughing nervously, Annie stared down at her hands, clasped in her lap. There was still black grease stubbornly lodged beneath her short, almost nonexistent nails. No matter what she did, she could never get rid of all of it. "Yeah, but you're a woman, Ms. Caldwell."

Frowning, Rook asked, "Have the guys been teasing you over at the hangar?"

"Ahh, no more than usual, ma'am. It's just that—well—you see, there's this guy on Lieutenant Caldwell's cutter by the name of Dave Harper, and I really like him." Her voice fell to a whisper. "But he won't even look at me. I see it in his eyes when I try to talk to him sometimes. He thinks I'm ugly."

Taking a deep breath, Rook's heart squeezed with Annie's pain. "Was it something he said?"

"Oh, no, ma'am. You see, Dave takes night classes over at the same college I do, and I see him a couple times a week." She licked her dry lips. "I watch how he looks at other girls who are really pretty. I'd like to get him to notice me, but I guess I'm pretty poor at figuring how to do it. My ma had eight of us young ones to raise, and she didn't have the time to teach us girls how to go about looking attractive."

Rook looked at the piece of note paper in front of her for a long minute before speaking. "I'm afraid I'm not the best one to ask on that account. I don't wear any makeup, either. My hair's so short, I don't have to figure out whether I should curl it or blow dry it."

"But you're awful pretty, ma'am, with or without all that gunk some women put on their faces."

"Thanks, Annie. I've always believed beauty comes from inside a person, and no amount of war paint can make the difference. Women shouldn't be judged on their looks or their body."

"Ain't that the truth? I just wish these men would look at our God-given talents, instead of those dumb things."

Rook smiled absently. "It would make things easier on our kind of woman, wouldn't it?"

"Yes, ma'am. Since you've come here, I've sure felt better about myself. You're an inspiration."

Rook tried to gently turn the conversation back to Annie. "Thanks. Just be careful you don't put me up on any pedestals: I fall off real easy. Annie, have you talked to the dental officer about your jaw and tooth alignment problem?"

"Just this morning." She brightened, her eyes brimming with hope. "He said my jaw would have to be busted and reset, and he'd have to do a lot of work on my teeth."

"And the outcome?"

Softly, "No one will be able to call me Bucky Beaver anymore . . ."

Rook took a deep breath, realizing what it had cost Annie in terms of pride to admit that she knew the nickname the men had given her. She wanted to rap each one of those insensitive clods in the mouth. If only they could see the hurt in Annie's eyes and the pain in her voice, they wouldn't ever call her that again. People were so cruel to one another.

"Know the nickname I have for you?"

Surprise flared in Annie's wide eyes. "Why—no."

Rook held her wavering gaze. "I've always called you Sunny behind your back. The name has sort of stuck, and the rest of the pilots call you Sunny, too. So, sometime, if one of us slips up and refers to you as that, you'll know who started the whole thing."

Tears stung Annie's eyes, but she fought them back. Her lower lip trembled and she tried to smile. "Thank you, ma'am."

Rook became more businesslike, on the verge of tears herself. "Well, when will you start the dental work? I think it's a great idea. But I think if you do it, you should do it for yourself, Annie, not for a man. We women need to learn to do things for ourselves, not for what some man might want of us. We have to learn to *be* ourselves. What do you think?"

Annie's trembly smile became stronger. "Yes, ma'am, I think you're right. Even if Dave Harper still continues to ignore me, at least he was the reason to get it done."

"I like the way you think, Annie. You're on top of things."

The woman rose. "I owe you one, Ms. Caldwell."

Shaking her head, Rook murmured, "We're even, Annie, believe me."

Annie cocked her head, silent for several seconds, trying to digest and understand her veiled comment. Not succeeding, she raised a hand in farewell. "I'll probably be seeing you again before tomorrow morning."

"Maybe we'll get lucky," Rook countered, and watched Annie leave.

Rook hoped not, trying to concentrate on the P.R. items in front of her. She didn't want a SAR case with Logan. He was on the verge of exploding, and Rook didn't want any part of it. Right now, she wished she was on board the *Point Countess* with Noah. His crew had gunnery practice this morning outside the mouth of the straits. Her relationship with Noah was subtly changing. Rook rested her chin on her hand, staring at the wall. Noah . . . he was like a shadow in her life—always there if she needed him, but never intrusive. By leaving her alone and not pressuring her, he'd made her feel free to come to him on her own. She wasn't sure how she felt about that. She was still uneasy about the past, yet Noah had so far given her no reason to distrust him. He was smart, Rook decided, getting back to work.

CHAPTER

Thirteen

A knock on the door made Ward turn, and he scowled. It was eight o'clock on the morning of June 26. Judging from the urgency of the knock, he sensed something had gone wrong. "Come in."

Lieutenant Rook Caldwell walked in, a newspaper in hand. She was pale. "Captain, I was running some errands this morning, and I saw this on the newsstand. I think you'd better take a look at it." She handed it to him, preparing herself accordingly.

Ward's eyes narrowed as he read the front-page headlines of the *Star*: *Whale Shot, Coast Guard Responsible?* There were three large black-and-white photos. One of them clearly showed the *Point Countess* and Scanlon's helo. The next was of the wounded calf, which had ten stitches of bullet holes across its body. The third showed the mother whale trying to keep her dying calf afloat. He stood there, rapidly perusing the five-column article, anger growing. He flicked a gaze at the byline, and realized with a sinking feeling that Eve Logan had written the article.

"Sir, is there anything I can do?" Rook asked, thinking that the P.R. officer should get involved immediately on this sort of situation.

"No . . . not just yet." Ward glanced up at her. "Thank you for bringing this to my attention, Ms. Caldwell."

Rook tilted her head, noting Stuart's agitation. "All right, sir."

"Dismissed," he told her, trying to keep the angry edge out of his voice.

Rook released a breath of air, only too glad to leave. She shut the door quietly behind her. My God, that was the *Point Countess*, Noah's cutter, in the photo! The article practically said that he had shot the whale. She slowed her pace down the hall, lost in turmoil. He wouldn't do that—Noah was gentle. She'd never seen him angry enough to strike anyone or anything. And God knew, they'd had plenty of verbal battles before—the worst kind. If he'd never raised his hand to her, he'd never harm a defenseless animal—especially a whale. Rook recalled the look on Stuart's face and a chill ran up her spine. Helos had no guns on board, so the only possible culprit to shoot the whale was the cutter, which did carry weaponry.

Rubbing her brow to stem a headache that was beginning, Rook rushed back down to her office. Noah's career would be destroyed if he was proven guilty. The photos and story were blatantly incriminating. She knew little of her brother, but one thing she did know was his dream of being the skipper of a large cutter in the Coast Guard. That dream had not wavered in his mind since the time he was a youngster. Noah would never jeopardize his career like this—never. Restless, Rook looked around her office. She wanted to help him, but didn't know how. Earlier, she had heard from the SAR desk that he had been called to participate in a case out in the straits. Was his cutter back in port yet?

Noah noticed both Captain Stuart and the Ops officer, Bob Nelson, waiting for him and Dave Harper when they arrived at the office. The silence was turgid.

"Reporting as ordered, sir."

Ward gave a brusque nod. "Sit down, Mr. Caldwell. You too, Harper."

Noah perused the officers' faces. Stuart looked positively angry, barely in control of his emotions, if he was any judge. What the hell was going down?

Stuart looked to his Ops officer. "Read them their rights, Mr. Nelson." Ward sat down.

Stunned, Noah looked over at Stuart, and watched Nelson drone on. He sat up tensely afterward as the C.O. put the newspaper into his hands.

"Read that, Mr. Caldwell," Ward ordered him.

Scowling, Noah read the account, studying the photos of the dying calf. He handed the newspaper back to Nelson, his attention focused on Stuart.

"You held gunnery practice out at these coordinates yesterday, Mr. Caldwell?" Ward asked, shoving the order to conduct target practice in Noah's direction.

Noah glanced at it. "Yes, sir."

"How many rounds did you expend? And how?"

"Harper and his team fired five bursts at one-minute intervals at a floating target we'd placed earlier."

"With fourteen bull's-eyes," Harper added, sensing that the captain was hunting a scapegoat. He liked his skipper, and immediately defended him.

Ward drilled a warning look in Harper's direction—one designed to tell him to keep his mouth shut until spoken to.

"Who was in that immediate vicinity with you, Mr. Caldwell?"

"Just the Coast Guard helo that was ordered out with us to conduct basket hoists."

"Did you or any of your men sight *anything* else in your vicinity?"

Noah kept his voice firm and unruffled. "No, sir. We had perfect visibility, and the seas were calm."

"Like glass," Harper added quickly.

Stuart snapped a look at him. He asked Caldwell, "Were there any other weather conditions present?"

Noah shrugged. "The normal fog bank we get this time of year, sir. It was southwest of us, about five miles away."

"Four and a half," Harper corrected, giving his skipper a swift glance.

"All right, four and a half," Noah amended.

Ward stared down at his notes. Either both his flight and

cutter crew were lying, or the newspaper was—specifically, Eve Logan. But how could she rig the whale shooting? She couldn't. There had to be an explanation—a logical one. He lifted his eyes, staring hard at Caldwell. He was composed, unruffled—at least, outwardly. If the man had something to hide, he'd give himself away. His gaze shifted to Harper, who had his jaw clenched, and was sitting forward aggressively. Ward almost smiled. Harper was protecting his skipper, which was commendable, up to a point, but foolhardy if Caldwell was lying. Harper's career would go down the drain, too.

Ward nailed Caldwell, speaking very slowly and very clearly. "For the record, did you see any whales anywhere near the area where you were practicing gunnery?"

"No, sir." He looked over at Dave. "Did you or your crew?"

"No, sir." Harper shifted his gaze to the captain, his voice shaking with anger. "We saw no whales, Captain."

"Very well. How about a twenty-foot yacht?"

Noah shook his head. "Sir, by the manual, I'm charged with making sure there is no boat traffic in the immediate area where we practice and CG 1224 confirmed this before we started to fire."

Ward sat back, studying the two men for a long time. The air grew oppressive in the office. "Lieutenant, I want you and Harper to go with the Ops officer right now and make out a full report of your activities yesterday. Leave nothing out. I'll expect that report on my desk within the hour. Understand?"

Noah rose, struggling with his shock. "Yes, sir." He turned. "Let's go, Dave."

"Yes, sir." Harper gave the C.O. a scowl, and then left with his skipper.

The office had just emptied when the phone rang. Ward answered it. "Captain Stuart."

"This is Admiral Savage. Just what the hell is going on down there?"

Ward's hand tightened around the phone. "Sir?"

"The *Seattle Dispatch*'s main headline reads: COAST GUARD ACCUSED OF SHOOTING WHALE.

"Admiral, I just saw the story myself. It's in the Port

Angeles paper, as well. We weren't notified that it was going to run, or given a chance to respond to the allegations."

"Do you realize it's been picked up by AP? Jesus Christ, it will be on the front page of every newspaper in the U.S.!" Savage's voice lowered to little more than a snarl. "Not only that, you can bet you'll have television crews on your doorstep within hours. Dammit, Stuart, I want action on this, and fast!"

"Nobody agrees with you more, Admiral."

"Have you talked to the helo and cutter crew?"

"Yes, sir. They just left my office."

"Did they do it?"

"I don't believe so, sir."

"What do you mean, you don't believe so?"

Ward held on to his disintegrating temper. His words came out chopped. "Admiral, the *Point Countess* arrived in port less than thirty minutes ago. My cutter captain is writing out his report right now. I'm moving on this just as fast as humanly possible. My next call is going to be to that newspaper, to find out why the hell they didn't wait on this story until they had all the facts."

Savage was breathing heavily into the phone. "I want to be updated as soon as you find out who did this. Good God! We've got enough problems without having the public think we're a bunch of a whale murderers."

Ward listened to the tirade, closing his eyes. What a can of goddamn worms. Eve Logan was going to pay for this.

By noon, Rook had fielded dozens of phone calls from newspapers from around the U.S. Stuart had told her that Admiral Savage was sending over his special P.R. team from Seattle to deal with the crisis. He didn't think it would look good to have the sister of one of the suspects handling the press. She hoped they would arrive soon.

The door to her office stood open and various people filed in and out, running to answer the ringing phones in the outer area. Rook had just given Jody a statement to read to an East Coast television station when she looked up and saw Eve

Logan, dressed in a chic gray suit, walk through the outer door. Her eyes narrowed with anger.

Rook stood up, slowly, her combat instincts rising dangerously. Gil Logan had already come by twice to apologize profusely for his wife's actions. Rook didn't blame him. Fists clenched, she waited.

"Hello, Lieutenant Caldwell," Eve announced soberly. She came in and shut the door to the office. "I understand you're the acting P.R. officer, so as a reporter from the *Star,* I demand some answers to my questions regarding the whale shooting."

The urge to wrap her fingers around Eve's white throat was very real. Rook stood there, tense, her feet slightly apart. "First, you'll answer mine. How'd you get those photos of the whale?"

"Simple. I was out sailing with another reporter and her husband yesterday morning when it happened. And like a good journalist, I had my camera along."

"A good reporter would have allowed the Coast Guard to respond to the charges before printing the article," Rook ground out.

"Three people *saw* the whole thing."

"I talked to Julia Edwards, the other reporter, earlier. Your sailboat was in a fog bank at the time the shooting occurred, Mrs. Logan. How the *hell* could you see *anything*?"

Eve shook her head. "Don't you raise your voice to me—" After torturous months of insecurity, wondering if Gil loved this woman, she finally had her revenge. But the victory left Eve feeling empty and scared.

Rook moved forward, punching her finger into Eve's shoulder. "I know the real reason you're doing this, Mrs. Logan. And so do you," she breathed harshly. "But you've made a mistake. You've gone after my brother, in order to get to me. No one gets away with that. Do you understand? For your information, there is *nothing* going on between your husband and me—there never was. It's all up in that jealous head of yours."

Shaken, Eve took a step back. Gathering her stunned

thoughts, she gripped the tape recorder in her left hand. "You're threatening me, Lieutenant!"

"You've threatened me, and my brother's career!" Rook shouted back angrily. She was losing it. Backing away, Rook dragged in several deep breaths. This wasn't the way she should be reacting, but she couldn't help it—the injustice of what Eve Logan was doing was too much to bear. Rook could see her career destroyed over this one confrontation alone.

The door opened. Rook turned, expecting Captain Stuart or some other officer to step in and break up the disintegrating situation. Her eyes widened enormously. Gil Logan stood in the doorway, his face thundercloud dark as he looked first at his wife, then at Rook.

"Eve?"

Eve's lips parted, her fear turning to anguish. "I'm here on official business as a reporter for the *Star*. I have every right to interview Lieutenant Caldwell." Eve shrank against the wall. After the newspaper had decided to run the story last night, she'd gone to stay at Julia's, wanting no confrontation with Gil.

The embarrassment of having the entire office watch the scene was too much for Gil. Lips pulling away from his teeth, he snarled softly, "You're coming with me, Eve," and he gripped her arm firmly, pulling her out of the office.

Rook stood open-mouthed. She saw Gil snap a look in her direction.

"I'm sorry this happened, Rook. It's going to be settled right now." Logan shifted his attention back to Eve. "Come with me," he whispered tautly, pulling her along with him.

Eve resisted his powerful grip once they were outside the main building and walking toward the parking lot. "Gil! Let me go!"

Gil released her in the center of the parking lot. At least out here, there were fewer eyes and ears. He rounded on her.

"You didn't come home last night. And you didn't bother to call to tell me where you were!" He shook his head, his face full of hurt and anger. "Now I know why. You wrote this pack of lies about Noah Caldwell and his crew killing whales and you were afraid of my reaction to it! You're a coward, Eve—a vindictive, vicious coward."

Lifting her chin, her green eyes flashing with pain, Eve whispered, "You're protecting *her*! You're in love with Rook Caldwell! I can tell!"

"You can't tell a goddamn thing!" Logan roared, gripping Eve by the arms. "You're so jealous and scared of losing me that you've concocted this stupid and untrue scenario involving me and Rook! Nothing could be farther from the truth, Eve. She's been dating Jim Barton since she arrived here."

Blinking, Eve turned her face aside. "Let me go," she sobbed.

Gil stepped away, hands on his hips, breathing hard. "You've really blown it, Eve. You've upset this entire station. The lies in that paper are hurting a lot of innocent people." He laughed darkly, shaking his head. "The sad thing is, we're all innocent."

"I *saw* the Coast Guard kill those whales!" she shrieked.

"You *heard* shots being fired in the fog, for Christ's sake," Gil roared back. He jabbed a finger in her direction. "That isn't proof, Eve. That's lousy journalism, from a woman who has allowed her own immature emotions to color what she really saw and heard." Taking a breath, Gil looked around. Their voices were echoing off the buildings.

"Dammit, I'm not washing our dirty laundry out in public," he muttered. "When you get home tonight, we're going to have a long, serious talk."

Rattled, Eve drew herself up, dashing the tears from her cheeks. "That's fine with me," she wept. "Now, if you'll excuse me, I've got to get back to work."

"Leave Rook and Noah Caldwell alone," Gil whispered lethally. His eyes hardened on Eve. "This fight is between us, no one else. Understand?"

Gil watched her face crumple with agony before she whirled around, running for her car. He stood in the parking lot, the day gray and overcast, mirroring how he felt. Running his fingers angrily through his hair, he watched Eve drive off toward the gate in the distance.

How could all of this have happened? Where had he gone wrong? He had always considered his parents' marriage good. They never had this kind of uncertainty. Dammit, a husband and wife ought to be able to fight constructively, and yet keep their marriage together! Other Coast Guard officers had problems, too, but they surmounted them. Why couldn't he? What the hell kind of flaw was in him that he couldn't reach Eve and get her to understand that?

Agitated, he turned and stalked back to the hangar. There had to be a way to salvage his marriage. Humiliation flowed through Gil, creating a bad taste in his mouth. How much more could go wrong?

By nine o'clock darkness had fallen over Port Angeles. Rook's phone had been ringing steadily all day. Commander Joe Malone had arrived at eleven that morning and had given her a statement to read to the various reporters who called. Both she and Gil had been pulled off SAR duty, and replacements chosen to fill their duty slots. Gil was working out of his office with two other commanders.

She was relieved that Malone knew his job well. The place was a zoo. She saw Stuart everywhere; had the man cloned himself? If he wasn't with the investigation team, he was giving her guidance, and sometimes support. Rook began to hate the Press. They were demanding to speak to the crews involved. To Rook's relief, Malone dealt adroitly with them. Noah and his crew were in the Admin building, waiting to be questioned individually by Pete McCall, the lawyer who had come in from Seattle with Malone.

Wiping her sweaty palms, Rook managed to grab a fifteen-minute break. She knew that she had to find her brother.

Noah glumly looked up from the table at which he was sitting in the deserted accounting office. He brightened when he saw Rook.

She shut the door quietly, leaning against it. "How are you doing?"

He snorted and stood, thrusting his hands into the pockets

of his one-piece dark-blue uniform. "At this point, I'm surprised there aren't armed guards at the door."

"This is the craziest thing I've ever heard of. I'm sorry, Noah. I know you'd never hurt a defenseless animal."

He paced the office, running his fingers through his black hair. "Then, you're the only one."

She watched him, feeling helpless. "Captain Stuart is maintaining your innocence to the press, Noah. He's a hundred percent behind you and your crew."

Barely turning his head, Noah gave her a dubious glance. "Until he can prove otherwise."

"He's not saying it just to the press. He's fighting for you. So are the commanders from the 13th District."

"Yeah, I heard the admiral sent his boys down to head up this three-ring circus. You know your career is screwed when the head honcho gets involved. What a mess."

She walked over to him. "Listen to me—I know you're innocent."

Noah lifted his head, studying Rook's exhausted features. A hint of a smile tipped his mouth. "This is a new twist: my sister finally believes something I said."

"Look, I know there's a lot of bad blood between us, Noah, but . . ." She hesitated.

Noah waited, watching her struggle with her feelings. "What?" he asked gently, breaking the strained silence.

Rook met his dark-gray eyes. "Well, I've gotten to know you better in the last month. You've never lied to me—"

"Like I supposedly did before?" Noah couldn't keep the hurt out of his tone.

Rook ignored his question. "My instincts tell me you had nothing to do with the shooting of the whale."

Noah eyed her speculatively, his voice thick with carefully controlled emotion. "Rook, if nothing else comes out of this stinking mess except the fact that you trust me again, that's more than I ever expected."

She stared down at her flight boots for a long time. "There's a difference between belief and trust, Noah. I don't believe you shot that whale."

He looked away, his face drawn. "And trust?"

"No. At least, not yet."

He nodded. "Okay, that's honest."

Rook gave an exasperated sigh. "Look, let's just call a truce between us for now. I don't want to get into another fight with you about our past while this thing is hanging over our heads."

Wondering if she realized she'd said 'our heads,' Noah nodded. "I've been wanting to settle this war between us ever since you got here."

"Noah—"

"Okay, okay. Thanks for coming up to see the prisoner. He appreciates it."

"I—do you need anything?"

Noah smiled slightly, some of the tension easing from the planes of his face. "You'd better get out of here. If one of the investigation team finds you 'conspiring' up here with your brother, they're liable to think you had something to do with the whale shooting, too."

"If I was worried about that, I wouldn't have come in the first place."

"My crew and I haven't eaten since noon. Could you get someone to bring us some dinner, and maybe coffee? We'd all appreciate it."

"I'll make sure that you're all fed."

Noah nodded, watching Rook wrestle with her feelings. Maybe something good would come out of this jam. Something already had. Rook hadn't abandoned him totally.

"Thanks."

On the way back down the stairs to her office, Rook ran into Jim. The look on his face mirrored the way she felt.

"Rook?" Jim took the last few steps two at a time. There were people walking rapidly here and there, so he stopped a few feet from Rook. As much as he wanted to hold her, it would be impossible, under the circumstances.

"You're a sight for sore eyes. I hope you know that." Rook heard the wobble in her low voice.

He managed a slight smile. "I've been trying to reach you

all day, and the phones to the station here have been busy. That's why I came over. You didn't answer your phone at your apartment, so I figured you were involved in this whale emergency. The whole town is in an uproar over it."

She fought an urge to fall into his arms. Right now, she needed a harbor of protection. "There's an empty room down the corridor. Let's talk in there," she suggested wearily.

Jim studied Rook's drawn features in silence as she closed the door and then rested her back against it. "You look like hell."

"I feel like hell, too," Rook murmured. She gave him a confused look. "Right now all I need is to be held for just a moment."

"Come here," Jim coaxed, opening his arms.

A broken sigh escaped Rook when she sagged against Jim. His arms were strong and supporting as they slid around her shoulders and back.

"Better?"

"Much," she whispered, closing her eyes, sliding her arms around her waist.

Jim rested his jaw against her hair. "Just knowing you, I don't think your brother could do something like that."

Wearily, Rook barely opened her eyes, her cheek against the rough cotton weave of his shirt. She could hear the slow, steady pounding of Jim's heart beneath her ear. "Noah and I have our problems, but he's never been a killer of animals. Never."

Stroking her hair with his hand, Jim muttered, "Then, what's behind this? The newspaper story I read this morning has gaping holes in its allegations. How could someone in a fog bank see a Coast Guard cutter shoot a whale?"

Each caressing stroke dissolved another layer of tension from Rook. "Eve Logan is using her newfound power as a reporter to get at me because she thinks Gil and I are having an affair."

"Christ," Jim grated, his arms tightening around Rook. "Can she prove the Coast Guard shot the whale?"

Rook shook her head. "I don't know. This whole thing is

a terrible mess. Eve came in here this afternoon to have a showdown with me."

Jim looked down at her, worried. "Tell me what happened."

She snorted. "I lost my cool, to begin with. I jabbed her in the shoulder with my finger. Then Gil showed up unexpectedly and literally dragged Eve out of the office. I understand from Jody Theron that they had a huge fight out in the parking lot behind the Admin building, and everyone could hear it."

Shaking his head, Jim held her at arm's length, studying her critically. "You've been through hell."

"It's not over yet, Jim. The captain is in a marathon session with Gil and the Seattle P.R. crew to try to find out what really happened."

"What can I do for you?"

"Have you got a white horse and some armor?"

He grinned, caressing Rook's stubborn chin. "I'd say you have your own white horse and armor. You're standing and fighting, instead of running. That's a good sign."

"How's your dad?" she asked.

"Getting along fine. In another week, he should be released from the hospital."

"At least that's good news."

Jim slid his hands down her shoulders and squeezed her arms. "I know all hell's broken loose around here, and I'm sure they're probably trying to find you right now. I'd better go . . ."

Rook gazed up into Jim's face. "You're so strong all the time. I wish I had that ability."

Jim tilted her chin upward, kissing her lips gently. "There was a time not so long ago when your strength was my strength," he reminded her huskily, relishing the returning warmth of her mouth. "I'll be yours now." Pulling away, Jim held her gaze. "Call me when you get home tonight, all right?"

"Yes."

"I'll wait for your call, Wild Rose. Hang in there."

CHAPTER

Fourteen

IT was midnight. Ward looked around the conference table at his team. Cups of half-drunk coffee, ashtrays heaped with cigarette butts, maps, photos, and anything else that might concern the investigation was in evidence. Everyone was grim.

Commander Pete McCall, the lawyer who had been called in, pointed to the tape recorder. "I think we've got to listen to your conversation with the *Star* one more time. Maybe we missed something in that meeting."

Nodding, Ward depressed the button on the tape player and the four of them listened.

Gil, who had been resting his brow against his hands, jerked his head up. "Wait!" and he signaled for the recorder to be stopped. He turned to his captain. "Did you hear what Eve said? She heard bullets being fired at a *high* rate of speed the first two times, and then a third time at a slower rate." He glanced at the commanders who sat opposite him. He liked McCall, who had proven to be sharp and helpful.

McCall sat up. "No cutter can fire a .50 caliber at a high rate of speed," Gil continued. Their max rate is five hundred rounds per minute. But as you all know, we always slow-fire at a hundred rounds per minute to keep the barrel of the gun cooled down."

"Besides," he added, pulling out Caldwell's report, "in

here, Noah and his crew both stated that they fired five bursts at one-minute intervals. I think what Eve heard the *third* time was the cutter firing."

Ward rubbed his jaw, which needed to be shaved. "So, who fired the first two times?"

McCall tapped his blunt fingertips against the highly polished surface of the cherry table. He looked over at Stuart. "Is it possible that a Canadian military helicopter flew over the yacht, fired at the whales, and then took off for the border?"

Ward sat up. "Wait a minute!" All heads turned in his direction, waiting.

Hope charged his voice. He leaned forward on his elbows. "Why just look at the Canadian military? Channing Helicopters has just opened up a manufacturing plant here in Port Angeles. They produce a small helicopter that is sold to Third World countries. Some of them are equipped with weapons."

Gil grinned. "Yes, sir, that's right! Christ, why didn't I think of that before?"

McCall smiled grimly, his green eyes thoughtful. "Because we were all so busy trying to locate the guilty party among our own people, that's why."

Ward agreed, relief flowing through him as never before. "McCall's correct. What we need to do is get a ballistics expert to look at those photos of the calf to figure out what *kind* of round was used to kill it. Then, we can match that against the *Point Countess*'s gun and the type of weapon Channing puts aboard its helos."

Gil sat back, excitement thrumming through him. "If the caliber matches what Channing arms that helo with, we've got our first real suspect."

The table quieted, each man gauging the other. Ward rose and cursed softly. He walked the perimeter of the small, carpeted room, thinking. He finally halted and studied the team.

"Channing has a group of test pilots who fly each new model that comes off the line. They've always notified us when they planned to hold target practice over the Pacific." A gleam came to his eyes. "What if some pilot went joyriding out there and decided to take a couple of pot shots at a whale?"

Gil got up. "Remember what Mrs. Edwards said: they were in a fog bank when the shooting took place. The helo she heard roared right over them. Whoever did the shooting had to be armed. Ballistics will give us the information to identify the type of slug used. Number two, not all helos are equipped with the kind of instruments that it takes to fly in fog. But, unless I've slipped a cog, Channing has been developing an all-terrain, all-weather helo. With an all-terrain screen, the pilot would be able to see not only landmasses, but boats or anything else on the surface, including whales. He may have been using the fog on purpose, to test that particular piece of equipment."

"The fact that there was a whale nearby was gravy," Ward added.

"Or," Malone added, "he might have wanted fog *and* a moving target to test both the radar equipment and the weapons system simultaneously."

Ward smiled. "Well, it's a reasonable explanation, gentlemen—something to sleep on tonight. Let's close up shop. I'll meet with all of you here at 0800 tomorrow."

Gil was walking across the deserted Admin parking lot when he heard his name called. Turning, he saw Rook Caldwell running toward him, her face contorted. What now? It was two in the morning, and he was trying to emotionally prepare himself to talk to Eve when he got home.

"Gil . . ." Rook said breathlessly, coming to a halt.

"What's wrong?"

Gulping for breath, she gasped, "It's Paula . . ." Rook choked on a lump in her throat, on the verge of tears. "I just talked to Tag a few minutes ago. She's slipping in and out of consciousness. Tag said her doctor didn't think she would last much longer—maybe a couple of hours . . ." Rook looked away, trying to hide the tears in her eyes. "Tag asked both of us to come over, if we could. I tried to find you in the wardroom, but you'd already left. I told the captain about Paula, and he said to find you."

Logan closed his eyes, using the car as support. The day had been a ball buster, and now it was going to get far worse. His confrontation with Eve would have to wait. And right now, the way he felt, he wasn't going to call and tell her where he was. "Come on, let's get over there."

Rook took a deep breath. "I know how close you two are."

"Like brothers," Gil admitted hoarsely. "We went through Pensacola and Mobile together."

She nodded, too emotional herself to try to find words that might comfort Gil. "I'll meet you over there," she whispered.

When Gil walked into the Welsh house, he knew that Paula had died. Rook gave him a strained look, as if she sensed it, too. Walking down the hall, they saw Paula's doctor and a nurse emerge from her room. The physician confirmed what they already knew. He gestured them toward the living room. Once there, he said, "Tag asked to be left alone for a few minutes with his wife . . ."

"Of course, Doctor." Gil swallowed against a barrage of tears. He gripped Rook's arm, leading her to a couch. "Come on, Rook, we'll wait in here until he comes out."

Rook wiped the tears from her eyes and sat down. The house was quiet. She glanced over at Gil. His face was drawn and his cheeks glistened with spent tears. Covering his hand, she choked out, "I think I'll make some coffee. I can't stand sitting around and waiting."

He nodded, avoiding her gaze. "Yeah . . . good idea."

Rook was working quietly in the small kitchen when she sensed, rather than heard, someone enter the room. She turned.

"Tag?" He appeared waxen, his eyes dark and lifeless, skin stretched taut across his cheekbones. Automatically, Rook set the percolator aside and walked over to him. Tears blurred her vision as she put her arms around him and drew him close. "I'm sorry," she muffled, "so sorry."

Wordlessly, Tag embraced her, burying his head on her small shoulder. Rook's womanly strength triggered a deluge of withheld grief. He'd been the steady one for Paula in her last hours. She had broken down and cried, telling him she never wanted to leave him. He'd stroked her hair and soothed away her fears. Tag didn't know what real courage was until now, when he'd controlled his own grief and fear of loss to give Paula peace of mind. A sob ripped through him, like a fist welling up through his guts, shattering his heart. Tag wasn't aware of exactly what Rook was crooning to him. It didn't matter. Just the solace in her voice, the care she was extending to him, was enough. Hot, scalding tears welled up in his tightly shut eyes. He gripped Rook hard, needing her support, her strength.

Gil heard Tag weeping and got to his feet, heading for the kitchen. He stood at the doorway for only a split second before moving to his friend's side. He saw the vulnerability in Rook's wide, tearstained eyes as she held his sobbing friend. He read the plea in her expression and came over to help.

The three of them stood in the center of the kitchen, arms around one another, crying.

Eve heard the door slowly open and then quietly close. She glanced at the clock on their bedroom dresser. It was 4:45 A.M. Anger, more chilling than she'd ever experienced, moved through her as she slipped into her silk robe. Opening the door, she met Gil halfway down the dimly lit hall.

"Just where have you been? Do you know what time it is?"

Gil staggered to a halt, his mind spongy with fatigue. Eve's face was shadowed with fury. He stared down at his watch for several seconds before the time registered on him.

"Things happened too fast—"

"And you forgot to call. Sure you did! Like you always do. This is it, Gil. I've had it. No more wondering where you are or for how long. I'm through worrying about you. For all I know, you could've been drowned on a SAR case!"

He tried to shake off his fatigue and held up his hand. "Wait . . . Eve, a lot has happened tonight. Paula—"

"You bet it has!" she whispered, walking up to him, her eyes blazing with torment.

He leaned against the wall, exhausted. "Look, dammit, Paula has—"

"I don't want to hear about Paula or the Coast Guard! I want to talk about us! Our problems! This is the last time that you'll—"

Gil grabbed her arm, jerking her to him. Her neck snapped back and Eve opened her mouth to scream. "Paula," he sobbed, "is *dead*!"

He released her, disgust written on his drawn face. Gil shouldered by her, stumbling toward the bedroom.

Shocked by his unexpected outrage, Eve rubbed her bruised arm, pouting. "I don't care!" she shrilled, her cry echoing down the hall. "Do you hear? I don't care anymore! Not about you or your precious Coast Guard family!" She began to follow him, her voice rising to a crescendo. "I'm sick and tired of playing second or third fiddle to whatever you think is more important than me!" She took a breath to launch a second verbal assault at him when Gil rounded on her.

It took every vestige of his control not to strike her. "This is it," Logan rasped. "I'm divorcing you. I can't take this emotional merry-go-round you like to ride, Eve. My best friend's wife just died. I feel like hell." His eyes watered dangerously with tears, and Eve's taut features wavered before him. He pushed her away.

"I'm going to pack a few things and get out of here. I won't be back. Whatever we had is dead. I'm too tired right now to figure out how it happened." Turning, he trudged into the bedroom, hunting for a small satchel. Gil would drive over to Reno's house and stay the night. Tomorrow, his head would be clearer and he could think—maybe.

Eve glared down the hallway. "Fine," she shrieked. "I can hardly wait 'til you tell your precious parents, who have a thirty-year marriage going, that you failed! You didn't marry me, Gil Logan, you tried to live up to *their* idea of what a marriage should be! That's where you made your mistake, damn you!"

Whirling around, Eve ran down the hall, sobbing.

When Rook pulled in the driveway of her apartment building, Jim Barton was there, waiting in his car. He got out and came around to her Toyota, opening the door for her. Crouching down, Jim studied her face.

"What's happened, Rook? I tried calling the station, and they said you left at two in the morning. I got worried when you didn't answer your phone at home a half hour after that."

Rook sat there, absorbing his concerned, drawn features. "This has been the most hellish twenty-four-hour period I've ever experienced," she admitted slowly, "except for when my mother died." Her voice cracked. "Paula Welsh died this morning. Gil and I were with Tag until just a while ago." She stared at her watch. The luminous dials indicated it was four-thirty.

Jim nodded and rose. He took her arm. "Come home with me, Rook. Let me take care of you tonight." Jim saw her begin to protest. "We can stop by your place and get you some clean clothes on the way. I don't want anyone at the station to be able to call you. Right now, you need plenty of rest."

Beyond exhaustion, Rook agreed in a hushed voice.

Inside her apartment, Jim turned on one of the lamps in the living room and sat down on the couch while Rook packed an overnight bag. When she rejoined him, Jim placed his hand beneath her chin, forcing her to look at him. He wanted to say, *I know you're fragile, Rook, even if you don't. And you scare so easily.* Instead, he murmured, "Okay, let's get going."

Rook was unable to sleep on the way over to Jim's house. She'd never felt like this before; her nerves were taut and screaming. Jim guided her into the house, taking her directly to the guest bedroom. While he hung up her uniform, she stood forlornly in the room, watching him.

Turning, Jim walked back to Rook. She was in shock, he realized. Taking her into his arms, he saw tears form in Rook's eyes and trickle down her cheeks.

"Tell me everything," he commanded softly, caressing her damp cheek. "Get it out, sweetheart, before it eats you up alive."

Words came haltingly at first, wedged with Tag's pain and loss. And then, Rook voiced her concern for Noah's predicament. Her emotions had left her raw and aching.

Gently using his thumbs, Jim dried her cheeks of tears. He looked deeply into her eyes. "Honey, you need to sleep."

"I have to be back over at the station at eight, Jim."

"All right." He kissed her brow, trying to ease the explosive tension he felt within her. "First, I want you to get washed up. Go put on your nightgown. I'll wake you up at half past seven, make you breakfast, and then drive you over to the station."

"Thank you, Jim." Rook leaned tiredly against him and he pressed a kiss to her hair.

"You're in shock, Rook, from everything that's happened. That station is rocking with disasters from one end to another, and you're caught in the middle of it all. If you need anything, call. I'll be in the den for a while."

Rook didn't have the strength to argue. Gratefully, she nodded. "Okay."

The hot shower didn't help her any. When Rook was done, she stood on the rug, water dripping off her. Every movement became an incredible physical effort. The numbness she was feeling began to disappear, and in its place, trembling began. Alarmed that she had no control over it, she sat down at the vanity, the huge pink bath towel wrapped around her.

The first sob caught her off guard. Miserably, she looked at herself in the mirror. The face that stared back at her wasn't the Rook she knew. There was such devastation in her eyes. The second sob came, and Rook was powerless to halt the building storm about to break within her. Tears jammed into her eyes and she buried her face in one hand, letting the torment run through her.

Jim heard Rook's weeping. Earlier, he'd taken a shower and put on his pajama bottoms. Too upset to sleep, he was in the den reading over some business contracts when he heard her begin to cry. He hurried down the hall, opening the bathroom door. His heart wrenched. Rook lay sobbing against the vanity. The pink towel was pressed against her breasts, pooling around her thighs, her naked back gleaming beneath the lights.

"Rook . . ." he whispered hoarsely, going over, gathering her limp, shaking form into his arms.

"Oh, Jim . . ." she wept, looking up at him. "I-I don't know what's wrong. All of a sudden I felt the numbness go away and I started shaking and crying uncontrollably."

He realized the traumatic emotional events had finally broken even Rook's stubborn reserves. "Sshh, it's all right, honey. You're just having a good old-fashioned letdown." In one easy motion, Jim lifted Rook into his arms. Like a hurt child, she collapsed against him, head tucked beneath his jaw, arms moving around his neck. "Everything's going to be fine. Just keep crying . . ." and he carried her across the hall to her bedroom. The bed stand lamp cast a small circle of light into the lavender room. Depositing her on the bed, Jim swung himself over to Rook's side, and pulled her into his arms.

"Let it go," he coaxed, caressing her damp back with his hand. Her flesh was firm and pliant beneath his fingers. He held Rook tightly against him, feeling each sob rack through her like a brutal ocean wave pounding against the beach. Words started to flow from him—words meant to soothe and heal her—as he kissed her temple, cheek, and finally, her mouth. Jim tasted the salt of her tears, evidence of the incredible pain that she'd borne so valiantly. The instant her lips molded to his, a groan tore through him, dissolving all his carefully monitored control.

Blindly, Rook absorbed the strength of Jim's mouth. She felt directionless, in a pit of nothing but pain and loss. She clung to him, focusing on his arms around her naked form, his calloused hands arousing far greater needs within her. Her breath became chaotic as she unconsciously revolved away from all the agony within her and moved toward the sunlight of his strength and tenderness.

Her fingers slid along the expanse of his chest, and her mouth hungrily matched his. The fresh scent of her recently washed hair and the taste of her skin as he ran his tongue across her bare shoulder culminated in a fiery splendor of fragrance coupled with texture. Pulling the towel from between them, he pressed her length against him, and felt her tremble violently as they met and molded together.

"Jim," she whispered raggedly, finding his mouth.

He removed his pajamas. His urgency mounted. Each time he kissed her, she wildly returned his ardor, her body pressed pliantly beneath his. Her long, curved thighs opened and he felt her fingers dig deeply into his shoulders, silently begging him to complete the union.

As Jim's hand slid beneath her hips, lifting her, Rook abandoned herself to him. He thrust deeply, repeatedly into her. A cry slipped from her parted lips as she absorbed his masculine strength, flowing rhythmically into each powerful thrust, burning away all the darkness that had claimed her soul.

Her body slid wetly against his as they became two animals locked in a primal coupling that tore away the veneer of civilization and carefully shielded emotions. Rook lost herself within the ever-spinning vortex of taste, smell, and fire. A building pressure quickened deep within her and she whimpered, sensing that the sunlight enveloping her was becoming brighter, more blinding. Fingers sinking into Jim's bunched shoulder muscles, she cried out, stiffening within his arms as that pressure became a volcanic rele[illegible] scalding heat throbbing rhythmically through her like molten sunlight, flowing in a river between their fused bodies.

Gasping for breath, Jim rested heavily upon Rook in the seconds after his own release within her. She lay limp beneath him, and he moved to one side, gathering her against him. He reached over, shutting off the light. Sinking against the pillows, he buried his face in her fragrant hair. He almost told her he loved her, but something warned him not to—not yet. Instead, Jim simply held her, smoothing the perspiration from her back and shoulders.

Exhaustion stalked Rook as she lay against him. It was impossible to talk, only feel. His pounding heart sounded like a sledgehammer beneath her ear as she nestled her cheek against the wiry texture of the hair on his chest. *Sleep . . . I have to sleep . . .* and Rook spiraled into darkness.

Rook jerked awake. She froze when she realized Jim lay at her side, his arm draped limply across her hip, still sleeping. What had she done? Why? Panic set in as she lay there in the dawn light. Gradually, the events of the last twenty-four hours flashed before her. Her heart began a painful pounding in her breast. It was six o'clock.

She closed her eyes, turmoil mixing with her newly awakened feelings. My God, what had she done? They'd made wild, hungry love. Last night, Rook felt as if she were drowning in a morass of hellish feelings. The grief she felt over the death of her mother had been triggered by Paula's death and Tag's reaction. Noah's predicament had forced her to realize that she didn't hate him, and that there was still love that bound them to one another.

Groaning inwardly, Rook carefully sat up. She looked down. Jim's face was shadowed by his beard, and his hair was tousled. He looked boyish. Panic began to eat away at Rook as she got up, moving quietly about the room to pick up her belongings. How could she face Jim? What would he say about last night? Something kept telling her to run from him.

Torn, Rook hesitated at the open door to the bedroom. The dawn cast gray shadows about the room. Memories of her other two affairs smashed back into her barely functioning mind. They had been swift, impersonal couplings designed to satisfy the man, not her. Last night had been different. Something beautiful had blossomed and then been released within her when she had allowed Jim to love her.

Unable to sort through everything, Rook left to take a

shower and then dress. Realizing she needed a ride to work, she called a taxi. Sitting at the table, she wrote Jim a note and placed it on the drain board, next to the coffee maker. Then Rook hurried out the front door, the need to escape overwhelming her.

At seven-thirty, Ward discovered that Paula Welsh had died. He stared down at the note on his desk from the senior duty officer on watch. Tag Welsh had requested him to say a few words at her funeral, which would take place three days from now. Rubbing his recently shaven face, Ward took a deep breath. There was a lot to do—not only for the funeral, but for Tag, as well. He was about to buzz his secretary when Gil Logan appeared at his door and knocked softly.

"Gil. Come in." Ward saw the dark circles beneath the pilot's eyes. Had he slept at all?

"Captain, I just wanted to let you know that Paula Welsh died last night. With everything up in the air, I didn't know if Tag had called you yet."

Ward lifted the note from the desk. "Yes, he called earlier and left a message. Thanks, Gil."

Fighting bone-deep exhaustion, Gil murmured, "Rook and I arrived there right after Paula died. We stayed with Tag until about four this morning. The doctor gave him some tranquilizers." He looked down at his watch. "He said Tag would probably sleep until noon today."

Ward critically assessed his pilot. "You haven't had much sleep yourself."

"No, sir."

"I understand." That meant Rook Caldwell was in equally bad shape this morning. Neither would be of any use to the investigation effort, in their condition. "I want you and Rook to go home right now and get some decent sleep."

Gil couldn't hide his surprise. The other C.O. hadn't cared if anyone lived or died. "Sir?"

"I said, get out of here. I need both of you for this investigation, but awake and alert. Be back here by 1700 today.

By that time we'll have put more together, and you two can take over at that point."

"Yes, sir."

"One more thing, Gil. Does Tag have anyone to support him through all this?"

"The people from the local hospice are helping him, sir. There's a lady there now, a Mrs. Collins, who's staying over at the house. She's coordinating all the funeral arrangements the way Paula wanted them."

"Good." Ward would make a point of going over to see Tag later today. "Is there anything else we can do from our end?"

"I'm sure Chaplain Moore needs to be notified."

"How's Tag doing?"

Gil shrugged. "He broke down last night when Rook and I were there. Right now, he's just kind of numb, and going through the motions."

"I see."

"If we didn't have this damn investigation cranking up," Gil said, "I would have liked to take some time off to be with him until he's past this funeral, sir."

"Is he close to Rook, too?"

"Yes, sir."

Ward searched his mind for a way around all the problems. "I'll make it known to the investigators that you'll be dividing your time, as you see fit, between them and helping Tag during this period."

Gil's eyes widened. "Do you think they'll understand, sir?"

Ward nodded, his mouth thinning. "I'll get some temporary personnel in here from Seattle. Also, if Rook feels up to it and wants to volunteer, she can help Tag when you aren't available."

"Thank you, Captain."

"Notify Rook about all this, will you? And tell her I don't want to see her face in the office when I go down there later."

Logan wanted to smile, but was simply too exhausted to do much of anything. "Yes, sir."

Gil found Rook in her office with a cup of coffee in hand.

Next door, he saw Malone hard at work. He stuck his head in the door. "Hey."

Rook dully looked around. "God, Gil, you look terrible."

He grinned tiredly. "Want to place a bet on which of us looks worse?"

"No."

"Smart lady. Listen, the captain has ordered us to go home. He found out we were up with Tag until four-thirty. Said to show up here at five tonight. How's that sound?"

"Too good to be true," Rook murmured.

"Stuart's turning out to be a pretty good dude, after all. At least the man has some humaneness in his bones. He's going to tell these commanders that we'll be splitting our time for the next three days between our office duties and helping Tag. That is, if you want to help?"

Rook brightened considerably and nodded. "You bet I do."

Gil gave her a warm look, filled with pride. "Welcome to the Coast Guard, Rook. You're now, officially, a Coastie."

She tilted her head, trying to tease him. Right now, she needed a smile from someone. "What brought this on?"

He pursed his lips. "You're acting like one," he explained. "Coasties stick together. We're family. You proved that last night by going over there to help Tag when you didn't have to."

Tears swam in Rook's eyes. Embarrassed by how easily her emotions were touched, she wiped them away and picked up her purse. "Thanks, Gil. You really know how to say the right thing at the right time."

No, Gil thought, *I don't. At least, according to Eve, I never did.* He forced a smile for Rook's benefit, realizing that she was suffering heavily from the strain of her brother's investigation, on top of Tag's problems. "Come on, let's get out of here. We're both running on reserves."

"My car is at my apartment. Can you give me a lift home?"

"Sure. Come on."

On the way to the car, Rook asked, "Did you ever call

your wife? I remember asking you about that after we got Tag settled down."

The day was cool and cloudy; typical straits weather. Gil watched a couple of sea gulls sail overhead toward the hangar. "Seems like this is the time for new beginnings for everyone."

Slowing her pace, Rook gave him a guarded look. "Beginnings? What are you talking about?"

Gil stopped at his car, digging for the keys in his jacket pocket. "I walked out on Eve last night after I got home. As soon as Paula's funeral is out of the way, I intend to file for divorce."

Automatically, Rook placed her hand on Gil's arm. He looked as lost as she felt inside. "I know how much you wanted to save the marriage."

He grimaced. "Yeah." Rubbing his face tiredly, Gil muttered, "I don't know, Rook. Something's screwed up inside me. I can't figure out what it is. Why can't I save my marriage? My father was in the Coast Guard. I'm in the Coast Guard. It's a family tradition. If my folks kept their marriage together through the pressures of this business of ours, I should be able to."

It was so hard for Rook to find the right words to say. She felt Gil searching for answers. Hell, she couldn't even figure out why she had fallen into Jim's arms last night. Moistening her lips, Rook gave him a sympathetic look.

"Don't take all the blame, Gil. If you hadn't gotten out of it, Eve would have eaten you up alive emotionally."

He snorted, digging the toe of his boot against the pavement. "It's not all her fault. I don't know . . . I was running on empty emotionally with her. I kept trying to talk to her, and we always ended up fighting. And when she joined the newspaper, that was the straw that broke the camel's back." He gave Rook an apologetic look. "I feel so bad about Eve implicating Noah in that whale shooting. She did that out of vindictiveness, to get my attention. Eve felt she was second in my life. Of all the stupid things, she thought we were having an affair."

"I know," Rook admitted softly.

Gil laughed sharply, raising his face, studying the moody

sky above them. "Hell, we're friends. Pilots are a fraternity —an extended family—but Eve couldn't accept that."

"We are a tight-knit group," Rook agreed. "All the pilots support one another." Jim's words came back to her about having a man as a friend. She looked at Gil in a new light. The last couple of months, she had evolved toward true friendship with him. How little she really knew of men and women, Rook mused. It struck her hard that all her life she had struggled to make something of herself by working hard. Social contact with men or women was strictly a secondary thing. Now, Rook was finding out she was like an infant in the world of complex and confusing relationships.

Gil opened the door for her. "Why couldn't Eve be happy at home, raising a family?"

Rook got in, and waited for him to enter the car. "Not all women are born homemakers, Gil."

"My mother found complete happiness raising the four of us kids. She loved to sew, and she took pride in her family."

There was little Rook could say. "First Tag loses his wife, and now you."

"Don't waste your pity on me, Rook. This has been brewing for a long time."

She held Gil's bloodshot gaze. "I never pity anyone, but you have my compassion and understanding."

He shoved the key into the lock. "Let's get out of here, little angel of mercy."

Rook had been taught the value of avoiding serious commitments with a man. She had seen what Jack had done to her mother. It had shortened her life, and more importantly, destroyed her mother's will to live. Gil was equally devastated. Nothing in life was ever solid or stable, especially in the realm of relationships. Jim's features wavered in her thoughts. What would he think of the note she had left him? Fear clutched at her heart, and all Rook could do was feel panic.

Jim awoke slowly, the fragrance of Rook in his nostrils. Happiness ribboned through him and he lay there savoring her all over again. As he drew out of the folds of sleep, he frowned. Automatically, his hand went out, searching for her. Prying his eyes open, he raised up on one arm. Rook was gone. He glanced at the clock: it was eight o'clock—time to get up and go to work.

Why hadn't Rook awakened him before she left? Puzzled, Jim slipped on his terry cloth robe and padded down the hall in his bare feet to the kitchen. At the coffee maker, he found her note.

No! Slowly, Jim crumpled up the paper. Pain jagged through his chest and he bowed his head, both fists clenched. "Dammit!" he breathed savagely, turning and glaring out across the silent kitchen. He'd screwed up, badly. Rook's words burned into his heart:

Dear Jim:

Please forgive me. Last night shouldn't have happened. I'm scared. Just leave me alone. I need time to think.

Rook

Throwing the note in the trash, Jim stalked into the den. He always found peace out on the sun deck. As he pulled open the sliding glass door and walked out on the cedar expanse, his heart contracted with more agony. Rook was running away from him.

Glaring out across the quiet, foggy expanse of Port Angeles, Jim ruthlessly examined himself. Last night, Rook had needed to be held and comforted. He'd mistaken her cry for help as a signal to make love. *No*! Jim had wanted to love Rook for as long as he could remember. In her need for comfort from the death of Paula Welsh, and pressure on Noah, she'd reached out for reassurance. Her act was *not* a signal that she had wanted to make love.

Or was it? Jim leaned against the cedar rail, frantically trying to sort out what happened. It struck him that Rook was in shock over the death of Paula Welsh. Had it brought back the memory of her mother's death? Jim knew Rook hadn't worked through all the grief of her mother's passing. Death and dying . . . of course!

"You stupid sonofabitch," he muttered harshly. Why hadn't he realized that? Why? Turning, Jim rested his face in his hand. Unconsciously, Rook must have identified having sex with him as the opposite of all the death and trauma she'd suffered through in the last twenty-four-hour period.

Miserably, Jim shook his head. Like a fool, he'd misinterpreted her needs. If he'd been smarter, he'd have refused to make love with Rook, and just held her, instead. Because he loved her, had ached to take her to bed to show her how much she meant to him, he'd made what may have been the biggest mistake in his life.

Pacing back into the den, Jim felt the walls close in on him. Rook must have awakened this morning, realized her mistake, and fled. Dammit, deep down, Jim knew she loved him, but she was afraid to admit it, afraid to run *toward* a man who might give her laughter and happiness, instead of pain and sorrow. All her conditioning, throughout her life, had taught her that men were something to avoid.

Last night, he reminded himself sharply, he'd seen love in her lustrous gray eyes for him. It *was* love, dammit! In his heart, Jim knew that, clung to that one indisputable fact. Rook had been incredibly wanton and willing, equally assertive in her need of him as he was with her. Looking back on it, Jim realized that she was naive in her lovemaking.

With a sinking feeling, he realized Rook probably had had very few experiences with men. With a shake of his head, Jim dragged in a ragged breath. He'd taken her swiftly, with no preparation, no warning. They'd come together like oil and fire, exploding violently within one another. It hadn't been an act of love between them as much as it had been a fierce, hungry need that demanded satiation. They were two starved human beings who had fed upon one another for very different reasons.

It was the reasons that bothered Jim the most. He'd come to her out of love. His act, no matter how violent or swift, had still been motivated by his love of Rook. She had come to him out of a need to prove that she was not dead inside. For Rook, it was a primal, unconscious need, not necessarily an act of love.

Jim sat down on the couch, staring at the woven tapestry hanging on the opposite wall. It depicted two great blue herons on a quiet pond, surrounded by cattails. Clasping his hands, he rested his chin on his knuckles, recalling details of their lovemaking. No, Rook *did* love him. It had shown in her eyes before and after experiencing that shatteringly beautiful climax with her. Something told him that Rook had never experienced an orgasm before, judging from the look of surprise and awe in her eyes.

A trickle of hope flared to life within him. Maybe Rook had come to him seeking to prove she could still feel, that she was still alive. But somewhere in their fiery coupling, all those feelings she'd been trying to deny toward him had escaped. The need to live, along with the need to love him had woven themselves together within her, and she hadn't yet separated the difference.

"I'll be damned," he muttered, hope surging within him. *That* was why Rook was running! Whether she admitted it consciously or not, last night in his arms had brought her in direct contact with her love for him. That had to be it! He squeezed his eyes shut, his brow resting against his clenched hands. "God, please let it be that," he rasped harshly. Because, if he was wrong, Rook would never see him again. She would run away from him, just as she had run from the men in her past.

What to do now? Jim clenched his teeth, feeling his way through that tricky question. Time—Rook had to have time to assimilate what had happened. Maybe she would be able to figure out, like he had, what had happened and why. If he tried to barge in on her now, Jim knew any chance of a further relationship with her would be completely destroyed. No. He had to wait. But, God, it was the last thing he wanted to do! Loving Rook last night had set him on fire, made him twice as hungry to fulfill them both again.

Rising, Jim felt the helplessness slough off him. There

was resolve in his blue eyes as he padded back to the kitchen to make coffee. Patience was the key. And if there was anything he had plenty of, it was that, thanks to his mother's Scottish blood. Let Rook settle down and accept Paula's death, and in reality, her mother's passing. Let her and Noah make amends. Then, and only then, would he step back into her life . . .

CHAPTER

Fifteen

THE doorbell was ringing. Rook groped to wake up as the chimes sounded throughout her small apartment. What time was it? She rolled over, the cotton nightgown twisted and tangled about her legs. Prying one eye open, she looked at the red dials on the large clock face: 4 P.M. It was time to get up anyway. The doorbell rang again. Fear seized her. Was it Jim? Hands trembling, Rook reached for her robe.

"I'm coming!" Grumbling, Rook threw on her well-worn white chenille robe, then stumbled out of the bedroom. Rubbing her eyes, she went to the door and pulled it open.

"Noah . . ."

"May I come in?"

Rook stood there, trying to collect her scattered thoughts. "Uh . . . yeah," and she stepped aside. Noah was in uniform: a light blue shirt and dark blue slacks. He gave her a slight smile as he took off his garrison cap and walked past her. He carried a bundle of envelopes in his left hand. Shutting the door, her normal defenses not in place yet, she asked, "What's going on?"

Noah looked around the comfortable apartment. Rook had good taste in color as well as furniture. Right now, she looked like a lost waif, her hair mussed, eyes sleep-ridden, standing there in that threadbare robe that should have been discarded long ago. Rook, like himself, kept things out of loyalty, long past their usefulness. Maybe she applied that same philosophy to him. Noah hoped so.

"I've got some good news for you."

Rubbing her puffy eyes, Rook headed toward the kitchen. "I need some coffee. What's the news?"

Noah swallowed his smile and followed her. He made himself comfortable at the pink Formica table, setting the bundle and his garrison cap aside. He watched Rook who, barely awake, dropped the parts to the percolator a couple of times on the counter before she got them correctly assembled. She was unfailingly human, and the love he felt toward her mushroomed fiercely in his chest.

"It's about the whale investigation," Noah baited.

"Oh?"

"Yeah. You've been out of the office all day, and the worm took an interesting turn while you were away."

Rook plugged in the percolator and turned, wrapping her arms against her breast. "What happened?"

Noah heard the underlying fear in her voice. Was it for him, or the helo pilots? He'd like to hope that it was for both of them. "This morning the captain went over to Channing and confronted the general manager. Stuart was able to confirm that they had a flight scheduled the morning in question. They were testing the radar guidance system of their helo in fog conditions."

"Great!"

"It gets better," Noah promised, cracking a smile. Unconsciously, he toyed with the large pack of letters. "The pilot, John Trevor, also had a load of ammunition on board that helo. He tested the radar device according to the flight plan, and after the test was completed, he spotted the whales. That's when Trevor decided to have a little fun."

"Fun?" Rook grumped. "I don't call killing a harmless baby whale fun."

He shook his head. "Few do. Anyway, Trevor, using the newly installed radar, saw the yacht was far enough away and used the whales as target practice. He was only intending to fire close to the adult whales. He says he never saw the baby in between them." Noah shook his head, bitterness in his voice. "Looks like their radar isn't perfect, doesn't it?"

Rook cursed softly. "No kidding. Did Trevor realize the Coast Guard was also conducting an exercise out in the warning area?"

"Yes."

Rook ran her fingers through her hair, trying to smooth it down into place. "The bastard."

"Channing officials are offering to make full restitution, and are as sorry as hell, according to their spokesperson. But it makes you wonder whether they would have let us take the rap if Stuart hadn't questioned them closely."

"From all appearances, it looked like they were going to lie low and let us take the heat." Rook sighed. "Are Ty and his crew off the hook, then?"

Noah tried to mask his hurt when she didn't ask about him or his cutter crew. "Officially, as of 1530 today, we're all cleared."

Smiling, Rook went to the cupboard. "Wonderful!" She brought down a cup for the brewing coffee. And then, she remembered her manners. "Do you want some?" Rook really didn't want Noah hanging around; she was uncomfortable with his presence.

"Please."

Rook made him a cup, and he took a sip of the steaming coffee. "By the way, the captain was going to contact you, but when he saw me, he figured you'd like to have all this good news in person. He said that he'd see you at 0800 tomorrow."

Brightening, Rook sipped her coffee. "You mean I don't have to go in today at all?"

"You get the night off. The air group's been laboring under a lot of pressure," Noah said. "The captain's asking the admiral for two more pilots to be assigned here on temporary duty so that he can get that duty roster straightened out."

Dramatically, Rook placed her hand against her heart. "I don't know if I can stand all these positives!"

He laughed with her. Setting the coffee aside, Noah cupped the bundle of letters in his hands. His smile dissolved.

"There's more news, but I don't know if you'll consider it good or not."

Frowning, Rook said, "What else?" She was thinking it concerned Tag or Gil. "Is it one of the guys?"

"No." Noah held her worried gaze. "It's about us. I think it's time we talked, Rook."

Silence hung between them.

Setting the cup aside, Rook crossed her arms defensively against her breast. "This isn't a good time, Noah."

He rose, holding the letters gently between his fingers. "I don't think you'll ever feel there's a right time to settle things between us."

Rook watched apprehensively as he slowly walked around the table and confronted her. "There's nothing to discuss," she countered defensively. "We've been over all this before. What's done is done. You and I have nothing to build on except the present."

"You're wrong. We have a past, a present, and a future. Together. As family."

She allowed her arms to drop, and walked to the living room. "Just leave, Noah. I'm tired, I've had one hell of a couple of days, and I want to rest."

He followed Rook and reached out, gently bringing her to a halt. When she whirled around, he saw the pain and anger in her features. "I'm tired, too. This investigation hasn't exactly been easy on me, either." He tried to ignore the tremor in his voice. "I'm not leaving this apartment until you hear me out, Rook. There are things I need to discuss with you. Please . . ."

Rook hated herself. Why did she have to be such a sucker for someone who looked desperate and in need of help? She glanced down at the package in his hand. "I won't discuss the past with you. We've hashed it over too many times already."

"This is something you don't know about, Rook." Noah looked at the letters. "Something that I think will change how you feel about me, and maybe, our family."

"Our family" grated across her exposed nerves. "Let me get showered and dressed. I've got to wake up before I tackle this."

"Fine."

Rook took her time in the shower, dread filling her. She hated confrontations, especially over family matters. She dressed in a pale pink blouse, a pair of jeans, and her Puma jogging shoes. She combed out her damp hair with a shaky hand. *Why am I so nervous? Calm down, you idiot. Just because Noah looks stricken and hurt doesn't mean a thing. He's pulled this act on you before.* She saw the high color in her cheeks, and avoided the fear etched in her wide gray eyes as she glanced in the bathroom mirror. Palms sweaty, she walked quietly to the living room.

Noah stood looking out the window, hands deep in his trouser pockets. She sat down in a chair and crossed her legs.

"Let's get this over with," she muttered, watching him turn around.

Noah sat on the couch, opposite Rook. His mouth was suddenly dry, and he could no longer hide his nervousness. Normally, he was an efficient and capable leader who usually had the right words for his crew. But he was vulnerable to Rook's distrusting look, and her defensive attitude.

"When Jack broke up with our mother, you were six and I was eight," he began.

"Yes, and you chose to stay with him," she reminded Noah. "I wasn't about to after he beat Mom up that one time. And she was smart enough to get out from under him and his tyrant rule."

"I wanted to come with you."

Rook snorted. "It sure didn't look that way, Noah. Father

and son stuck together like glue, while Mom and daughter left. Penniless, I might add. Mom asked for no alimony when she headed for Texas."

"Jack pulled me aside one day, Rook, before Mom and you left," he told her quietly. "He told me he was dying of cancer, and that I owed it to him to stay behind to help him."

Rook sat up, her eyes rounding. "What?"

Noah gave her a twisted smile. "I found out much too late that Jack was a chronic liar."

"And a wife beater."

"That also."

She tilted her head, trying to penetrate Noah's open features to see if he was lying to her once again. "You said Jack made you believe he had cancer?"

"Yes. Looking back on it many years later, after another incident, I began to piece things together. He lied about a lot of things, Rook."

"When he didn't die of cancer, didn't you stop to think about it?" she challenged.

Leaning forward, Noah pleaded, "Rook, I was eight at the time. You know how naive children are. Jack came into my room one night just before Mom left and started sobbing. It was the first time I'd ever seen a man cry. He begged for me to stay. I didn't know what to do."

Rook got up, pacing the room. "Why should I believe you, Noah? Jack was a chronic liar. Why shouldn't you be, too? You lived with that monster. It's a well-known fact that what the parent does, so does the child."

He held on to his anger. "I have proof, Rook."

She halted. "All right, go on with your story."

"When Jack took me back East, and he remarried, he hired detectives to hunt you down."

"Those were the right words. Mom and I felt like felons on the run from the law. She couldn't keep a job in some small jerkwater town for more than six months to a year because Jack had the power, the prestige, and most important, the money to locate us."

Noah nodded. "Jack had a brittle ego, and he couldn't

stand the thought that Mom had run out on him. It was like a wound that never healed in him."

"You bet it didn't. Jack taught me what hate can do, Noah."

"He taught us all," he agreed wearily. "Right after we moved back to Washington, D.C., I started writing letters to you and Mom, as soon as the detectives found your address. I couldn't leave Jack because I still thought he was dying of cancer, but I wanted to let you and Mom know how much I missed you."

Rook stared down at the letters. "We never got any of them."

Noah got up and thrust his hands in his trouser pockets, walking over to where Rook stood tensely. "Jack promised me that each and every one of those letters would be sent to you. So, over the years, until I was eighteen, I kept writing. For a long time, I couldn't figure out why you didn't write back. Every time I asked that question, Jack hammered it into me that you and Mom didn't love me. He tried to make me think Mom had abandoned me for you."

Rook heard the agony in Noah's voice. She saw it in his eyes. This was no act he was putting on, her gut told her. "Go on . . ."

"You remember the times the detectives found you and brought you back East?"

"How could I forget? Locked in my room all day, and only allowed out when Jack or his wife was there to keep an eye on me."

"The first time they brought you back, you were eleven."

Rook felt old anger stirring in her. "Yes, and you were nowhere to be found. Jack kept telling me how much you had missed me, but I sure as hell didn't get to see you."

"Know why?"

"No," she muttered, refusing to meet his eyes. "I figured you hated me as much as I hated you, and you were avoiding me."

Noah fought the urge to place his hands on her drawn

shoulders. His voice dropped to a rasp. "Jack had me locked in my room, too, Rook."

Jerking her chin up, Rook stared at him. The anguish was clearly etched in his eyes. "What?"

"If he'd allowed us together, the first thing I would have asked you was why you and Mom hadn't answered all my letters over the years."

Rubbing her chest because it hurt, Rook stepped away from him. "Jack said during the next visit that you were away at a military academy, and weren't allowed home."

"That was a partial lie. I was sent to a military academy five days a week, but I was allowed home on weekends. The week you were brought home, Jack told the officials to keep me at the academy. He wanted to make sure you and I didn't get together."

Rook's mouth fell open. Noah, who was always so warm and giving, wasn't the type to adjust easily to a military lifestyle. They had been so close as a family before the divorce. He had always been a toucher and hugger. Rook could vividly remember the time when she and Noah were inseparable. Her mother had reinforced their closeness, showering them with constant love and attention.

Rook's distrust warred with the new information. They were no longer children, but that didn't stop the hurt she was feeling for Noah—if he was telling the truth.

"Jack kept saying that if I was a good little girl, he'd let me see you—eventually."

"The only reason he wanted you back East was to hurt Mom, Rook."

"I believe that! He never did like me. You were always his favorite."

"Lucky me," Noah grated.

"What about when I was twelve? They tracked us down in Odessa, Texas, and I spent two lousy weeks back there."

"I was kept at the academy again. This time, I knew something was up and hitched a ride home with one of my friends' parents. Remember that time I got to your room before we were discovered together?"

"Too well. You were like an excited puppy, hugging and kissing me."

He managed a slight smile. "No one was more excited than me at discovering you were there, Rook. I loved you. I was lonely, and I couldn't figure out why you hadn't answered my letters. Remember, just as Jack found us together, I asked you why you never wrote back?"

Rook searched her memory. "Yes," she admitted slowly. "I didn't understand what you were talking about."

"I was eighteen before I found out the extent of Jack's lies. I had just gotten to the Coast Guard Academy, and had sent you a letter at the address the detective agency had on you. I got it back ten days later, unopened. I called the agency and they said it was your last known address. It wasn't, of course. Jack had given them orders to lie to me. By this time, Jack had pretty much given up on harassing Mom. The letter should have reached you, Rook. When I went home on leave that summer, I cornered Jack about it.

"He tried to weasel out of giving me an explanation. I had grown up believing that neither of you wanted to hear from me, but this letter indicated something far different." Noah rubbed his square jaw. "It was one of the few times in my life I lost my temper. When I did, it triggered something in Jack, and he started screaming at me. He told me how much he'd hated Mom, and how he was going to make her pay for leaving him. When he started calling her names, I jerked him up by the lapels of his sport coat and slammed him against the wall. I told him to never speak about our mother that way again. We ended up in a fight." Noah pointed to his broken nose as proof. "While I was lying semiconscious on the floor of the den, he went over to the desk, opened this drawer he'd always kept locked, and flung this bunch of letters at me. He told me that none of the letters I'd written over the years had been delivered to you." Noah's voice faltered, and he looked deeply into Rook's eyes. "All those years he'd lied to me, Rook. He said you had gotten the letters, but that you refused to answer them. He'd convinced me that neither of you had ever loved me."

Rook blinked once, pain of an insurmountable nature moving through her. She opened her mouth, but Noah interrupted.

"Look, do me a favor. Just read the letters. They're all dated. Let them prove to you that I didn't hate you . . . or Mom."

Before she could say anything, Noah went to the kitchen, picked up his garrison cap, and left. Rook stared down at the stack of letters. Oh, God, what was happening? The ache in her heart multiplied as she went over and carefully picked up the pack. She saw a number of envelopes that had turned yellow with age, and ran her fingertips reverently across them. Her hands shook as she sat down and carefully unknotted the red yarn that bound them.

It was ten o'clock by the time Rook finished reading the eighty-five letters. They lay scattered all over the coffee table. She picked up one of the early letters, studying Noah's wide scrawl. What hurt the most was the fact that Rook could still see the tearstains splotched on the yellowed paper. Other letters made her cry. Noah thought he'd been abandoned by his mother. "Why don't you love me anymore, Mom? I still love you. I want to come home to you and Rook, but Dad says he's dying and he needs me . . ."

Taking a deep, unsteady breath, Rook reread another one. Tears blurred her vision. It had been a letter Noah had written to her when she was thirteen. By then, he'd accepted the fact that they might not want to write to him, but he was persistent in believing they liked to hear from him. "Today's a special day, Sis. I've been chosen to carry the flag at our next academy graduation ceremony. I wish you were here to see me. I miss you and love you so much. When the other guys talk about their sisters, I don't say much. If you could maybe write just a few lines and let me know how you are, I'd have something to brag about to them about you, too."

Miserably, Rook looked at her watch. She had to talk to Noah. The June night was cool and windy. The sky was clear, for once. As she walked to her sports car, the stars hung above her, cold and silent—just as she had been to Noah. Placing all the letters on the seat, she started up the car.

Rook knocked until her knuckles were sore, but Noah didn't answer the door of his apartment. She turned, tucking her chilled hands into the pockets of her white jacket. Looking toward the town of Port Angeles below her, she could see the wharf where the *Point Countess* was docked, and decided to go to there next.

Dave Harper was on duty, and allowed her on board.

"Where's Lieutenant Caldwell?" she asked.

"Last I saw him, ma'am, he was in his cabin, working on some reports." Harper pointed down the well-lit hatch opening and stairs.

"Thanks."

The cutter was small and economically built. She could smell oil and diesel fuel as she tread through the quiet boat. Heart pounding in her chest, Rook located Noah's stateroom and knocked lightly. No answer. Again, she knocked.

Nothing. Rook looked around, chewing on her lower lip. Was Noah avoiding her? God knew, he had a right to be angry with her. Could he forgive her for all those years she refused to see or even talk to him? Taking a deep breath, Rook climbed topside. Harper was up on the bridge. She walked to the aft end of the boat, searching.

The shadows swallowed her up as she walked on the starboard side of the cutter, heading toward the bow. She spotted Noah. Shoulders hunched forward and wearing his foul weather jacket, he had his back to her. He was staring up at the stars. Noah looked so alone—abandoned. Rook girded herself. It was her turn to ask for his forgiveness. She stepped toward him.

Noah heard Rook approach, but barely turned his head in her direction. Even in the darkness, the light defused by the cutter's bridge above them, he could see the anguish written on her face. Would she understand? Would she forgive him and herself for their twisted past? A lump formed in his constricted throat.

Rook moved to his side, inches separating them. Her voice was unsteady when she spoke. "I read them. All of them . . ."

Noah steeled himself. "And?"

Tears scalded her eyes and she swallowed, her voice thick. "I—was wrong, Noah."

He turned to Rook, looking at her for a long moment. Two silvery paths of tears glistened down her cheeks. Gently, Noah wiped them away with his trembling fingers. "Can we start over?"

"If you want to . . . "

He nodded, no longer able to trust his voice.

With a muffled sob, Rook blindly threw her arms around her brother. They stood there a long time, the darkness shielding them, absorbing their old pain and loss.

Finally, Noah released his grip on Rook. "Come on," he urged thickly, "let's go to my cabin. I think we could both use some coffee."

Rook nodded, trying unsuccessfully to smile. His face was tortured with so many emotions, but new hope burned in his dark-gray eyes. "Yes . . ."

In his cabin, Rook sat on the tiny bunk, the mug gripped tightly between her cold hands. Noah sat on the chair, the desk behind him. This time, the silence wasn't stilted.

"You never gave up on me," Rook said, her voice still raw. "Why?"

"Because you were my sister. How can you ignore your own blood, Rook?"

"I did a pretty good job of it, didn't I?"

"It wasn't your fault."

"No, it was Jack's." Her voice hardened. "He was sick, Noah. Sick!"

"Right now he's in a mental hospital. Did you know that?"

Rook gasped and looked over at Noah. "No, I didn't know."

"Yeah, last year my stepmother had him committed. He

was diagnosed as paranoid schizophrenic. Even the medication hasn't helped him."

"My God."

Noah nodded thoughtfully, sipping his coffee. "He did a lot of damage to all of us, Rook."

"Worst of all, to you. He made you think Mom didn't love you, and she did—always."

"I know that now," he whispered, "thanks to you."

Rook rubbed her face, emotionally exhausted. "God, so much suffering, so many lost years that we'll never be able to make up." Her eyes softened as she held her brother's red-rimmed gaze. "Worst of all, you never had Mom's love."

"I had a stepmother."

Rook shook her head. "I don't care what you say, Noah, it had to hurt you—deeply." Forever . . .

"I survived." He mustered a sad smile. "We both did, despite some pretty awful circumstances. And look at us. We've both grown up, we're responsible adults who care about others . . . Things could have turned out a lot worst. No, we're well off, despite all that other stuff."

"Noah Caldwell: the eternal optimist."

He grinned. "And you the eternal pessimist."

"Guess we're a good balance for one another, huh?"

His smile widened, warmth shining in his eyes. "Yeah."

"Why didn't you show me those letters sooner?"

"It was obvious to me that if I tried to push you too hard, I'd destroy any chance of getting you to sit still long enough to hear me out. I had to wait."

"You always did have patience."

"And you never did."

"No, it's not one of my strong points."

Noah cleared his throat, holding Rook's softened gaze. "You'll never know how much it meant to me for you to show up yesterday when all hell was breaking loose."

"I fought myself all afternoon. I knew they'd brought you and your crew in. I kept telling myself I didn't want to see you. Why should I go hold your hand? You'd never held ours." Rook shrugged, giving him an apologetic look. "I was trying to punish you for past transgressions."

"In the end, you came, Sis."

"Yes . . ."

Noah reached out and gripped her hand. "You were there for me because I was your brother, and I was in trouble. That's when I knew it was time to show you those letters. I was going to show them to you as soon as the incident was cleared up, one way or another."

She squeezed his hand. "In my heart, I knew you'd never shoot a whale." And then Rook smiled shakily. "You were always so chivalrous. I swear, in some ways, you're a throwback to the days of knighthood."

Laughing, Noah stood, feeling the last of the weight he'd carried for all those years slipping free of his shoulders. "Come on, you need to get home and catch up on some sleep. You've still got dark shadows under your eyes."

Rook moved off the bunk, placing the mug on the desk. "Uh-oh, there you go, starting to act like a mother hen."

Noah opened the cabin door. "Wrong," he told her with a devilish grin. "It's called acting like a brother. You might as well get used to it, Rook Caldwell."

With a dramatic groan, Rook laughed freely. The sound carried throughout the cutter. "Just remember, there's only eighteen months difference in our age, so don't go getting too pushy and know-it-all with me."

"Agreed. But from now on, let's use each other's strength in times of need, okay?"

"Okay."

CHAPTER

Sixteen

IT was time. Chappie glanced out the window of his office toward the quiet hangar bay. The doors were closed against the weather, which had turned foul, with rain and winds exceeding thirty-five knots, and thirty-foot waves at sea. Gale warnings had been posted throughout the day. A powerful Alaskan cold front was bearing down on them. He'd purposely stayed late, until the day crew had left. The only ones on duty now were Lieutenants Scanlon and Caldwell. A grizzled smiled pulled at his mouth. Annie Locke was flight mech for tonight. Good. Everything was in order.

He'd waited with the patience of a hungry wolf, watching his quarry for the last three weeks. Chappie had been smart: he'd let the station settle down after the whale incident and the funeral for Welsh's wife before making his move. When Locke's error came to light, he wanted the whole station to be focused on it, not detoured by some other crisis. The watch on his wrist read 11 P.M. By now, the SAR pilots were asleep. Locke was already in the duty quarters across the way, with the door shut and lights off.

Moving to CG 1224, the helo that was prepped and ready for SAR call, he stole through the open fuselage door. Making his way forward, he halted before going into the cockpit, looking right and then left. The hangar was buried in deep gloom; only a few necessary lights illuminated the area.

Chappie settled into the right-hand seat. His hands trembled as he unscrewed the top of the channel monitor panel to the right of the pilot's seat. Glancing around again, he pulled the wires that led to the hardover switches of the Automatic Stabilization Equipment (ASE). Scraping one wire carefully with his penknife, he then put two drops of saltwater over it. Satisfied, sweat beading his wrinkled brow, he screwed the plate back into place.

The nose of the '52 had a tendency to turn in the direction of flight. That was due to a large, flat, plate area aft of the main rotor shaft. The ASE improved the helicopter's basic flying qualities in conjunction with the cyclic stick trim system and was capable of maintaining a desired attitude with minimal assistance from the pilot.

Chappie slid out of the seat, making sure his presence in the cockpit would never be discovered. An electrical ASE hardover could occur now. The ASE could become a critical item—especially at night, or if the SAR was taking place during high winds or dangerous conditions. If any of those combinations occurred, the pilot could get vertigo and lose his sense of direction. Then, the helo could crash. Or, if the SAR was at a critical phase when the hardover occurred, it could push the pilot over the edge, snapping his concentration, and he might create an in-flight emergency.

Jarvis didn't anticipate anything as dangerous as that happening. The ASE had only ten percent control over the flight attitude of a helo. If the pilot was on top of things, and he didn't doubt that Scanlon would be, the hardover would be overridden with a simple flight correction on his part, and then the channel could be disengaged—or, if that didn't work, the ASE Off switch could be punched on the cyclic stick, and the system would be shut down.

He checked the maintenance record on CG 1224, and saw Locke's initials signing off a previous ASE discrepancy. Earlier that day, she had also done the normal inspection on the helo. When Scanlon got back from the SAR case, he'd have to down the aircraft. Then Chappie would have Locke's ass right where he wanted it. He would put her on report for failing to do a complete and proper Q.A. check on her helo, and endangering the crew, as well as potentially losing a five-hundred thousand dollar helo. Letting the maintenance record fall back on the board, Chappie smiled. He'd get even with her for squealing on him. One way or another, she'd pay—in spades. Now, all he had to do was wait and hope for a SAR case tonight. With this kind of weather, there was bound to be some boat or yacht caught in the grips of high seas and the hammering wind. Someone would need assistance out there.

"Hey, Rook, wake up." Ty leaned over, giving her a good shake. Rook was in her rumpled flight suit, sleeping on the couch in the ready room. The television was on, but had gone off the air a long time ago. It was 2 A.M.

"I'm up," Rook mumbled, sitting up. Automatically, she slipped into her flight boots while Ty went back down to the SAR desk. She stumbled after him, sleepiness quickly replaced by alertness. Adrenaline was pumping through her now.

A cup of hot coffee was waiting for her when she joined Ty at the desk, falling into her normal duties as copilot.

"What have we got?"

"An SOS from a disabled yacht with three people aboard. They're going to need to be airlifted out." Ty answered. "This is going to be a rough flight."

Rook turned and looked out the rain-glazed window. "Ugly might be a better word."

He nodded, his mouth thinning as he wrote down the necessary information. "Winds are thirty-five knots out there. We've got a report from a tanker twenty miles west of where the signal was picked up, and he's reporting thirty- to forty-foot waves."

Her heart started to pound. All her previous cases had been fair-weather rescues. "You're joking."

"Wish I was."

"But—this is July. They said—"

"This is typical Northern Pacific weather," Ty muttered

unhappily. "We've got heavy head winds, and it's going to slow us down getting to the spot. They're sending a Falcon jet from Astoria to assist us. They'll locate the distressed boat and lead us to it."

Rook tried to ignore the chill that stalked her. Nightmare cases like this one made her uneasy. Undetected turbulence could test even the most experienced pilot's abilities. Pursing her lips, she reached for the charts. "Okay, let's get this show on the road."

Ty shook his head. "What a mother of a night for a case . . ."

Annie Locke's face was grim. It made Rook even jumpier. She had less than three months of SAR training under her belt, and this rescue worried her. Ty knew she wasn't fully trained to help if they got in trouble—at least, not in the rescue portion, if something happened to him.

Getting the helo checked for flight and lifting off into the darkness helped settle Rook's nerves. As they flew past the last Washington landmass and headed out over the Pacific Ocean, Rook strained to see the water five hundred feet below them. She could see nothing. The rain pounded furiously against the cockpit windows, severely limiting visibility. The soft red glow of the panel lights bathed their faces. Nothing but blackness lay outside the thin skin of the struggling, shuddering '52. What little Rook could see was evidenced by the lights on the fuselage, blinking rapidly in the turgid darkness of the howling storm.

Scanlon glanced over at Rook and saw the tension on her face. Christ, what was he going to do? He'd better be able to pull this case off on his own. It wasn't her fault, he reminded himself. Both Logan and Welsh, who had flown with Rook on a couple of other rescues, had high praise for her touch with a helo. They said she was a pro, and not to worry about her being behind a stick. That was good. This was the first chance he'd had to fly with her. The duty roster had been so screwed up lately that copilots flew frequently with the same pilots.

Tonight, he'd need everything Rook had to give him. From his own years of experience, he knew a basket hoist would be the only way to rescue the people on board that yacht. Scanlon's eyes narrowed as he concentrated on his instrument flying. The cyclic vibrated in his right hand, but the collective, which sat on the left side of his seat, felt good and solid. The '52 was working well. He breathed another bit of relief: Annie was tops in flight maintenance. Not that the other flight mechs weren't. He simply trusted her a bit more because she was such a stickler for details when she worked on a helo. And right now, Ty knew he was going to need all those infinitesimal extras to pull off this SAR case. With the present weather conditions, they would have to refuel at Neah Bay and La Push, in order to go out over the rescue site with a full load on board.

Jarvis could hardly wait for the '52 to land. He'd sat in his office, following the rescue on radio. The transmissions from CG 1224 had been sparse and terse. He was delighted when he heard Scanlon on the radio instead of the copilot. So, Caldwell had had to take over the rescue. The electrical hardover must have occurred, or Scanlon wouldn't have given the controls to such a green copilot. Two ambulances from Mercy Hospital were standing by near the hangar bay doors, waiting to transfer the three survivors once the helo landed. It was 0310. Chappie rubbed his hands together, congratulating himself.

CG 1224 returned to the station at 0400. While Annie slid the fuselage door open, Rook sat limply in the left-hand seat, completely wrung out. Her flight suit was damp with sweat. Her hands ached and so did her forearms, shoulders, and neck. Midway through, the helo had had unexpected flight difficulties. Ty Scanlon had developed a case of vertigo and had handed the controls over to her. Thank God she had been able to complete the rescue and fly them back without further incident.

Ty leaned back, closing his eyes for a moment, silence

filtering into the cabin. They should go through their checks, but right now, they both needed a few minutes to collect themselves.

"You did a good job, Rook."

She snorted softly. "Yeah, if you call five tries before I got the basket on the deck good."

"You got the men off safely and hoisted them; that's all that counts."

"Did you see how much fuel we have left?"

"Not much. It's okay."

Gradually, some of the knots were beginning to work out of Rook's fingers and lower arms. She turned her head and sat up. "How are you feeling?"

"I didn't have vertigo again after we discovered it was the ASE hardover."

"Good." A pilot with severe or continuing vertigo would have to go to the medical officer and be examined. A pilot could be grounded until a doctor was convinced that he wouldn't experience the dangerous condition again. "I'm sure it was caused by the hardover."

"It had to be. I've never had vertigo before—ever."

Rook stirred and unstrapped, beginning to feel shaky now as the adrenaline left her bloodstream. Annie had gotten the survivors into the ambulance. Rook watched as the flight mech climbed back into the helo.

"Ms. Caldwell, what happened up here?" she asked worriedly, crouching between the two seats.

Rook's heart went out to Annie. Her freckled face was waxen looking, her eyes dark with concern. The flight mech who rode in the helo was also responsible for servicing it properly. She knew what Annie was thinking: that she was responsible for the malfunction.

"We experienced an ASE electrical hardover."

Annie reached out, touching the lower radio console with her trembling fingers. "I can't figure it out. I did my periodic check on this bird only two hours before the call. The ASE was working fine then." She turned to Ty, apology in her strained voice. "I'm really sorry, Mr. Scanlon."

"Annie, it's a fluke. I know how well you maintain the helos. You've got a clean record. Don't worry about it." He managed a weary but genuine smile for Annie, giving her a well-deserved pat on the shoulder. "You did a hell of a job out there. We couldn't have done it without you, Annie."

Rook nodded. "You were the greatest, Annie. Now, I see why all the pilots pray for you to be on the duty roster when a case comes in."

Annie lowered her lashes, a blush bringing color back to her features. "Gosh . . . thanks . . ."

Rook saw anxiety in her drawn features. "We'll have to down the bird," she told her.

Locke nodded, understanding. "As soon as I can get a dry set of clothes on, we'll bring the helo in, take off that plate, and see what went wrong."

"Fine," Ty agreed, beginning to unstrap. "Go get cleaned up."

"Yes, sir."

Annie ran through the rain, visor down on her helmet to shield her eyes from the deluge. She halted just inside the now-quiet hangar and shoved the visor back up into her helmet. With shaking hands, she unsnapped the chin strap and pulled the helmet off. When she straightened up, Chief Jarvis was standing no more than ten feet away from her. She saw a savage gleam in his eyes.

"Looks like you fucked up real good, Locke," he began softly. "An ASE electrical hardover? What's the matter, you cheating on your Q.A. checks and just signing them off instead?"

Anger roared through her as she stood there with the helmet in the crook of her right arm. Exhausted physically, mentally and emotionally drained, Annie struggled to hold on to her temper. "The day I sign off a discrepancy on a helo without checking it first will be the day I die, Chief."

Chappie smiled wolfishly. "You damn near just killed two fine pilots, not to mention the three men you picked up." He walked slowly toward her, his face mirroring his pleasure. Jabbing a finger into her shoulder he snarled, "You didn't do your job, Locke. You got lazy because those Q.A. checks are boring, and you damn near cost a lot of lives, not to mention a helo."

"Now look here, Chief, I *checked* that helo out two hours before we flew!"

"Doesn't appear to be that way, Locke." He gloated as Annie started coming loose, like an unraveling ball of yarn. "One thing I learned about you, Locke, a long time ago, was your false pride in your work. Of course, with your looks, maybe work is all you have to take pride in."

Annie gripped her helmet hard, wanting to throw a punch into the chief's smiling face. "You bastard," she hissed, "you've been waiting for this, haven't you? You've been wanting me to make a mistake for so long that—"

Jarvis stepped up to her, his face inches from hers. "You're on report, Locke, for insubordination."

Shaken, Annie took a step back, realizing what she had done. After taking a year of Jarvis riding her almost daily, she'd done the one thing she swore she wouldn't do: talk back to the mealy-mouthed bastard. "But, I—"

"You're on report, Locke. I'm also pulling you off duty as ready crew for the rest of the night."

"But, Chief, I want to pull the ASE apart and check it out—"

"I'll do it. I'm the chief here. I'm going to find out what really happened."

Annie stood open-mouthed, at a loss for words. Jarvis check her work? If she couldn't check it out first, herself, he could rig it so that something would be wrong to get her into a hell of a lot more trouble. "I want Mr. Welsh to look at it. He's the engineer."

Rook stepped into the hangar, realizing belatedly that there was a confrontation going down. She frowned and walked over. "What's going on here, Chief?"

Jarvis nodded deferentially in the officer's direction. "I just placed Locke on report for insubordination to a superior, ma'am."

"What?" Rook glanced over at Annie's stricken face and

then back to Jarvis, who was barely able to keep a somber look on his grizzled features.

Jarvis explained the incident, omitting his part in the conversation with Locke. "Further, I'm going to pull that ASE apart and look at it myself."

Rook nailed him with a glare. "No, you won't, Chief. I'll notify Lieutenant Welsh, and he'll come out and investigate this."

Jarvis stared up at her. *The bitch.* "I'm line chief here," he reminded her angrily.

"Not anymore," Rook parried. "Not according to Captain Stuart's orders. You push paper, Chief—you don't have anything to do with a helo on the line."

Heat soared up through Jarvis. He wanted to take a swing at Rook. He hated her confidence and authority. No woman had any business being a pilot!

"What's going on here?" Ty came up, standing at Rook's side.

Rook explained.

Jarvis smiled slightly, turning to Scanlon for help. "Look, Mr. Scanlon, I know these helos like they were my own children. All I wanted to do was check out the ASE, that's all. How about it?"

Automatically, Rook tensed. Would Ty become a "good ole boy" and stick with what another man wanted, instead of following the orders Stuart had issued? He was senior duty officer for the night, and what he decided became law. She could see the feral pleasure in Jarvis's eyes as he looked at Annie. He'd already put her on report for insubordination. Dammit! Rook wished she'd gotten to the hangar sooner. Maybe she could have prevented this. The case had been particularly hard on Annie. She had had five other lives in her hands as she orchestrated the rescue. It was one hell of a load on anyone's shoulders.

"Sorry, Chief. That's not your job any longer," Scanlon said.

Rook relaxed. Thank God Ty wasn't going to side with

the wheedling chief. "I already told the chief that Lieutenant Welsh would come out and do it."

Ty nodded. "That's correct procedure in a case like this. Chief, do you understand?"

Jarvis quelled his fury. "Yes, sir." That was all right; he had Locke right where he wanted her, anyway. When Welsh saw the bare wire and dried saltwater on the cable and below it, Locke would be implicated immediately. Besides, to add to it, she was now on report. He silently celebrated.

"Come on," Ty told Rook, "we've got paperwork ahead of us."

Rook gave Annie a silent look that said: *relax, we'll help you as much as we can.* "Okay." She wondered why the chief was here at this time in the morning. He didn't have duty tonight. Dismissing it because of encroaching exhaustion, Rook followed Ty to the line shack.

"Look at this," Tag said, pointing down at the wiring in the opened channel monitor panel. One of the hardover switch wires was bare, and there was dried saltwater on it, plus a small pool of dried crystals beneath it.

Rook, who was sitting in the left-hand seat, stared over at it. Tag had come on duty at 0800 and gone straight over to the hangar to inspect CG 1224. Annie was up, moving around in the hangar, going about her normal duties for the day, but Rook could see the strain in every feature of her vulnerable, pale face. Flicking a look over at Tag, sitting in the pilot's seat, she said, "You know what this implies."

"Yeah, that Annie didn't do her required inspection," he answered heavily. Writing down his findings on his memo pad, the scowl increased across Tag's brow. "This isn't like Annie. She's a stickler for detail. I've seen her tear into a wiring panel when something was within normal range and she wasn't satisfied with it."

"I know." Rook looked up and saw Chief Jarvis watching them from his office. Compressing her lips, she returned her attention to Tag. "I've got an ugly feeling about this, Tag."

He completed his report. "What are you talking about?"

"Last night, when we got back from that SAR case, Jarvis was waiting here for us. I checked the duty roster this morning, and he didn't have the duty. He looked positively happy when I came into the hangar while he was confronting Annie." She shook her head. "It's as if he knew. . ."

Leaning back in the steel pilot seat, Tag studied her in the gathering silence. "Knew what?"

Shrugging, Rook muttered, "I don't know. I mean, why would he be waiting for us, like a buzzard ready to jump on a carcass, if he didn't know something was wrong? Annie said she had barely gotten in the hangar before Jarvis jumped all over her case about the ASE hardover."

"Poor kid, she's devastated," Tag murmured, watching Annie walk slowly back to the metal shop. "She's got an impeccable performance record."

"I know. She's got all kinds of commendations. No one works harder than she does, Tag." Rook rubbed her aching temple. "I smell a rat, and I know Jarvis is connected with it, but I can't prove anything."

"Well," Tag said, getting up, "I've got to report this directly to the captain today. This little mistake almost cost six lives. He isn't going to be happy."

Rook chewed on her lower lip. "This is going to wreck her chances of getting OCS. You know that."

"I know," he said softly, apologetically.

Following Welsh out of the helo, Rook said, "I'm going to have a talk with Annie and tell her your findings."

"Okay. See you later." And then Tag grimaced. "The captain will call all of us in on this one sometime today."

And poor Annie will die of embarrassment, Rook thought. "I know. See you later, Tag."

Annie sat at the table with the ASE manual in front of her. She looked up to see Rook enter the empty shop. When Rook gave her a slight smile, she rallied.

"What did Mr. Welsh find, ma'am?"

Rook came over and sat down opposite her, folding her

hands on the table. As gently as possible, Rook told her of Tag's investigation. She saw Annie pale even more.

Collecting herself, Annie stammered, "B-but, was there any indication of saltwater on the covering?"

"No, it was clean."

She frowned, staring down at the opened manual. "I've been going over and over the electrical schematic on the ASE, Ms. Caldwell. I've been racking my brain as to how a hardover could have occurred." She swallowed, her voice thick. "I swear to you, I checked CG 1224 two hours prior to our takeoff. I lifted that plate on the channel monitor panel and checked for dirt, debris, and water. It was clean. Clean!"

"Mr. Welsh checked the overhead and pilot's window just to be sure there wasn't any evidence of water leaking through it and dropping onto the console," Rook said, trying to soothe her anguish.

"And?" Hope rose in her voice.

"It was dry. No evidence of leaks."

Annie buried her face in her hands. She sobbed softly, her shoulders hunched and shaking.

Wanting to console her, but not daring to, Rook sat there and waited until Annie's weeping abated. She got up and pulled a Kleenex from the pocket of her flight suit pocket.

"Here," Rook said, handing it to her. "Dry your eyes. We're going over everything that happened one more time."

Sniffing, Annie said, "But, I've put it down on my report, Ms. Caldwell. Mr. Welsh read it this morning before he checked out CG 1224. You've already heard it all."

"I know, Annie, but run over it one more time—for me, please?"

Eyes reddened, Annie sat there, the tissue clutched between her fingers. "A-all right, Ms. Caldwell."

Chappie waited happily out in the hall. To his right stood a very unhappy Locke. Right now, Stuart had the three officers in his closed office, asking, he was sure, plenty of questions about the ASE hardover. He could barely maintain the proper stoic attitude. Occasionally, he glanced over at Locke. She was suffering, that was apparent. Feelings of triumph soared through Chappie as he perused her dejected posture, shaking hands, and reddened eyes. This was one time the captain would have to go by the book. He'd bury Locke's career on this one. No OCS for her. No more dreams of becoming an officer. Bucky Beaver was finally going to get that well-earned kick in her crooked teeth that she so richly deserved.

Ward winced inwardly when Annie Locke came in. He'd already studied her personnel file, and was well acquainted with her record of excellence. He also saw the request for OCS that would have been approved by him and sent in next month. She looked devastated.

"Sit down, Petty Officer Locke." His voice was firm, but he kept a gentle edge to it. There was no need to be tough with her; she was obviously suffering enough.

"Thank you, sir." Annie tried to shore up the broken state of her emotions. Under no circumstance would she break down and start weeping in front of Stuart. She'd already accepted her fate, fair or not. All that remained was for the captain to go through the expected motions. Her dream of OCS was gone—forever.

Ward leaned forward and softened his tone. "I've read Mr. Welsh's report on CG 1224, and I've read Chief Jarvis's report regarding your insubordination to him. What do you have to say about all this?"

Clearing her raw throat, Annie faithfully repeated everything she had said to Welsh and Caldwell, leaving nothing out. She wondered why the captain had his tape recorder on, and why he was taking such copious notes. Who would believe a flight mech's word against such heavy proof in the opposite direction? Was Stuart trying to make her feel as if she were getting a fair hearing? If she didn't know the outcome of such an error, Annie would have taken hope. As it was, the evidence was simply too powerful to negate and clear her.

"I'd like your side of the story as to why Chief Jarvis placed you on report, Ms. Locke."

Annie's brows fell. Her voice grew tight with barely veiled anger. "He jumped on me the minute I came in the hangar, Captain. We'd all just come off a very rough SAR case, and I was still high with adrenaline—shaky and jumpy. The chief came running—"

"Running?"

"Uh, no, sir. He walked in a hurry toward me. Sorry."

"Go on."

"He said, 'Looks like you fucked up real good, Locke. An ASE electrical hardover? What's the matter, you cheating on your Q.A. checks and just signing them off, instead?' "

Ward's eyes hardened. Any form of cursing was banned—especially that four-letter word. Jarvis would say something like that. "You're sure those were his exact words?"

"Yes, sir."

"What happened next?"

Ward listened closely to the rest of Annie's explanation. "He says in his report you called him a bastard. Did you?"

"I did, sir."

"What did he say to draw that sort of response from you, Locke?"

She avoided Stuart's incisive gaze, her throat closing with tears. "Do I have to tell you, sir? I admit I called him that name. Isn't that enough?"

Ward saw the tears glittering fiercely in her eyes. "Annie, how can I decide whether or not Chief Jarvis should have put you on report if I don't know the reasons for such a serious charge?"

Struggling with a deluge of tears that wanted to fall, Annie stared down at her tightly clenched hands in her lap. "I—uh, he said, 'Of course, with your looks, maybe work is all you have left to take pride in.' "

Ward straightened up, stunned. Annie sat there, head bowed, tears dribbling down her cheeks and collecting on her chin. He clenched his fist. Expelling a breath of air from his flared nostrils, Stuart said, "Is there anything else you want to add?"

Annie shook her head, afraid that if she spoke, she'd cry. Captain Stuart sounded furious; his voice was lined with steel.

"Very well, dismissed."

Annie quickly got up, stood at attention, and did an about face, blindly walking out of the office. She avoided Jarvis's sharpened look and the laughter in his eyes. She hurried to the bathroom, where she could cry without anyone hearing or seeing her.

Jarvis eyed the damning tape recorder that Stuart turned on after he sat down. Feeling fairly confident of his position in the matter, he relaxed, crossing his legs.

"All right, Chief, tell me what you know about the ASE hardover on CG 1224."

Happily, Chappie said, "Yes, sir," and launched with enthusiasm into the entire sordid incident that would ruin Locke's promising career. Maybe then Stuart would change his opinion of him—see that he was a real watchdog, on top of things—and give him his rightful authority back as line chief.

Ward compared his notes to those of the previous people he'd interviewed. "You say you overheard Lieutenant Scanlon tell Lieutenant Caldwell that the CG 1224 had an ASE electrical hardover?"

"That's correct, sir. I've been telling Mr. Welsh all along the Locke's been sluffing off on her Q.A. duties, but nobody would believe me. I'd see her out in that helo, just sitting around. I knew what she was up to—daydreaming about becoming an officer someday and not paying proper attention to her duties—"

Ward glowered at the man, barely holding his anger in check. "Let's move on to the next topic: Locke's insubordination to you."

"Yes, sir."

Ward pulled out a paper. "Did you say the following to her, Chief?" And he read what Locke had stated.

Chappie tried to look properly shocked. "Why, no, Captain. I'd never say any of those things to her! That's against regulations, sir."

"That's called harassment," Ward growled, pinning him with a black look.

"Of course it is, sir. I didn't harass her. I just questioned her about the ASE problems I heard over the radio, that's all. She got real defensive and started yelling at me. She called me a bastard, just like I stated in my report to you. Sir."

"She admitted calling you that name." Ward reached over to his intercom. "June, get Lieutenants Scanlon and Caldwell up here, will you, please?"

"Yes, sir."

Chappie cocked his head. He almost blurted out, "Why are you calling them back in?" but didn't. He saw the blackness in Stuart's eyes and the harsh line to his mouth. What the hell was he up to? Nervously, Chappie uncrossed his legs, and let both hands rest on the arms of the leather chair.

Ward waited five minutes while the officers were located and directed to his office. Both gave him a quizzical look as they stood at ease in front of his desk.

"Mr. Scanlon, did you mention the ASE hardover on the radio to Ms. Caldwell?" Ward asked.

"No, sir."

Stuart looked steadily at Ty. "Were you on hot mike?"

"Yes, sir."

Chappie gasped and nearly came out of his seat. He gripped the arms of the chair.

Rook's mouth fell open. She stared at the captain and then turned to Ty, realizing what the C.O. was getting at.

"Were you on hot mike, Ms. Caldwell?" Ward asked.

"Oh, yes, sir, we were. We were!"

"And did you, at any time after that, mention the hardover over the radio to the base, Mr. Scanlon?"

Ty's eyes widened with realization. He barely checked a smile. "No, sir, we never spoke of it on the radio."

Briskly, Ward said, "That will be shown as soon as the radio transmissions are checked on the radio room tapes. Thank you for that valuable piece of information."

Ward slowly stood up, facing Jarvis. "Then, just how the hell did you know that CG 1224 had an ASE electrical hard-over, Chief? The ICS is not broadcast by any radio and is strictly an interphone system in the helo used by the crew. You, by your own testimony and that of Locke, asked her about the hardover the moment she entered the hangar." He walked around the desk, lording over the cowering Jarvis, who was now drenched in sweat. His voice came out in a low snarl. "The only way you could have known about that hardover was to have caused it yourself. Not only that, but you weren't supposed to be anywhere near the hangar last night. Why were you loitering around until that hour of the morning? Were you waiting for the ASE hardover to occur so you could blame Locke and get her into hot water?"

"Well—I, uh . . ." Jarvis stammered. And then he shoved the chair back. He stood up with such force that he nearly knocked it over backward. Breathing hard, he rasped, "I want legal counsel! I demand to see a lawyer before this goes any further. Sir."

Ward didn't quite smile, knowing he'd discovered Jarvis's plan. "I have no objection to you getting a lawyer, Chief. In fact, I'd encourage you to get one—a damned good one." Ward jabbed a finger toward him. "But I am placing you on report. And mister, you're going to need a battery of lawyers for your despicable conduct. Nobody messes with my people like this, Chief—no one. You're on restriction, as of this minute. You are not allowed near the hangar, the helicopters, or any of the personnel. Understood? Report to the Officer of the Day for your next assignment."

Chappie wiped his brow, his breath coming in sharp breaths. "You can't do this! I've got eighteen years in!"

"You're restricted to the base limits, Chief," Ward said

icily. "I suggest you call the District legal officer. You're going to need him. Dismissed!"

Rook felt Stuart's rage. She'd never experienced tangible anger in a room, as she did now. She wanted to whoop for joy. Why hadn't she or Ty remembered that they were on hot mike? Her admiration and respect for Stuart soared. He'd just saved Annie's entire career. Barely able to stand still, she waited until Jarvis stalked out in a huff, slamming the door to the office behind him.

With a cry, Rook threw her arms around Ty, giving him an unexpected hug.

Ward watched her antics, a grudging smile coming to his mouth. Pretending he'd not seen her enthusiastic display, he walked back around his desk and sat down. Gathering up all the papers and shutting off the tape recorder, he said crisply, "Lieutenant Caldwell, how'd you like to find Ms. Locke and bring her back in here."

Grinning, Rook said, "Yes, sir!"

"You'll probably find her in the women's head."

Rook smiled at Ward. She liked the man, his sensitivity. He knew Annie would probably be bawling her eyes out in private. "Right away, Captain."

Ty's grin stretched ear from ear. After Rook had left, he cleared his throat. "That was a fine piece of work, Captain. Both of us felt bad about Annie . . . I mean, Petty Officer Locke, getting written up."

"Thank you, Mr. Scanlon. I think the only reason it escaped you and Ms. Caldwell was because you're tired from the flying. It was a rough case."

"Just the same, sir, thank you. Annie Locke's special."

"Yes, she is." Ward sobered and held Ty's gaze. "But don't forget, Mr. Scanlon, even the best of people can make errors. No one's perfect."

"You're right, sir." And then Ty brightened. "Annie's a little more perfect than most flight mechs, though," and smiled, adding, "sir."

"Get out of here, Lieutenant. I'm sure you've got some work to catch up on."

Ty left, feeling happy. This captain was beginning to show his true colors, and Ty liked what he saw. If the other captain had been here, Annie would have been written up and convicted at a Captain's Mast, and her entire career would have gone down the drain. Whistling as he walked down the hall, Ty smiled. Wait until Annie found out!

Annie's face positively glowed as Ward said, "The evidence I just discovered vindicates you in my eyes, Petty Officer Locke—and the Coast Guard's. However," he went on in a serious tone, "I'm sure that Chief Jarvis will hire a civilian attorney, and he'll try to prove himself innocent at your expense. No one saw him tamper with the ASE. It's basically his word against no hard evidence on our part. He may be able to get off on that charge, as a result. However, corroboration of testimony given by Lieutenants Scanlon and Caldwell makes it clear that you did check out the ASE before the flight, according to procedure, and I'm satisfied, as a result." He scribbled his signature at the end of the report and then looked up into Annie's happy face. "Next time, Annie, don't be afraid to tell what you know. If I hadn't dragged some of that information from you, you might not have been cleared. Another C.O. might not have dug as deep. Understand?"

"Yes, sir, I do. It was a good lesson." She grinned, exposing her wide, uneven teeth. "Thanks, Captain—from the bottom of my heart."

Ward smiled warmly. "You're a credit to the Coast Guard. And just to keep you from worrying or losing sleep over it, I've already approved your request for OCS."

Annie came forward and extended her hand. She pumped Ward's a long time. "Gosh, sir, thanks. You don't know how much it means to me."

Ward retrieved his hand, noting she had a healthy grip. Flight mech responsibility was hard, demanding physically, and requiring a sharp mind. Annie was strong in both. "Lieutenant Caldwell mentioned in passing that you're scheduled for major dental surgery in a month. I've approved the request and sent it over to Dr. Harrison."

Distressed, Annie resumed her at ease position in front of the desk. "But, sir, with Chief Jarvis on restriction, isn't that going to put an extra burden on the other mechs?"

Swallowing his smile, Ward nodded. "Yes, and since you're in a key slot as Mr. Welsh's assistant, that means we'll have to move someone else up temporarily, or get someone from another air station to take your place while you're recovering." He looked up at her. "Does that meet with your approval, Ms. Locke?"

Annie fairly beamed. "Yes, sir, it does."

"Get out of here. I've got work to do."

Happily, Annie came to attention and turned, fairly bouncing out of the office. In her eyes, Captain Stuart was the finest officer she'd ever had the privilege to serve under. It was only going to make her work harder so that he'd continue to be proud of her.

Ward's intercom buzzed. He depressed the switch. "Yes, June?"

"Captain, your wife is on line two."

Ward frowned, thinking that June sounded odd. He picked up the phone. "Hi."

"Ward?"

"What is it, Marcia? You sound upset."

"I just got a call from the sheriff's department."

Ward tried to prepare himself. He muttered, "It's Kenny, isn't it?"

"Yes." She hesitated, then dove on. "They just picked him up at school for buying coke from an undercover agent."

CHAPTER

Seventeen

ROOK was hard at work in her office at five o'clock. Most of the office personnel had left. Tiredness lapped at her. The case from the night before had drained her completely. She wished Noah was around, so she could tell him about the rescue.

"I'm not taking no for an answer."

Rook's head snapped up. Jim Barton stood before her. A gasp escaped her. An entire month had passed, and he'd made no attempt to see her. Rook's eyes widened considerably as she saw him give her a slight but warm smile of welcome. His blue eyes grew amused.

"Jim . . ."

Barton leaned against the doorjamb, dressed casually in a pale pink shirt and gray slacks. He wanted to appear at ease, but inwardly, his gut was tied in aching knots. There were so many fine lines to tread with Rook . . . Jim wasn't sure he could do it, but he had to try. He loved her. "You look tired. Did you have a case last night?" he guessed. Rook's short hair was ruffled and feminine-looking, despite the fact she wore no makeup. The olive-green flight suit de-emphasized the fact she was a woman, but not in his eyes. When he saw her cheeks color, Jim responded to the unspoken invitation.

Rook dropped the pencil on the report and shoved her

chair away from the desk. That same old panic came back. "A nasty one." Nervously, she asked, "How's your dad?"

He watched her stand. There was a feline grace to Rook. Jim wondered if she was even aware of the powerful sensuality that lurked just beneath the surface. "Dad's doing fine. He's chomping at the bit to get back to work again."

"Tired of being confined to his house? Bored?"

"You got it." Jim grew serious. "I'm sorry I had to drop in unannounced like this. I know you don't like mixing business with pleasure here at the office, but I haven't been able to get hold of you any other way."

Rook frowned, avoiding his searching gaze. "I always forget to turn my answering machine on when I leave the apartment." That was a lie.

"You've been busy." His heart started beating faster. "Look, we need to talk, Rook. I'd like to take you to dinner tonight."

Chewing on her lower lip, Rook winced. Her treatment of Jim was worse than callous. He deserved better. Expelling a breath of air, Rook nodded. "Okay, dinner."

Relief swept through him. "Great."

Rook retrieved her garrison cap and purse, walking up to him. "You don't want to take me like this. I smell like hell. I'll have to go home and get a shower."

He wanted to lean those few inches and claim her compressed lips, but squelched the idea. "How about if I pick you up at six-thirty?"

The urge to run was almost overwhelming. "Fine," Rook said in a strained tone.

After Rook changed uniforms, Jim walked her out to the parking lot. She fought feelings of apprehension. A large part of her was ecstatic at seeing him once again. She'd missed his sensitivity and intelligence, his laughter and keen humor. Jim had made her lighten up when no one had ever been able to do that before. By coming over to the air station and confronting her he'd caught her off guard. She halted at her sports car, Jim at her shoulder.

"Jim, where are we going to eat?"

He leaned an arm on the Toyota's roof, looking down at her. He wanted her so damn bad—and more than just in bed. "Ma Maison—it's right outside Port Angeles. Have you been there yet?"

Doubtful, Rook shook her head. "Are you kidding? I've been living on McDonald's hamburgers and Wendy's chili the last couple of months. What's a restaurant?"

He reached out, gently caressing her flame-colored cheek. Her skin was soft and inviting. "It's run by two San Francisco caterers who moved north to escape civilization. Pat and Dennis Perry are the owners, and they're a nice couple. Plus, the food is good."

Her flesh tingled beneath his grazing touch. Rook lowered her lashes, suddenly thrown into a quandary. She sensed Jim's hunger and saw it in his eyes. Taking a step back to escape, she murmured, "Well, I mean, is it a fancy place, where I have to dress up, or can I go casual?"

Jim gave her an enigmatic smile. "You might want to dress up a bit."

She gave him a pained look.

"I've never seen you in a dress, Rook."

"Poor baby." She laughed a little nervously and unlocked the car, sliding into the seat. "Men," she muttered. "I'll see you at six-thirty."

Unsure whether the pale mint linen blazer and matching skirt were appropriate, Rook chafed to herself. The pure Pima cotton blouse with the silk Venice lace yoke made her business suit a bit more feminine. She fussed with her hair, then placed her hands flat on the sink, staring at herself in the mirror.

"Why are you acting like an eighteen-year-old? This isn't a date. We have things to talk over." She stared down at the comb in her hand. What did Jim want from her?

She owned one set of earrings—her mother's. They were simple gold clip-ons that were small and circular. "Lipstick. Where the hell did I put the lipstick?" She rummaged for a full minute through a drawer, trying to locate the only tube she owned. "There you are . . ."

Unhappy with the overall effect of her efforts, Rook stared at the mirror. With a pang, she wished she looked better. *Why, you idiot? Who are you trying to impress? Just be yourself.*

The doorbell rang, and the knot in Rook's stomach grew proportionately. It rang again. Taking a deep breath, walking carefully in her three-inch heels, Rook answered the door.

"Say. . ."

"*Don't* say it," Rook warned Jim, frowning as she stepped aside to let him enter.

Jim handed her a small bouquet of summer flowers. "Don't say that you are attractive?" Jim leaned over, taking a glance at her. "Or that you've got a gorgeous set of legs—"

Heat fled up her neck and into her cheeks. Nervously, Rook took the flowers, walking to the kitchen to find a vase. "Jim, spare me the macho comments, okay?"

Jim sauntered into the kitchen. How shy she really was, he mused. It made her that much more enticing to him. "Take it easy, Rook."

Rook tried to hide her nervousness. Placing the flowers in a vase, she fled back to the living room to pick up her clutch purse. Jim caught up with her, reaching out and catching her by the arm, bringing her to a stop. "Whoa," he said. He placed his hands on Rook's shoulders, inches separating them. "Slow down," he coaxed huskily. "I'm taking you out to eat, that's all."

She eyed him. "I'm not the main course, Jim."

He raised his eyebrows. "Dessert?"

With a moan, Rook broke free of his entrapment. "You're incorrigible!"

Laughing lightly, Jim walked toward the door to open it for her. "So I've been told by a certain pert young lady who's a Coast Guard officer."

As she passed him on the way out, Rook muttered, "Yeah? Well, you'd better take it to heart."

"Threats! Threats!" Jim pretended to be properly frightened. Rook gave him a dirty look, but finally burst into laughter. Then she relaxed. That was the way Jim wanted her: laughter in her dove-gray eyes, that luscious mouth of hers curved upward in a smile, all the tension of her job erased from her features. Tonight was special, and he wanted Rook with her defenses down toward him.

"You know, the last four months of my life have been the best and worse I've ever had," Jim confided to Rook, easing into the relaxed atmosphere between them. They had finished a very good dinner and were languishing over liqueur after dessert. Jim held Rook's gaze. Throughout the evening, she had alternately been defensive and then unguarded, allowing him to see familiar and endearing facets of herself. He swirled the contents of the crystal goblet. "The worst, because I caused an accident that could have killed you. Plus, my dad's injury." Setting the glass aside, Jim captured Rook's hands. They were cool and damp between his. "And the best, because I met you and my dad's recovering."

"Jim—please . . ." Rook tried to pull her fingers free, but didn't succeed.

"Stop running from me," he told her softly.

Rook sat there, eyes downcast on the white tablecloth. His hands were warm and dry. Hers were clammy. "I'm not running!" she whispered tautly between her thinned lips. "If this is going where I think it's going, it's no good, Jim."

"Where do you think this is going?"

Rook could have died as she felt heat rising once again to her cheeks. Mercifully, Jim allowed her to reclaim her hands. "Look, I'm just not cut out for the bedroom scene."

"I'm not into one-night stands myself, Rook."

She lowered her lashes, her heart beating hard in her chest. "Well . . . I thought you wanted . . . that is, I mean—"

"Rook, look at me."

She met Jim's unwavering blue eyes.

"I'm not saying things too well, myself. You mean a hell of a lot to me. When we first met, I thought you were the most brazen spitfire I'd ever met, and I liked you for it."

"We had a terrible fight."

Jim smiled slightly, his voice faltering. "Yeah. And when

I brought those flowers over to you and you blushed," he reached over, barely grazing her cheek, "like you are now, I realized you were more than just the tough broad you pretended to be."

"It's not exactly easy working and living in a male-dominated environment," she began defensively.

"I realize that more and more every day, Rook. Being around you has taught me a lot." Jim toyed absently with his glass, staring down at it a long time before he spoke again. His voice came out roughened with emotion when he did. "When you helped rescue my dad over by Thatcher Ridge, something snapped inside me. Too much was going on at the time for me to analyze it properly. And then, when you showed up at the hospital that night . . ."

Jim took a deep breath, holding her wavering stare. Her eyes were like soft, gray diamonds, filled with compassion. "Dammit, I'm not saying this well at all." He placed both hands on the table and said, "I know we got off track with one another the night we made love, but I'm not sorry we did. I want the chance to explore a relationship with you. I'm asking you to think about it.

"Christ, I can't go to sleep at night. All I do is toss and turn and think about you. You're different—unique. Sometimes I feel like a moth flying directly into a flame." Jim slid his hands forward, covering her tightly clenched ones on the table.

"I'm thirty-two years old, Rook. I've been around, and I know the score—at least, I thought I did. You careened into my life and turned it upside down." His hands tightened around hers. "Please, can you give me—give us—a chance?"

His honesty shattered Rook's defenses. "Oh, Jim, I'm not a safe bet."

"Who said I wanted a safe bet?"

Rook begged him with her eyes to remain silent. "I can give you a hundred reasons why this won't work—can't work . . ."

His mouth tightened, more authority in his voice. "Then, you'd better start giving those reasons right now, Rook."

"I'm in the Coast Guard."

"So?"

"They move me from station to station every two to three years."

"We'll cross that bridge when we come to it."

"I put in hellishly long hours."

"So do I. We'll see each other at night, or when you don't have duty. I want to be your friend, too, Rook—your confidante. I want you to be able to lean on me like you did before. I want to lean on you when I need to. We're a team, you and I. We've proven that between us already."

"I don't know that," Rook stated, pulling her hands away from his and tucking them in her lap beneath the tablecloth.

Patience, Jim warned himself. She was getting ready to run. He could see it in every feature of her face. "You will if you give us a chance."

Rook gnawed on her lower lip, her heart beating so hard she wondered if she was going to have a heart attack. "You're macho and I'm a feminist."

"So, we'll both learn to bend to one another. That's what a relationship's all about: compromise. But both people have to want it and be willing to bend, Rook."

"I don't know. . ." She began to rub her temple.

"You won't until you give us a try, Rook."

"You're rich—filthy rich."

"And you come from a poor family. So what? You make decent money in the Coast Guard."

"You could've married a lot of women before you met me. Why didn't you?" Rook challenged.

"Because I knew most of them were after my money, or security, or both," Jim said patiently. "You didn't give a damn about my money. You cared what happened to me, as a person, after my dad got hurt."

Panic set in. Rook grabbed her clutch purse, rising from the table. Rushing past the smiling owners, Rook opened the door. The damned heels—she couldn't run in them! Frustration curdled in her as she hurried as fast as she could into the parking lot. The night was windy and chilly, with a slice of moon peeking from behind the turbulent clouds overhead.

Hearing Jim's heavier footsteps behind her, Rook halted and turned.

Jim halted, breathing hard, his hands open, question in his eyes. "Rook, don't run."

Her breath came in gulps as she stood tensely, as if waiting for a forthcoming attack. "Leave me alone," Rook begged. "I'm not right for you, Jim."

The tears glittered like shards of diamonds in her eyes. Jim heard the anguish in her unsteady voice. He shook his head, slowly approaching her, his hand held out to her. "No, I won't believe that. Too much has happened between us, Rook. There's something there and we both know it." He laid his hand on her slumped shoulder.

Rook trembled as his hand settled on her. Jim was tall, powerful, and so confident about himself and his future. Fighting back tears, she looked up at him, his face contoured in the shadows.

"Talk to me, Rook," he pleaded huskily. "I'll listen—I promise. Just tell me what it is that's making you run from me, and we'll take the hurdle together. Please . . ."

Choking back a sob, she rasped, "I'm afraid, all right?"

Startled, Jim cocked his head, studying her. "Afraid? Of what?"

She tore her gaze from him. "I told you before, I'm not a veteran at this game, Jim. I'm not a virgin, but I sure as hell don't have the experience you have. All my life, I've had to fight for what I wanted. My mother and I moved from one town to another so often, I was never able to make any lasting friends of either sex. I worked summers to make money so we could survive. When I started flying helicopters, the boys didn't want anything to do with me. By the time I got to college, I had a purpose and a goal. For four years I busted my tail to graduate. I took courses during the day and worked until midnight, sometimes one in the morning, at a part-time job to earn the money to pay for my education." Rook's voice steadied. "In those four years, I had exactly two affairs." She grimaced, avoiding the look in his eyes. "Real quick ones that I won't bore you with, because they were one-night stands that I was stupid enough to walk into." Bitterness tinged her tone. "So I took the consequences. Lesson learned."

Jim nodded, allowing his hand to slide off her shoulder. He felt her pain, her vulnerability. "And, since then?"

"Eighteen months learning how to be a damn good Coast Guard helicopter pilot didn't leave me any time to myself." She risked a look at him, some of her anger and fear dissolving. "Eighteen months of pure hell, where you busted your ass on a daily basis, and you weren't sure whether the Navy instructor pilots were going to wash you out one day or the next. No, I didn't have time for a relationship, as you call it."

"I understand."

Rook shook her head, wrapping her arms about herself. "No, you don't. Ever since I can remember, men and I have been at odds with one another." She gestured in the direction of the station. "God knows, I'm having to learn how to get along with them as never before. All my experiences with men, up until recently, have been disappointing or bad, Jim."

He stepped forward, gently cradling her face between his large hands. Her mouth and eyes broadcast her pain, her unsureness. "I can't promise I won't ever hurt you, Rook, because I'm human. But what I can promise is to always be honest with you. We can talk, explore, and find out about one another in many ways. And yes, sharing ourselves in bed can be a part of that, too. We don't have to rush into anything. One of the many things I like about you is your honesty. You don't pull any punches."

Tears blurred her vision and Rook fought them. His hands were calloused and roughened against her face, but they sent a protective, good feeling through her. "I'm not such a hot deal."

"I don't want a hot deal. I want you."

Rook shut her eyes and laid her hands against his arms, suddenly dizzy with fear. "I'm so afraid, Jim," she wobbled.

"So am I," he whispered, leaning over, brushing her parted lips. "Let's be frightened together," and he gently drew Rook to him, kissing her as if she were fragile glass. This woman, who put her life on the line on almost a daily basis, who had nerves like a steel cable behind the stick of a helicopter, was hauntingly human through his heart's eyes.

Rook tried to pull away, tearing her mouth from his.

"No," Jim whispered hoarsely, holding on to her arms. "If you're going to run, run *to* me, not away from me, Rook."

Tears glittered in her eyes. The fear shot up through her, and she struggled.

"Listen to me," Jim ordered, pulling her against him, "you might as well stop fighting me. We're going back to your apartment and hash all of this out—right now."

Miserably, Rook looked away. Without a word, Jim tucked her under his arm and walked her back to the Corvette.

Jim switched on the lamp in the living room of Rook's apartment. He saw her slip off her shoes and sit dejectedly on the couch. Grimly, he joined her, taking her clenched hands out of her lap and holding them.

"I'm going to tell you why you're afraid of me, Rook," he began unevenly. "You care for me, don't you?"

His voice was deep, soothing to her chaotic state. "Y-yes."

"How much?"

"A lot."

"More than any man in your life?"

She nodded, biting her lower lip. "This isn't your fault, Jim. It's mine. I'm treating you the way I was treated. That isn't right." She lifted her eyes, forcing herself to hold his compassionate gaze. "So much has happened in the last month. I-I've tried to figure out why I wanted to leave you."

He gripped her fingers more firmly. "Rook, this is important. In your heart, do you want a long-term relationship with me? Don't listen to your head, just your heart. Please . . ."

The silence throbbed around them. Rook's shoulders fell, and after an agonizing minute, she whispered, "Yes."

Jim wanted to embrace her, but he didn't dare—not yet.

"I feel the same way about you," he began unsteadily, watching her lashes rise, those gray eyes filled with hope instead of fear, as before. "Rook, we can surmount this problem—together."

Giving a jerky nod of her head, Rook rasped, "This is my fault. You never did anything to me. I—it's all from the past."

"I know that. Tell me about these two affairs. I don't need the sordid details, but how did they end up?"

With a little laugh of embarrassment, Rook looked away. "In my senior year of high school I was terribly lonely for some kind of social life. I worked my newspaper route morning and evening in order to bring in extra money for Mom and me to survive on, so I never had time for boys. Then, this guy, Frank Helman, asked me to the senior prom. I'd never had a boyfriend, never been to a dance before, so I accepted."

"Anyone in your shoes would have to want some form of companionship in a situation like that," Jim said, keeping his voice low. How lonely Rook must have really been as a teen-ager girl, forced to grow up long before she should have, and shoulder adult responsibilities.

"Yes." Rook glanced over at him. "To make a miserable story short, I ended up going to the dance. Afterward, Frank took me to a secluded spot outside town." Her voice lowered. "The next morning, it was all over school: Frank had slept with me. He'd made a bet with his friends that he could do it."

"The bastard," Jim hissed. Gently, he forced Rook to sit and face him, his hands remaining on her slumped shoulders. "And the second time?"

"Just as stupid and foolish. I was a junior at college. Same kind of thing: working day and night and every summer. I got lonely. A senior, John Trevor, asked me out. I accepted. Only this time, I got drunk. I wasn't into drugs or the drinking scene. He'd brought along rum and Coke. The next thing I knew, I was back in the attic room where I lived, in this old house not far from the campus. It was over in minutes. John got up and left without a word. When I saw him on campus after that, he just ignored me." Rook closed her eyes, unable to stand the look of suffering on Jim's features. "I felt as if every time I tried to get close to a man, it turned sour—just like the relationship with my father."

Sliding his hand along the line of her jaw, Jim whispered, "Look at me, Rook." As her eyes met and held his, he leaned over, barely brushing her lips, wanting to ease all her pain. Pulling inches away, he framed her face with his hands. "I think you see the pattern that was set up from your past."

It hurt to swallow, and Rook choked out, "Yes . . ." A ragged sigh came from deep within her. "For the last month, I've thought a lot about why I ran from you, why I wrote that note begging you not to contact me."

"When I came along, that wounded part of you wanted nothing to do with me because I was a man. I was capable of abusing you, and then walking away, just like those two jerks did."

For the first time, Rook took the initiative, some of her panic dissolving beneath their searching conversation. She slid her hands up Jim's arms, allowing them to rest on his broad, capable shoulders. "Exactly." There was such undeniable love in Jim's eyes. "After I figured out what I'd done, I thought I'd lost you . . . lost whatever we might have."

"And because of your inexperience with relationships, you didn't know how to approach me or tell me that," Jim guessed, caressing her flushed cheeks with his thumbs. Her skin was incredibly pliant. His breath snagged as she laid her cheek against his palm, an unmistakable sign of trust.

"You mean more to me than any other person in my life, except for Mom and Noah. I-I've never felt like this with anyone before, and that scared the hell out of me, too." Rook closed her eyes as he threaded his fingers through her hair, stroking her as if she were a beautiful woman to be worshiped.

Whispering her name, Jim eased Rook into his arms. She came without a fight, her gray eyes filled with adoration. "It takes courage to admit that," he said huskily, smoothing strands of hair from her cheek, placing them behind her small, delicate ear. "I was waiting—hoping that you'd realize what happened after that night we'd made love. I knew you were running again, Rook, and I was helpless to stop you."

"I know."

"We have something special, Wild Rose—something that sets my heart pounding every time I think of you, talk to you, or touch you. Only you can give us the time we need to explore it—together."

Together. Rook looked into Jim's eyes, and found incredible warmth lingering in them. "This is all so new to me, Jim."

"And you're scared."

"Very."

"So am I." A slight smile tugged at his mouth—a smile of self-deprecation. Rook wasn't ready to admit she loved him, any more than she was ready to hear from him that he loved her.

"Feel like exploring this new territory of our relationship?"

"Yes . . ." Her nerves tingled as Jim kissed her ear, her neck, and then, the base of her throat. Automatically, her fingers curved around his powerful neck. As he kissed her cheek and brushed her lips lightly, she looked into his burning blue eyes.

"This time," Jim murmured, rising to his feet, "we're going to make slow, passionate love with one another. I want to show you how much you mean to me and how beautiful you really are."

Dazed by the catch of his lowered voice, Rook allowed herself to be pulled to her feet. Within seconds, he had picked her up in his arms and walked to her bedroom. As he laid her on the bed and removed each of her shoes, he came and sat down beside her. Rook gave him a look of awe.

"What is it?" he asked, sliding his hands beneath her blazer, easing it off her shoulders.

Rook marveled that he was able to know that she had made a discovery about herself. "The panic's gone. I don't feel it anymore." He set the blazer on the cedar chest at the end of the bed. In the shadowy darkness of the room, Jim's features were rugged-looking, filled with an intense longing that made her pulse leap raggedly.

"That's because you had the courage to stop running from your past and face a much better future." He smiled, kissing her parted lips with great restraint. "A very happy one—with me." The blouse was next, and Jim began to patiently unbutton each button, holding her shimmering gaze while he did so.

Rook's eyes shuttered closed as the blouse fell away, exposing her lacy bra. She felt his fingers trace her neck and shoulders, sliding the material away.

"You're so incredibly beautiful," he quavered, tracing her prominent collarbones, feeling her unfettered reaction to his exploration. "Undressing you is like unfolding layers of petals from a flower..."

A whisper of need rushed from her as the bra was freed. Oddly, Rook felt no shame as she opened her eyes, sitting exposed before Jim. As his calloused hands cupped each of her straining breasts, tremors of heat flooded her, anticipation beginning a slow, throbbing beat through her.

"A flower," Rook murmured unsteadily, her hands coming to rest on his muscular arms. She had missed Jim's way of seeing the world. He saw it in a far less harsh light than she, teaching her how to see beauty, instead of darkness. His eyes were hooded and smoldering with hunger. Just the way he worshiped her breasts, holding them as if they were priceless treasures, she felt what it was like to be loved completely as a woman, not an object to be used and then cast aside.

Jim marveled at the firm, rounded beauty of her breasts. He ached to lean down and taste each of those taut, beckoning nipples. There was time, he reminded himself, gently releasing them. Holding her warm gray eyes, he began to undress before her. First, his shirt came off, exposing his powerful chest. Could she hear the beat of his heart? He felt it pounding through him. Jim was aware of the ache centered below. As he stood up, unbuckling his belt and opening his slacks, he watched Rook intently.

"Tonight," he told her in a deep voice, as he placed the slacks on the cedar chest, "is for us. The last time we came together was for different reasons." He approached Rook, tunneling his fingers through her hair, watching her lashes drop to her fiery cheeks, her lips parting. "We belong together, Rook. You and I," and he cradled the back of her head, guiding her down upon the bright quilt on the double bed.

A sigh of anticipation stole through Rook as she felt Jim loosen her skirt and pull it down the length of her legs. His large hand settled on her hip, then moved slowly, provocatively down her thigh. Each touch, whether firm or feathery, sent prickles of expectation racing through her.

Jim absorbed her glowing features as he brought the half slip downward. And last, her silky panties. The shadowy light caressed Rook's naked form, reminding him once again of her wonderful figure. Moving to her side after he disrobed, he lay above her, his hand cupping her breast. Rook inhaled sharply as he moved his thumb across her taut nipple. Her arms lifted, resting on his shoulders, her eyes dazed with desire.

"My Wild Rose," he whispered, claiming the nipple, drawing it gently into his mouth.

A wild, jagged heat raced through her. Rook moaned, feeling the hot moistness of his mouth closing over her nipple, sucking gently upon it. Mindlessly, she pressed herself to his naked form. Her hip came in contact with his male hardness, sending more shafts of molten fire through her. His rough hand pressed against her spine, following it all the way down, capturing her hips solidly against his own.

"Sweet . . . my God, you're sweet . . ." Jim rasped, sampling the other nipple reverently. She was writhing within his arms, moaning, her fingers alternately digging and restless upon his shoulders. Humbled by Rook's naive response, he felt an overwhelming sense of love toward her. She hadn't allowed the cruelty that men had played upon her to repress her own femininity. As she arched willingly into his arms, it took every bit of control not to take her as he had before.

A gasp of pleasure escaped Rook as she felt his mouth trail a path of building fire down across her belly until finally, his hand slid between her taut thighs, asking her to part them for him. Breath coming in gulps, Rook dug her fingers into the quilt as she felt his tongue explore the most secret parts of her. Her head thrashed from side to side, and a pleading cry tore from her as molten heat built violently within her core, the ache heavy and throbbing.

Give yourself to me, Wild Rose. Trust me enough to give yourself to me. All of you . . . Jim nuzzled her womanly sweetness, teasing her, driving her into a frenzy of mindless wanting. Gripping her hips, he continued his tender assault, drawing the honey from her. Joy flooded him as her back arched like a bow, a ragged cry tearing from her. It was a cry of discovery, coupled with incredible pleasure.

Sobbing for breath, Rook rolled her head to the left as Jim settled back at her side. He was smiling. It went straight through her like blinding sunlight. He licked a trickle of perspiration away from her temple. The fragrance of her body mixed with his male scent intoxicated her, making her want more of him. "I . . . never realized. . . ."

Cradling her cheek, he kissed her ripe, willing mouth. "You've given me the greatest gift a woman can ever give her man," he breathed against her. He saw the confusion in Rook's eyes. "Not every woman experiences a climax, Wild Rose. To a man, it's a wonderful, rare gift."

Weakness was replaced by a building sense of urgency as Jim stroked her breast, teasing the nipple. Her mind had shorted out; thinking was almost impossible. "The first time," she whispered.

He nodded, running his tongue across her full lower lip, tasting her essence, probing into the corners, feeling her unbridled response. "I know," he murmured, realizing Rook was referring to a month ago when they had made love. "And now, this time." Bringing her hip against him, he smiled with pride. "You're as rare as your name, Wild Rose. I only hope I can bring as great a gift through myself to you, because you deserve only the best . . ."

"Love me, Jim . . ." she pleaded, sliding her arms around his corded neck. His body gleamed in the semidarkness, each group of muscles standing at taut attention, sheathing powerfully into the next set. Rook realized how beautiful Jim was as he covered her with his body. His weight was like a trembling, hot blanket, creating urgency within her. She opened her thighs, welcoming him, asking him to meet, meld, and become one with her.

He quivered, trying to hold back the hunger of wanting to plunge into her. Gritting his teeth, Jim held his breath, perspiration standing out on his pained brow. Rook's voice fell over him, bidding him to come to her. Her fingers moved downward from his chest until she came in contact with his narrow, tense hips. He felt her thighs open more and he plunged into her. In those precious seconds after he thrust deep, he watched her, soaking up her expression. Joy vibrated through him. This time, Rook's eyes widened with pleasure, not surprise or pain, as before.

A low, animal groan began deep within him, rumbling up through his chest and out his mouth as she moved her hips against him. The moment was sacred, built upon trust, upon love. Each thrust drew him deeper and deeper into her moist, liquid depths. Gripping the quilt on either side of her head, he strained forward, asking her to reach that incredible pinnacle of pleasure with him.

The rhythm increased, like a storm gathering power before it unleashed all its might. Rook savored Jim in all aspects as she moved with him. They were thunder and lightning, the life-giving rain the liquid they shared between their bodies. Each stroke brought her higher, closer to the blinding brilliance of the sun once again. She reveled in his sheer beauty, his masculinity, and surrendered herself to him, feeling the second explosion unfold like a swiftly moving storm within her.

Gripping her hip, Jim groaned, her cry spurring him on, prolonging the sensation for her. At the peak of her cry, his own release came and he tensed, frozen against her wet, giving form. Seconds spun into a world of fiery reward and gratification, his eyes shut tightly, savoring their burning union, their fulfilled promise to one another.

With a groan, Jim rested his head next to hers, breathing hard. He didn't want to hurt Rook with his weight so he moved off her and onto his side. Slipping his hand around her hips, he brought her back into his arms, her head resting weakly against his sweaty chest.

Rook could do nothing but gulp in breaths of air. She was too weak to move, much less speak. Jim was warm and strong and sleek where she ran her fingers down across his waist and hip. The hair of his chest was like a wiry pillow beneath her cheek. Nuzzling him, she kissed him, inhaling his wonderful male scent.

Jim lay on his side, the woman he loved in his arms. Words were useless for what he felt as he stroked her hair, feeling the silky strands flow through his fingers. After several minutes he spoke, his voice hoarse.

"We've crossed the last hurdle, Rook. Together..."

She nodded, sighing softly, feeling cherished beneath his stroking hands.

"Scared?"

Barely opening her lashes, Rook looked upward, meeting, melting beneath Jim's tender gaze. "Not anymore."

Whispering her name, Jim leaned down, placing a kiss on her lips. Time was on their side now. One day, he would hear her say, "I love you." One day...

CHAPTER

Eighteen

"SHERIFF Cole?" Ward stood stiffly in the sheriff's office. Cole, a gray-haired man of fifty-five, with pale blue eyes and a thin mouth, rose.

"Yes. You must be Captain Stuart." He extended his hand.

Ward shook it. Inside, he was shaking with humiliation and anger. This time, Kenny had done it. "I understand my son's here."

Cole gestured to a chair. "Yes. Sit down, Captain." He drew out the arrest report. "For over a year, we've suspected that there was a coke ring among the students of Danvers High School. With the aid of the Drug Task Force, we planted an agent who assumed the role of a senior in that school. She set herself up to buy coke and, over the last six months, has been able to identify everyone in the ring." Cole pushed the report toward Stuart. "We busted the ring today. Your son wasn't a dealer, but he was caught buying from the agent."

Great, Ward thought. That was Kenny's luck. "And the charges against him?"

"Possession of coke, Captain." Cole gave the Coast Guard captain a measured look. "When we ran a check on him, we found out this isn't his first offense."

"No," Ward answered heavily, "it isn't." He quickly read

the police report. The drug bust had gone down minutes after Kenny had bought the coke. Christ, what bad luck.

"Your son has a drug problem." Cole said it matter-of-factly.

Ward stared down at the report. "I could never prove it, Sheriff."

"Most parents don't want to," the sheriff said gently.

Stuart was on his feet. "Are you implying that I didn't care if my son was on drugs or not?"

"Take it easy, Captain. Sit back down." He saw the flash of anger in the officer's eyes and added, "look, I'm aware of your stature in this town and the surrounding area. And because of that, I'm going to do everything possible to help your son. But one thing you have to promise is that you'll send him to a rehab clinic in Seattle and get him cleaned up. Once he does that and comes back home, then I'll expect you to deal with the situation."

Relief flowed through Ward. He closed his eyes momentarily and then looked at Cole. "That's more than fair, Sheriff. Thank you."

With a nod, Cole stood. "Your son's in solitary. I don't like putting juveniles in the jail. Talk to him. When you get done, come back to see me and we'll get the paperwork started. In the meantime, I'll have one of my deputies contact the rehab clinic."

Kenny's head snapped up, his eyes widening when the door opened briefly and his father walked in. He slumped back against the wall, one foot drawn up on the wafer-thin mattress of the bunk. Bracing himself, he muttered, "I fucked up, okay?"

Ward stood there, staring down at him. Memories of Kenny when he was born, when he was seven, ten, and thirteen flashed through his spinning mind. Where had he gone wrong with him? How could he efficiently run a base of two hundred and fifty divergent people and yet be unable to raise his son properly? Shattering layers of anger, hurt, and betrayal simmered through him. More than ever before,

Ward knew he had to handle this properly. He had to think, not feel, where Kenny was concerned. He had to treat him with impartiality, like he did his people at the base, without allowing his emotions to get in the way of his judgment. He leaned against the door, his arms at his side.

"The deed's done," Ward began quietly. "What remains is to pick up what's left."

Kenny glared up at him, steeling himself for his father to erupt at him. "They caught me red-handed, so there are no pieces up in the air. Are they gonna send me to juvie hall?"

"Is that where you want to go?"

"Hell, no! In six months I'll be eighteen, and I won't have to put up with all this shit."

Holding on to his anger, Ward said, "What do you want out of life, Kenny?"

"First of all," he snapped, "I hate being called Kenny! You've called me that since I was a baby. Everyone at school calls me Ken."

"All right, Ken, you tell me what you want out of all this."

His eyes rounded at his father. "What new psyche game are you laying on me this time? I know you're pissed off as hell. Go on, start yelling and screaming at me like you always do."

"Is that what you want?"

"It's just a matter of time," he growled, slumping even further down on the bunk, pouting.

Stuart shrugged. "I'm not going to waste my breath on you, son, if you don't care enough to talk with me."

"This is just too outrageous. My old man suddenly wants to be nice to me. What happened, Father? Is the bad old sheriff gonna lay the big one on me? Will this one sandbag your precious career, once and for all? I can see the headline now: SKIPPER'S SON ARRESTED ON DRUG CHARGES. Wait until your Seattle head honcho reads that." Kenny slapped his hands together, the sound cracking through the chilled room. "Bam! Torpedoed by your useless son. Outrageous."

Ward stared down at Kenny. He knotted his fists. "Right

now, I don't give a damn about my career. It's you I'm concerned about," he gritted out.

"Sure you are. I'll bet you're trying to figure out different ways to talk the editor out of printing anything about my infamous arrest."

"You're going to a rehab clinic in Seattle, Ken. I'm signing papers tonight that will send you down there to clean you up from the coke you've been sniffing."

Kenny was off the bunk in a second, screaming, "No! I'm not an addict! I don't have a problem!"

Tensing, Ward got ready in case his son attacked him. Kenny's face turned purple, his eyes wild and vacant. My God, how could he have been blind this past year to his problem? How could he have missed it? The answer was easy: Ward was rarely home to notice these changes in Ken, or to lend Marcia assistance with their son. She wasn't to blame for this, he was.

"We've got a problem!" Ward roared at him.

Kenny staggered back a step, shaken by his father's unexpected action. It took a few seconds to regroup from the shock. His lips lifted away from his teeth. "Forget it! This is just your way of getting rid of me. You've wanted me out of that house and out of your life for the last couple of years. Ever since you made captain, you've walked on eggs. I had to live the life of a goddamn choirboy. Well, forget it! I am who I am! And if you think that rehab outfit is gonna do anything for me—"

Ward advanced on him. He grabbed Kenny by the collar of his damp, sweaty shirt and slammed him up against the wall. He heard the air knocked out of his son's lungs as he pinned him. "Now, you listen to me," Ward breathed hoarsely in Kenny's face. "Coke is *your* problem. Until you turn eighteen and are of legal age, this is *our* problem. Your mother and I will do everything in our power to help you, Ken. But if you don't want help, there's nothing we can do to push it on you."

Releasing his son, Ward held his petulant glare. "Now, you sit in here until you can figure out whether you want our help or not. When the sheriff comes to get you, I'll be waiting outside. At that time, you give me your answer. Understand?"

Kenny slowly pushed himself away from his father. In all his years, Ward had never physically touched him. Shaken, he stared at him mutinously. "Forget it. You stopped giving your help a long time ago. Don't start playing concerned parent now. It's too late."

Pain of incredible magnitude moved through Ward. He could taste bile in his mouth. "Okay, if that's the way you want it—"

"That's the way it's going down. I'm not some poor slob who needs rescuing, so just forget about me. I'll be in Seattle having a great time."

Ward halted at the door, weight pushing downward on him. "We'll be in touch, Ken," he rasped.

CHAPTER

Nineteen

RENO didn't say anything when he walked into the Logan residence. The September morning was pleasantly warm, and already the blue summer uniform he was wearing was beginning to cling to him. For the last week, Reno had picked Gil up because his car was in for repair. Reno thought that marriage was the pits, and was glad to be free of any serious entanglements. Divorce had sure played hell on Logan, and it was something he never wanted to experience personally himself.

"Gil?" The words echoed down the hall. Usually, he'd find Gil in the kitchen, reading the morning edition of the *Star*, coffee in hand.

"In here," Gil said, indicating he was in the bedroom.

Reno sauntered through the kitchen. The place was a disaster. Eve had moved out, leasing a townhouse in Port Angeles. Logan had struggled in vain to keep the house clean. Stacks of clean dishes were piled on the counter around the sink.

"You about ready?" Reno asked, halting at the bedroom door. Logan was retrieving a clean flight suit from a drawer and folding it up. They had SAR duty for the next twenty-four hours. Lucky them. It was Labor Day, one of the biggest tourist holidays up here in Port Angeles, and he'd gotten stuck with duty. Reno had wanted the day off to go to Victoria, like everyone else, for the festivities. The women over in British Columbia were some of the prettiest he'd ever seen, and he wanted to sample them, like ripe plums. Usually, Reno would hitch a ride on the *Flyer*, the ferry that operated between Port Angeles and Victoria. It was a one and a half hour trip across the straits. Even the ride on the *Flyer* gave him ample opportunity to appreciate good-looking women. Tourists swamped Port Angeles, which sat at the base of the Olympic National Park. Many of them crowded onto the ferry, motor homes and all, to camp up in the splendor of British Columbia's forests. This year, it wasn't in the cards for him to have the day off.

Gil walked back to the kitchen, throwing the newspaper down on the table with disgust. He slugged down the last of a cold cup of coffee and then jabbed a finger at the *Star*. "Did you see the social section yet?" he growled.

"No." That was dangerous territory to tread as far as Reno was concerned. Of late, with the divorce settlement negotiations going on strong and heatedly, Gil was a bear. Reno had no desire to step into that messy quagmire of discussion with him.

Shutting off the kitchen light, Gil muttered, "Eve's doing a real hatchet job on the C.O.'s son."

"I thought Ken was at the rehab clinic in Seattle?"

"I guess the kid's getting out today, and is supposed to come home." Anger burned in Logan's eyes. "You'd think Eve would have the common decency *not* to say anything about it. Stuart and his family have suffered enough bad press over this." Gil picked up his flight suit and attaché case and headed toward the rear door. "Eve always did like gossip. Now, she's in hog heaven."

Reno couldn't agree more. "Sure looks like she's got it in for us Coasties."

"Did you see her column yesterday? It was devoted exclusively to Rook and her boyfriend, Jim Barton. Christ, what an embarrassment. If I were Rook, I'd sue Eve and that goddamn rag of a paper."

Reno went down the steps and walked over to his dark blue Camaro, opening the door. "How did she take that column?"

"Not very well. I caught her just as she was coming out of the head. She looked like she'd been crying."

Settling in the car and strapping on the seat belt, Gil glowered out the window, immune to the apricot sunrise and the beauty of the mountains on one side, and the calm waters of the straits on the other. "Eve's been needling Rook ever since she got that job on the paper and moved out of the house. She always thought there was something between Rook and me. There wasn't."

Reno smiled and backed the car out of the driveway. "My friend, in my vast experience, I've found that some women are just naturally jealous little minxes."

"Eve excels at it."

"Rook doesn't need that kind of pressure on her."

"No one does," Gil said. "Can you imagine accusing Rook of chasing Barton for his money?"

Glumly, Reno shook his head. "Rook's in a unique position. It's part of paying her dues, I guess."

With a shake of his head Gil said, "Another one paying a lot of unfair dues is Captain Stuart. Seattle District must be having cardiac arrests with the kind of trash in the paper. You know Admiral Savage doesn't like this kind of tawdry press. It could hurt his chances to become the next commandant."

Reno agreed. "Well, I'd say Stuart is on the razor's edge."

Ward's gut tightened when the phone rang at ten o'clock. Marcia was sitting across from him at the kitchen table, her face drawn. They planned to leave in fifteen minutes to pick up Kenny from the bus station. They both wondered if the time in rehab had helped their son. Once a week, Ward and Marcia had driven down to visit Ken. And, every week, Ken had become more withdrawn from them, until six days ago, Ward no longer recognized his son. The rehab clinic, in Ward's opinion, had only made Ken more embittered and angry.

"Captain Stuart speaking."

"This is Admiral Savage's office calling, Captain. One moment while I connect you."

Ward slid a glance to Marcia. "It's Savage," he whispered, placing his hand over the phone.

"Oh, no . . ." Marcia got up, worry in her eyes. Even though the morning was warm and the breeze off the straits wafted through the open doors of the house, she was suddenly cold. The last two months had been hard on everyone, but especially on Ward. He was a man of immense pride, and she had watched the newspaper attack over Kenny's rehab cut him to the bone. The guilt Ward carried was beginning to give him an ulcer. As a military wife, she knew that an admiral calling on a holiday spelled trouble. Just what kind, she'd find out shortly. That was all Ward needed, on top of Ken's return home today.

"Admiral?"

"Good morning, Ward. I'm glad I caught you at home. We've got a problem that I've been trying to politely ignore for some time now, but I'm afraid this can't go on any longer."

Ward sat stiffly, a sinking sensation moving through him. "What problem is that, sir?" He knew without asking. Why fool himself?

Clearing his throat, Savage said briskly, "The *Port Angeles Star* has run a number of highly embarrassing articles about your problems with your son, Kenny. Unfortunately, these articles have reached Washington, and they're not happy. Now, I'm sure you're as upset about this as we are, and I would like to suggest a few steps to be taken to counteract the bad publicity."

"What kind of steps, sir?" Ward had images of Savage discreetly removing him from command and "hiding" him in some shit job where he could finish out his career—out of sight, out of mind. That was how that political game was played.

Ward pulled the note pad toward him, prepared to write.

"The suggestions are Lieutenant Commander Malone's. He feels a positive publicity campaign is needed by the Coast Guard. I'm aware of your involvement with local organizations, but this would be a good time to increase that involvement. Set up a speaker's bureau, and give talks at ladies clubs, luncheons, and other such events. *Show* the people of Port Angeles that the Coast Guard cares. Invite the public onto the base for an open house. I've already talked to our Canadian SAR contingent, and they're willing to bring some of their helicopters, cutters, and other equipment down for such an event. We can promote good feelings with the Canadians and the public simultaneously." Savage sounded rather pleased with himself. "Lastly, Malone said you needed some more national headlines. That whale shooting buried us, even though your people were proven innocent. Malone says to try and produce an event or idea that will *make* the wire services want to pick it up and run it."

Ward almost laughed. What did Savage want—a multiple disaster where the Coasties went zooming in like the good guys to the rescue? "Yes, sir, I'll follow your recommendations immediately. And I'll try to think of something the wire services would want to carry."

"Excellent! Excellent. We'll be looking forward to some positive articles on you and your people from the *Star* soon, then."

I'll bet you will. Ward was sure Savage had his assistants combing the *Star* daily. His career was sandbagged. All he could do was poke his fingers into the dike and try to stop the most serious leaks.

"Ward? It's time to leave for the bus depot," Marcia said gently, coming over and standing behind her husband. She rested her hands on his shoulders. "You can tell me on the way over what the admiral had to say."

The *Flyer* sat at dockside, ready for the seven o'clock trip to Victoria. Captain Roland York, a rotund man of sixty-six, studied the traffic waiting on the wharf. His experienced eye took in the trucks, motor homes, campers, and people waiting patiently below. They'd have a maximum load: three hundred people and one hundred autos and trucks. Turning, York was pleased that the straits were calm this morning. It was a cloudless, sunny day, one of the few that the Olympic Peninsula enjoyed.

Having lived fifty years in Port Angeles, York absently perused the waiting line of people. He spotted a couple of individuals from the Coast Guard base, dressed in civilian clothes, among them. And there was that gossip columnist from the *Star*, Eve Logan, with her inseparable companion, Julia Edwards. His white brows drew downward. What did those two biddies want? They never crossed to Victoria. Now, Jim Barton and his girlfriend, Rook Caldwell, were another thing. He often saw them come over on a Friday night and take the ferry back from Victoria on a Sunday afternoon. He didn't blame them for escaping from Port Angeles to pursue their private lives with one another—especially after all the sticky press they'd received from those two gossips at the *Star*.

York rubbed his belly. *That's it,* he thought, *Logan and Edwards are following Barton and his girlfriend.* With a snort of disgust, he turned around to Craig Green, his helmsman.

"Ask Tony to get up here," he ordered.

"Yes, sir."

The first mate, Tony Knox, appeared a few minutes later. Opening the glass-and-oak door, he handed his skipper some official-looking papers.

"We've got two trucks boarding with hazardous material. One is carrying swimming pool chemicals—HTH—and drums of brake fluid oil. The second is a fuel oil tanker. There's also a truck carrying scrap copper, but that doesn't pose any problem."

"Chlorine and fuel oil on board, eh?" York asked. Hazardous materials weren't to be transported unless declared before they reached Canadian customs in Victoria.

"Yes, sir." Tony pointed to the bill of lading. "Inert. He's carrying thirty-pound canisters of HTH in dry form. I've placed all three trucks together up at the front of the bow. They'll be the first off."

York put on his wire-rim glasses, studied the paper closely, and then grunted his approval. "Five hundred canisters of HTH?" And then he smiled. "You wouldn't think any fool would own a swimming pool over in Canada, would you?"

Tony's long face broke into a grin. "There are a lot of rich Canadian retirees over there, Skipper. *A lot*. They can all afford pools, even if they can only use them three months out of the year."

York agreed, flipping through the rest of the papers. Satisfied that customs wasn't going to give him heartburn over what was being transported, he said, "Let them board, Mr. Knox."

"What's that smell?" Jim leaned over, sniffing Rook's hair, as they waited to board the ferry. Rook had let it grow the past few months and it was curling around her face, making her just that much more feminine in his eyes. She gave him a dirty look, but her mouth pulled into a smile.

"What? God, Jim, quit acting like a bloodhound on a scent. What's the matter with you?" Rook laughed, slipping her arm around his waist and hugging him as they began to walk up the ramp that would lead them to the upper deck of the ferry.

"Perfume. You're wearing perfume, aren't you?" They followed the foot traffic across the boarding ramp of the *Flyer*. Below them, vehicles of all makes, sizes, and descriptions were beginning to load quickly and efficiently, thanks to the hard-working crew of the *Flyer*.

"I thought I'd try some," Rook muttered self-consciously.

Jim gripped her hand and they walked through the open hatch. Pointing to one of the large red vinyl booths, he said, "let's grab this one."

Rook agreed. The ferry was going to be crowded, but that was typical on holidays and weekends. She tolerated the sardine feeling because once they were over in Victoria, away from prying eyes, they were free to enjoy themselves. Jim sat down and Rook settled next to him, content with his arm around her shoulders.

"I like the perfume," Jim told her, meeting her glance. "It becomes you."

Rook wondered if she'd ever stop blushing. In the last few months, Jim had brought out a side in her she never realized existed—a softer side. He had taught her not to be afraid, but to reach out and be all of herself. Rook slid her hand down his powerful, curved thigh, the denim a delightful texture beneath her fingertips. "It's Giorgio. I bought a bottle last time we were in Victoria. Remember?"

Jim nodded, relaxing as he absently watched the crowds of vacationers, tourists, and locals from Port Angeles walk past them to find seats. "Even shopping is fun with you."

Rook jabbed him playfully in the ribs. "I don't buy that much, Jim Barton, and you know it."

"Just sexy, beautiful things that drive me crazy, that's all . . ."

A shiver of expectation feathered through Rook when he lowered his voice. He made her feel womanly, sensual. "Stop that."

Jim studied Rook's tilted face, from her sparkling gray eyes to the curve of her lush lips. Wanting to lean over and kiss her, but not daring to, Jim embraced her, instead. "Stop what?"

"You know what, Barton. You're such a terrible tease."

"I thought only women got blamed for doing that."

"I thought so, too, until I met you."

"But you like the way I tease you," Jim whispered against her ear.

Rook colored fiercely. The ferry was filling up rapidly. "If you don't quit . . ."

"You'll do what?" Jim lightly kissed her clean, apricot-scented hair. Rook looked incredibly appealing to him in a loose-knit cranberry tank top and white cotton slacks. She wore a bright pink silk scarf that was the same color as her cheeks right now. The sandals were delicate on her small, but oh-so-perfect feet. He sighed dramatically, sliding down a bit more in the seat, content. When Rook didn't answer him, he glanced over at her. She was smiling, and if he was any judge of her feelings, very happy.

"You know," Jim confided to her quietly, "I can't ever recall being this happy. Can you?"

Rook shook her head, languishing in the warmth of the sunshine that came through the huge windows around the upper deck of the *Flyer*. "No."

"Kinda nice, huh?"

"The best."

Jim met and held her warm gaze. He ached to kiss Rook, to feel the sleek, soft warmth of her body against his. She was such a passionate, giving woman. "Kinda glad you took that fearful step and decided to let our relationship develop?"

"Now, yes." Rook ran her fingers through Jim's thick brown hair. In the sunlight, his hair picked up reddish highlights. There wasn't anything not to love about him. Rook frowned. Love... There was that word again. She wasn't sure what real love was, and it was too soon to say that was what they felt for one another. Time...they had time, and Rook was satisfied to let all these new feelings Jim was effortlessly bringing to the surface blossom naturally. Rook didn't want to put words on what she felt toward him, or what he felt toward her.

She grew thoughtful as she leaned against him. Sometimes, especially after they had made love, she would see an indecipherable emotion linger in his dark-blue eyes. Rook had the intense feeling that Jim wanted to tell her he loved her, but didn't because he knew she still might run from him.

Jim sighed and smiled. "Just think, we've got a whole two days to ourselves."

"Where are we going today?"

"A special place for a special lady."

She smiled. "Where?"

He raised his eyebrows in mock horror. "And spoil the surprise?"

"Jim!"

Grinning, he murmured, "How can I keep a secret from you when you give me that sexy look of yours?"

Rook had never thought of herself as sexy—until lately. "Well?"

"Okay, I've got us a room at the Empress Hotel. She's the grande old dame of buildings in Victoria. We'll have an elegant, typically English room with more antiques than you can shake a stick at—and their restaurant is excellent." Jim reached over, caressing her cheek. "At four today, we'll have high tea in the lobby. It's a very proper, English thing to do, you know."

Delighted, Rook sat up. They had often walked by the huge stone edifice that greeted everyone when the *Flyer* pulled into the docks of Victoria. Rook leaned over, giving him a quick kiss on his curved mouth. Jim smelled so male, so wonderfully inviting. She had to control herself. This wasn't the place to show too much affection. Rook was jumpy about Eve Logan possibly writing another embarrassing column on her. "Wonderful," she whispered.

Jim patted her thigh. "We're going to have the best two days of our lives," he promised her huskily. "We're celebrating our ten-week anniversary."

Rook's laughter pealed through the aft section of the ferry. "You're crazy, Jim Barton! But I like you anyway."

"That's good to know," he gloated, matching her smile.

Eve sat with Julia, scrunched down in her vinyl booth seat at the rear of the ferry. From her vantage point, she could easily watch Jim Barton and Rook Caldwell.

"Juicy," Julia whispered to her. "She's all over him."

Eve diligently wrote her notes. "Wouldn't you be, too, if he was worth that much money?"

"You bet, sweetie," Julia laughed.

Excitedly, keeping her voice purposely low, Eve said, "This was a great idea, Julia. Who would have thought to follow them to Victoria? This will make our editor *very* happy."

"Just don't forget to take some discreet photos every now and then."

"Don't worry, I won't." Eve raised her head, scanning the

crowd of passengers who were now settling into the rows of booths and seats. There just might be another story here, Eve decided. Three long blasts on the ferry horn announced that they were now underway. Soon, they'd be leaving the deep-water bay, chugging past Ediz Hook, where the Coast Guard station sat, and moving out into the open waters of the straits. Eve spied two other Coasties.

"Psst!"

"What?" Julia sat up, alert.

"Look, over there! There's Annie Locke. If I remember correctly, I think that's Dave Harper with her."

Julia craned her neck in that general direction. "Isn't Locke the one who had major dental surgery about six weeks ago?"

Eve snickered. "Yeah. Gil told me they used to call her Bucky Beaver over at the hangar. I talked to Jody Theron the other day about Annie. Her surgery was *very* successful—that Harper guy is a hunk."

"No kidding. Wish I was in my twenties again," Julia commented. "I wouldn't mind making a play for Harper myself. You know, Annie looks pretty good. I thought you said she was homely."

"She was, believe me!" Eve pushed up a bit more in the seat, using the back of the booth and her legs to steady her as she stared across the way at Annie. She sat back down. "She's hardly homely anymore." Eve wrote some more notes. "Her jaw was broken and reset. I guess she has to wear braces for the next year or so, but that's all."

Julia watched Annie Locke, who was on the port side, and quite a few booths in front of them. "She'll never be beautiful."

"No, but at least she isn't ugly anymore. This is great. We've got two couples to watch. This trip is turning out to be fantastic!"

"I have a feeling it's going to be a great one," Julia agreed, patting herself on the back for the idea in the first place.

"Where the hell is he?" Ward barely ground out the words from between his clenched teeth. Marcia stood at his side, just inside the bus terminal. All the passengers on the bus from Seattle had disembarked and were now leaving the small station.

"Oh, Ward, what do you think happened?"

Stuart headed in the direction of the phone in the stationmaster's office. "I don't know, but we're going to find out."

Marcia stood off to one side, listening, as Ward talked on the telephone with the rehab clinic. The man he spoke to told him that the clinic driver had put Ken on the bus and left the station before it had pulled out for Port Angeles. As far as they knew, Ken had been on board.

Marcia followed Ward outside. The July morning was warm, the sun taking away the chill she felt. She saw the worry and anger in her husband's face. Marcia voiced what he was thinking. "Do you think he slipped off the bus after the rehab people left and stayed in Seattle?"

"I don't know," Ward began irritably. "That goddamn kid! He's causing us so much pain and embarrassment!"

Gripping Ward's arm, Marcia wisely led him away from the terminal and any ears that might overhear them speaking. As they walked toward their car she said, "Let's call Sheriff Cole. He said if we needed help to contact him."

Ward rubbed his chest angrily. "I'm not dragging the damn sheriff into this, Marcia! Jesus Christ, my career is hanging by threads now. The sheriff has to log in all complaints. Once he does, they're public information. The goddamn *Star* would have a field day, and so would Savage."

"Well, what are you going to do?"

He turned to her, his brown eyes burning with anger. "I'm going to give Paul Beirne a call, over at District Legal. He'll keep this quiet." Ward drew in a shaky breath. He and Beirne had flown fixed-wing aircraft up in Alaska together. Their friendship spanned decades. "I'll ask him to do some unofficial checking with local authorities to see if we can track Ken down."

CHAPTER

Twenty

KENNY braced himself as the ferry moved out into the straits. The behemoth rocked unsteadily through the four-foot waves as he walked between the rows of cars and trucks on the lower deck. Good, everyone had gone topside, to look out the huge glass windows that enclosed the upper deck.

He smiled and stopped in front of a truck with a tarpaulin over the rear, weaving unsteadily. He could feel the high that the coke had given him slowly beginning to fade. He could climb in there, smoke a couple of joints, take a nap, and wake up refreshed in Victoria. Kenny had spotted a couple of Coasties on board the ferry and didn't want them to identify him, so he had decided to stay below.

Kenny climbed into the rear of the truck. It was dark, except for a bit of light between the tarp that hung over the rear and cargo compartment. He looked around. Gathering up some loose cardboard and one of several gunny sacks, he created a makeshift bed for himself and lay down. He had already used up his supply of coke between Seattle and Port Angeles. All that was left were a couple of joints of marijuana. Rolling the first joint with a good, thick portion of grass within the paper, Kenny struck a match and lit it. Inhaling deeply, he held the smoke in his lungs for as long as he could, letting the marijuana work its magic.

God, he was tired. After hitching four different rides to get to Port Angeles, he was beat. Kenny sucked contentedly on the joint until it burned down to his fingers. He dropped it on the wooden floor beside him and rolled another. The first one had ironed out all the kinks in his body. He was hungry, but that could wait. Grinning, Kenny settled back. Wouldn't his old man shit if he found out he'd robbed a liquor store in Seattle before hitching his way to Port Angeles, and that the first thing he'd done with his money was buy drugs? He patted the bulge of bills in his pocket contentedly.

The second one relaxed him to the point of sleep. His hand slipped off his chest, the half-smoked joint dangling loosely between his fingers. Closing his eyes, Kenny sighed deeply. He'd get off in Victoria, show his driver's license to the unsuspecting Canadian customs agents, and he'd be free —free of his old man, free of a school he hated, and free of people trying to tell him what to do. He'd live in Canada, get a job, and become a nameless American. No, no one was going to tell him what to do, ever again . . .

The joint slipped from between his fingers as he fell asleep. The motion of the waves made the glowing tip roll into a stack of loosely tied burlap bags. First one thread, and then another, smoldered. The burlap was dry and old; the smoke rose in thin wisps. The ferry continued to rock, moving the glowing tip back and forth in the stack of bags. Soon, the threads had enough oxygen to catch on fire.

Burlap is like sawdust; it burns hot and deep. Smoke rose in the upper portion of the eighteen-wheeler, then descended like a heavy white blanket, trapped within the confines of the truck cavity by the tarp. Kenny, who was in a deep, exhausted sleep, breathed it in. Suddenly, small tongues of flame, reaching for oxygen that slipped between the tarp and the rear of the vehicle, leaped upward. The flame moved slowly from the twine around the burlap down toward the rear, to the tarp.

A thick cotton cord, nearly an inch in circumference, lay by the opening. The flames greedily ate into the cotton, moving silently up the rope. The instant the flame came in contact with the fresh air, it leaped hungrily to the tarp itself. Within minutes, the tarp caught on fire, followed by the smoldering pile of burlap. Kenny awoke, coughing violently. He felt heat; his skin pricked. Disoriented, still floating in a cloud of drug-induced euphoria and exhaustion, he couldn't move fast enough to save himself.

The burlap exploded into a wall of flame that completely enveloped the entire rear of the truck. The cardboard containers carrying the powdered chlorine quickly burned. As the white crystals spilled out, mixing with the flames and heat, yellowish green clouds of smoke began pouring from the rear of the truck. The heat rose quickly—first a thousand degrees Fahrenheit, and then fifteen hundred. When it reached two thousand degrees, the brake fluid barrel lids starting popping off. The hydrocarbon fumes from the brake fluid mixed with the oxidizing agents contained in the chlorine. The five canisters in the first row exploded like a chain of firecrackers.

Ward's beeper went off just after he arrived at the house. Already upset over Ken's disappearance, he jerked the device from his shirt pocket. Marcia rolled her eyes, wondering what had gone wrong now.

"This is Captain Stuart, Chief McDonald. What's going on?"

"Sir, we've just gotten a mayday call from the *Flyer*," he gulped. "There's been a chain of explosions on the lower parking deck and the ferry is in trouble. She's got three hundred people on board."

"My God," Ward whispered. Suddenly, his mind went into overdrive. He steadied his voice, hearing the panic in McDonald's. Both realized the implications of this disaster.

"All right, Chief, get all available resources underway and start an immediate recall of all base personnel. I'll be there," he glanced down at his watch, "in fifteen minutes."

Relief came through McDonald's voice. "Yes, sir!"

Ward turned to Marcia. "The *Flyer*'s on fire out in the straits. There are three hundred people on board."

"Oh, my God," she whispered. "Oh, Ward . . ."

He kissed her quickly, running toward the back door to the garage. As he drove down toward Port Angeles, he could see the *Flyer*, no more than five miles off Ediz Hook. Huge, rolling, yellow-green clouds were mixing with black, oily smoke. Green smoke? What the hell could that be? And then he remembered Jody Theron telling him on Friday afternoon that Rook Caldwell was supposed to be on that ferry. So were Annie and her new boyfriend, Harper. He cursed softly, stepping on the accelerator. In the history of the Coast Guard, there had been only one other rescue this large that he knew of—the *Prinsendam*. Ward's head spun with possibilities, probabilities, and reality. How many ships did he have available to him? How many helos? The water was cold; anyone who jumped overboard would not live any longer than about an hour in the straits, even in the summer. That meant any rescue he attempted to mount had to be swift and orderly, and would require a lot of manpower, which was at a minimum today because it was a holiday.

The moment Ward entered the Admin building, he began to issue orders. Chief McDonald's bearded face was pale, his eyes large, as he waited for Ward's assistance.

"Have you hit all SAR alarms, Chief?" That would bring all available air and ship crews back to their specific areas so that they could prepare for the SAR case.

"Yes, sir! The ready helo is preparing to launch right now. Lieutenant Logan is the air commander, and Mr. Gunnison his copilot."

Good, Ward thought, *I've got one of my best pilots here already.* "Ready the 41-foot UTB and the patrolling 82-footer."

"The *Point Countess* just came in from patrol, sir."

"Excellent. Locate Commander Nelson, and have him hightail it over to the *Countess*. Then, send the cutter to the ferry immediately. Nelson will be the on-scene commander."

"What if I can't locate Commander Nelson, sir?"

"Then have Lieutenant Caldwell be the OSC. We can't waste time waiting for Nelson if we can't locate him fast enough."

"Yes, sir."

"Have you alerted every SAR facility in the entire area?" District Seattle's SAR Coordination Center would take charge of the overall case and direct resources from the U.S. Coast Guard and Navy, and their Canadian counterparts. Ward saw the chief nod. His mind raced. Could he get civilian tugs and other vessels docked here in Port Angeles to help evacuate passengers under his direction?

"Link me to the *Flyer,* Chief. I want to talk with the captain."

"Yes, sir."

Noah Caldwell had been on the *Point Countess's* bridge when the first of three distinct explosions had boomed, like heavy artillery being fired at a very close range, from the vicinity of the straits. His eardrums ached. Standing there, Noah felt a fist squeeze his heart. It was the *Flyer* that was in trouble. Yellow and black smoke spewed out of the bow area of the ferry. And then, terror drenched his shock. Rook and Jim were aboard! He'd had dinner with them the night before over at Jim's house and they'd tried to talk him into going to Victoria with them today. Noah had had to decline because he was on duty. And Harper, his first mate, was on board, too. It was Dave's first date with Annie Locke, and they were going to spend the day over in the Canadian city.

Turning, Noah hit the intercom switch that would connect him to the engine room and his machinery technician, Mike Sitka.

"Crank up the engines, Mike," he shouted, his voice terribly off key. "The *Flyer's* dead in the water. She's on fire." Luckily, the rest of his crew was on base, showing some visitors around the facility. He had them recalled to the *Countess* immediately. Without changing stride, Noah picked up the radio and called the communications center on base to apprise them that the *Point Countess* was prepared to cast off within the next ten minutes to help in the rescue of the ferry. Captain Stuart gave his approval. Commander Nelson couldn't be located, so Noah became the OSC.

Rook! Noah screamed silently. *Rook, are you all right?* Tears wedged into his eyes. *Dammit, I just found her! You can't take her from me! You can't . . .*

Jim Barton smelled the chlorine first. He sat up in the booth, suddenly alert. Rook had been dozing, head resting against his shoulder. She roused herself.

"Jim, what's the matter?" she asked sleepily.

He gripped Rook's shoulder firmly, taking another sniff of the air. "I don't know. Something's wrong. That smell . . . I know it, but I can't identify it . . ."

Alarm spread through Rook. She'd never seen Jim so worried. The planes of his face had grown tense, and his mouth had thinned. She sniffed the air. "Yes . . . I smell it, too." She glanced around. Apparently no one else had, but she knew Jim had an incredibly sensitive nose. Everyone else was laughing or talking quietly; there was an air of anxious excitement in the upper deck of the ferry. A number of children raced between the clumps of booths and chairs, playing happily. A baby cried somewhere up front, near the bow.

He rose, pulling her up with him. "Come on, let's go investigate."

Rook tried to still her alarm. "What do you think is wrong?"

Jim led her toward the rear doors of the ferry. "This wouldn't be the first time there's been a car engine catch on fire. It doesn't happen often, but when it does, it can throw one hell of a panic into the ferry. Come on."

Rook stayed at his heels. Her eyes widened when she recognized Eve Logan and Julia Edwards. She opened her mouth to say something, but Jim tugged at her hand, pulling her outside with him.

The air was warm and salty as they exited from the air-conditioned upper deck. Passengers were standing at both rails, simply enjoying the balmy day. The water sparkled, a dark green, sun dappling the surface. Sea gulls cried and circled above them, begging for a few handouts, as they always did.

They were aft, starting to walk toward the open hatchway that led to the below-deck parking, when the first of the three explosions ripped through the ferry. The first sent clouds of chlorine gas through both ends of the lower deck. Jim was thrown off his feet. Rook screamed and was flung backward, into the steel bulkhead, knocked unconscious. The next explosion ignited the second row of chlorine containers positioned up against the brake fluid drums at the front of the truck. Thick, choking clouds of yellow-green gas tunneled out the bow entrance. The steel plating on the ferry was adequate, but the edges of the ramp openings to the car deck provided outward channels for the exploding force. Chlorine gas shot through them, and into the air conditioning ducts. Instantly, the gas was funneled through the enclosed upper deck, where two hundred and fifty people were thrown into a panic by the first blast. The instant the gas filtered into the contained area, people began choking and dropping to the deck. Panic set in, and the rest of the survivors ran for the hatches at the bow and stern of the ferry, trying to escape the deadly gas.

Jim shook his head, blood running out of his nose and mouth. He crawled on his hands and knees toward Rook, who lay unconscious against the bulkhead. Just as he reached her, covering her with his own body, the third and worst detonation occurred. The temperature rose. Lids popped off more brake fluid drums. The resulting explosion ripped through the steel-plated decks. The engine room was destroyed, and the personnel on that deck were killed instantly. The air conditioning system failed. The water pumps, which might have been used to fight the fire by the surviving crew of the *Flyer*, were inactivated.

First Mate Tony Knox was the only officer to survive the series of blasts. Captain Roland York had been going down the ladder from the helm when the first explosion had occurred. The chlorine gas he'd inhaled had burned the lining of his throat so badly that the tissue swelled up and closed off his bronchial tubes. He fell to the deck, gasping for air, and suffocated to death three minutes later.

Knox grabbed the radio microphone. "Port Angeles Coast Guard Base—mayday! Mayday! This is the *Flyer.* We've been hit by two explosions, and our captain is dead. We need help immediately! Over!" Sweat dripped into Tony's eyes as he crouched down, seeking protection behind the bulkhead in case another blast occurred.

"*Flyer*, this is Port Angeles Coast Guard. Give us a status report."

Gasping for breath, Knox blurted out, "We've got chlorine gas filtering up from the car deck! People are dropping like flies. I gotta have help! That gas is poisonous. We need oxygen. The *Flyer* is dead in the water. We're drifting."

He gasped, hearing and feeling a third explosion, hugging the bulkhead for protection. "We're carrying five hundred canisters of HTH, along with forty 55-gallon drums of brake fluid on one vehicle, fuel oil for furnaces on another."

"Any other hazardous materials on board, *Flyer*?"

Tony riffled shakily through the manifests. "Wait . . . just one more, but it shouldn't be important. I had a scrap copper truck parked in between the fuel tanker and the HTH truck. Over."

"Roger, *Flyer*. We're dispensing all available units to your position immediately. Have your crew get the people into life rafts. Our on-scene officer, Lieutenant Caldwell, will be arriving shortly on a cutter, the *Point Countess*. He'll start coordinating the rescue effort with you. Over."

Getting to his knees, Tony nodded, daring to look out the shattered windows. In the distance, he saw a white cutter with an orange stripe across its bow hurrying toward them. "Roger, Coast Guard. God, get medical help! There are three hundred people on board, and at least half of them are injured! Hurry!"

The *Flyer* now drifted helplessly, whim to the straits' changing mood, listing to starboard as seawater began to leak into the lower deck through cracks created by the third and worst explosion.

"Rook!" Jim shook her. He sobbed for breath, keeping his body as a shield against her in case there were any more explosions. Screams of terror, pain, and anguish bombarded his ears. "Rook! Wake up!" Jim glanced around. Of the thirty people on deck, half of them were hurt. He felt pain drifting up his left arm, but ignored it.

Rook's lashes fluttered. She tasted the metallic flavor of blood in her mouth. Jim's urgent voice cut through her semiconscious state. She tried to rise, but he kept her down. "W-what happened?" Her voice sounded so far away to her ears. She heard terrible cries of distress, and the shrieks of children.

Gasping for breath, Jim glanced over his shoulder. Clouds of gas were pouring out of a side hatch that led down to the parking deck. "I don't know," he rasped. "Three explosions. That's chlorine gas. It's deadly. Jesus Christ . . ."

It took her long seconds to digest all of it. Chlorine? She saw the wind taking the billowing clouds that spewed out the bow, carrying them high above the crippled ferry. "Help me up," Rook croaked. Dizziness washed over her, and she felt her left temple. There was a cut there, and it was bleeding heavily.

Jim gathered her into his arms, helping her stand. He took Rook to the stern of the ferry, the farthest point from the fire and gas. As long as the wind didn't shift direction, they would be safe there. He saw people staggering and stumbling blindly out of the upper deck; others were diving through the shattered windows, directly into the water.

"We've got to help," Rook cried, gripping his arms. She pointed to where two struggling crewmen were trying to release the life rafts that were stored on the roof. The huge plastic cylinders sat on six different ramps, at various points, and each needed to be manually released. The rest of the *Flyer* crew jerked bin lids open along the bulkheads of the ferry, and tossed out life preservers. "If we could get up there and help release those rafts, people could get off this ferry faster."

With a nod, Jim said, "You stay here. I'll help them."

"But the gas! It's poisonous!"

"I'll be all right," Jim said patiently. "Look, keep an eye on the wind direction and stay out of the gas. Try and get the survivors back here, and into life jackets. As we release the barrels, have enough people to fill the capacity of one raft jump overboard." Jim gripped her hard, looking anxiously down at her. "Do you understand?"

Rook blinked, her eyes watering. "Yes—yes . . ."

Jim smiled gamely and leaned down, kissing her hard. "I love the hell out of you, lady," he said, and then he was gone, climbing up the stairs to tackle the release of the cylinders, along with two crewmen. The black clouds were rolling across the roof. Very quickly, all three of them were swallowed up in the acrid smoke.

Fear rooted Rook to the spot for an instant. And then, her training as a SAR pilot took over. Weaving drunkenly across the slanted deck, Rook began guiding the shocked, terrorized survivors to the safety of the stern. Once, she glanced toward Ediz Hook, some six miles away now. The air station *had* to know what happened! *Hurry, oh, please, hurry with help!* she prayed.

"Cast off!" Noah shouted to the man below. He went to the conn and took the helm himself. Placing one hand over the twin throttles, he eased the cutter forward, slow ahead. The huge, throaty roar of the diesels rumbled across the dock, and the ship quivered with barely leashed power.

Noah gripped the chrome wheel hard, his knuckles white. Urgency thrummed through the cutter crew. He saw the anguish on his men's tension-lined faces. It hadn't been lost on them that his sister and Dave Harper were on board that sinking ferry.

Noah wore the mandatory orange life vest over his one-piece, dark-blue uniform. Looking to port, Noah saw the

41-foot UTB roar full throttle out of its berth, creating huge wakes of white turbulence behind it. Captain Stuart had organized them quickly and efficiently. With Noah's crew already at the air station, they'd gotten a jump on the plans set in motion.

As the *Point Countess* plowed through the straits, Noah saw that one helo was already airborne. He knew that the other three were being prepared for launch. The air crews were running around like ants over at the hangar bay. He clenched his fist, his eyes dark with anguish as he looked toward the *Flyer*. Was anyone left alive?

Rook and the four *Flyer* crewmen had gathered over 150 survivors on the stern. She had screamed orders for the panicked civilians to put on the life jackets until her voice was little more than a croak. Jim had crawled up on the roof of the ferry, and Rook anxiously tried to divide her attention between the passengers and his location. Sometimes, black clouds of smoke rolled across the roof, totally obliterating him and the other two men. If the wind changed, the deadly yellow-green clouds would roll across the roof, and she knew that it would kill all three of them.

The first cylinder rolled down off the ramp, dropping into the water with a terrific splash. Rook raced to the rail.

"All right, all right! I need a volunteer—a good, strong swimmer to jump in and grab that cylinder. Once you get to it, open the latches. The instant those latches are opened, the raft will inflate."

Dave Harper, who had been struck by flying glass from the explosions, elbowed through the huddled, stunned crowd. "I'll do it, Ms. Caldwell."

Rook stared up at him in disbelief. "Dave . . ."

Annie squeezed through. Her face had been cut by flying glass, her trousers burned. "We'll help you, Ms. Caldwell. Just tell us what to do."

Tears blurred Rook's eyes. She hadn't realized they were on board until just now. Grateful, she gripped Dave's arm.

"Okay . . . thanks. Dave, can you jump in and get that first raft out and righted?"

"Yes, ma'am." He climbed up on the edge of the rail and then made a graceful dive into the straits. Surfacing, he swam strongly toward the cylinder and quickly opened the huge, hinged latches. The first raft popped out and began to fill with air.

Rook gave Dave a thumbs up, and then turned to Annie. "Can you see if any more people are unconscious on the upper deck?" Rook grabbed a black crewman. "You two go together. Whatever you do, don't get near that gas. Back off, understand? But, if you can reach any more victims and drag them back here to the stern, do it."

Annie nodded and flashed the crewman a slight smile. "Let's get to work," she said to him.

"Stay out of the gas," Rook warned her again. She was well aware of Annie's unflagging courage in the face of a disaster. And Rook knew of the times that Annie had disregarded her own safety to save the life of another. This was one time that ignoring the threat could kill her almost instantly.

Annie threw Rook a thumbs up. "I'll be careful, I promise."

The second and third cylinders were released from the first ramp slide on the roof. Harper swam to both and released the rafts, then climbed in one and pulled the three close to the hull of the ferry, waiting for the passengers to begin leaping from the rail.

"Come on, come on," Rook cried, waving her arm at the crowd, "I need fifty people to jump! One at a time. Hurry!"

Desperately, Rook looked back toward the air station. Her heart raced. She saw one helo lift off. Never had a '52 looked so good to her. Now Rook understood what it meant to be rescued.

CHAPTER

Twenty-one

"IT'S imperative that all pilots stay upwind of the ferry to effect their rescues," Ward told his people, who were gathered in the busy hangar. "Rotor wash could suck that chlorine gas back across the ferry, possibly killing more survivors. Thanks to several volunteer fire departments in the area, you've all been issued oxygen tanks and masks. Extra tanks are being put on board for yourselves and any survivors who'll need them. Questions?" Ward looked hard at the strained faces of his pilots and flight mechs. The hangar crackled with tension. "All coordination efforts go through Lieutenant Caldwell. He's the OSC. He'll then call me for final permission. You want to do something different from the plan I've sketched out, call first for approval." Grimly, Ward added, "There's going to be a lot of panic, and a lot of dying around you. Keep your heads. Dismissed."

As Gil jogged toward CG 1300 with his copilot, Reno, on his heels, he thought again of Rook and Annie. Angelo Marchetti met them at the open fuselage door, already in his mask, the tank strapped on his back, the harness around his upper body. Getting settled into their seats, they also donned the new equipment.

"Christ," Reno grumbled, moving rapidly through the

preflight check, "I feel like a fighter pilot wearing one of these things."

Gil nodded, throwing a thumbs up to alert the mech he was ready to start the engine. "We're going to war, all right. Okay, let's roll." The '52's engine whined to life and the rotor blades began to turn slowly. The sunlight was bright through the cockpit windshield, and Gil drew down the dark visor to protect his eyes. He tried to put himself in the right mind frame for this SAR case. It wasn't going to be a one-shot deal—they would be making landing after landing on the water's surface to pick up the survivors. It would strain their concentration and test their physical limits of endurance. Already, the wind was picking up, like it always did midmorning, and the waves were five to six feet high out in the straits. That meant water landings would be difficult.

As they roared toward the disaster scene, at an altitude of three hundred feet, Reno whistled. "My God, that's a mess down there."

"Radio back to base. Tell them what we've got," Logan ordered tersely. Sometimes, Reno's excitement got in the way of his normally good judgment. The ferry was on fire. Huge tongues of red flames were mixing into the angry black clouds erupting from the bow area. Gil could see people in orange life vests bobbing a half mile downwind of the listing behemoth, all of them beneath the malevolent cloud of yellow-green gas coiling endlessly from the *Flyer*. There were at least four rafts in the water, and he saw approximately twenty people in each one of them. Good, at least someone down there was thinking on their feet. The more people in rafts, the fewer hypothermia cases they would have.

Logan spotted three men on the roof of the ferry, crawling around, but black smoke obscured any further view of them. Most of the survivors were huddled on the stern of the upper deck. The hull of the *Flyer* near the bow looked warped and cracked. The *Point Countess* and the 44-footer were upwind, already beginning to pluck survivors from the water.

Over his headset, he heard Stuart's voice as he called to all skippers and air commanders.

"This is Captain Stuart. You are advised *not* to approach the ferry. Repeat: do *not* approach the *Flyer*. We've just gotten word from a haz-mat expert that chlorine will explode when it comes in contact with copper. According to the first mate aboard the *Flyer*, there is a truck filled with at least five tons of copper scrap. It's parked near the truck carrying HTH and brake fluid. If the fire gets hot enough, the copper will begin spontaneous ignition. Until I can get more information regarding this potential danger, you are to stay as far from the ferry as possible when you pick up victims. Acknowledge this order. Over."

"Great," Logan muttered, making the mandatory call to the captain. "Copper and HTH? Who would guess those two things could create a problem? That whole mother is probably going to blow right out of the water."

Reno glanced at him, his eyes widening. "I wonder what the radius on an explosion like that would be?"

"Who the hell knows?" Gil snorted, easing the '52 down to a lower altitude as he approached the first group of survivors, upwind of the ferry.

"Oh, man . . ."

"Yeah," Gil muttered. "I hope that haz-mat expert the skipper's got is going to tell him how far away we have to be so we don't end up in little pieces if that ferry decides to blow."

Wiping the sweat accumulating on his brow, Reno muttered, "Man, this is worse than combat."

"You're right. It's a barbecue, and we could all be crispy critters before it's over." Gil looked at the *Point Countess* below them. "Noah had better watch his ass, too."

On the bridge of the *Point Countess,* Noah was in constant radio contact with civilian boats and tugs who had answered Captain Stuart's emergency call to help in the rescue. He kept the cutter a half mile upwind of the *Flyer*. From his stationary post, he began to direct the awaiting boat traffic that had lined up, waiting for his orders. He'd send them in, one at a time, to either pick up survivors who were in the water, or pull alongside of a raft and begin to transfer people.

Whether he wanted to or not, Stuart's latest communiqué over the radio bothered the hell out of him. What did it mean? How long did those people on the *Flyer* have if that copper and HTH combined? And how large an explosion was Stuart talking about? Anguish moved through Noah as he steadied the binoculars to his eyes. He could see Rook on the stern, helping to direct the evacuation, along with several other *Flyer* crewmen.

"Captain Stuart," Bob Bancroft began, tapping the map of the straits with his finger, "if we didn't have the threat of that copper coming in contact with the HTH, you could get your 41-footer in there to start spraying water on that fire. As it is, we can't even begin to guess when or if those two will combine to create that explosion."

Ward stared at the tall, gangly man. Bancroft had volunteered his services, having heard the bulletins regarding the *Flyer* disaster on the radio earlier. He was a haz-mat technician for the state of Washington who happened to be on vacation in the area. Frustration ate at him. "You're telling me I can't put out the fire on that ferry?"

Apologetically, Bancroft scratched his thinning blond hair. "I'm afraid so, Captain."

"And there's no way to estimate the size of such an explosion?"

"None. But five tons of copper is a lot of metal to put in contact with that much HTH. Right now, every effort should be focused on getting the people off the *Flyer*. No one can estimate when or if that copper will ignite. According to the first mate, Knox, those two trucks are parked close together. It's a crapshoot, Captain."

Ward turned and stared out the window of his office. He could see the smoke rising from the ferry. Six miles separated them from the disaster. Hospital ambulances were lined up on the tarmac, waiting for the first load of survivors to arrive in the helos. Mercy Hospital had geared up for a triage emergency situation. The city of Port Angeles had responded en masse to the emergency. Local residents were bringing pickups, vans, buses, and even newspaper trucks to the air station to help transport the injured to the hospital. Red Cross volunteers from several local chapters waited tensely out on the tarmac, ready to assist the *Flyer* survivors to the vehicles. Medical personnel from six Seattle hospitals were being flown in by a local airline to help at Mercy. Coast Guard helicopters from adjacent stations were flying in, prepared to take the more seriously injured, after they were stabilized at Mercy, to Seattle hospitals.

Surprisingly, Chief McDonald had managed to scare up one hundred and fifty Coast Guard personnel, and all of them were working on the coordination effort. Ward was proud of his people, and he was worried about his cutter and helo crews. "Dammit, I thought we had enough to worry about with my people exposed to that chlorine gas. Now, there's the possibility of an explosion of unknown proportion," he growled.

Bob nodded understandingly. "Look, Captain Stuart, I don't want to belabor this point with you, but I think you need to understand the size of such an explosion."

"Spell it out for me," Ward said, "clearly."

"We're talking an explosion so powerful that it could make that ferry look like nothing but pieces of shrapnel when it was all over."

Ward sucked in a breath. "What's the radius on that kind of detonation?"

"I'd say anyone within half a mile would be killed instantly. Three-quarters of a mile, serious injury."

"And one mile?"

"Injured, but alive."

"What about my aircraft?"

"They'll take one hell of a pounding. I don't know much about choppers, so I can't realistically answer that. The shock wave would be tremendous. Like a tsunami, only an invisible one made of air."

"All right, you've spelled it out for me, Bancroft." Ward paced, running his fingers through his damp hair. He was sweating profusely. He glanced over at the haz-mat technician.

"Give me your best educated guess on how long we have before this could happen," he demanded tightly.

"Depends upon a lot of variables that we have no way of knowing, Captain."

"According to the first mate, those trucks are parked within five feet of one another."

"Then," Bob offered softly, "those poor people on board may not have much time at all . . ."

"Next!" Rook shouted, helping several of the walking injured to the rail. One hundred people had climbed over the rail and found safety in the rafts that Jim and the *Flyer* crew had been able to release from the ferry roof. Dave was still in the water, releasing canisters and helping the passengers climb into the rafts. It was a tedious, time-consuming effort.

Rook had seen the *Point Countess* slicing through the water. The cutter had stationed herself a half mile upwind of the ferry to pick up those in the water. She saw at least forty to fifty small craft around the cutter, helping in the evacuation of wounded. The small, valiant '52s were landing on the water, plucking three to four people at a time from the water. The rescue was well underway.

Rook's head ached fiercely where she had sustained the gash on her temple. She moved through the hundred people left on the stern, all the time keeping an eye on which way the wind was blowing. And always, she tried to spot Jim as he crawled from one cylinder ramp to another on his belly. Most of the time she lost sight of him and the other two men in the roiling, twisting smoke as it poured more heavily out of the starboard hatches.

Rook felt the heat under her feet, and realized that the fire was spreading. Gagging on fumes from other chemicals burning, Rook staggered toward the starboard side. Annie Locke and Bill Stone had worked without rest, hauling out one unconscious victim after another from the upper deck lounge. Several other men, the least injured, were doing the same. Sooner or later the helos would have to initiate basket drops to the deck of the ferry to take away the worst cases. They couldn't be lifted overboard to the rafts below.

Annie groaned, tugging and pulling an unconscious two-hundred-pound woman. Rook met her halfway across the deck and came to her side.

"You take one arm, I'll take the other," Rook gasped.

Annie nodded, sobbing for breath. Together, they managed to get the woman down the ladder and to the knot of people on the stern. Others were administering CPR to those who had quit breathing after inhaling the deadly chlorine fumes.

Rook saw Annie gag from the chlorine fumes, then fall to her knees, retching. Leaning down, Rook held her.

"T-thanks." Annie wiped her mouth with the back of her torn sleeve. Slowly, unsteadily, she got to her feet.

"Go over there, Annie," Rook begged, "you're not well. Rest."

Stubbornly, Annie shook her head. She managed a lopsided grin. "Take a look at yourself, ma'am. You're a sight for sore eyes, too. You can barely stand . . ."

Rook ignored her, straightening up. The ferry suddenly groaned, the plates screeching and rending beneath them. They clutched at one another to stay upright as the deck slowly listed more and more. Another explosion occurred below. Annie cringed. Rook ducked.

Fire spewed out of the closest hatch, and shrapnel from an exploding car parked near the opening shot outward in a narrow arc. Another explosion! Rook jerked Annie along, trying to stay upright as they made their way back to the stern.

Two more cylinders were loosened and trundled down the steep ramps, splashing into the water. Rook brought Annie to the rail. They both clung to the steel bar, gasping for breath. Rook's attention was drawn to Dave. His movements in the water were slow and uncoordinated as he swam toward the cylinders. He was going hypothermic. Annie sobbed, leaning over the rail.

"Dave! Get out of the water and stay out!" she screamed.

He didn't hear her above the roar of the fire, the helicopters buzzing around like bees, and the loudspeakers blaring from the cutter upwind of them. The water was pulling at him. His legs were tired; he felt as if he was carrying thirty-pound weights. He opened his mouth to grab a breath of air, but instead, he swallowed water. Choking, he vomited and struck out more determinedly toward the next four cylinders, only feet away.

Annie checked out her life vest, making sure it was good and tight around her body. "I'm going in after him," she told Rook, climbing unsteadily up on the rail. "The damn fool is already past reason. He'll die if I don't get him out of there."

Rook grabbed her arm. "Get him *and* yourself out of the water—*now*. That's an order, Annie. Do you hear me?" she demanded, her voice strained.

Annie was going to argue with her, but then thought better of it when she saw the set of Rook Caldwell's jaw. "Yes, ma'am. In and out. I'll get these rafts down to you as soon as I can and then stay out of the water."

"Do that."

Annie held her breath and stood. She leaped, feet first, into the icy water. The life vest she wore popped her quickly to the surface. Shaking the water out of her eyes, Annie swam strongly toward Dave, who was weakly trying to keep his head above water. Her years of rescue experience made it easy to slide her arm around his chest and beneath his arm to keep him from drowning.

"I've got you," she gasped.

Dave gagged, and stopped flailing around. He relaxed immediately when Annie's strong, thin arm went about him. His throat and nose burned from the saltwater he'd inhaled. Barely coherent, black dots danced before his half-closed eyes. "Annie . . . I-I'm losing . . ." He blacked out before he finished.

Alarmed, Annie twisted a look down at him. Taking powerful strokes with her free arm and legs, she reached a half-filled raft of people. Hands stretched downward to help Dave as soon as she maneuvered him so they could reach him. Sucking in huge gulps of air, she moved aside as two men hauled Dave into the raft.

"Cover him!" she shouted up to them, trying to be heard over the cacophony of sounds. "He's hypothermic! Put your coats or anything else you have around him." And then she pushed off, striking out for the cylinders floating aside the *Flyer*.

Rook divided her attention between her coordinating the passengers with Tony Knox and trying to search for Jim. There was one more ramp, near the bow, that had to be released. He knew, as she did, that the hundred people left on deck would have no way of getting off the ferry to be rescued without the remaining rafts. Tears blurred Rook's vision. She wanted to scream for Jim to get back to her. He'd been up there for so long. She'd seen wisps of chlorine gas slide across the roof. Had Jim breathed in the poisonous fumes? Was he unconscious somewhere up there? She ached to go find him, but when she saw the anxious, shocked looks on the passengers' faces, she knew her duty was here, with them. No one else knew about emergency rescue procedure like the Coast Guard, and she couldn't jeopardize all of them for the sake of one life . . .

Noah heard the announcement over the radio, and his blood turned icy. He gripped the console, staring hard at the ferry. Captain Stuart had just ordered everyone to remain one mile away from the *Flyer*, because of the danger of an explosion, which could occur at any time. Already, the *Flyer* was listing twenty degrees to starboard. It was only a matter of time before it slid into a watery grave, if that explosion didn't do it first. Earlier, he'd spotted Rook, Harper, and

Annie Locke, but not Jim Barton. With Commander Nelson now acting as on-scene commander from the 250-foot cutter, the *Osprey*, Noah was relieved of his extra duties. He'd taken the *Point Countess* very close to the *Flyer* to pick up survivors. And now, he waited impatiently for the last of them to be helped off the cutter to dockside.

"We're ready to roll, Skipper!" the bos'n shouted from the dock. The last person had been led down the ramp to awaiting volunteers and medical people.

Good. Noah gave orders to place a large, heavy gangplank on the cutter. He eased the *Point Countess* from the berth, pointing her bow out toward the straits once again. Noah had a plan, and he prayed that the Captain would approve of it. Rook didn't know the danger she was in, and he was damned if he was going to lose her like this. He picked up the microphone to call Stuart.

Ward rubbed his tired eyes, listening to Noah's plan. He wanted to say no, but he couldn't. The first mate, Knox, had reported twenty gravely injured people lying on the stern of the *Flyer*. Right now, all helos were busy either picking up people in the water or refueling. The injured who could walk or move were the last of the passengers to be transported. There was no way to get the last twenty people, except to send someone or something in to pick them up. Noah wanted to take the *Point Countess* alongside, drop the gangplank on the *Flyer*'s slanted deck, and rescue them. Should he risk a million-dollar cutter and the lives of eight men? Ward rubbed his eyes again.

"Stand by, Lieutenant Caldwell," he ordered gruffly, trying to analyze the best way to handle the situation. Noah was right: they had to get the critically injured off the ferry in a hurry, or they'd all go up with the coming explosion. What way was best with minimal risk of life and property—helos or a cutter? The blade wash from a '52 could pull the chlorine gas to the stern of the *Flyer*, endangering everyone. His air crew would be jeopardized, too. They were running low on extra oxygen tanks from the fire departments. If he chose wrong, people could die because of his decision.

"Captain, I've *got* to have your answer," came Noah's anxious voice. "I'm one mile to port of the *Flyer*."

"Get the *Point Countess* in there and get her out, Lieutenant Caldwell," he snapped.

"Yes, sir!"

Ward cursed, setting down the microphone. He stared over at several officers manning other phones and radios. Had he made the right decision? The rescue of twenty people, plus those few attending them, would take too long by helo. The '52 could only hold four, maximum, plus a crew of three. The cutter, on the other hand, could take all survivors, minimizing the time factor, but maximizing the loss of people if that ferry exploded while they were in the act of evacuating them. Turning, Ward glanced out the window toward the straits.

Rook's eyes widened as she saw the *Point Countess*'s clean, sleek shape turn and bear down directly on the ferry. And then, she understood. A sob escaped her and she quickly returned to her role as leader for the group.

"Listen! Everyone, listen! They're going to move the cutter alongside the *Flyer*. We'll all be able to cross over and make it to safety. Do you understand?" Her voice cracked with emotion. The few people who were still coherent nodded. Twenty lay unconscious or seriously injured at Rook's feet. Blood covered the deck. Others were administering CPR. Their faces were worn, their arms tired, but they continued the life-saving procedure.

Anxiously, Rook looked toward the roof. Where was Jim? Both *Flyer* crewmen had already climbed down and had just joined the group. Their faces were glistening with sweat, hair plastered against their skulls. The clothes they wore clung to their bodies. She made her way to the two weary men.

"Jim—the other man up there. Where is he? Why didn't he come off the roof with you?"

The older man, his arms and knees burned badly from crawling around on the roof, leaned over, talking loud enough so that Rook could hear him. "He said he was gonna try for that last ramp. I told him he was crazy, but he said we needed that last cylinder when he saw how many people were left down here." The crewman lifted his blistered forearms for her to look at. "He's got more guts than we have. Frank and I couldn't take the heat up there anymore."

Tears jammed into Rook's eyes, and she fought them back. Her voice wavered. "D-did he say he'd come down after releasing the cylinders?"

"Yes, ma'am," the younger crewman vowed. "Said he'd be down straight away."

Rook strained to see through the heavy smoke which was increasing every minute. Torn between a desire to find Jim and stay with her group, Rook looked back toward the fast-approaching *Point Countess*. *Hurry, oh, God, Noah, hurry!*

Noah gave orders to his crew as they approached the tilted deck of the ferry. Ordinarily, no gangplank would be long enough to reach that upper deck from his cutter, but with the degree of list, it would work. His men had been with him for over a year, and knew their stations. Sitka cast lines over the rail of the ferry. A couple of *Flyer* crewmen caught them and quickly wrapped them around the steel bar rail.

"Ease her in," Noah ordered Dixon. The ferry was listing badly to starboard. They had to place that gangplank between the cutter and the unstable, slanted deck. Noah ordered that the knots placed in the lines between the cutter and ferry be the type for quick release. If that ferry decided to sink, he didn't want the *Point Countess* going down with it. As it was, the gangplank was going to be precarious as hell on the ferry deck. There was no way to secure it. Noah saw Rook waving wildly, her face bloody and swollen from the injury she had received. There was terror in her eyes. He ordered the throttle pulled back to all stop, watching as the cushioning fenders were thrown over the side of the *Point Countess* to prevent any damage when the two ships moved next to one another.

"Jerry, get Steve to help you maneuver that gangplank onto the *Flyer*."

"Yes, sir!"

A ladder with rope handrails and solid oak planking was laid gingerly between the two ships, creating a passable bridge between them. Noah stepped out on deck with the microphone and used the ship's PA system to direct the *Flyer* survivors.

"Prepare the injured for transport. My crew will help you across."

Rook rallied beneath her brother's calm, authoritative voice, and so did everyone else. Fighting back tears of relief, Rook got down on her hands and knees and began relieving those who had been giving CPR for far too long. Two more explosions, deep in the belly of the *Flyer*, shook the deck. The heat was increasing, and so was the wind. Rook noticed a slight wind change.

"No!" she cried, seeing the chlorine cloud begin to turn and twist back across the bow—back across the roof, toward the stern. She felt a hand on her shoulder. Looking up, she saw a *Point Countess* crewman. He took the man she was working on across the plank to safety.

Dizzy, Rook watched in terrible fascination as the chlorine cloud changed direction. At first, yellow-green wisps mixed with the black column of smoke that crawled across the roof and then, the mixture thickened.

With a cry, Rook turned to Dixon, the nearest *Point Countess* crewman. "Get help," she told him. "Jim Barton's still up there on that roof! I'm going to get him." She lunged forward, slipping across the deck, falling several times, trying to make it to the upper deck stairs that led to the roof.

"Where the hell is she going?" Noah shouted to Dixon on the *Flyer*.

Dixon cupped his hands to his mouth. "She's going after a guy named Barton. He's still up on that roof!"

"Rook!" Noah shouted, using the PA system. "Don't go up there!" He called her one more time. Dammit, she either didn't hear him, or—Noah threw down the microphone, slid down the stair rails, and hit the deck of the *Point Countess* running. As he did so, he slipped the oxygen mask to his face and twisted the regulator so that cooling air pumped into the mask. He turned to Carter, the second mate. "You have command, Carter. If I'm not back by the time this evacuation is complete, you pull this cutter clear. Understand?"

Carter's mouth dropped open, but he nodded.

Noah leaped to the unsteady gangplank, making his way across it to the tilted deck of the *Flyer*. He screamed at Rook to stop as she climbed the stairs. She had no oxygen tank—there was no way she could enter that wall of smoke up on the roof and survive.

Rook gagged, gasping for breath. The smell of chlorine was overwhelming. She wriggled onto the roof and lay there, gasping for breath. The metal beneath her was hot. Hands bloodied, she pulled herself forward.

"Jim! Jim, where are you?" Her cry sounded like a weakened kitten mewing. Coughing violently, Rook felt her consciousness slipping. No! No, she couldn't faint. Jim! He was in trouble. She knew it. She could feel it. Crawling forward, covered by the clouds of black smoke, she disappeared beneath the thick veil.

Noah lunged forward, making a grab for Rook's foot. He lay on the roof, gasping for breath, his eyes smarting badly. Pulling on her ankle, muscles straining, he brought her back toward him—back out of the clouds of dark, greasy smoke. Dixon was waiting at the bottom of the stairs as he handed his semiconscious sister to him.

"Get her back to the cutter!" Noah ordered, his voice muffled badly by the mask he wore.

Dixon supported Rook, who slumped against him. "Yes, sir!"

"Jim!" Rook cried, weakly raising her hand, pointing toward the roof.

Noah nodded his understanding of Rook's entreaty and searched the angry smoke, feeling the heat scorch his skin. Crawling quickly up on the roof on his hands and knees,

Noah went to the port edge of the deck, snaking his way along it. The smoke was opaque, and he could see nothing. Every few feet he'd stop, hang on to the edge, and move his long legs back toward the center of the roof, trying to locate Barton. If he didn't have a point of reference, Noah knew he could become disoriented and lost in the viscous clouds. And then, he might be like Barton: wandering around on the roof, unable to find the stairs and safety.

Noah kept shouting for Jim, but the mask made it almost useless. The roar of the fire was like a freight train bearing down on him. The closer he inched toward the bow, the hotter the surface became. Noah could feel his skin begin to burn where he touched the metal. By mental calculations, he knew there was one ramp left, and it should be only a few feet ahead. What if the ferry blew? Sweat ran into his eyes, making them sting.

There! Noah froze. Wildly, he searched with his right hand. It was Barton! It had to be. The man was unconscious and slumped over the ramp. Gripping Barton by the left arm, Noah got to his knees, tugging hard. Christ, the man was heavy! Noah had forgotten Jim was six-four, and probably weighed at least two hundred and thirty pounds. Urgency thrummed through him. How much time had elapsed?

Saliva drooled from the corners of Noah's mouth as he gasped for breath, and he dragged Barton toward the stern. A series of new explosions sent an arc of fear through him. His knees were burning, and so were his legs. *Dear God, get us out of here. Let us live. Let us—*

Rook screamed as a monstrous explosion shattered the bow of the *Flyer*. The *Point Countess* was in the process of backing away when it occurred. She had yelled at the second mate to wait, but Carson had disregarded her order. Rook staggered out of the bridge, clutching at the rail, watching as fire vomited three hundred feet into the sky. The bow steel plates peeled open, massive fireballs belching upward. Metal buckled. Plates were bent and sent hurtling hundreds of feet in all directions. Her second scream was drowned out by the sound of the roof wrenching free of the *Flyer*, erupting skyward into the black smoke.

Rook took a step forward, hand outstretched, a raw cry tearing from her throat. She staggered, blackness engulfing her as she sank to her knees.

The *Point Countess* was far enough away from the explosion to avoid serious damage. Carter, the second mate, was shaken, but kept his presence of mind as he swung the responsive cutter to stern. The ferry was rapidly sinking, the clouds of chlorine and black smoke extinguished in a hissing roar and billowing clouds of steam as it slipped beneath the waters of the straits.

"Look!" Dixon cried, pointing five hundred feet away from where the *Flyer* had sunk. "Two men!"

Carter gawked. He saw his skipper floundering weakly in the water, getting pulled under by the forty pounds of oxygen equipment strapped to his back. The other man was floating facedown in the brackish water not more than five feet away from Lieutenant Caldwell. Throwing the throttles to all stop, Carter screamed at his men to begin recovery procedures immediately to rescue them from the straits.

CHAPTER

Twenty-two

BLACKNESS . . . it engulfed Rook, held her in its clutches, until she thought she was going to suffocate. She tried to drag in deep breaths of air, and choked.

"Easy, Rook, easy . . ."

Rook frowned, hearing the male voice and feeling something being clapped over her nose and mouth. Cool, fresh air flowed up into her nose and open, gasping mouth.

"Take nice, deep breaths. Nice and deep. That's it . . ."

Rook fought the darkness, fought to wake up. She hungrily sucked in the oxygen, feeling the last of the anxiety leave her tightened chest. Forcing her eyes open to bare slits, she looked up. Gil Logan, his face bathed in sweat, was crouched over her. Where was she? Other sounds impinged on her consciousness. She was lying on something hard and unforgiving. She felt Gil's hand on her shoulder, the other clapped over the mask he held to her face. *Jim?* Her eyes widened. *Noah?* She sobbed, lifting her arm, trying to remove the mask.

"No, Rook, don't. Lie still. You're going to be flown by helo to Seattle in a minute." He was breathing hard, kneeling on the concrete of the dock. Everywhere he looked, there were injured people. Most of them were being tended by either Coasties or ambulance personnel. At the hangar,

'52s from neighboring air stations and the larger HH-3Fs from Seattle were making flights to area hospitals just as soon as they got enough stabilized victims on board. Gil had just picked up the last survivors from the straits and landed. He had heard Cole's plea over the loudspeaker at the hangar for all personnel to get to the dock to help with the twenty seriously injured survivors that would be docking in ten minutes. When Gil recognized Rook among the injured, lying as-yet unattended on the dock, anger ripped through him. She was damn near gray, indicating a lack of oxygen. Gil had raced over to a nearby ambulance and taken an extra bottle and mask. Her color was coming back.

"Lie still," he begged, leaning closer, thinking she was in shock. *Dammit, why couldn't they at least get her a blanket?* She was shivering and going, it appeared, into deeper shock.

With a moan, Rook clawed at Gil's hand on the mask. Jim! Noah! Where were they? She shut her eyes, tears squeezing out from beneath them.

"Easy, Rook," Gil soothed unsteadily. He awkwardly stroked her dirty, smoky hair. When he saw her tears, it tore him apart. There was so much carnage around them. Stretcher bearers were running in all directions with gurneys. Nurses with I.V. bottles lifted and carrying along the worst cases as they transported them to the awaiting fleet of helos.

"Hey!" he shouted to a passing medic. "I need help over here!"

The doctor hesitated, and then turned in Gil's direction. He was out of breath as he knelt at Rook's side.

"What's her condition?" he gasped, immediately feeling for a pulse.

"Critical. Can't you get her aboard one of those choppers? She needs help. Now."

Hesitating fractionally, the doctor nodded. "Okay, Lieutenant." He placed a red triangle, indicating she was a critical case, on her dirtied tank top. "If you can get her over to the H-3 at the hangar," he said, pointing toward the tarmac in the distance, "she can go with us this trip."

Gil grinned belatedly. "Don't worry, Doc, she'll be on board. Thanks."

Logan left the mask on Rook, placing the small oxygen bottle on her stomach. He slipped his arms beneath her. Her breath was uneven, coming in gasps. "Okay, babe, hang on. You're going for a ride."

Rook sobbed for breath, her lungs on fire. It hurt to breathe. She couldn't find her voice; her throat was raw, and felt as if it had been scalded. Once in Gil's arms, she collapsed against him and fell back into semiconsciousness.

Gil hitched a ride with the closest ambulance, to make damn sure they took first-class care of Rook. Her eyes were glazed and she was having a lot of trouble breathing on her own. He'd heard about her bravery on the deck of the *Flyer* already, from people she had helped save. He patted her hand, holding her tightly in his arms as the ambulance swerved off the road and headed directly to the H-3. Gil braced Rook as the vehicle screeched to a halt parallel to the open door of the fuselage. He heard the H-3's engines whine louder, indicating it was preparing for takeoff.

The driver got out and ran around to the rear of the ambulance, swinging both doors wide. With his help, Gil was able to get Rook on board. He made sure the medical personnel on board knew she was a Coastie, like them. Gil watched as they threw two blankets around Rook, and quickly placed an I.V. into her left arm. He gripped her hand, the wind whipping around them. Raising his voice, he shouted into the cabin, "Rook, we'll be in touch! Everything will be all right."

She tried to raise her head to speak, but fell back.

Tears squeezed from beneath her tightly shut eyes. Noah . . . Jim . . . they were dead. Dead . . .

Stuart looked around the grimly silent room. The men and women of his station were whipped. The *Flyer* rescue had begun at 1000. It was now 1500. In five hours, they'd rescued and dispatched 240 survivors to different hospitals in the area. Pride for his people welled up through him. At the same time, raw grief serrated his heart. Annie Locke had just found him ten minutes ago, and told him that she had seen Kenny on board the *Flyer*. Was he among the survivors? Anguished, Ward had to wait, just like everyone else, to find out. The Red Cross people were doing everything humanely possible to compile a list of victims and survivors. As soon as it was completed, he would be notified. Ward flexed his hand, trying to hold back his fear, his anxiety.

In a monumental effort of will, Ward placed his own personal grief aside and looked at his people. Never had he seen or been part of such a heroic, nonstop effort as this one.

"I want you to know," Ward began, his voice scratchy with feeling, "that I think you're the finest group of people I've ever had the privilege of serving with." He saw their exhausted faces, their reddened eyes. His pilots all had that two-thousand-yard stare indicative of battle fatigue. And that's what this had been. "That was one hell of a war you fought out there today, and we won. So far, we've lost sixty people. I'm sure that number will climb. But under the circumstances, you all performed above and beyond the call of duty."

"I'd like to say something," Admiral Savage interjected, coming forward. He had flown in from Seattle an hour ago. Savage studied the assembled personnel. "In all my years in the Coast Guard, I've never seen anything like this. Air Station Port Angeles has made the headlines of every paper in the nation today. Your bravery has not gone unnoticed. By tonight, every major network will carry this rescue as their lead story. I know that one network is planning a half-hour special on it. Again, I say, well done."

Ward swallowed his nausea over Savage's little speech. His people didn't give a damn about the publicity. Many of them had friends or family in that lead story, or were worrying about their comrades who had been hurt during the rescue. A number of Coasties had serious injuries from inhaling chlorine gas. Right now, all Ward wanted to do was call Seattle to find out how his people were doing. Logan and Welsh had flown down to the city with a medevac for Montieth Hospital. He suspected that they would check on the wounded officers there from Port Angeles before they returned to the air station.

Tag Welsh and Gil Logan walked quickly down the halls of the hospital in their flight boots and smelly flight suits. It was nearly five o'clock and they had just unloaded their medevac cases. Gil had deliberately volunteered for the flight, anxious to find out about Rook and Noah. He had grabbed Tag, who eagerly went along, for a copilot.

"What do you think?" Tag asked, walking at Logan's shoulder.

"About what?"

"About how many of them survived. I heard Dixon from the *Point Countess* say that they pulled Noah and Jim Barton out of the straits after that ferry blew. I don't see how anyone could have survived that blast."

Gil shrugged his aching shoulders. "We'll know in a minute." They swung around to the busy nursing station on the operating floor. One of the nurses stared at them briefly.

"May I help you, gentlemen?"

"Yes, ma'am," Tag said, taking off his garrison cap. "We're Coast Guard pilots from the Port Angeles Air Station. You've got two of our people here. A brother and sister—Lieutenants Rook and Noah Caldwell. And there's a civilian by the name of Jim Barton here, too. Can you tell us how they are?"

Her mouth thinned in displeasure and she reached over, grabbing a sheaf of papers that needed to be sorted. "I'm sorry, our hospital rules don't allow us to tell anyone but family members about the condition of our patients." She gave them both an irritated look, obviously very busy with duties brought on by the *Flyer* disaster. "If you gentlemen will just—"

Gil stepped forward. "Just tell us how they're doing, goddammit."

The nurse stepped back, her mouth falling open. The nursing station froze, all eyes on the Coast Guard pilots. The nurse snapped her mouth shut, and glared contemptuously a Gil.

Tag put his hand on Gil's arm. "Sorry, ma'am, but we're mite tired. You can understand, can't you? Rook, Noah, an Jim are close friends of ours." He managed a slight, persuasive smile. "Coasties stick together like family."

Shaken by the rage in the other officer's voice, and hi continued black stare, the nurse dropped the sheaf of paper and reached for a clipboard that contained the names of patients on the floor. "Dr. Marhefka is assigned to their cases You can see him right now. He's down there at the end of th hall in the visitors' lobby. I can't give you permission to se these people, but he can."

Tag nodded. "Thank you, ma'am. We're deeply grateful."

Gil swung into the lounge first. A short man of abou forty-five, with broad shoulders, was talking to . . . H gawked. That was Howard Barton—Jim Barton's father! H started forward, but saw the old man sag back down into hi chair, a look of devastation written across his features. Th doctor reached out, placing a hand on the man's shoulder.

"Shit," Logan whispered, gripping Tag and forcing hin out of the lounge, back into the hall. Gil lowered his voice "That's Howard Barton, Jim's father," he explained.

Tag frowned. "Don't tell me—"

"Jim didn't make it. Sonofabitch."

Wrestling with his own feelings, Tag muttered, "Don' jump to conclusions. Let's wait and see. Noah Caldwell wa up on that roof with him, you know."

Raking his fingers through his dark hair, Gil muttered "Yeah, I know. Let's wait out here. We'll nail Marhefka when he comes out. I don't want to disturb Mr. Barton. H looks prety upset."

Gil grabbed the doctor the instant he came out of th lounge. "Dr. Marhefka, we're friends of Lieutenants Rook and Noah Caldwell. Rook's boyfriend, Jim Barton, is here too."

The doctor looked up at both men, his face lined anc somber. "I see."

"How are they?" Gil asked, barely suppressing his anger over the doctor's hesitation.

Tag gripped Gil's arm, giving him a warning glance.

"Ms. Caldwell suffered mild chlorine injuries to her respiratory system. She's sedated, but conscious. Jim Barton has a concussion, multiple rib fractures, second degree burns over thirty percent of his lower legs and arms. He's still in the recovery room."

"Thank God," Gil muttered, suddenly limp with relief, grateful that they had both survived. He leaned against the wall, fighting off the exhaustion that wanted to claim him.

"Can we see them, sir?" Tag asked.

"You can certainly see Ms. Caldwell. She's in Room 22."

Fatigue was lapping at Gil. "Hold it. What about Noah? You haven't said anything about him." His gut tightened.

"I'm sorry. He didn't make it through surgery. His sister just regained consciousness. I haven't told her yet."

Gil glanced over at Tag. "Go on down to her room." He turned back to Dr. Marhefka. "I'll do it, Doctor. Rook and I are good friends."

The doctor shrugged. "If you're sure you want to."

Grimly, Gil whispered, "I do." He looked over at Tag. "I'll be there in a minute." He wanted to talk to the doctor further, alone.

Tag nodded sadly, his garrison cap crushed in his tightly knotted fist. "You bet."

Gil waited until Tag had left and then turned to Marhefka. "Look, Rook is one of us, Doctor. She's a Coast Guard pilot. She and Noah were close. Did Noah say anything before he died?"

Marhefka studied the pilot's slack face and saw that his eyes burned with barely leashed emotions. "Yes, he did, just as we prepped him for surgery." The doctor told Gil what the cutter captain had said. "If Lieutenant Caldwell needs a sedative afterward, just ring the nurse."

Grateful, Gil's voice cracked when he spoke. "Thanks, Doctor." He turned away and began the long walk down the hall, trying to contain his escaping grief. Rook would need their strength now, not their tears.

Rook's black lashes were beaded with spent tears when Gil quietly entered her room minutes later. Tag was standing by her bed, talking to her quietly. Logan saw the I.V. going in her left arm and the oxygen bottle on the right. At first, he thought Rook was asleep; her skin matched the white color of the sheets that surrounded her. Her head had been bandaged, and the blood cleaned off her face. The bruise on her cheek was purple and had turned puffy. Swallowing hard, Gil approached her bed and Tag moved around to the other side.

"Rook?" Gil called softly, placing his trembling fingers on her hand, which rested across her stomach. Her skin was clammy.

Wearily, Rook lifted her lashes. Blinking, she stared up at Gil, her lips parting.

"Hi, there," Gil said softly, squeezing her hand. He smiled down at her. "How's our favorite lady pilot?"

"Gil? Tag?" Her voice was raw, and she could barely make an audible sound.

"Sshh," Gil soothed, leaning down, resting his arms on the steel tubing that surrounded the bed. "We just wanted to let you know that your friends are here. How do you feel?"

Overwhelmed by their appearance, Rook sobbed once, and weakly gripped Gil's fingers. Images, flashes of the *Flyer*, blipped in front of her groggy memory. "Noah . . . Jim?"

Logan leaned over, placing his hand on her hair. "Jim is in serious condition, but he's going to make it, Rook. He's just two rooms down from you, still in recovery. Jim's father is here, too. I'm sure he'll want to see both of you."

Relief surged through Rook. She shut her eyes, taking in a jerky breath of air. Reopening them, she stared darkly into Gil's shadowed features. His mouth had become a thin line, like it always did when something was wrong. Rook recognized that set look. She felt Gil's hand become firmer on hers.

Taking in a deep breath, Gil bit down on his lower lip, unable to stop the awful pain surging up through his chest. "Noah didn't make it, Rook. We're sorry—so damn sorry . . . he was a hell of a man. Special—like you . . ."

A rasping cry tore from Rook. She tried to sit up, but was too weak. She fell back down on the pillow, wild cries tearing from the very reaches of her soul. "No! It can't be . . . tell me it isn't so, Gil! He can't be dead. That just isn't fair!"

Tag winced as he leaned over to stroke Rook's hair, and whispered, "Hush, honey, it's all right. He loved you—that's all that counts. You two got to patch up things between you . . . that was important . . ."

Gil was unable to remain impervious to Rook's anguished weeping. He straightened up, tears burning in his eyes, and looked over at Tag. There were tears in his eyes, too. "Take care of her for a minute," he ordered thickly, and then spun around, heading for the door. Goddamn this rotten little world anyway! He jerked the door open, and began to walk blindly and aimlessly down the hall. Everything blurred in front of Gil, and he slowed his pace. Goddamn this whole stinking situation! Stumbling to a halt, reeling with weariness, Gil sank against a wall and buried his face in his hands.

CHAPTER

Twenty-three

A crisp November breeze blew across the tarmac outside the hangar. Jim had just been released from the hospital two weeks ago and was recovering nicely. Rook was still pale and gaunt.

The ceremony honoring the many people who had helped in the *Flyer* disaster was over. Jim heard Captain Stuart dismiss the two hundred and fifty Coast Guard personnel who were attired in their blue dress uniforms. The ranks that stood at attention on the tarmac relaxed and began to break up into smaller groups. Reviewing stands, brought in days earlier to line the adjacent area, were now filled to overflowing, with five thousand people in attendance. The 13th District Coast Guard band struck up another patriotic tune. Jim eyed the reporters who raced toward the small cluster of people who had just been awarded medals. His only concern was for Rook.

"Come on," Jim urged, taking her by the arm and pointing her toward the parking lot. Admiral Savage, and even the Commandant of the Coast Guard were present. It was a political field day for all the high-ranking officers of the district who had been involved in the *Flyer* rescue. Their career advancement was assured. Jim didn't care about that. All he wanted to do was protect Rook from the hungry hordes of reporters and get her away from the air station. Ever since the disaster, the press had been hounding her for an interview. She had refused, too grief-stricken over Noah's death to discuss the disaster. Senator Rufford and his daughter had made peace with Rook earlier, and today she appeared to receive her DFC medal, as well as Noah's medal.

They wove through knots of people, trying to dodge the reporters. Let Annie and Dave field their questions. Jim tried to nod, to appear pleasant as they received murmurs of "thank you" and "you were all wonderful," along with pats on the back. He perused Rook's features, his heart wrenching.

So much had happened since the disaster—so much. He saw Rook clutch the DFC medals in her fist, her mouth stretched in pain. He hurried her to his Corvette and opened the door.

Rook laid her head back, barely controlling the tears that wanted to fall. When Jim slid into the driver's seat, she whispered, "Take me to the cemetery, will you?"

Frowning, Jim hesitated and then nodded. He started the car and carefully backed out. Air Station Port Angeles was crowded to the maximum with visitors. All he wanted to do was escape.

A fresh breeze blew through the car window, drying some of the perspiration on Rook's face. She didn't see the colorful fall splendor, the dazzling sunlight, or the intense dark blue of the sky. Reaching out, she sought and found Jim's right hand. His fingers were damp and cool, like her own. She turned her head, studying his tension-lined profile.

"How are you doing?" she asked.

"Better than you." Jim glanced at Rook. "You were weaving around at attention. I didn't know if you were going to make it through that damn ceremony."

"It was too long." The words came out bitter.

"It was a dog and pony show," he agreed.

"It really wasn't that bad. Captain Stuart went to great efforts to keep the presentation of the medals simple and quick. It was the admiral and his bunch that turned it into a sideshow."

Jim squeezed her hand gently. "I just wanted to get the hell out of there. I felt like I was suffocating."

"Me, too." Rook managed a sad smile. "At least Annie, Dave Harper, and the crewmen got medals, too. They all deserved them."

"Yeah," he whispered tiredly, "a few good things came out of it. That disaster sealed Annie and Dave's relationship."

"That was the only good thing." Rook looked out over the straits. Today, the water was a marine blue, with sunlight dancing off the gentle swells. How much the sea knew and kept to herself, she mused. "Somewhere down there at the bottom of the straits are twenty people," she murmured. "People who will never be found."

"Yeah. I felt especially sorry for Captain Stuart. They never did recover Kenny's body."

Rook stared up at the roof of the car. "He was hit hard."

Jim's voice lowered. "So were you."

The reference to Noah sent a veil of tears to Rook's eyes. Automatically, she reached in her pocket where she always carried tissues. Blotting her eyes, she mumbled, "I've never cried so much, Jim—ever. Now, that's all I can do."

"It's only been two and half months," Jim said gently, dividing his attention betwen Rook and driving up the twisting, turning road.

"I—I know." She sniffed and blew her nose, clutching the tissue between her fingers. "I'll be at my desk, working on some P.R. releases, and all of a sudden, I'll start sobbing. My mind won't even be on Noah. I—I don't understand it . . ."

"Your heart's on him, Rook."

She looked at Jim through the blur of her tears. "My whole family is gone."

"We have each other. At least that's something," he told her quietly. His head was aching like a reverberating drum through his skull. The doctors had told him he'd probably have headaches for at least a year after receiving the concussion—maybe two. Jim redirected his attention to Rook. He ached to lift her out of her grief, but didn't know how.

"I talked to Captain Stuart just before the ceremony," he told Rook. "He's approved an additional two months of convalescence for you, plus thirty days of leave." Jim gave her a hopeful look. "It will give you three months to heal, Rook—really heal."

Rook responded strongly to his care. Since the ferry disaster, they had become emotionally inseparable. She'd had to remain in the hospital for five weeks. Still, it didn't stop them from visiting with one another and having long, and sometimes painful, talks. She clung to his strong, steady hand wrapped around hers. Sometimes, their talks were a natural high for both of them. This relationship gave strength and support to her life. Jim had provided a way for her when she felt utterly lost without Noah—without any family at all.

"I've got plans for us, you know," Jim teased lightly, trying to raise her spirits. Rook's smile was wobbly, but it was there as she met his blue gaze.

"I knew you were plotting and planning away in that hospital room of yours. Even your dad was complaining that you were running the company from that bed."

He laughed softly. "I was bored, Rook. You only visited me at night, and I had all day on my hands. Sure, I have plans for us. The company paperwork kept me from going completely stir crazy in that place."

Rook managed a strained smile. "Just what kind of plans have you got for me, Jim Barton? You've been awful secretive about them."

He raised her hand, kissing the back of it. Her flesh was cool to his touch. "I'll tell you in a little while," he promised.

The cemetery, located on top of a hill overlooking Port Angeles and the straits, came into view. Jim slowed and guided the Corvette into the well-kept area. Glancing over at Rook, he saw her eyes go dark with pain, with remembrance. Following a narrower asphalt road, they drove to the crest. The sycamore and elm trees that were scattered throughout the cemetery were now bleak, their branches bare, awaiting the coming winter.

Rook sat there, staring at a small headstone to her right. It was the exact shape and size of all the rest—only the name identified it. The car came to a stop, and she felt Jim's arm come around her shoulders.

"Okay?" he whispered.

Tears jammed into her eyes and her fingers closed around the medal. "Yeah . . ." Rook sniffed and looked over at Jim. "W-will you come with me?"

"Sure."

As they got out, Rook noticed the sunlight lancing through the naked, up-raised arms of the elm above her brother's grave. Jim placed his arm around her, drawing her close, and she trembled. He walked with her on the springy, manicured grass. Because of their injuries, neither had been able to attend Noah's funeral. Jim knew that since Rook's release from the hospital, she had visited his grave only once before. He took a deep breath, feeling her pain and loss. Noah had saved Jim's life by giving his own in trade for it. If only he'd survived. If only . . .

Rook knelt down by the headstone, staring at it through her tears for a long time. Above them, a sea gull cried, the sound lonely, serrating. The wind was cool, drying the tears as they streamed down her cheeks. She opened her fingers, Noah's medal gleaming in the sunlight.

"Noah knew his chances when he went up on that roof," Rook began hoarsely.

Jim walked to the other side, kneeling down opposite her. "I think he did."

A sob tremored through Rook. "And the one man who would think the least of medals isn't here to receive his."

He nodded, a lump forming in his throat. "Noah was special," he agreed softly.

"Th-that's what he always said about me—that I was special. I never believed him, because in my heart, I knew he was the one who was really special." Rook pressed her hand against her tightly shut eyes. "That day he came over to my apartment with those letters . . . I felt as if someone had chopped my heart up after I read them. When I went to ask his forgiveness and start all over, he pretended as if it was the easiest thing in the world for him to do." She sobbed harder, tears running between her fingers and plopping on the grave below. "A-and now I know why. He'd always love Mom and me . . . when you love your family that much, it's easy to forgive them."

"He loved you, Rook," Jim rasped, and reached across the grave to grip her slumped shoulder. "He loved you with his life."

Rook sobbed hard. Struggling to control the gamut of unleashed emotions, she finally succeeded. Raising her chin, she met and held Jim's suffering gaze. "You know the worst of it, Jim?"

He shook his head. "No, tell me."

"I—I never told him I loved him!" Rook cried hoarsely, and she bent double, burying her face in her hands.

Jim got up, moving around the grave, kneeling at her side. Gently, he gathered Rook into his arms. She came, burying her tear-stained face against his suit, her arms wrapped tightly around him. He held Rook and rocked her, stroking her hair and whispering words he hoped would help. Words were so useless sometimes, Jim thought, tears squeezing from beneath his closed eyes.

"Sshh, Rook, it's all right," he crooned. "Noah knew. I know he knew. He could tell by the look in your eyes, your laughter." Jim blindly pressed his mouth to her temple, kissing her. "Don't tear yourself up over that, sweetheart. Please don't . . ."

Three white gulls with black-tipped wings sailed overhead, crying out forlornly. Jim had no idea how long he held Rook. Time didn't matter, anyway. She did. Gradually, her sobs lessened, and so did her trembling. Jim continued to stroke her hair, holding her tight against him, trying to take away her pain. She clung mutely to him, and he could feel the rapid beat of her heart against his chest. Gradually, Rook's heartbeat slowed.

"We're all so fragile," he whispered, looking down at her. "Love makes us fragile, Rook, but it also makes us strong in ways that we'd never be, otherwise. You've had such a rough life, and you thought no one loved or cared for you except your mother." Jim managed a faint smile, pressing a final kiss to her hair. "Noah was happy because you buried the past between you. At least you had the chance to right the wrong done to all of you. I know he's happy about that, Rook. Do you understand?"

Rook barely moved her head, wanting, needing Jim's strength right now. His arms felt good around her. She could hear the heavy, steady beat of his heart beneath her ear. There was no more strength left in her; she'd hit bottom emotionally. What would she have done if Jim hadn't been here? Slowly, Rook pulled out of his arms and looked up at him. She saw anguish in his dark blue eyes. Jim was suffering no less than she, and that revelation shattered another wall that she'd built around her heart to protect herself a long time ago.

Rook opened her hand to show Jim the medal. "He deserves this."

He squeezed Rook gently. "Yes, he does. Noah was one hell of a man."

Rook leaned over, placing her ribbon and medal next to the headstone. She laid her hand on the cold earth, whispering in a choked voice, "I love you, Noah . . ."

Gil Logan waited impatiently at the entrance to the cemetery. He'd seen Rook and Jim drive away right after the ceremony was over. No one had told him where they were going, but he knew. Gil laughed, remembering how insensitive Eve had accused him of being. He paced near his car, still in uniform. They'd been up on that hill for an hour. Having attended Noah's funeral, he knew exactly where the grave was located. Gil tried to remember what it had been like when he and Eve had fallen in love—that intense, breathtaking emotion that had hurled them into one another's arms.

He frowned, leaning against his car, staring moodily out at the straits. He felt Rook and Jim's relationship was more stable, more enduring than his and Eve's had been. They had real love. All he and Eve had shared was a set of rose-colored glasses. Gil laughed derisively. What was left after the romantic love faded from their marriage wasn't worth one brick, much less a foundation. Maybe that was the reason for the divorce. His family was still distraught over his decision—and so was he for their sake.

Logan took off the garrison cap he was wearing, setting it on the roof of the car. He hated to wear the thing. Running his fingers through his short hair, he tried to still his own inner restlessness. He hadn't realized Eve was on the ferry until he'd seen the list of survivors the next day at the office. He closed his eyes, allowing the sunlight to warm him. He was so damned cold and empty inside. Memory of that final confrontation between them came sharply back into focus. He'd found out she was at the same hospital that Rook and Jim had been taken to.

"What are you doing here?" Eve had whispered as he entered the room.

Gil stood there, dressed in civilian clothes, staring over at his wife. Eve was in a wrinkled white cotton hospital gown. Her face was devoid of makeup, and she looked waxen. He saw the bruises on her forehead and right cheek. Her right arm was in a cast and sling.

"I didn't know you were on board or I'd have come sooner," he began haltingly.

"You wouldn't care even if you had known," she muttered, refusing to look at him. "Just get out of here, Gil! I've had enough shock and trauma the past few days to last me a lifetime. I don't need you here, too."

He opened his hand, palm outward, as he walked over to her bed. Eve looked so helpless. "But—"

She whirled toward him, her lips contorted with anguish.

"I said, *get out of here*! I hate you! I hate what you did to us!"

His eyes widened. Pain twisted through his heart. It took long moments for him to collect his thoughts and get his emotions back under tight control. "How long have you hated me, Eve?" The words came out in a naked whisper.

She sobbed and blurted out, "I thought when I married a Coast Guard officer, that life would be great. I'd get out of that dirty little Southern town and get respect. I'd be important. I'd be somebody." Eve's eyes veiled with fresh tears. "Instead of somebody, I became a nobody again. You might have been married to me, Gil Logan, but the Coast Guard was your *real* wife. All I was to you was a mistress—someone to come home to when the Coast Guard felt like releasing you."

"That's not true, Eve! Nothing could be further from the damn truth!"

"Don't you start shouting at me!"

His breath was coming in uneven gulps and he knotted his fists. "I love you, Eve. I never *stopped* loving you. I can't help it if I have long hours. That's the way it is, and you knew that before you married me!"

Her eyes flashed with resentment. "*You* ruined this marriage. You and your real wife, your beloved Coast Guard." Clumsily, Eve worked the wedding ring off her left hand. "That ferry disaster jelled a lot of things for me, Gil. I found out how much I wanted to live, really live—not just be some secondhand castoff. Oh, sure, we were great in bed together, but that was all. It's not enough!" Eve threw the ring at him with all her strength. It bounced harmlessly off his chest, clattering to the tile floor and rolling toward the door, where it finally tinkled to a stop.

Gil stared openmouthed at her, grief tearing at him. "Eve," he rasped, taking a step forward.

Eve cowered and screamed, "Get out of here! Get out of my life! I never want to see you again!"

He reined in his escaping feelings. He wanted to talk, to try and figure out where they had gone wrong. But just as he stood there, Gil realized she wasn't going to cooperate. Could he blame her? No. "Get those divorce papers over to me," he rasped thickly, his voice unsteady.

"Good!"

Gil turned and stalked toward the door. He picked up the wedding ring and jerked the door open, stepping out into the hall and out of Eve's life. Forever.

Gil roused himself from his thoughts when he heard a Corvette coming down the hill. He turned. It was Jim and Rook. Swallowing hard, realizing that he was probably doing the wrong thing at the wrong time by being here, he waited until they drove up alongside his vehicle.

Jim rolled down the window. "Gil?"

Gil leaned over so he could see both of them, and forced a tight smile. "Hi. I—uh, just thought I'd come up here. There was something I needed to say to Rook, and I thought the time might as well be now."

Jim saw the anxiety and unsureness in his eyes. He looked over at Rook. She was pale and silent. "Rook?"

"It's all right, Jim. Meet us at the bottom of the hill. I'll walk down with Gil."

"Are you sure?" What did Gil have to tell her? He didn't want her any more upset than she was already.

Rook reached over, touching his arm. "I'll be all right."

Relief fled through Gil. He saw Jim start to scowl, and sensed his concern. "Look, I'll take care of her. Don't worry," Gil assured him in a low voice.

"She's fragile, Gil. Don't do anything else to push her toward the edge. She needs to heal."

"I understand. Or, at least, I think I do." Gil patted the door. "See you later."

Gil waited until Jim's Corvette had disappeared down the winding road before going over to Rook. She stood there, ashen, looking as though she felt abandoned. He swallowed hard, trying to hide his own nervousness. Giving Rook a game smile, he walked up to her.

"Hell of a day, wasn't it?"

She nodded, her emotions numb after the weeping earlier.

"Hell of a day," Rook agreed scratchily. She searched Gil's face. "A-are you okay?" She reached out to rest her hand on the sleeve of his jacket.

How like Rook, even when she was hurting herself, to ask about others. Trying to hold his smile, Gil came to her side, slipping his arm around her shoulders. "Yeah, I'm fine." Liar. "Come on, let's go for a little walk. You look like you need to get some color back in those cheeks."

Rook slid her arm around Gil's waist. She leaned against his strong frame, grateful for his care. They walked along a small asphalt path that encircled the lower part of the cemetery.

"You were smart to escape when you did," Gil said brightly, trying to maintain a lightness he didn't feel. "You should have seen all those reporters try and get to you and Jim."

She looked up at him. "I'm afraid I didn't notice." Her voice was raw.

"Yup." Gil winked down at her. "Only, Reno, Tag, and I used a classic football tactic and provided pass protection for you." He chuckled, pleased with himself. "You know how much of a clown Reno can be?"

"Yes, he's always in hot water."

"Well, he ran up to this network reporter and grabbed his microphone, begging to be interviewed. He made a complete ass out of himself. And then Tag grabbed another reporter. By that time, the cameramen, cables, and equipment were entangled and they were tripping all over themselves. I tackled a cameraman and we stopped them cold." He chuckled again. "You'd have been proud of us, Rook."

Rook managed a strained laugh, giving him a hug. "What would I do without you guys? You're all like big brothers to me." She slowed to a stop and turned, somberly studying him. "For a long time, I didn't have a brother. Then, Noah and I patched things up between ourselves." Rook reached up, picking a piece of lint from his uniform. "I was so afraid when I came to this station. I thought the other pilots were going to be against me because I was a woman." Rook took a deep breath and continued. "I was wrong. You guys have taken me under your wing and been like the brothers I'd always daydreamed about, but never had. Now, with Noah gone . . ."

"We can't replace him entirely, Rook," Gil began awkwardly, "but we are your brothers in another sense. You're a part of our Coast Guard family." Gil placed his hands on her slumped shoulders. "We think you're kinda special, too."

Rook winced. Those were Noah's words. She rallied, searching Gil's suffering features. "Gil, what's wrong? You're nervous and jumpy. That's not like you. Is it Eve again?"

He rubbed her shoulders in a nervous gesture. "No, that part of my life's behind me now." That wasn't the complete truth. The divorce haunted him daily, but he knew it had been the only answer. Gil cleared his throat. "Look, there's something I've been meaning to tell you for a long time." He looked up at the sky. "Eve always accused me of being insensitive, saying I never had a good sense of timing on much of anything." Gil lowered his gaze, holding her dove-gray eyes, which were now velvet with spent tears. "Jesus, Rook, I hope I haven't screwed up with you—with what I had to tell you. At first, I didn't want to because you were in the hurt locker there at the hospital. And when you got out and came back to the base, you looked awful." He compressed his lips, the words coming hard. "Sometimes, I'd see you in your office crying. And then, I'd back off again, afraid it might not be the right time. I know how much you loved Noah, and I felt terrible for you."

Gently, Rook reached up, touching his cheek. "Gil, it's all right. Just tell me. I wish you wouldn't be so hard on yourself. We're all human, for God's sake. We bumble around, fall down, make mistakes, and then get back up again. I've never seen you like this before. Just tell me and get it over with . . ."

Gil dropped his hands, shoving them into his pockets. A tidal wave of emotions threatened him, and he wrestled with it before speaking. Looking down at his highly polished shoes, he began, his voice low and tortured. "When we first got to the hospital to see how the three of you were doing, we cornered Dr. Marhefka and we squeezed the info out of him about your condition." Logan cleared his throat, risking a look up at Rook. She had clasped her hands, as if holding herself rigid, waiting. Unable to stand seeing her suffer anymore, Gil blurted out the rest. "I buttonholed him about Noah. I asked him if he had regained consciousness at any point."

Rook gasped, taking a step toward Gil. She gripped his arm to steady herself. "Did he?"

Gil nodded, holding her anxious gaze. "Yeah, and that's what I've been waiting to tell you. Christ, I'm sorry, Rook, I probably should have told you sooner, but I thought it might hurt you even more."

Her fingers tightened on his arm. "Gil, what did Noah say? I have to know..."

"He was calling out for you. And when the nurse leaned over, she heard him say: 'love frees.'" Gil glanced up at her. "That's all he said. After that, he lost consciousness." Automatically, Gil placed his hand on Rook's arm. Was she going to faint? Cry? God knew, he was a lousy one to be around when tears started to fall. Eve always said he was like a bull in a china shop around emotional women, and didn't know how to comfort them.

Love frees... Rook closed her eyes, leaning on Gil for support. Her heart suddenly exploded and an inexplicable number of emotions rushed through her—consuming her, releasing her. For a long moment, she wasn't aware that Gil was holding her as if she were a fragile egg that might shatter in his arms. Tears scaled her eyes, but they were tears of happiness this time, not sadness.

Gil saw Rook's tears, and dug unsuccessfully for the handkerchief in his pocket. Cursing, he transferred her beneath his left arm and started digging again.

"I got a handkerchief here somewhere," he muttered apologetically.

Rook caught his arm. "No, it's all right, Gil," and she smiled through her tears at his distraught features.

Perplexed, he asked, "It is?" Rook was smiling, and she was crying. Was she happy or sad? What the hell was going on? He'd never forgive himself if he'd wounded Rook even more. She didn't deserve that kind of pain, and misery was all he seemed capable of giving to women lately.

Choking back a sob, Rook threw her arms around Gil, hugging him tightly. "Thank you, Gil," she whispered, "thank you for telling me that. It means so much to me . . . so much . . ."

"It does?" He scowled, holding her at arm's length, tears running freely down her flushed cheeks. "How? I mean, it's none of my business, but I don't understand."

Taking a well-used tissue from her pocket, Rook dabbed at her reddened eyes. "Of course you wouldn't," she whispered. "Noah used to call me his little cocoon, promising me one day that I'd hatch into a beautiful butterfly and fly free, and we'd have a new beginning between us, as brother and sister." Rook sobbed, still smiling. "I—I never told him I loved him, Gil. I was holding back saying it until I felt strong enough to mean it." She sniffed. "I thought he died not knowing that I really did love him. He said that when I left my cocoon, we'd be able to express our love for one another freely." She shook her head, gripping Gil's arm. "Don't you see? Noah was telling me he knew I loved him, even though I'd never admitted it. Thank you, Gil. Oh, thanks so much. You'll never know how good this makes me feel . . ."

Logan stood there, stunned. "You mean, you're not sad?"

Rook looked toward the hill where Noah's grave sat. "I'll be sad for a long time over his death, but now I can be at peace with myself because my brother knew I loved him, just as much as he loved me." She turned back and held Gil's wavering gaze. He looked like a lost little boy in that moment, so unsure of himself, of her. Wiping her eyes one last time, Rook murmured, "I'll never forget Noah . . . I loved him so very much . . ."

"They say," Gil began awkwardly, "that time heals everything, Rook." And then he shrugged. "Well, I've got a divorce to get over and so does Eve. Maybe I'll find out if that saying is true."

Rook slipped her arm through his, heading down the hill where Jim stood beside the Corvette, waiting for them. "Tag's with us on this, too. We'll all find out together, Gil. Each of us has suffered a terrible loss."

Heartened that his message had had such a wonderful effect on Rook, Gil's step became its normal, cocky self. Patting her hand, he said, "Listen, misery loves company. We're family, and family helps their own. The three of us and the rest of the crew at the air station will help us through this."

Family . . . the word hung gently before Rook's open, feeling heart. A wobbly smile touched her mouth as she gazed up at Gil. He looked suddenly years younger. Hope burned in his blue eyes again. "Yes."

CHAPTER

Twenty-four

"WARD?" Marcia looked around the darkened bedroom. She ran her fingers across the sheets where he normally lay. They were cold. She called him again, but there was no answer. It was 3 A.M. Slipping on her robe, Marcia tried to shake off the grogginess that always haunted her upon waking. She padded noiselessly through the living room, moonlight streaming through the windows, muted by the curtains. She found Ward standing in his robe and slippers on the patio, looking out toward the black waters of the straits. She slid the door open and stepped out into the chilly night air.

Ward turned, sensing his wife's presence before she opened the door. He saw the worry in her eyes as she walked up to him. Holding his arm out, he invited her to his side. She came, pressing herself to him, wrapping her arms around his waist.

"Couldn't sleep?" she asked.

With a sigh he murmured, "No."

"It's a wonder I did. I thought the commandant and all those admirals were never going to leave. What a zoo," Marcia admitted in a whisper.

Ward rested his chin against Macia's hair, eyes hardening. "It was just what Savage ordered: national headlines guaranteed to make the Coast Guard look good." Anger vibrated through his voice. "He got what he wanted. Nobody in America remembers the whale incident. All they remember is how we rescued those hundreds of people."

Marcia squeezed him. They had both suffered terribly over the shock of Kenny's death—Ward particularly. His guilt and helplessness over their son's demise was being focused elsewhere. "Ward, they weren't happy that seventy people died in order to get those headlines," she soothed. "I know sometimes you think Savage is publicity-hungry, but it's his nature to make a lot out of something like this. And something should be." Marcia pulled back enough to catch and hold Ward's smoldering gaze. "Why won't you take your plaudits? You were the man who coordinated the entire rescue." Her voice grew husky with emotion. "You *deserve* the medal they gave you, Ward. You've earned everyone's respect and admiration."

Ward avoided her pleading eyes. He absently rubbed Marcia's slumped shoulder, glaring toward the straits—a silent black ribbon in the darkness. He shivered, never forgetting for one second that somewhere on the bottom Ken lay in a cold, watery grave, gone, but never forgotten—ever. "It doesn't mean a thing, Marcia—not a damn thing."

"Then, what does?"

His mouth was set in a line of anguish, and the words came out forced. "Ken meant something, but he never respected me. And I never understood him, either." Shutting his eyes tightly, Ward gripped his wife to him. "Why, Marcia? Where did I go wrong?"

"Hush," she whispered fiercely, giving him a shake. Tears glittered in her eyes. "I know how much you're suffering over Ken's death. We both are, Ward. But remember what Father Davis said: we can create them and bring them into this world. That's our responsibility. What they turned out to be is up to them. We gave Kenny our love, our guidance and help."

"I failed," Ward whispered harshly. "I failed Ken."

"Kenny failed himself!" Marcia cried, giving Ward a shake to try and make him understand. Tears streaked down her cheeks. "Don't buy into that premise, Ward. I can see what it's doing to you—it's eating you up alive. You've got a bleeding ulcer. Please . . ."

Ward shut his eyes, tears squeezing from beneath them. "My God, Marcia," he rasped. "Ken robbed a liquor store in Seattle. He was heading to Canada. What was he going to do—run away? Do you realize he probably had no intentions of ever seeing us again? He was skipping out of the country for good."

She gripped Ward, forcing him to look at her. "Kenny never loved himself, so how could he return our love? He was like a bucket without a bottom, Ward. He'd been that way since the day he was born."

"I should have paid more attention to him."

"You did as much as you could, under the circumstances. What Kenny refused to accept was that the Coast Guard demanded long, hard hours from you. Remember when we were stationed in Alaska; that was a nightmare."

"Yes, and Ken paid for it, too."

Marcia stepped away from him, her mouth set. "We all did, Ward! *All* of us. Do you think I liked two years up in that godforsaken place? You hated it, too! The children weren't happy, either."

Rubbing his brow, Ward walked across the tiled patio. The moon was gliding through the silent sky, shedding a silver blanket over the straits and the town of Port Angeles. He leaned against one of the rough-cut oak beams that supported the roof overhead. The air was damp and he shivered, cold clear to his soul. Ward felt Marcia come up behind him; he needed her warmth. She pressed herself to his back, sliding her arms around his waist.

"I love you, Ward Stuart, faults and all. Don't look at just your weaknesses. Look at your strengths. I was at that ceremony, and I saw the light shining in the eyes of those kids under your command. They adore you."

"They respect me."

"They think you walk on water."

"They know my bite's worse than my bark."

She buried her face against his back, smiling softly. "You're so hard on yourself, darling. Don't be, because they aren't. All your career you've worked toward this moment."

Ward closed his eyes, soaking up her love, her effortless warmth. "What are you talking about?" he demanded gruffly, trying to camouflage his own escalating emotions.

Marcia pressed a kiss against his flannel robe. "The *Flyer* rescue pulled every ounce of training, knowledge, and experience from you, Ward. All those stations we moved to and all those long hours behind the stick of a helo, or stuck in some back room at an air station slaving away, were utilized. Without all those sacrifices, those awful duty places out in the middle of nowhere, SAR cases that ripped your heart out, you couldn't have coordinated this one like you did." Her voice grew fervent. "You saved so many lives, Ward. Don't count the ones who died—count the living. Did you see how many of the survivors were there today? I've never seen so many grateful faces, or heard so many thank yous." Her voice wobbled. "We lost a son, but we'd lost him long before the ferry accident. We've gained by saving others who will still have their families whole and healthy."

Turning, Ward pulled Marcia into his arms, crushing her against him. He buried his face beside hers. He struggled not to cry. He'd cried so much in private already because of Ken. His voice was roughened when he spoke. "I'll try to see it your way, honey, but it's going to be tough. I'm carrying so much guilt over Ken—what I should have done, could have done, instead of what I did do. Sweet Mother of Christ, how can I command a station, and yet, not even be able to talk with my son?"

Marcia understood; she held Ward tightly. "We have one son left," she muffled against his chest. "Let's try to learn from our errors. We're still a family."

He sighed and nodded. He loved Marcia fiercely. She was so soft and flexible, and yet, incredibly strong, in ways he was presently not. "And don't forget, we've got our extended family."

Marcia lifted her chin, managing a thin smile, her face

damp with spent tears. "Our Coast Guard family is one you can always be proud of, Ward—people like Dave Harper and Annie Locke. If it weren't for Rook and her brother, Noah, so many more would have perished in that awful ordeal."

Ward nodded. "And don't forget Jim Barton. Without him, fewer people might have survived."

She smiled gamely. "Jim is a credit to all of us. He's a fine human being."

"He epitomizes the best of us," Ward said, watching as an owl flew silently through the sky, heading for a pine tree in the distance. And then, he looked down at her. "Our people are the best, Marcia. Christ, I was proud of them—all of them. They worked so hard . . ."

Relaxing because Ward appeared to be momentarily over his own crisis with Kenny, she patted his arm. "Well, Captain Stuart, I think you need to get some sleep. There are two hundred and fifty people at that air station that are looking to you for continued guidance for another year and a half."

Ward leaned down, placing a kiss on her smiling lips. "You're right. That air station has come a long way in a short time, but there are still things to be done and people to help."

As Marcia led him back toward the bedroom she murmured, "I'm so glad that Rook has Jim. She's taken so many emotional shocks, so close together."

Patting his wife's shoulder, Ward nodded. "But like a Coastie, she'll rally and come out of it."

"Can't sleep?" Jim padded out on the sun deck toward Rook, who stood leaning against the rail looking down at the lights of Port Angeles. In her thin robe, she looked lost on the huge expanse. She turned toward him.

Rook managed a smile that could be misconstrued as a grimace. "No. Did I wake you when I got up?"

Jim placed his arms around Rook, drawing her against him. She looked like a lost waif to him. Her eyes were slightly puffy from crying earlier that day, her skin pale and drawn, her once-proud shoulders drawn downward in defeat. "I was awake anyway."

A sigh escaped Rook as she sagged against him, snuggling against the nubby texture of the terry cloth robe he wore. "You were pretending, then."

Smiling, Jim closed his eyes and rested his cheek against her mussed hair. "For your sake. You need rest, Rook, not me tossing and turning, keeping you awake."

Her heart mushroomed with a fierce love for him. Gently disengaging, Rook gazed up at Jim. The moonlight cascaded down on them, soothing to her highly emotional state. "You're still healing, yourself," she whispered, her eyes darkening with concern.

"Now, don't start worrying about me," he chided, kissing her lips tenderly. "You're the object of my concern."

His mouth was warm and enticing. Since the ferry disaster, they had had no opportunity to be alone, or even make hungry love to one another. Rook drowned in his offering, losing herself in the taste and texture of his mouth.

"Mmmm," Jim said, drawing inches away, smiling down into her eyes—eyes that now held a spark of life, for the first time in months. "You taste pretty good."

Breathy laughter escaped Rook as she framed his face between her hands. Jim was haggard. His face had aged and he now had lines of pain around his mouth. Part of it was due to weight loss, she realized. The burns he had suffered were terrible, and his ongoing therapy was far from over. "Pretty good for a Coastie, huh?"

"Not bad," he agreed. Rook's laughter feathered through him. It was the first time he'd heard her laugh since Noah had died. Her gray eyes were luminous, and he ached to make love with her.

"Jim, I need to talk to you," Rook began slowly. "I don't even know where to begin . . ."

He slowly began to massage her shoulders and upper back, feeling the tension in them. Fear gripped him internally. Rook's eyes grew shadowed, and he wondered if all the trauma and crisis she'd suffered would drive her away from him. Would she run again? "Okay," he murmured, "let's talk."

Closing her eyes, Rook rested her hands against his chest, feeling the beat of his heart beneath her palms. "You've been so patient and understanding with me . . ."

"You invite that kind of response, Rook."

"I was scared of personal commitment to a man—any man."

"And you've had the courage to overcome that, Rook."

She gazed at him through her lashes. "With you, yes." She slid her hands around his neck. "Noah's death taught me something I'll never forget."

"What, sweetheart?" Jim's breath snagged as he watched her wrestle with words that seemed impossible for her to say. Was she going to leave him? His hands stilled on her shoulders.

Hot tears filled Rook's eyes as she held his shadowed blue gaze. "To always say what I feel, Jim." The tears overflowed, trailing down her cheeks. "I love you . . ."

Lifting his head, Jim shut his eyes tightly and crushed Rook against him. He held her hard. Relief and incredible joy cascaded through him.

Rook buried her head against him, holding him just as tightly as he held her. "I don't know what my future holds with you," she went on, the words tumbling out, "but I'll *never* not tell you how I feel, from now on. I withheld so much from Noah that he'll never know about. I cheated him. I cheated myself. I won't do that to you."

"Life's too short and too unpredictable not to be honest," Jim agreed hoarsely, kissing her hair, her temple, her damp cheek.

Rook filled with happiness and met his burning gaze. Her spirits lifted and her heart began a yearning beat in her breast. She loved him fiercely. "You taught me how to love, Jim. You gave me the time and space I needed."

Laughing softly, he cradled Rook's face between his hands. The glow in her eyes told him everything. There was a new softness to Rook, even in her contralto voice. "I was lucky enough to read between the lines of what had happened to you, Rook."

"That, plus you have a wonderful insight to people and their motivations."

Jim nodded, resting his mouth against her smiling, welcoming lips. "I love you, Wild Rose. We're going to have ups and downs in the future, but together, we can handle them."

A moan vibrated in Rook's throat as he cherished her lips, worshiping her. The next moment, she found herself lifted off the sun deck and into his embrace. Placing her arms around his shoulders, she was content to relax against him as he walked back into the quiet, darkened house.

"This is a beginning," Jim told her in a hushed tone as he walked down the hall toward the master bedroom.

Resting her head against his jaw, Rook whispered, "Is it? Everyone around us has lost so much in the last six months, Jim. Gil lost his wife in a divorce. Tag lost Paula to illness. The captain lost his son."

"And you lost Noah." Jim drew to a halt just inside the bedroom, not wanting to let her down, content to hold her close and give her comfort. Gazing down at her, he added, "But every one of us has been given a chance for a new beginning. Gil, Tag, and the captain will have a lot to wrestle with and work through." His arms tightened around her. "We're just a little ahead of them, that's all. Your courage gave us our beginning months ago. It could have floundered, with all the things that happened to you after the ferry disaster, but you didn't let it. You didn't run away from me, Rook."

Leaning upward, Rook placed a tender, warming kiss on his mouth. "I'm running to you, darling. I want this night to be our beginning . . ."

Jim gently deposited Rook on the bed and joined her. Tunneling his fingers through her glorious, ebony hair, he murmured, "I want you to be my best friend, my lover, my confidant." He didn't add *wife*. Although he had purchased an engagement ring and had planned to ask Rook to marry him in Victoria the day the ferry blew up, Jim had decided to wait. Right now her shining, dove-gray eyes sparkled with tears of utter happiness. Jim smiled down at her. Someday, and he'd know when, he would ask this woman to marry him. Right now, this was their beginning, and he needed nothing else.

Rook moved further onto the bed, watching as Jim turned out the light. She opened her arms to him. "I want to be all those things to you," she said in a hushed voice. As his weight settled gently upon her, his mouth molding teasingly against her own, she pleaded, "Love me, Jim . . ."

Rook's scent entered his nostrils and Jim inhaled it deeply as a man dragging life into his heart, his soul. He pulled the sash to her robe open, exposing her lovely form. "Every day of our lives," he promised her huskily, a catch in his voice.